AT THE TRADING POST, Star had observed the white women closely. Now she quickly tied about her waist the lengths of blue calico she had sewn together in an imitation of their full skirts. Just as she finished arranging her tightly braided hair up in a knot at the back of her neck, she heard Hugh's familiar footsteps approaching the lodge.

"Star!" he called, a hint of alarm in his voice when she did not come from the lodge to greet him.

"Here," she answered from inside. Her mouth was dry and her heart pounded as she arranged her calico skirt and waited for his reaction.

Hugh ducked into the dim interior. "Well, I'm damned!" he said, staring at her, dumbfounded.

When he burst into laughter, her heart plunged and the expectant glow she'd felt faded and died. "I dress pretty for you . . . like white woman," she told him in a pained voice. Tears of disappointment stung her eyes.

At once contrite, Hugh drew her toward him. "You ain't a white woman," he said softly, his big hands working loose the thongs that bound her hair, so that it fell in a dark cascade about her shoulders. "I don't want no white woman." He held her close, looking into her face with such love Star felt her heart turn over. "Don't never change, Star . . . never."

"A BITTERSWEET STORY OF A WOMAN WITH TREMENDOUS STRENGTH AND COURAGE . . ."
—*Publishers Weekly*

"A BREATHTAKING EPIC SAGA . . ."
—*Rave Reviews*

Falling Star

ELISABETH MACDONALD

POCKET BOOKS

New York   London   Toronto   Sydney   Tokyo

Another *Original* publication of POCKET BOOKS

POCKET BOOKS, a division of Simon & Schuster Inc.
1230 Avenue of the Americas, New York, N.Y. 10020

ISBN: 0-671-66798-X

First Pocket Books mass-market printing June 1988

10 9 8 7 6 5 4 3 2 1

For Mac

Prologue

Within the years of memory, the tribe would speak of it as the Night of Falling Stars. Safe in time from dread of the Great Spirit's vengeance in deadly catastrophe, they would forget the terror of all heaven descending upon them.

The sound of Old Grandmother's voice calling her name startled the girl. Alone of her family she sat before her father's lodge, staring enthralled at the flaming sky. Inside the tepee, even her warrior father, Many Horses, trembled before the fire, his robes clutched about him as he awaited the dreaded outcome of this heavenly display.

"Come, girl," said Old Grandmother, standing beside her and holding out her hand. Together they moved away from the village. The old woman's aged limbs were stiff, and she leaned heavily on her stout oak staff. It was said that Old Grandmother had the sight . . . that she saw the future. Some of the tribe feared her for that reason. The future was an unfathomable secret.

Talks-with-Horses did not fear her grandmother. Already she knew she had been chosen, already Old Grandmother had taught her the use of herbs for healing, the lore of the medicine lodge, and how to look within herself for guidance. She had always been aware she was different from the other young girls in her village. She learned not to mind, to absorb Old Grandmother's wisdom, and to have pride that her father valued her for her empathy with his horses. Since she was a child, her village had never lost a horse, for she always knew where to find them.

Painfully Old Grandmother climbed the hill above the village. At last she sat down upon a flat rock, indicating that the girl should sit beside her.

"Look, child," Old Grandmother ordered, pointing her staff at the sky. "Look well . . . and remember."

The village and the forest beyond lay illuminated by an unearthly light. Phosphorescent streams poured earthward, filling the night sky with brilliance. Every star in the heavens seemed to be falling from its place.

Talks-with-Horses lifted her face to the magnificence of the blazing sky, unafraid, glorying in its beauty. At last she felt her grandmother's eyes on her and turned to meet the piercing gaze in the dark wizened face. Their eyes held as though in that look Old Grandmother imparted to her some eternal wisdom.

"You are fourteen summers now," the old woman said. "It is time." From about her neck, she took the small beaded doeskin bag she always wore. Cupping Talks-with-Horses' hand in hers, Old Grandmother revealed its contents for the first time . . . her *wyakin*. In the girl's hand lay a small rough blue stone flecked with veins of creamy white. It seemed to burn Talks-with-Horses' palm as she held it, transfixed by this gift of Old Grandmother's power.

"It was given me long ago by a warrior from a tribe far to the south." Old Grandmother's voice was low and strong. "He spoke of its value and magic among his people. When our chief sent him away, he wished me to go with him, but I could not leave my people . . . even for him."

Returning the stone to the bag, she carefully hung it about Talks-with-Horses' neck. "Its power will be yours," she said, "but you must be alone to find a vision." With the aid of her staff, she struggled to her feet and set off down the hill.

Unaware of the chill autumn air, or the cold of the stone where she sat cross-legged, Talks-with-Horses gave herself up completely to the spectacle before her. Fire raining from the heavens seemed to engulf and possess her until she was no longer earthbound, but lifted up to become one with sky and stars in the Great Spirit of the universe.

It seemed a long time had passed when she became aware of a light moving along the forest trail. Slowly it came toward her out of the darkness. At last she could perceive its form and saw that it was a horse and rider. It was a fine strong horse, and when the rider became clear to her, somehow she was neither surprised nor frightened. The bear sitting astride the horse was a great golden-colored creature with fur that curled down over his huge chest. In that unearthly light he seemed to shine, golden as the sun, bright as the falling stars above. As he drew nearer, she saw that the great bear's eyes were blue. Now she knew him, as surely as though he were kin to her. Drawn to this strange and beautiful creature, Talks-with-Horses rose and held her arms out to him. At once the vision disappeared.

The heavens quieted as morning came, the sun rose, and the world remained whole. Relieved at their deliverance, the village began the business of the day. Smoke rose from the cooking fires, children tumbled in play, dogs barked and fought over scraps. Women chattered incessantly, calling to each other from their lodges. Every man insisted on telling the others his perception of the Night of the Falling Stars.

Aching with cold from her vigil on the hilltop, Talks-with-Horses came down into the village. The doeskin bag with its blue stone hung warm and comforting between her breasts. Old Grandmother greeted her silently.

"Where have you been, girl?" the women asked from their cooking fires.

The pressure of Old Grandmother's hand on her arm told her she must watch her tongue. "Watching the falling stars," she answered, and the women laughed, teasing her.

Her brother's wife called out, "That should be your woman name . . . Falling Star."

"Yes," said Old Grandmother. "She is a woman now and her name will be Falling Star."

Beside the cooking fire at Many Horses' lodge, they sat apart from the others.

"You must not speak of it," Old Grandmother spoke in a

3

low voice so no one else would hear. "It is given to only a few to know such visions, even among the warriors. I have had many visions and I have better medicine than old Talking Crow the medicine man. My gift has been passed on to you, but you must guard it and hold the secret close until there is one born after you who shall have the gift too."

Falling Star listened, hoarding the words for the future. She longed for Old Grandmother to interpret the vision, but she had said she must not. The truth of it would unfold in the future. While Falling Star could not yet guess its true meaning, she knew the depth of its significance. So she listened to Old Grandmother, all the while holding warm in her heart the vision of the Shining Bear.

Book I

✖✖✖✖✖✖✖✖

Shining Bear

Chapter 1

Rendezvous, 1834

Gasping for breath, her chest aching with exhaustion, the girl fell forward into the underbrush. Trembling, she huddled against the moist rocks hidden by the choke-cherry bushes. The rocks were cold and damp from the overflow of the spring they contained, but the chill was welcome against her perspiring body.

The crashing in the underbrush had ceased and the woods were quiet. Falling Star pressed her flushed face gratefully against the chill stone, sick with relief that she had eluded her pursuers. How she hated those bearded, stinking fur trappers. Nausea swelled in her throat as she thought of their grinning, lustful faces, their clutching hands. If her father sold her to such a one, she swore in her heart, she would kill the man on their marriage bed.

As her breathing eased, she stared out through the choke-cherry tangle at the aspen trees trembling green against the deep blue sky. Pressing her fingers against the mossy stone, she wet them, touching them carefully to the bruised place on her breast where the trapper had pinched her. Under her breath she muttered a Nez Percé curse on the man.

Underbrush cracked and snapped beneath the approach of man and animals. Falling Star cringed back against the rocks in the desperate hope that this man, surely another trapper, would not see her. In frozen stillness, her breath came quick and shallow.

Hugh Cameron plunged his bearded face into the spring, grateful for its icy coldness after the long trek across the desert from South Pass. Beside him, a bay horse and two pack mules shared the refreshing draft just as they had shared his life for the past year. On the mules' backs, the parfleche carry-alls were filled with pelts from his beaver traps . . . a year's catch to trade at the annual rendezvous.

Filling his floppy leather hat from the spring, he poured the cold water over his head, snorting with pleasure as the icy liquid cascaded down his long blond hair and his unkempt curly beard. Quickly, he pulled the blood- and grease-stained leather tunic over his head and splashed the cooling water over his muscular body.

In her hiding place beneath the chokecherry bushes, Falling Star stared at the thick golden hair on his chest and arms glistening in the sunlight. Her heart leaped and began to pound wildly against her ribs. She recognized him . . . the Shining Bear of her vision last autumn beneath the blazing sky. Without thought, she stood up.

At once the young trapper turned, half crouching, a long-bladed Green River knife instantly in his hand. Their eyes met and held. Falling Star was pierced by a deep and pervading joy. His eyes were blue . . . as deep blue as the Wind River mountains towering far to the north of the rendezvous. The Shining Bear had found his way to her.

"Well, I'll be damned," he said in a deep rumbling voice. "Ain't you a pretty one." The blue eyes took in her slender form in the pale doeskin dress, her soft face with high cheekbones and dark almond-shaped eyes, the smooth fall of her shining black hair. He'd not had a woman since he'd stayed some days with a band of Shoshone in their winter camp south of the Laramie. This one was that rarity among Indian women . . . a real beauty. At once, Hugh felt the stirring in his loins and he took a step toward her.

Overjoyed at the fulfillment of her vision, Falling Star did not immediately hear the inner voice. Not yet, it said, not yet. The white man doesn't know what is to be the future. Go now. And the voice became urgent as the man moved toward her. Like a deer startled from cover, Falling Star turned and fled into the forest.

Shrugging his shoulders, Hugh Cameron pulled the filthy tunic back over his head, then picked up his horse's reins. There would be women enough at the rendezvous, eager and compliant for the price of a few yards of scarlet cloth and some bright beads.

Mounting his horse, he rode through the aspens, pausing at the edge of the hill to enjoy the scene spread before him on the wide flats of the Green River. Dust rose from hundreds of horses moving constantly from one camp to another . . . from races taking place on a course set farther upriver. Each tribe had created its own village wherever there was room for lodges, wood for cooking fires, and forage for animals. Snake and Crow, Nez Percé and Flathead. Smoke from their fires drifted lazily in the air, bringing a scent of cooking meat that made Hugh's stomach growl.

This year's rivals for the fur trade . . . the Rocky Mountain Fur Company and the American Fur Company had set up their trading tents a mile apart. Both were crowded with trappers anxious to trade their furs for liquor, as well as for the beads and mirrors and bright cloth needed to lure the squaws to their bed.

Indians crowded in, bartering their furs and skins for the doctored alcohol the companies sold as whiskey. Already, half the camp was roaring drunk on the filthy stuff. Already fights had broken out among intoxicated trappers. Those still sober enough challenged each other to wrestling or shooting matches. Circles of seated, shouting men played the Indian hand game, gambling the year's earnings away.

Hugh allowed himself a bitter grimace. None of that for him. He'd learned that lesson long ago. And an old revulsion rose in his throat. Fourteen years old and running away from the miller he was bound to, he'd been plied with liquor by the degenerate flatboatman and buggered while he lay too drunk to resist. In the pale dawn light Hugh killed the bastard as he slept, with his own knife, then dumped the body overboard for the fishes at the bottom of the Ohio River.

"Whar you been, ol' coon?" a booming voice hailed him from the Rocky Mountain Fur Company tent.

"Fitz, you ol' hoss!" Hugh swung down from his saddle and returned the older man's enthusiastic bear hug.

"Purely thought them Blackfeet had lifted yer hair. Wagh!" Old Broken Hand Fitzpatrick stood back to survey his friend. Fitz was a tall man, his hair heavily streaked with gray, his leather-colored face creased by lines from a lifetime in the mountains. He was clad in a bright-colored northwest wool capote fresh from St. Louis. It had never handicapped him in his chosen trade, but his withered hand earned him the nickname "Broken Hand" from the Indians.

"Not this one," Hugh replied with a grin. "You taught me too good for any Injun to get close enough to my scalp."

"Larned ya good, *well* I did!" Fitz gave the younger man an affectionate look. "We missed ya on the hunt this winter. How'd you like bein' a free trapper?"

"Damned lonesome doin's," Hugh replied. "I been studying on buying myself a wife."

Fitz stepped over to the mules and examined the parfleche carry-alls filled with beaver skins with a critical and expert eye. "Had a woman to dress yer skins, you'd a done better."

"Figured you'd help me find one by paying mighty handsome for my beaver."

"You ain't gonna make me bid agin the trust fer your catch, boy? Why I bin like a pa to you!" Fitz turned his grizzled frown on Hugh.

"Ain't likely I'd trade with Astor's varmints," Hugh answered quickly. "I know you'll do me right."

Fitz chuckled and began untying the parfleche packs. "Enuff to buy yerself a wife, anyways. Wagh!"

While Fitz inspected and priced the plews, Coburn, the

company clerk, stood by to keep record of Hugh's credit. Hugh kept his own tally on a piece of white buckskin, trusting Fitz but not the clerk, who was half drunk. When they had agreed on the total, Coburn drew a measure of whiskey from a barrel and handed it to Hugh.

Fitz threw his head back and roared his laughter. "Not this hyar chile, Coburn. He don't like that stuff . . . nor gamblin' either. Jes comes to rendezvous and drowns hisself in wimmen."

"We all got our weakness," Coburn said, and drank the whiskey himself.

"Damn yer eyes," Fitz growled. "I won't have no drunk clerks givin' my trade goods away. Sleep it off and I'll run the store." He turned to Hugh. "You wanna job as clerk?"

"Not me," Hugh grinned. "Just now I want new clothes, a shave, and a squaw."

Fitz's laugh boomed out. "Wal, you kin stay at my lodge tonight. My squaw'll be cookin' fat cow jes fer you."

As he splashed himself clean in river water muddied by the passage of horses, Indians, and trappers, Hugh grinned with anticipation. From the camp came the familiar noise of a drunken spree . . . shouts, gunshots, bawdy songs. It was good to be in company again, he thought, and good to see old Fitz.

Fitzpatrick had been his friend since the day four years ago when he signed on with him in St. Louis, a sixteen-year-old man contracting to come up the Missouri with trade goods for the rendezvous. For three years, he'd trapped with Fitz's brigade, learning the mountains, the ways of the beavers and the Indians. After losing everything he owned in the Indian hand game that first rendezvous, he'd forsworn gambling. Because he neither drank nor gambled, he came away from rendezvous with his profits intact . . . except for the year's supplies and the foofaraw necessary to buy a squaw for his bed. Last year he'd set out on his own, a free trapper beholden to no fur company.

"Damn!" he said, seeing that he was already hard with

anticipation. Scrambling up the river's sandy bank, he quickly pulled on new wool pants and shirt. Then he stuffed the beads and scarlet cloth into his pocket and went to find a woman.

Many Horses sat at ease before the cooking fire, a thick buffalo robe padding his woven willow backrest. Puffing silently on his pipe, he stared into the flames, well pleased with the day's events. His spotted-rump Palouse horses had won handily in several races. Tonight he would have the wherewithal to join in one of the many hand-game circles.

Through half-closed eyes, he watched his eldest daughter, Falling Star, bring more wood to the cooking fire. He valued this girl now that Old Grandmother had died, for she had inherited the old woman's medicine. Still it was well that the young warrior, Bull Head, would have this rendezvous to rid himself of wildness before he and Falling Star were wed. Content with his thoughts, he glanced idly up at the two horsemen approaching his lodge.

"That the one?" Fitz asked, nodding his head toward Falling Star.

Hugh nodded, unable to speak. It had never happened to him before. For two days he had reveled in women, and every time, at the moment of climax, this girl's face had flooded his mind. It was as though that brief encounter at the spring had left him bewitched. Finding less pleasure in each of his sexual contacts, Hugh decided the only way to be rid of his obsession was to take the girl for his wife. Fitz had finally located her.

She stood now beside the lodge, away from the fire, so that only a faint flickering light touched the soft planes of her face. Their eyes met and Hugh's throat tightened painfully.

So he has come at last, Falling Star thought. She had known it was inevitable, and yet now that he was here, she was suddenly afraid. Perhaps he was too late. Only yesterday, her father had promised that when the Nez Percé returned to their own mountains, she would be wife to Bull Head. She disliked Bull Head for his careless and wild ways. He would not be a kind husband, she was sure, but Many

Horses said the young warrior was a great hunter, brave in battle, and rich in horses.

Looking into the young trapper's blue eyes, Falling Star felt as though she were drowning in them. Behind the lust she saw there, she knew her destined love would grow, for this was the Shining Bear of her vision.

"Ask him!" Hugh's voice was low and tense. Beneath the flannel shirt his body was bathed in perspiration and he could not seem to draw air into his lungs. Nor could he tear his eyes from the face of the girl. A woman was a woman, he tried to tell himself. Why should this girl affect him so mightily, in a way no other woman ever had?

"It won't shine," Fitz growled. "You know that. You don't jump right inta things with an Injun. A little smoke first."

The pipe passed around as Hugh and Fitz sat before the fire with Many Horses. Falling Star and her stepmother, Blue Feather, brought the bark dishes and served the men from the stew pot. Fitz, whose command of Indian lingo was prodigious, carried on the desultory conversation with Many Horses.

While he listened, Hugh's body ached and burned as with a fever. He had never trapped the Nez Percé country and knew little of their language, so he had to wait for Fitz's translation. As the conversation ebbed and flowed, he watched Falling Star, admiring her quickness as she moved about her work, the swell of her bosom beneath the doeskin frock, the turn of her slender ankles. . . .

Sitting with Blue Feather away from the fire, Falling Star tried to eat and could not. Her eyes remained on the Shining Bear, watching him watching her. Help me, she prayed silently, her fingers clutching the medicine bag about her neck. Inside the delicate beaded bag was the blue stone that had been her grandmother's strongest medicine and now was her own *wyakin*.

She could hear Broken Hand delicately leading up to the purpose of his visit.

"I have many daughters," she heard her father reply in a boastful tone. "And many warrior sons."

"That one." Broken Hand indicated Falling Star.

"No . . . no . . . no." Many Horses shook his head and waved his arms in denial. "That one is promised to Bull Head."

"Hugh Cameron is a rich trapper," Fitz protested. "He kin pay more than Bull Head . . . a heap more."

For a moment Many Horses was silent, staring into the fire as though contemplating possible enrichment from the sale of his daughter. Then he somberly began to shake his head. "Not this one . . . not her." His glance went carefully over Hugh, but he did not even look at his daughter. "The Old One died last winter. Now Falling Star is our medicine woman. She must stay with her people." Brightening, he gave Hugh a hopeful grin. "But I have other daughters."

Fitz glanced at Hugh and translated. Hugh shook his head. He wanted no other daughter of Many Horses, only this one, sitting there with the flames lighting her slender face, her dark eyes fixed on him. Suddenly he felt sick and lost, and was angry for the unaccustomed feeling. Back at Fitz's lodge there would be other women, he didn't need this one.

Many Horses rose, urging the two trappers to come join him at the hand game. Offering a gift of tobacco, Fitz declined.

In the darkness beside her father's lodge, Falling Star watched the two men ride away. With one brief glance of longing and frustration, Shining Bear had set his now-beardless jaw, mounted his horse, and rode from her life.

Bitterness welled in her. What had been only dislike for Bull Head burgeoned into hatred and her throat was clogged with anger at her father. How could he promise her to Bull Head when the Shining Bear had offered more? Now she knew how much he valued her medicine. He would not let her go from the village for any price.

Struggling to appear unconcerned, she strolled idly toward the staked horses. When she whistled, her favorite horse broke from the others and came to her. Nuzzling the little mare, scratching her ears, Falling Star told her softly,

"We will go to him this night. I know where the lodge of Fitzpatrick is and we will find him."

A deep pervading joy filled her as she realized she had made a momentous decision. Nothing her father could ever do would keep her from the Shining Bear, for he had been foretold in her vision and her life was inextricably bound to his.

Chapter 2

Reflected starlight shimmered in the dark waters of the river. Wading into the swift, cold water, Hugh let it swirl about his nude body, washing away all trace of the woman who had shared his bed for a string of bright beads. The rendezvous was quiet now in the depths of night, only an occasional dog barking, the snort of horses in answer to the distant wailing of coyotes.

Restless and unsatisfied, Hugh stared back at the camp where low banked fires gleamed through the darkness. She has bewitched me, he thought, seized by fierce longing for the daughter of Many Horses. The squaw he had just sent away from his bed had given him no surcease from that longing, and he knew with deep certainty no other woman ever would.

Stepping out of the swift-moving water, Hugh reached for the trousers he had left on the sandy bank. With a grin and a sudden determined lift of his chin, he strode back toward camp. Tomorrow he would offer Many Horses everything he owned for Falling Star. Indians were a greedy lot. Surely the old man would consent to sell his daughter for that much booty. Even though he'd no longer be a free trapper, the Rocky Mountain Fur Company would outfit him on credit. It didn't matter . . . nothing mattered but Falling Star.

"Greedy slut," Hugh muttered when he saw that his

bedroll was still occupied. He'd given her beads and a length of scarlet cloth . . . more than she deserved . . . and he'd thought she left when he did. Angry because she was not the woman he wanted, Hugh gave the figure a sharp kick.

With a soft cry, the woman sat up, dark hair falling about her shoulders. Starlight reflected in the soft luminous eyes of Falling Star as she stared at him in dismay.

"Oh God!" The words burst from Hugh. Quickly he knelt beside her, drawing her into his arms. "I'm sorry . . . sorry . . ."

Gently, she held him away, her dark eyes glowing in the pale light as she studied his face. "You . . . Shining Bear," she murmured in a voice as soft as her eyes. "Want wife . . . me . . . Falling Star."

"Want you?" Hugh managed to choke out, totally in thrall now to the obsession that had grown inside him since he'd first seen her at the spring. If her price were his very soul, he would pay it gladly.

A slow sweet smile lifted the corners of her young mouth and her eyes glowed in the starlight. Without once taking her eyes from his, Falling Star pulled off her doeskin gown. Rolling it into a pillow, she lay back and held her arms up to him. Her pale nakedness seemed to have an incandescent glow of its own.

A kind of madness possessed Hugh as he sank into her embrace, her soft young body hot against his, firm young breasts burning his chest. His mouth claimed hers and the sweet, smoky taste of her brought his passion to fever pitch. All day he had thought of her, wanting her, and he could wait no longer. When he entered her, she gasped with pain.

Hugh froze into perfect stillness, his face against her warm throat, her loose dark hair like silk threads against his cheek. She was that incredibly rare thing among Indian women . . . a virgin . . . and he had hurt her in his haste to possess her.

Carefully he withdrew from her in spite of her soft protests. Gently he began to woo her . . . with light kisses on her throat, her eyes, his tongue teasing at her soft mouth. Her breasts responded to his lips, the nipples hardening as

17

she moaned softly and clutched at his back, pressing him closer.

Slowly, with his lips and hands exploring, caressing, he aroused her until her breath came quickly and her body strained against his. When her low cries pleaded with him, he moved gently into her, his own pleasure doubled in the knowledge that this time he had not hurt her.

Falling Star instinctively lifted her hips to receive him and he clasped them in his hands, holding her against him. His mouth covered hers as she answered his movements, whimpering with passion as their joining grew more frenzied. Hugh burst within her, crying out in triumphant fulfillment. Seconds later, her cry answered his. Even then she held him, fiercely embraced by arms and legs, kissing him wildly as they descended into satiated stillness.

A coyote howled in the far distance, and an Indian dog answered from nearby. Faintly, Falling Star could hear the raucous voices of the gamblers still at the hand game by some campfire beyond her vision. The vast dark bowl of the sky arched above her, gilded now by the late rising moon.

Falling Star smiled up at the golden moon hanging low in the eastern sky, certain that the Shining Bear was bound to her now for all time. Reluctantly, she relaxed her fierce hold on him, her body slack and damp against his warm and hairy one. With a contented sigh, she stroked the thick curls on his head lying upon her breast, inhaling the pleasantly musky odor of him.

Even though Old Grandmother had guarded her from the young men who would have had her as soon as her flow began and she was a woman, Falling Star was not ignorant of the act of sex. Many a winter night she'd awakened to the groaning and panting of her father and his wife, many a time come upon a couple in the forests heaving their bodies together. It had made no real sense until now when all her being yearned to be part of this man. She had come to him because it was destined, but his unexpected gentleness had won her completely.

Stroking his hard-muscled back with loving hands, she

felt him stir and mutter sleepily. Again she sighed, knowing
the sun would soon burn away the late rising moon and that
she must leave him before first light. Her heart tripped and
began to pound anxiously. Would he understand what she
meant to tell him? She had picked up a little English from
listening to the trappers who traded with her father. Shining
Bear must understand. Their destiny together depended
upon it.

"Hugh Cameron," she tested the name softly.

"Aye," he answered, turned, and began to kiss her throat.

A hot ache leaped between her thighs. Wanting the kisses
and all that came with them, Falling Star pushed him away
reluctantly. "I go now."

"No!" Hugh's arms tightened possessively about her.

"Saus . . . Quiet. You listen . . ." She cupped his face in
her hands and looked into his eyes. "Tomorrow you go . . ."
And she pointed toward the Wind River mountains black
against the northern sky. "I follow."

"No!" Hugh pulled her close against him, his mouth
taking hers in a long deep kiss.

Breathless, they broke apart. Falling Star felt his hardness
pressing urgently against her belly.

"No," he said again. His hands began to move gently over
her body and she caught her breath as her flesh began to
warm and quicken in answer to his caresses. "I'll go to your
pa tomorrow," he continued, his words punctuated by
kisses. "I'll up the ante until he cain't say no. If we run,
there'll be trouble."

Falling Star understood only part of his words, the
vehemence of his tone making the message clear to her. Hot
rivulets of desire coursed through her as his mouth covered
her breast. All her being yearned toward him, aching with
her newfound need. Drawing a deep breath, she forced him
to look at her by holding his face in her two hands. It must
be settled now between them, before they were lost once
more in each other's body.

"Father not sell. You go tomorrow. I follow. Only way."
As Hugh silently studied her earnest face, Falling Star called

on her *wyakin* . . . the blue stone . . . her strong medicine. Let the Shining Bear understand her stumbling words and let him hear her urgency in his heart.

Hugh covered her hand with one of his own, turning his serious face to kiss her palm. The touch of his moist mouth sent a flurry of sensation radiating through her, and Falling Star sighed as the ache grew in her body.

Frowning, Hugh looked into her serious eyes. "Only way?" he asked. When she nodded emphatically, he drew her close against him. "I'll go," he said as his mouth covered hers.

She wanted to cry out in triumph, but his tongue probed her mouth. The salty taste of him added to the flame consuming her. In one violent movement, she flung her legs about him, taking him deep into the hot aching depths of her.

Hugh grunted in surprise, laughed aloud, and kissed her again, his body responding to her frenzied movements. Then the late moon seemed to burst in her eyes into a million falling stars and she knew the vision was true and good.

"Ye're a crazy ol' coon," Fitz said with a puzzled frown as he watched Hugh loading his mules. "Ye got so fond of the big lonesome outen there, three days rendezvous enuff fer ye?"

"Got what I come for," Hugh answered, not meeting his friend's curious eyes. Fitz was right to call him crazy, he thought. The girl, Falling Star, had put a kind of craziness in him that sent everything from his mind but the need to possess her. Glancing at Fitz, he told himself it was best the older man not know the truth . . . in case there was trouble.

"Money and supplies . . ." he added vaguely as he pulled the parfleches tight on the mule's back.

Fitz laughed. "Never seen you git filled up on wimmen that quick." Nudging Hugh in the ribs, he added slyly, "Fire goin' out, chile?"

Hugh managed a grin in reply, knowing the fire in his

loins was for one woman now and only her. He was risking his scalp to steal her, that's how crazy she'd made him. But he didn't seem to have any will to resist. He had to have her and if this was the only way . . .

"Look at them dumb bastards," he told Fitz, waving a hand to indicate the hung-over trappers already starting on another day's drunk. The trading booths were busy dispensing whiskey even though the sun was only a hand's breadth above the Wind Rivers. "I'll have a load of beaver before they're even sober enough to pack up."

"Cursed with ambition, ain't ye?" Fitz chuckled as Hugh mounted his horse.

Hugh merely nodded, anxious to be on his way, his nerves singing with anticipation. He dared not ride by the Nez Percé camp, or even glance at it. "See you next July at New Fork," he told Fitz, lifting a hand in farewell and spurring his horse.

"Watch yer hair!" Fitz called after him in the mountain man's traditional farewell.

Shadows of the lodgepole pines lay long on the rocky hillside as Hugh paused to let his animals blow and rest. Wind stirred the pine trees in a faint sighing, but the only other sound that came to his listening ear was the faint, distant cry of mourning doves.

A sinking sensation ran through him, leaving what seemed a great empty hole at the pit of his stomach. Doubts had been growing all through the long day's trek up from the Green River into the foothills of the Wind River mountains. His ear was attuned to the sounds of the mountains, and he knew no one followed him.

He took a long pull on his canteen, then squinted into the wooded distance. Before dark, he had to find water and grass, a place to make camp.

"Damn her eyes," he cried suddenly, pounding his fist against the saddle so that his horse shied. Why had he believed her? All squaws were liars and cheats! Hell, maybe he hadn't understood her right. God knows, her English was poor enough to leave both of them confused. He'd been thinking with the wrong part of his body when he agreed to her crazy scheme.

So she wasn't coming, he told himself, surprised at how much that knowledge pained him. What in hell was different about this woman? he asked himself. It wasn't just her body he wanted, though God knew the thought of that set his loins stirring. It was something elusive . . . never encountered before.

"The little squaw sent me on a fool's chase," he told his horse as he mounted up. A faint sound of water over stones made him turn the horse in that direction. The mules picked up their pace, sniffing the air, anxious for a drink after the long dry day.

Chewing a piece of jerky, Hugh stared reflectively into his low campfire. Beside the small stream, his tethered animals cropped grass noisily. In the distance, a coyote howled, high and lonesome in the darkness.

He felt oddly disoriented, almost lost, although he knew perfectly well where he was and how he would strike eastward in the morning into the heart of the Wind Rivers. It was the girl made him feel this way, her and her lies about following him.

"She's a damn Injun witch," he muttered, and thought of the black conjure woman his stepmother had consulted back in Kentuck. The Indian girl was a magic woman too. She'd stolen his manhood, sent him like a whipped dog running before her. And she hadn't followed. "Damn!" He hated it that the knowledge left him so empty.

Adding a few sticks to the fire, Hugh pulled his new wool capote about him and leaned back against the trunk of a tall pine. He'd forget quick enough, he promised himself. Next Indian camp he came on, he'd buy a wife to help with the furs and forget that Injun witch. Even as the thought passed and his eyelids drooped as he stared into the coals of his fire, he knew he lied to himself.

A twig snapped. Startled into full awareness, Hugh instinctively grabbed for the loaded rifle leaning against the tree trunk. Then his hand fell to his side.

Across the little clearing where he'd made camp, at the very edge of the firelight, Falling Star stood, smiling at him. For a sick moment, Hugh thought he had conjured her image from his own longing. Then she laughed aloud. Crying out, *"Taz . . . taz . . .* good . . . good" and the name she had called him last night . . . Shining Bear . . . she ran toward him.

Hugh opened his arms as she flung herself against him. The world that had seemed empty only moments before was suddenly made whole.

Chapter 3

Sunlight streaming through the pine trees dazzled Falling Star's eyes as she came awake. It was far too late, she thought, with an inward start of panic. Already her father would have sent a party in pursuit of her. She would have been missed at the cooking fire last night, her bed robes empty. Perhaps then they would have found her personal belongings gone, her sewing equipment, her ceremonial dress, and the doeskins she had cured this summer.

Turning to look at the man sleeping heavily beside her, she touched the blue stone on its thong about her neck. Grant that her father had not noticed the stallion and mare missing from his herd of fine horses. He would be truly angry for that loss, but she did not care. He owed the Shining Bear for the insult of denying him herself in marriage.

Hugh muttered, turned, and was suddenly awake, his blue eyes staring into hers. The eyes softened and he grinned as he drew her against him, his body already hard with desire. Falling Star felt her own body turn soft and throbbing in response. All through the night he had taught her of love . . . sleeping, awakening to love again. Smiling as his mouth caressed her breasts, she recalled his puzzlement as she prompted him through the words of the Nez Percé marriage ceremony:

"Hamo hanisa . . . I take you for husband."

"Inepne hanisa . . . I take you for wife."

"Star," he murmured now against her throat. "My wife . . . my Star . . . mine . . ."

Her body took fire from the touch of his hands and his eager mouth. Falling Star forgot there would be Nez Percé pursuers on her trail, forgot everything but the sensations that grew and grew until her whole body seemed to explode in a white-hot fire of rapture.

"Koimze!" Falling Star called. "Hurry!" Mounting her mare, she winced. Her body was tender from the night of loving. As she watched Hugh scatter the ashes from their dead campfire, the skin at the back of her neck pricked with urgency. Somewhere between here and the Green River a search party followed them, of that she was as certain as she was that if they were overtaken it meant death for Shining Bear.

Furiously, she motioned at Hugh to mount and follow her. He would have been content to stay all day in this fine camp, with its good water and grass, lying in the bed robes making love.

She had risen quickly from their lovemaking to begin packing the animals, ignoring his protests.

"I'll be damned," he said, when she led up the horses she had brought. "You little horse thief! No wonder yer in a hurry." His amazed grin disappeared at once into a worried frown. "You shouldn'ta done it. Likely ye'll git us killed fer yer damn horses."

Without pausing for breakfast, Hugh helped load the horses and mules. They set off northward, making their own trail through the thick stands of lodgepole pine, each of them chewing at a piece of jerky. Falling Star's apprehension had communicated itself to Hugh and he kept a hard pace all through the day, pausing only to water the animals.

Dusk gathered beneath the tall pines and the last rays of sunlight gilded the trembling leaves of the aspen trees.

Hugh pulled his horse up and turned back to look at Falling Star. "The critters are plumb wore out," he said.

Then remembering how little English she understood, he used Indian sign language to tell her they should stop for the night.

Fear ran cold through Falling Star's veins. Inside her head following hoofbeats echoed . . . a sound she knew only she could hear. The warriors might take her back in dishonor, but they would not spare Shining Bear.

With a quick glance around, she took in their situation. Below the rocky hillside where they had paused, a small creek tumbled among boulders, half hidden in a tangle of willows and underbrush. She nodded at Hugh, motioning to him that they must ride further upstream, hoping to find grass for the animals.

When they had unpacked and tethered the animals on the small swatch of grass beside the stream, Hugh drew her into his arms. It was a thing he'd longed for all through the day, yet her tension communicated itself to him at once.

"Come," she urged, drawing away from him. Picking up the bedroll, she motioned to him to follow. Puzzled and protesting, Hugh followed her to the spot she had chosen for their camp, a hillside glade thick with aspen and choke-cherry bushes.

"We oughta stay with the animals," he growled, watching as she hurried to gather wood for their campfire. The meal of jerky and hardtack was eaten quickly. They had pushed so fast there had been no time to hunt along the trail, although Hugh thought even a jackrabbit or squirrel would have tasted better than jerky.

As the campfire burned down, its light scarcely penetrating the dark forest, Falling Star arranged the bedroll nearby, stuffing pine boughs beneath the blankets so that it seemed to be occupied.

"We wait there." She pointed to a thick growth of bushes just beyond the campsite.

Understanding dawned in Hugh's eyes and he grinned. "Ain't you the one?" he asked, drawing her into his arms. "We're gonna ambush 'em."

She nodded, yielding to his kiss for only a moment, before she pushed him away. Taking a skin robe for each of them, she made a kind of nest among the thicket of bushes. Hugh quickly loaded his rifle and his pistol, testing the sharpness of the Green River knife at his belt. His eyes widened at the sight of the skinning knife Falling Star inserted in her legging.

Darkness deepened as they huddled together in the damp bushes. Night creatures moved through the forest. A porcupine waddled past, dimly seen in the last glow of the fire. Somewhere in the far distance a coyote wailed and was answered by his mate.

Falling Star shivered, every nerve drawn tight. Hugh's arm came around her shoulders, drawing her close to share his warmth. In the blackness, she could scarcely see the gleam of his eyes in starlight filtering through the trees. This man was her heart, but now was not the time to think of love. It was *kiuala piyakasuisa* . . . time to fight. Time to ask *Hunyewat* for strength in the coming battle and pray that the warriors attacked before the rising of the moon . . . while the ambushers held the advantage.

She heard them before he did, the barest rustle of sound through the trees. The last coals of their fire gave faint light to the little clearing, to the seemingly occupied bed robes. Falling Star straightened, stiff and alert, carefully drawing the knife from her legging. She felt Hugh grow tense beside her, silently lifting the Hawken rifle in his hands, his own ears now aware of the sound of men creeping through the forest.

"Eeeagh!" A bloodcurdling yell echoed in the darkness, the sound bouncing back from the rocky cliffs, repeated in the blackness. Three Nez Percé warriors with painted faces leaped into the firelight, descending upon the bed robes with knives and spears.

Very deliberately, Hugh took aim. The Hawken spoke in thunderous tones. One of the warriors spun around, his chest suddenly scarlet. Falling Star gasped at the sight of Bull Head's dying face. Then the other warriors were on them, leaping across the space, crashing through the brush toward them. Hugh's pistol barked. Another warrior fell face down on the forest floor.

Guns emptied, Hugh grabbed for the Green River knife at his belt. Too late! The Nez Percé leaped upon him, knocking the knife from his hands, bearing him violently down upon the tree roots. The warrior's muscular arm raised, aiming his knife at Hugh's throat. Grasping that arm with all his strength, Hugh struggled to hold it away.

"Eeeagh!" He felt the warrior start and hesitate at the cry from behind him. Then the Indian fell, a dead weight across Hugh's body.

Caught between fear and relief, Falling Star sobbed as she struggled to drag the dead warrior from Hugh. Her skinning knife was sunk to the hilt in the man's back and bloody foam bubbled noisily from his dying lungs.

Freeing himself, Hugh scrambled to his feet. He grabbed Falling Star, holding her protectively until her trembling stopped. At a sound from the woods, he released her and grabbed his rifle to quickly reload.

"More of the bastards out there," he growled.

"No," she said, guessing his intent. "No more. All dead."

Frowning, Hugh repeated their spoken words in the Indian sign language. Then he shrugged. She knew her people, and she had the ears of a wild creature. Just the same, he finished loading the Hawken and leaned it against the tree.

Then he retrieved the Green River knife from the dirt where the Nez Percé warrior had knocked it from his hand. Bending over, he lifted the dead Indian's hair.

"Eeagh!" Falling Star's cry made him stop short of scalping the man.

"Sepekuse!" she cried. "Let be!" Her hands moved quickly in the signs, her face pleading. "No scalp."

Once more Hugh shrugged, allowing her to overrule him. These were her people . . . and he wasn't that fond of taking scalps anyway.

Quickly gathering wood, Falling Star built up the fire. A new kind of urgency possessed her now as she signed to Hugh that they must bury the warriors quickly. There was a small ravine on the rocky hillside beyond their campsite.

Together they dragged the three bodies there, then covered them with rocks.

Falling Star disappeared into the woods, returning with the three horses the warriors had tethered there while they sneaked up on their intended victims. Hugh stared to see how docilely the Palouse horses followed her to join their other animals tethered in the grass near the creek.

"I'm damned, woman," he told her when she returned, taking her into his arms. "You're a she-bear, an' a magic woman to boot." He kissed her, long and fiercely, then looked tenderly into her somber face. "This h'yar chile never bin so lucky as the day I first saw yer face."

He had shaken out the bed robes and laid them again beside the dwindling fire. Danger past now, he wanted her, and drew her with him toward the waiting bed.

Falling Star shook her head, making the sign to tell him he must wait. Hugh grinned indulgently, sure there must be some woman thing she needed to do before coming to his bed. Watching as she moved into the forest, where the faint light of the rising moon had begun to illuminate the landscape, Hugh shucked off his clothes and slid between the bed robes, waiting eagerly for her return.

A high thin cry struck terror to his bones. Then the sound dwindled and a mournful chant began. Hugh groaned, recognizing an Indian mourning song.

Three Nez Percé warriors had died this night, Falling Star told herself. She would do them the honor of sending them to *Hunyewat* with a mourning song to guide them. One of them might have been her husband had not her vision been fulfilled with the coming of the Shining Bear.

Yet as her voice rose and fell in the old, old chant, the sound lifting up toward the rising moon, Falling Star knew she mourned not just for the dead warriors of her tribe, but for the old familiar life she was leaving behind forever.

Chapter 4

Why in tarnation was he letting a girl, a Nez Percé from the far country across the Snake River, guide him in his own stomping grounds? Hugh asked himself. He knew the country. Tom Fitzpatrick's brigade had trapped north through this part of the Wind Rivers when Hugh Cameron was a greenhorn. They'd joined up with Jim Bridger's brigade at Jackson Hole, trapped clear to the upper Missouri, down Powder River and the Medicine Bow, into winter quarters at Fort Laramie.

Now Hugh grinned to himself at the memory of those days of plenty beaver, with fat buffalo cow to eat most every night. Afterward, he'd trapped the Wind Rivers by himself, and he'd been certain there was a map of the country engraved on his mind.

Hugh frowned at Falling Star's slender back as she rode her spotted mare down the trail ahead of him. She'd simply gone ahead of him after their brief nooning stop, her face intent. Her eyes had that dark, unfathomable look he'd come to know in their few days together. It was the look she'd had when she knew the warriors were following them. Now it seemed to be concentrated on something ahead of them, something she meant to find.

"Yer besotted, Cameron, crazy ol' hoss," he said aloud,

just as he'd always talked to himself when he was companionless.

Falling Star turned, smiling at him questioningly, and Hugh's throat tightened painfully. He'd guessed that the words she said with him that first night had been the Nez Percé marriage ceremony. No trapper was bound by such things, as he might have been back in the States. But this was not a woman for a season, this was his woman for all the rest of his life.

Falling Star knew her husband was vexed with her for taking the lead. The trail she'd chosen was a precipitous one, a rocky canyon so narrow they had to guide the animals down the creek bed, between boulders and overhanging willows. She led the pack mules behind her. Hugh led the horses she had brought with her and the three warriors' horses strung out on lead ropes.

Behind her, she could hear Hugh cursing, yelling at her in English, but she could not pause now. An insistent inner compass guided her as surely as the wild birds were guided north with the coming of spring. Steeling herself against his anger, she refused to look back at him. Women were supposed to follow, but he must come to understand that sometimes a medicine woman must lead.

She would have to learn his tongue, she thought. Only then could she truly share with him. For now he must trust her instincts and her gift. Even she wasn't certain of their destination, but something drew her there, something deep and compelling.

Scrambling up a fall of broken limestone, the mare broke through the willows to gain an outcropping of rock where she stopped to blow, her sides heaving. Below them, the creek tumbled down into a wide mountain-rimmed valley. In the hazy distance, rolling hills, gray-green with sagebrush, stretched to a horizon of low blue mountains. Here on the southeastern slope of the mountain they'd just crossed, water ran everywhere through wide green meadows. Even from this distance, Star knew the streams were full of beaver sign.

"Aikits palojami," she said in an awed voice, patting the

tired mare. *"Aikits palojami . . .* Fair land . . ." Falling Star let out a long sigh, knowing the gift of foreknowledge had led her truly. In this fair land, she would live with Shining Bear.

Hugh rode up beside her. Her heart stilled as she waited, watching his eyes survey the valley before them. Would he find it as fair as she? And would he share her sense of homecoming?

"Ya done good," he said, reaching across to take her hand tightly in his. "Had me worried fer a while there, but reckon ya know somethin' I don't." Dismounting, he held up his arms for her, drawing her close to him as she slid from the horse's back. "We'll stay," he said.

Even though only a few of the English words had meaning for her, Falling Star understood he was pleased.

Together, they rode down the rocky hillside to where the thundering creek slowed to slip peacefully between grassy, willow-lined banks. "Beaver!" Hugh peered at the pile of chewed lengths of aspen and willow damming one of the small streams. "Don't recollect this place," he mused, "but it's fine . . . mighty fine."

Falling Star chose their camp beside a clump of tall willow and red alder that would shade them from the midday sun. At once she began unloading the packs, for the sun had plunged behind the towering western peaks and dusk lay over the valley. While she made a fire and set up camp, Hugh tethered the horses further down the creek. He returned with four fresh trout still wriggling on a willow fork.

"Mighty tasty after four days of jerky and hardtack," Hugh told her when they had finished eating. He leaned back against a pack saddle, a satisfied grin on his face.

Cooking chores finished, Falling Star built up the fire and sat beside Hugh on the bed robes. Contentment filled her heart as she surveyed their neat camp, the warm fire lighting the darkness. Hugh drew her into his arms, nuzzling against her soft cheek. With a protesting cry, she moved away, rubbing her face where his newly burgeoning beard had scratched her. Hugh kissed the spot and she smiled, taking his face in her two hands, looking directly into his eyes.

"You . . ." She pointed at him. "Teach . . . me."

"I done larned you near everything I know." He gave her a lustful grin and attempted to pull her against him.

Again, she held him away. Taking his hand in hers, she pointed at it insistently. "What?"

"Hand," Hugh replied with a puzzled frown.

"Hand," she repeated carefully, giving him a dazzling smile.

Now Hugh understood and he laughed aloud, repeating the words as her pointing finger moved from hand to "arm" to "shoulder" to "face."

"Eye," he said, as her fingers gently stroked the blue eyes she found so compelling. "Nose," as the fingers moved down his face. "Mouth." Then he could wait no longer. Pulling her tightly against his aroused body, he murmured, "Kiss," and proceeded to demonstrate.

"Kiss," she repeated, enthusiastically returning his demonstration. The English lesson was forgotten as they slid together beneath the bed robes, communicating in the most universal language of all.

In the gray light of predawn Hugh was already at work setting his traps. Wading upstream through the icy creek water, he quickly selected the places experience had taught him there would be beaver. Anchoring the trap to a stout pole pounded into the creek bank, he baited it with a bit of twig drenched with castoreum, the noxious-smelling mixture of beaver gland he carried in a horn bottle at his belt. There was no time to be wasted, for winter came early in the mountains.

Legs aching from wading in the icy water, Hugh headed back to camp, across meadows drenched with morning dew. The horses cropping grass along the creek raised their heads to whinny a greeting. Good Lord, he thought, Falling Star had tamed the horses just as quickly as she'd tamed him. Magic woman . . . she'd enchanted the animals too.

The odor of hot coffee brought a grin of anticipation. By God, it was good to have a wife by the fire making coffee . . . good not to be alone. Coming up behind Star, he scooped her into his arms. She let out a cry and, wrinkling her nose, pushed him away.

"Wash!" she commanded, pointing at the creek. Hugh laughed aloud, wondering where in hell she'd learned that word. But he obediently went to the creek bank, bending over to scrub the stench of the castoreum from his hands with sand. It was the scent of the trapper, so pervasive he was used to it and surprised that she disliked it. Anxious to please her, he splashed the cold water over his face and head, then hurried back to seize her in his arms again.

There were hardtack biscuits dipped in the coffee for breakfast. At once, Hugh began loading his rifle.

"Gotta make some meat today," he told her. "My belly's plumb sick of hardtack and jerky."

"Meat," she repeated, looking pleased.

Hugh grinned. "Yer learnin' fast." Even though he knew meat was an almost universally understood word in the mountains, it pleased him that she was eager to learn his language. He'd been alone so long he was sick of the sound of his own voice. When she could speak his language, he could quit talking to himself.

With a full heart, Falling Star watched the tall straight-backed man ride away, his rifle held in front of him on the saddle. They were at the beginning of their life together and yet it seemed to her they had been together always. From the first there had been no strangeness between them. Except for the barrier of language they might have been one person.

Straightening the camp, she shook out the bed robes, rearranging them on the mattress of pine branches. Then she set the iron pot on the coals of her fire, adding to the water the wild onions she'd dug from the hillside and watercress from the stream. Before nightfall there would be deer meat to add, and perhaps a fat beaver tail.

Taking her knife, she walked along the creek, carefully selecting willow branches to be fashioned into a drying rack for the deer meat. They would need many skins, she thought, for winter clothing and moccasins . . . and for building a lodge. She was determined not to live in the kind of miserable dugout she had seen on other hillsides where trappers holed up for the winter. A skin lodge was the best of all homes, and the deer hides would be fine enough until they could go north for buffalo.

When Shining Bear returned from the hunt, they would explore the valley and choose the site for their winter camp. She paused in her work, laughing into the wind as she recalled how she had cried out that name last night in the midst of their lovemaking.

He had growled, "My name is Hugh. Call me Hugh . . . say it!"

And she had said it a dozen times, kissing him each time until neither of them could speak more for being lost in loving.

There was frost on the grass in the mornings now, and in the high canyons above the valley the aspen were already turning golden. They had moved to the head of the valley where the south sloping hillsides would provide cured bunch grass for the horses all winter. A stand of tall pines would provide shelter from the prevailing winds for the lodge she would build. Scattered all about the dugout Hugh had built to protect them from the cold autumn rains were drying skins and beaver pelts.

Streaks of gold and coral gleamed above the eastern hills as Falling Star stirred up the fire, setting coffee to boil. She shivered, wishing for a comfortable skin lodge and a fur wrap to cover her doeskin gown.

Hugh had gone to check his traps and she glanced up to see him returning, his breath like white smoke in the frosty air. He carried two fresh beaver pelts, and handed her the cutoff tails. Piercing them with a stick, she placed them in the coals to burn off the hair and the horny hide before she added them to her cooking pot.

He changed into dry leggings and they sat close to the fire, savoring the hot coffee and the fat roasted beaver tail.

Falling Star smiled contentedly, watching her husband eat

the food she had prepared. Sometimes she missed the village, the camaraderie of the women exchanging gossip, the traditional round of the seasons . . . going to dig camas roots, helping each other prepare skins. Her eyes followed Hugh as he rose and moved about the dugout, studying the supplies she had stowed neatly there. He was not like the men of her tribe, this Shining Bear who said she must call him Hugh. In the years he'd been alone, he'd cured his own beaver pelts, prepared his own meat, and now, unlike most men, he continued to help her with that work. It eased a burden that was shared back in the villages by the other women.

Love for him burgeoned in her heart. Surely *Hunyewat* had been kind in bringing her so good a man. The future was not yet entirely clear to her, but it would always be bound to the Shining Bear.

"There ain't enuff!" he said abruptly, turning to confront her after his inventory. "I took supplies fer one from the rendezvous. It'll be a starvin' winter unless I go to Fort Laramie fer more supplies."

By now she had learned enough of his language to make out the import of his words. Dismayed at the thought of a journey to Fort Laramie, she turned to look at all the skins and pelts still drying on their frames. Today she had meant to go into the forest and select the straight young pine saplings for lodge poles now that she had enough skins to make a lodge.

"Could ye stay alone?" he asked, studying her face.

"Alone." The very sound of the word gave its meaning to her, and she steeled herself.

"I could take two of the horses to sell and the pack mule. Two days goin', two days back if I travel by myself without all the foofaraw of a camp." Hugh took her shoulders in his hands, drawing her near him, his eyes intent. The thought of leaving her alone pained him as much as the thought of being without her for days. This girl . . . this wife . . . had become as necessary to him as the air he breathed.

"Yes," she answered, determined not to let him see how unhappy the prospect of staying here without him made her feel. She did not fear for his safety . . . he would return, yet she felt devastated at the thought of lonely nights ahead. "You go." Falling Star made her voice firm and steady. "I stay . . . keep camp . . . wait."

The heavily loaded pack mule occasionally brayed his protest at the fast pace Hugh kept north from Fort Laramie. The horses had commanded a fair price and the parfleche carry-alls contained coffee, sugar, and cornmeal, special treats for Star . . . new blankets, and what Hugh was certain Star would prize most: buffalo skins for her to work into warm robes for their winter bed, dried buffalo fat he'd traded from the squaws camping near the fort, and in his pocket, a sack of the bright glass beads all Indian women prized to decorate their clothing.

The cold autumn wind brought a shower of dead cottonwood leaves down on him, and Hugh shivered. Dried bunch grass blew among the gray-green sagebrush. The mountains where his inner compass was aimed were lightly dusted by the first snow of the year.

Fallen leaves rustled beneath the horse's hooves and Hugh was suddenly seized by a sense of dread. Memory of another autumn, long ago, rose to the top of his mind like the stink of the bubbling sulfur springs north of the Wind Rivers.

At twelve years old, young Hugh Cameron had suddenly grown tall, and his voice changed almost overnight to the deep baritone of a man. That was the year after his itinerant sharecropper father had moved from Kentuck north into Ohio . . . dragging along his young wife, Hugh's stepmother, and their barefoot, ragged children.

The corn crop had been a poor one that year. It seemed a gift from heaven when one of the neighbors offered a side of pork if his father would help with hog killing. Bo Cameron took the little children with him, for there would be plenty of food served at that farm.

Hugh and his stepmother, Bo said, must stay and get the corn in before the autumn rains started. Even now, after all these years, Hugh's throat clogged with revulsion as he remembered the woman's strangely burning eyes as she confronted him there between the rustling rows of dried cornstalks.

"Purty boy, Hugh," she said in a coaxing voice, then grabbed him, pulling him toward her, one hand seeking his crotch, rubbing his privates.

Humiliated and terrified, Hugh shoved her as hard as he could. When she fell, screeching, between the rows of corn, he fled into the forest, red-faced and sobbing with anger.

Carrying his razor strop, his father had come looking for him in the cold autumn dusk. "Hit yer ma, will ye, little bastard!" he cried. The leather strap fell again and again on the cowering boy. Hugh remembered nothing more until his father kicked him awake next morning.

"Git yerself down to the store," his father ordered. "Ma's plumb out of salt. Tell Old Man Werner to put it on my account." With his father's baleful eyes on his back, Hugh set off on that half day's walk without breakfast.

Now, descending the rocky hillside into his valley . . . his and Falling Star's . . . Hugh felt faintly sick at the remembrance of his homecoming that long-ago day. How silent the clearing had been. His dog, Blaze, didn't run to greet him. There were no mules in the makeshift corral . . . no sounds of children playing and quarreling.

The boy Hugh Cameron had been walked slowly into the low, mean cabin that was his home. It was empty, deserted. Stunned, he looked around for a note, some sign left for him. There was nothing. "Always trouble to me," his father had said. Barefoot in the cold autumn wind, with only the clothes he stood in, desolate and abandoned, the boy knew they had left him behind deliberately.

A knot of fear tightened in Hugh's chest as the memory tore through him. Whipping his horse, shouting wildly at the protesting mule, he dashed across the sagebrush hills. He'd let himself believe in home again after all these years. Would she be gone now, back to her own people, back to the company of other women?

Tears poured from his eyes as he and the animals rode out onto the wide meadows. The grazing Palouse horses raised their heads to sniff the new arrivals. And there, across the creek, sheltered by the hills and the trees, stood a fine skin lodge.

"Star!" he shouted. "Star!" And his heart almost burst from his chest as she ran toward him, holding out hands stained with berry juice from the medicine sign she was painting on their new home.

Chapter 5

1835

Hugh Cameron and Falling Star rode down into the valley of the Green at New Fork Creek in late July. They brought to rendezvous a string of horses with two new colts and two mules loaded with beaver. One of the horses pulled a travois made of lodge poles, loaded with camp goods and lodge skins. This was a new way of traveling for Hugh, quite unlike the brigades he'd traveled with at first, or his lonely free-trapper wanderings.

Falling Star chose the site for their camp, a distance from the noisy, dusty encampments of Indians and trappers. If there were no trees, there was forage and water nearby. Filled with pride in her skill, Hugh watched as Falling Star erected the stout skin lodge in the way she had been taught since childhood. Fate had dealt him a winner this time, Hugh told himself. He'd brought nearly twice the number of beaver pelts to trade this year, thanks to Star's hard work. And best of all, he thought, watching her lay out their bed robes, anxious to tumble her in them as soon as darkness fell, this woman loved him. The fruit of their love grew in her now . . . his child. With a sigh of contentment, Hugh decided it was too long until dark. Pulling down the door flap behind him, he drew his wife into his arms.

Tom Fitzpatrick was late to rendezvous. Indians and trappers drank and caroused and speculated for a month waiting for Fitzpatrick to bring in the caravan from Missouri. Captain Stewart, the wealthy Englishman who traveled in the mountains every summer, had brought a fine racehorse with him this year and there was no dearth of challengers.

To pass the days, Hugh visited around the camp, listening to the gossip and the rumors. Word had filtered in by the mountain grapevine; Fitz was now a company partisan for the American Fur Company. He was bringing Lucien Fontenelle, new owner of Fort Laramie, and some missionaries to the Nez Percé. There had been cholera on the Missouri, although any mountain man knew it never came to the mountains. The Sioux were moving onto the Laramie Plain, too close to the violent Crows. There might have been an Indian war. The wait for Fitzpatrick and the supply caravan went on.

Star pretended not to notice when Nez Percé from the tribe's nearby camp rode past her lodge, staring curiously. No doubt they returned to the encampment to report that Many Horses' daughter, Falling Star, who had run away, had returned with Hugh Cameron and that she was huge with child. Hugh had warned her to be careful of them, for he was afraid they might seek revenge, but she was not afraid. They were her people. The right time would come.

Returning from the river one morning with the day's water, she saw the spotted rump of a Palouse horse riding away from her lodge. Hugh stood beside the cooking fire, staring after the departing Indian with a bemused expression. She set down the skin bucket and looked at him, waiting.

"That there was old Talking Crow. You remember him?"

She nodded.

"He sez yer pa wonders if you ain't a Nez Percé anymore."

It was the invitation she'd been expecting, certain that her father's curiosity would overcome his anger at her. "I go to him now," she said simply, and stepped into the lodge to gather up the gifts she had brought as peace offerings.

"I'll jest tag along," Hugh replied, checking his pistol and picking up the Hawken.

Together they rode to Many Horses' lodge. He sat with Talking Crow before the cooking fire. For a long time he seemed unaware of their presence as the horses moved uneasily, waiting. Falling Star's eyes met the dancing glance of her stepmother, who was working at her sewing beside the fire, and knew at least there was a welcome. The wives of her brothers came running from their lodges, clustering nearby, whispering and giggling.

Finally Many Horses acknowledged their presence by making a sign for them to dismount and join him.

"I have brought presents for my father," Falling Star told him in their own language. With both arms, she held out the buffalo robe—a winter's work chipping away the thick hide until the robe was as flexible and silky as the finest doeskin —and the ceremonial shirt of soft bleached doeskin, beaded in the signs of Many Horses' own medicine, a garment only medicine women were allowed to make.

Many Horses grunted, but she saw the glow in his eyes as he accepted the shirt. He called Blue Feather to bring his pipe, indicating Hugh should join him and Talking Crow beside the fire.

Then Blue Feather drew Falling Star into the circle of chattering women. Questions flew as they touched her, patted her stomach, laughed at their own ribald jokes. Back in the winter lodge she had often thought herself lonely and longed for the company of the women of her village. But now, even as they gathered around her, she felt apart from them in the way she had always been apart.

When her own mother died at her birth, Old Grandmother had taken her into her lodge. She had grown up there, learning mysteries the other women only guessed at. Now she was in another lodge learning the mysteries of the white man. All winter she and Shining Bear had spoken only in English so that the cadence of the harsh Nez Percé tongue fell strangely on her ears, and she sometimes had to strain to translate meanings.

Finished with smoking and talking, the men strolled away

some distance where a shooting match was in progress. It was the only thing Hugh was ever likely to gamble on. As he started to follow Many Horses and Talking Crow and her brother Looking Glass, Hugh turned to look at Star. To the unspoken question in his eyes, she nodded. Yes, she would be safe here among her people, even though she had fled from them a year ago.

When the men had gone, the women crowded around, filling their bark dishes from the stew pot. Her brothers' wives, her half sisters, and Blue Feather kept up an incessant chatter, patting her pregnant belly, making ribald jokes about the sexual prowess of the golden-haired white man.

"Is he a good man?" Blue Feather asked when the other women had returned to their own fires, and they were alone.

Her face still burning from the sly remarks of the women, Falling Star merely nodded. Aware of Blue Feather's waiting silence, her kindly questioning eyes, Star finally spoke. "He is kind." She could not speak of what was truly between herself and Shining Bear . . . a love so powerful they were as one being.

"A better husband than Bull Head would have been." It was a statement from Blue Feather, not a question.

Again Star could only nod, a sense of guilt running through her like a sharp pain.

"Bull Head was very angry when you went away," Blue Feather continued. "He said the white trapper must have stolen you, forced you to go with him. He couldn't believe you would choose another man over him."

Star merely smiled to herself.

"He bribed some young men to go with him to follow you. The first day most of them tired of the chase and returned to our village. Bull Head and two others rode on and never returned." Blue Feather paused, her dark eyes probing Star's.

"It is said he met the *hattia tinukin* . . . the death wind." Her voice fell as she stared at Falling Star. "That it was sent him by a medicine woman of great powers."

A heaviness settled in the pit of Star's stomach. Bull Head was dead and she had helped kill him. But he would have killed the Shining Bear, and what he would have done to her afterward did not bear thinking on. It was done . . . past. New life stirred within her.

"Sepekuse," she murmured, staring into the fire. "Let it be."

Blue Feather shrugged. "At first your father was angry too, but now he thinks he will be rich with gifts from his daughter's white husband. Already, he brags to the other warriors of what will be his when the supply caravan arrives."

Falling Star laid her hand on her stomach where the child moved restlessly. Repressing a triumphant smile, she looked at Blue Feather. "The Shining Bear offered much for me and my father refused him. Now my husband has no need to offer gifts to Many Horses."

She saw the disappointment in Blue Feather's face and smiled openly, knowing her stepmother too had been bragging of the gifts that would be hers. Let them worry a bit, she thought, certain that Shining Bear would allow her to take beads and scarlet cloth to her stepmother, for the woman had always treated her kindly.

"Eeagh!" Falling Star cried out as the baby inside kicked furiously.

Laughing, Blue Feather reached over to lay a worn hand on Star's belly. "He will be a great warrior, that one," she said.

One of the women added some twigs to the fire; the light and flame of it filled Star's eyes. Within the fiery depths she saw the figure of a Nez Percé warrior, fierce and proud, the son she carried. Heat seemed to sear her heart as the fire blazed up and the warrior dwindled into ashes. The gift held her in a long silence as she stored in her head a knowledge of the future that was not to be shared. At last she said quietly, "Yes, he will be a great warrior."

Fitzpatrick brought the supply caravan in the first week of August to a greeting that rivaled a prairie thunderstorm in noise. Sitting before their lodge, Hugh and Star laughed to see the trappers and Indians riding wildly to greet Fitz, shooting off guns and shouting, dogs barking and running recklessly among the milling horses.

The partisans could scarcely set up their tent and unload the whiskey barrels for the trappers and Indians pressing in on them, eager to trade.

Smoking his pipe as he watched, Hugh grinned at Falling Star. "We'll trade tomorrow when they're all drunk. Ain't no call to hurry anyhow." The news had come ahead of Fitz; the American Fur Company had a monopoly now. The trappers had no choice but to sell their beaver at the company's rate. Fitz was a fair man, but the company . . .

Still, he was certain that after he bought his winter supplies, there would be plenty for new blankets for Many Horses, needles and awls and beads for Blue Feather, and some gifts for Falling Star.

"You gotta see this show." Fitzpatrick stood grinning down at Hugh where he sat in the shade of the lodge, mending the mule's bridle. His trading finished, Hugh passed the days visiting with the other trappers, cheering at horse races, even trying his luck in a shooting match. Falling Star had gone this morning to trade with the Nez Percé for the camas root they harvested in their country.

Struggling to his feet, Hugh joined Fitz, and they threaded their way among the lodges, the children, and the dogs. In the distance, near the company tent, a noisy crowd had gathered. The sun stared down from a hot blue sky, the air washed clean by yesterday's rainstorm that had blessedly settled the dust.

Fitz chuckled. "Last year, when the Nez Percé sent two of their young braves east to bring back missionaries with the white man's religion, I couldn't figger their bein' so blamed anxious fer civilization."

Hugh had already met Dr. Marcus Whitman, a decent enough man, and Reverend Samuel Parker, who seemed to be in a permanent state of shock from the goings-on at rendezvous. "Could be they ain't got any idea what they're in for?" he said.

With a glum nod, Fitz shrugged, then broke into a grin as

they neared the crowd of excited trappers and Indians. "You recollect couple years ago, Old Gabe got hisself an arrow in the back?"

"Yeah," Hugh replied, eyeing his friend curiously. "Blackfeet, warn't it?"

Again, Fitz nodded. "Wal, this Dr. Whitman's a white medicine man, a real doctor. He aims to take the arrow outa Jim's back."

"Damned if he does?" Hugh returned, amazed.

They pushed through the crowd of shouting, chattering Indians and trappers, to see Bridger lying face down on an improvised log table. He lay limp, with enough whiskey and laudanum in him to kill the pain. Marcus Whitman had placed his leather bag of tools on the table. Now he took up his scalpel and opened Bridger's back. Blood flowed freely, mopped up by Bridger's Indian wife. The self-possessed Dr. Whitman worked fast, ignoring the cheers of his audience, the shouts of free advice, and the blood spilling over his hands and on the table. Finally, he held up a three-inch barbed iron arrowhead and was rewarded by the loud and vociferous approval of his audience.

"I'll be damned," Hugh said, staring in amazement as the doctor bandaged Bridger's wound and helped him sit up.

"Thet's civilization." Fitz grinned. His face faded to disgruntled annoyance when a nearly sober trapper grabbed his arm and implored him to open the whiskey tent.

Just as Fitz and his customer pushed out through the crowd, a grizzled trapper confronted Dr. Whitman. "I got me an arrer in the hip," he announced. "Reckon you kin git it out good as ya did Jim's?"

With a smile, Dr. Whitman indicated the bloodstained table. The trapper shucked off his pants and lay down.

"Enuff of that," Hugh told himself. His stomach was growling with hunger. Falling Star should have finished her trading by now and have something ready to eat in her cooking pot.

Coming over the little rise to his own lodge, he stopped, staring in surprise. Falling Star had brought up the horses and was busy dismantling the lodge.

"You eat," she ordered, indicating the cooking pot still on the fire. "Then we go."

"Go . . . hell!" he protested. "I fixed it up to go north to the Yellowstone with Jim Bridger's brigade. We kin trap and hunt buffalo till time to make winter camp."

"You join them later to hunt the buffalo," she told him, mixing English and Nez Percé recklessly in her haste. "Now we go home."

Hugh's eyes softened as he looked into her determined face. "It's the babe, ain't it?" he asked. "Yer wantin' to be home afore it comes." A longing for the valley he had come to think of as his own private kingdom filled his heart. "Aye," he said, drawing her close to him, smoothing back her silky hair. "Aye, wife; fer now, we go home."

It was far more difficult than she had expected. Pain ebbed as the contraction faded and Falling Star lay back with a soft moan. Remembering how easily the women of her tribe seemed to give birth, she thought again there was something alien in her. When she said good-bye to her family at the rendezvous, she had known she would never go back again to that life. Those bonds were severed and her future lay here with Shining Bear.

Outside in the darkness, a cold autumn wind tore at the trees. It plucked at the skins of the snug lodge, but the heavy skin curtains Falling Star had hung around the edge of the room kept the inside snug and warm. The winter lodge had been made ready before the first snow. Everything was in its place. The willow framed bed covered by buffalo robes and warm new blankets, backrests of rawhide thongs beside the low fire.

Returning from rendezvous, she and Hugh had ridden into the valley from the south, over the low rolling, sage-covered hills. There were willow-rimmed springs for water, bunch grass for the animals, then the wide meadows along the creek and the pine-covered mountains rising to the north and west. Home.

Hugh had strung his traps while she set up the lodge. On the appointed day he had gone, reluctantly, to join Bridger's brigade where he would hunt for the buffalo robes that were rapidly becoming more valuable than beaver skins.

He feared leaving her there with her unborn child, so she had lied to him, promising him he would be back before the birth. She could not have ridden with him, knowing unhappily that she was not as strong as the other women of her tribe. Yet she had been certain the birth would be easy, as easy as those she'd observed in her village.

She hadn't guessed there would be so much blood. The moss couch she had prepared for herself was soaked with it. And still the child did not come.

Drowning in pain, she managed to force herself into a squatting position, straining with the last of her strength as the contraction shook her body. There was another rush of blood, a high sharp cry tore from her throat, and her son lay on the blood-soaked moss.

An overwhelming surge of love poured through Falling Star as she watched him flail his tiny fists, wailing as he filled his lungs with air.

"Little warrior," she murmured as she gently cleaned him and wrapped him in softest doeskin. As he lay on her breast, heart beating against heart, she softly stroked his dark hair. Falling Star gave herself up completely to the joy of this child. A child created from her destined love for Shining Bear. What she had glimpsed of the future in the fire beside her father's lodge, she set from her mind.

"Sepekuse," she told herself. "Let it be," and she bent to kiss her son's softly pulsing head as he nuzzled, blindly searching for her breast.

Chapter 6

1836

"White wimmen!" Joe Meeks shouted through his grizzled beard. Spurring ahead of his companions, he jerked his horse up short beside Hugh Cameron.

Just as they came down the divide, Hugh and Falling Star met the band of half-drunk trappers riding out from the rendezvous at Horse Creek. The Cameron pack mules were loaded with beaver and fine buffalo robes; the growing herd of horses trailed behind on lead ropes. The trappers looked to be on some kind of a spree.

Joe spat a brown stream of tobacco juice and grinned at Hugh. "I heard they's white wimmen comin' west with Fitzpatrick's caravan!"

The baby sleeping in his cradle board on Falling Star's back awakened, wailing at the sound of the rough trapper's raucous voice.

"Yer yarnin' agin, Joe," Hugh answered indulgently.

"Not this hyar chile," Meeks protested. "Me and the boys here are ridin' out to meet 'em."

"White wimmen," Hugh said, shaking his head as he watched the whooping riders gallop away across the sagebrush flats. He glanced at Falling Star trying to soothe the baby, and she lifted serious eyes to meet his. "Ain't no white wimmen gonna get west of the Missouri," he told her. "Not never."

Without answering, she urged her horse ahead, down into the crowded valley of the rendezvous. A faint chill touched her heart, for although Joe Meeks' love for tall tales was legendary, she also knew this time he did not lie. White women had come to the mountains for the first time, and nothing would ever again be the same.

Beneath the blazing midsummer sun, the rendezvous camp lay somnolent. Even the dogs were sprawled sleeping in the sparse shade of the skin lodges. The pale brown water of the Green River glittered as it flowed silently through the wide valley. Dust devils danced across the far plain, seeming to rush toward the cool blue of the distant Wind River mountains.

Holding the baby to her breast, Falling Star sat in the shaded doorway of her own lodge. The greedy baby clutched at her breast with one tiny fist as he suckled. Stroking his dark head lovingly, Falling Star smiled to herself. How beautiful he was, and how strong. Her husband had called the child Jed, for the greatest mountain man of all, he said. But until he grew of an age to find his own name, her name for him was Little Warrior.

Two days now since their arrival and Joe Meeks' startling announcement of the white women's coming. Even after she learned the women were the wives of the missionaries, Dr. Whitman, and another man, Falling Star had been unable to put away the sense of apprehension her gift brought. There had been no such premonition the first time she had seen a white man as a child. Those men lived as the Indians did, and it was joked among the tribes that there were no white women, which was why the white men were so avid for Indian women. With a sigh, Falling Star tried to smother her anxiety. The future would unfold what was to be.

Bending to kiss the baby, she thought that surely it was time for the caravan to arrive. As if in answer to her thoughts, a shouting horseman plunged down the divide, racing through the camp to announce the caravan. All at once, the camp seemed to leap into action. Dogs awakened, adding their barking to the sudden tumult. Mounting their horses, men rode wildly to meet the string of heavily laden mules coming down the divide with Tom Fitzpatrick riding ahead. Gunshots echoed a greeting through the valley.

A four-wheeled wagon lumbered down the sandy trail, a strange new vehicle in the west. Star stared as the riders wheeled their horses, jostling each other in their frantic haste to gape at the women inside the wagon.

It was always this way when the caravan came in, Falling Star tried to reassure herself. Covering her breast and cuddling the sleeping child against her, she strained to catch a glimpse of the women, but could see only the dirty white canvas top of the wagon. The horsemen, both Indians and white trappers, were reckless in their attempts to get near these white missionary wives, and Star knew this year it was not the same.

Dismounting, several of the trappers hurried to help set up the missionaries' camp at the choice spot saved for Fitz. Men stumbled over each other to make the fire, set up the tent, unload the wagon. Falling Star was uncertain whether to be amused or astounded at their behavior.

Hugh was watching from horseback. As though he felt her eyes on him, he reined the horse around and rode toward her. Falling Star's heart lifted as it always did in the knowledge of the bonds between them.

The morning's sickness had passed. She was certain now another child grew within her. Perhaps tonight she would share that knowledge with Shining Bear.

"Ain't you gonna come look at the white wimmen?" he asked, dismounting and regarding her with a grin. "Doc Whitman's wife is purely a beauty."

Jealousy flushed through her, leaving her as sick as the first symptoms of pregnancy had done this very morning. "You would rather have a white wife?" she accused, moving away from the touch of his outstretched hand as she tucked the baby back into his cradle board.

He captured her arm and drew her roughly against him, looking down at her with a lustful grin. "Come in the lodge with me and I'll show you which wife I want."

Feeling his hardness pressed against her thigh, Falling

51

Star laughed aloud. It pleased her that he wanted her this moment, as he always wanted her. Tilting her head to one side, she looked up at him teasingly. "I give you a new name, Shining Bear."

"What?" he asked, his voice muffled as he drew her inside the lodge and let the flap down behind them.

"Iron Tail," she answered, and broke into giggles as he pulled her down with him onto the bed robes.

Hugh's mouth smothered her laughter, hot and insistent. His hands tugged at the hem of her gown, pulling it upward. Star's whole being leaped into tingling awareness as it always did when he made love to her. She slid her hands down his body, pressing him to her.

"Give me a name like that," he muttered, his mouth hot against her throat. "Reckon I'll have to live up to it."

Star laughed aloud, lifting her hips to receive him, already aroused and eager.

Dressed in her finest beaded and fringed doeskin gown, Falling Star walked beside her husband, through the purple summer dusk. The white missionaries had rested and eaten. Fitz had sent word through the camp that now trappers and wives and Indians could come to greet their guests.

The women sat on camp stools in front of the tent with their husbands standing behind them. Making use of the awe the women evoked, Fitz managed to keep the crowd under control.

Rough old Joe Meeks, clean shaven and bathed, was trying to herd the Indian women through the camp. Each one of them insisted on greeting the two white women with a kiss, touching their hair, fingering their dresses.

Waiting her turn, Falling Star considered the strange women seated before their campfire. Narcissa Whitman, the doctor's wife, was indeed beautiful, with her red-gold hair and flashing eyes. The other woman, Eliza Spalding, looked pale and ill. Star thought their clothing impractical and ridiculous, with full unmanageable skirts and high collars. How did their men ever fight their way through those skirts, she wondered, smiling at Hugh as she remembered their joyous coupling this afternoon. No wonder white men were so eager for Indian women.

When her turn came, she approached the women, carrying Little Warrior in his cradleboard. Something in her held back from touching them, and she thought they seemed relieved.

"This hyar's Hugh Cameron an' his woman," Fitzpatrick's voice boomed out over the hubbub of the crowd.

"Howdy, Miz Whitman . . . Miz Spalding." Hugh removed his leather hat and grinned at the women. He had shaved since they arrived at rendezvous, and Falling Star thought he looked very handsome. Even the white women looked at him admiringly and Falling Star felt again the sting of jealousy. Did Shining Bear wish for such a woman in spite of all he'd said? Irrationally, she longed to be like them just to please him.

"I am Falling Star." She spoke in her best English, pleased at the surprise on Narcissa's face.

"You speak English?"

"I taught her." Hugh beamed proudly.

"Yes," Falling Star said. "This is my son." And she held up Little Warrior for the women's admiration.

Behind them the crowd, anxious to touch and stare at the white women, pushed forward, forcing them to relinquish their place.

"Wal . . . now you seen 'em," Hugh remarked as they strolled back toward their own lodge.

Falling Star frowned, wondering if all white women were treated in this manner, honored and respected as though they were chief of the tribe. "Will they stay here?" she asked, thinking perhaps she could learn from them how they commanded such service from their men. If she were like them, maybe her husband would look at her with the kind of admiration she'd seen in his eyes for Narcissa Whitman.

"Naw," Hugh replied easily, reaching to tickle Little Warrior's chin. "They're headin' fer Oregon territory. Gonna convert the Injuns there. You know whar that is, don't ya? The big river . . . the Columbia."

She nodded, remembering long-ago journeys the Nez Percé made to the villages of their cousins in the country of the Big River. There they speared and smoked the huge pink salmon to carry back into their own mountains for the winter. The white women would be far away and she was glad of it . . . glad her husband would not be tempted by his own kind. But while they were here, she could learn from them.

Next day, Falling Star hovered near the missionaries' encampment, watching the women . . . the way they moved and talked, the way they dressed and did up their hair. When Hugh traded his beaver and buffalo robes to Fitzpatrick, she surprised him by demanding a bolt of brightly colored calico.

The hot air smelled of dust stirred up by the horses of the constantly moving Indians. Lifting her arm to brush sweat from her face, Star hurried with her task. The yards of blue calico had been cut into even lengths and sewn quickly together with deer sinew. Now she gathered the fabric about her waist with a braided rawhide belt. Pleased with the effect, she whirled around, wondering how Hugh would react when he saw her dressed as a white woman. Now she must hurry to do her hair.

Hugh had spent the day watching horse races and shooting matches. Through the open flap of the lodge, Star could see that the merciless sun was just beginning its westward slide, and she knew he would return soon. Little Warrior slept in his cradle board propped against a lodge pole. From the pot over the cooking fire came the delicious odors of stewed deer meat flavored with the camas root Star had traded for with Blue Feather.

Just as she finished tying her tightly braided hair up in a knot at the back of her neck, Star heard Hugh's familiar footsteps approaching the lodge.

"Star!" he called, a hint of alarm in his voice when she did not come from the lodge to greet him.

"Here." She answered from inside the lodge. Her mouth was dry and her heart pounding as she arranged her calico skirt and waited for his reaction.

Hugh ducked into the dim interior. "Wal, I'm damned!" he said, staring at her, dumbfounded.

When he burst into laughter, her heart plunged and the expectant glow she'd felt faded and died. "I dress pretty for you . . . like white woman," she told him in a pained voice. Tears of disappointment stung her eyes.

At once contrite, Hugh drew her toward him. "You ain't a white woman," he said softly, his big hands working loose the thongs that bound her hair, so that it fell in a dark cascade about her shoulders. "I don't want no white woman." He held her close, looking into her face with such love Star felt her heart turn over. "Don't never change, Star . . . never."

His mouth came down on hers and Star gave herself completely to his kiss. Because of the love he bore her, she could forgive the laughter that had hurt her. He did not want a white wife, he wanted her . . . as she was, without white trappings. She had been wrong, and relief poured through her.

"Besides . . ." Hugh grinned down at her. "You git too refined, like those ladies, you won't want an ignorant trapper fer a husband." His hands worked loose the plaited belt and the lengths of calico fell to the ground.

Cupping his face in both her hands, Star looked into his eyes, so filled with love her heart seemed about to burst. "We are for always, Shining Bear," she murmured softly. "For always."

With his hands on her hips, Hugh pulled her close. "Remember that name you give me yesterday?" he asked, grinning. "Ol' Iron Tail?"

Afterward, as they held each other in satiated contentment on the bed robes, she told him she carried another child.

Hugh spread his big rough hand over her belly, and lay in awed silence as though he could already feel the being growing in there. When he spoke, his voice was choked. "I never thought to be so happy." He laid his face against her bare shoulder and she felt the wetness of his tears.

* * *

Sunlight glittered on the upraised lances and medicine tokens fluttered in the hot wind. The Indians, dressed in full ceremonial regalia and mounted on their finest horses, had gathered to parade for the white women.

"How the hell did all them Injuns git together fer this?" Hugh asked in amazement as they watched from beside their own lodge.

Falling Star smiled, certain that some arrogant young men had decided to show off. Word would have gone from camp to camp, and one tribe could not bear to be outdone by another in displaying their finery.

The missionaries sat on a rug spread in the shade of their tent. Fitz had joined them, and Captain Stewart, the Englishman who loved the mountains. The four tribes passed in review, shooting off rifles and shouting blood-chilling war cries. Feathered headdresses of the half-naked painted warriors blew in the wind. The horses pranced, galloped, curvetted, a fine dust rising beneath the pounding hooves. Each tribe tried to outdo the other in brilliant costume and noise for the benefit of the white women.

Yesterday's foolish jealousy had faded and Falling Star watched the colorful parade with smiling appreciation. She wondered if the women or their husbands appreciated the meaning of the medicines fluttering from the lances, many of them fashioned from white scalps. Their religious ceremonies, she had observed, were dull and ponderous compared to those of her own people. Still, an uneasiness fell over her.

"We go home tomorrow?" Falling Star asked Hugh that night as they walked back through the dark camp from their bath in the river. He did not need to ask where she meant.

"If you figger it's time to go," he answered, "we go." So he had come to trust her, she thought, pleased. Laughing, she raced him to their lodge to tumble with him on the bed robes.

Next day winter supplies were purchased, the parfleches packed, and arrangements made to meet Bridger's brigade for the buffalo hunt. In the morning, Falling Star would strike the lodge, load it on travois, and they would leave the rendezvous.

"Afore we go," Hugh began as he helped her pack the traps, "we oughta say good-bye to the white wimmen."

"Now?" Falling Star asked in consternation, for she was dressed in her dirty camp gown.

"Yes," was the firm reply, even though his eyes were questioning.

Rummaging through the packs, Falling Star found her ceremonial beaded gown. Dressing quickly, she combed her hair, smiling at Hugh's admiring words, "Yer awful purty."

Through the long shadows of a lavender twilight, they walked to the missionaries' tent.

Narcissa Whitman's red-gold hair gleamed like a misplaced sunbeam in the last rays of sunlight. She smiled at Star with innate courtesy and held out her hand in farewell.

The touch of the other woman's hand sent a coldness rushing through Star's veins. Drawing a deep breath, she tried to steady herself against the onslaught of her gift of vision. For what seemed an endless moment, the two women stood clasping hands.

Star closed her eyes against the pain flooding through her. Narcissa was an omen of the future . . . the first wave in a tide of white men and their women who would fill the mountains. Something seemed to shatter inside Star's head, and she foresaw Narcissa's violent and bloody end. Drained utterly, she let her hand fall limply from Narcissa's grasp, knowing she was powerless to change the future.

Chapter 7

Looking up from the moccasin she was lacing with deer sinew through holes punched with her awl, Falling Star smiled at the two boys tumbling in play on the skin floor of the winter lodge.

So it was, the sons she had known would be hers, strong and beautiful as she had dreamed. Each time she looked on them, her heart swelled in her chest, so filled with the warmth of love she could not speak. Her joy in them was never-ending.

"You love 'em too much," Hugh had once said, watching her impulsively gather them in her arms to hold and kiss.

"Among my people, all children are loved," she told him. A shadow of old pain darkened his blue eyes. She had long ago surmised that there had been no love in the childhood of Shining Bear. Releasing the boys, she went to Hugh and held him so that he would know her love for him was not diminished by her feeling for her sons.

With an affectionate chuckle, Star watched now as Little Warrior pinned his younger brother to the floor. Four years old, Little Warrior was already living up to the name she had given him. Wiry and tough, with boundless energy, he easily bested his smaller brother. Little Bear, as she called him because he bore the golden-haired stamp of his father, was a quieter child. He had even been quiet before he was born and brought her far less pain than her firstborn. Hugh had named him Alex, for a fur trader who had once been his friend.

By some strange trick of fate, these two unlike boys . . . Little Warrior, dark-skinned, black-haired, had Hugh's blue eyes gleaming in his small handsome face, while Little Bear's eyes were nearly as dark as those of his mother.

As she watched, the boys gave up their wrestling match to lie panting beside each other on the buffalo robes, gazing into the cooking fire that burned low, its smoke rising through the opening at the top of the lodge.

"Are you hungry?" she asked. They immediately sat up, waiting to be served, chattering in the mixture of English and Nez Percé that had become their language.

While they ate, Falling Star returned to the moccasins she was sewing for Hugh. He'd gone to tend his beaver traps, anxious to gather the prime pelts of early spring. Last year, at the rendezvous of 1838 at the mouth of the Popo Agie River, the price of beaver had been so low he sold only prime, and brought back the rest of his pelts for her to make the soft beaver robe that now covered their bed.

Their buffalo robes sold well, and there had been more missionaries on their way to Oregon territory anxious to buy their well-trained horses. Four white women this time . . . and Star allowed herself a sigh. Every year there were more whites coming west to stay. Not to hunt, but to take up residence on Indian lands, building cabins and farms. Two years ago they had brought with them the dreaded smallpox, wiping out whole villages of Mandan, and Assiniboin, and Blackfeet. Glancing possessively at her sons, Star thanked *Hunyewat* the plague had not spread this far west. Her treasured children had been spared.

Tying off and cutting the sinew, she laid aside the finished moccasin. Before picking up the pieces to make its mate, she let her hands rest, palms open, on her subtly rounded belly. A smile lit her face as she thought of the child growing there. A girl child at last, she was certain of it. The daughter she had longed for to share her work and her knowledge, to teach her medicine of the Nez Percé, to be her companion and carry her gift.

With a soft plop, snow fell from the pine branches onto the skins of the lodge. The first warming days had come, heralding spring of the year of her girl-child. Only a few weeks left before the beaver fur lost the thick gloss of its winter coat and could no longer be stamped "prime" by the traders for the fur company. She must hurry with the moccasin, for there would be beaver skins to clean and stretch when Hugh returned from his rounds.

Dazzling sunlight filled the great bowl of the valley, reflecting off the miles of snow-covered hills. From beneath the snowdrifts, rivulets of water rippled and sang running down to the creeks and meadows.

Spring runoff was beginning and the water in the creek was icy cold, high and swift, buffeting Hugh each time he waded into its waist-high depths to take a beaver from his traps. Already he'd replenished the glands in his horn bottle of castoreum. Grinning as he dabbed the stinking mixture on the twigs as he rebaited each trap, Hugh thought that fresh scent was always good luck. Only the prime pelts would sell at rendezvous now that silk hats were replacing beaver in the distant cities.

Floundering through the wet snow, he gathered up the bloody beaver pelts to load on the mule. Shivering, soaked to the waist from wading in the icy water, Hugh tightened the rawhide ropes about the strangely uneasy animal.

A twig snapped. Hugh froze, his startled eyes on the creature moving out of the trees. The bear looked gaunt and hungry. He moved sluggishly, awakened too soon from hibernation by the warm day. Animal and man stared at each other across the muddy clearing. A rank odor stung Hugh's nostrils. He watched the bear raise his massive head and sniff the still air. Fear trickled down his spine. There was enough beaver blood on his clothes to arouse a hungry grizzly.

Slowly, carefully, his eyes still on the bear, he reached out for the loaded Hawken leaning against a fallen tree. In one swift movement, he seized it, aimed, and fired. The mule brayed and fled.

The bear shambled forward, growling menacingly, its huge chest spurting blood. Its eyes glowed with primitive ferocity.

"Damn!" Hugh muttered, his Green River knife instantly in his hand. A wounded bear was the most dangerous critter on earth. Even with a bloody gaping hole in its chest, this one came onward.

Suddenly, the bear lunged. His terrible claws skimmed along Hugh's cheek and down the uplifted arm. Pain roared through him as he plunged the knife into the creature's throat. Foamy blood bubbled from the bear's wound as Hugh backed away, panting, his knife dripping gore.

Weaving groggily, the bear still came on, growling with pain and fury. Damn critter should be dead with all that blood running from him!

Blood poured from Hugh's wounded arm, his fingers turned nerveless, and the knife fell from his grip. For an instant he stood frozen. Driblets of scarlet-stained saliva hung from the bear's sagging mouth, the huge teeth gleamed terrifyingly. Horror poured through Hugh's veins. The creature would not die, and it would surely kill him. Star and the boys . . . his heart twisted painfully at the thought . . . they couldn't survive without him. Nothing for it now but to run like hell. He turned to flee, slipped on a patch of snow, and felt the awful claws rake his leg. His own cry of excruciating pain echoed in his ears. He couldn't move. Clenching his teeth he waited for another blow.

From behind him came a strange whistling sound, then a grunt, and he heard the bear fall heavily to the ground. In the distance, he could hear the mule still braying in terror. It was the last he knew.

Falling Star cut off a chunk of dried buffalo fat to add to the simmering pot of deer meat and dried berries. Glancing out the open flap of the lodge which she had lifted to air the place while the sun was warm, she realized dusk was coming on. A faint thrill of fear ran through her.

Hugh always took the pelts early, so that the rest of the winter daylight could be spent in cleaning and stretching the skins. She'd been so caught up in her work today, and in playing with the boys, the hours had run away from her. She realized she had closed off that inner sensitivity that was always with Shining Bear, and sudden apprehension clogged her throat.

Pain shot through her and she stood up, giving a soft cry. The boys turned toward her with wide fearful eyes.

"Stay here!" she commanded. "Don't move!" Quickly, she pulled on her outdoor moccasins and leggings, flinging her buffalo robe about her shoulders. With one last admonishment to her sons, she slipped the skinning knife into her legging and stepped out into the cold winter dusk.

A sense of danger, so pervasive she could almost smell it, filled the air. Her heart stopped as she looked across the meadow and saw the mule, loaded with bloody pelts, grazing peacefully among the horses.

Blood pounded wildly through her veins as she raced along the trail to the creek and the beaver pond. "Shining Bear!" she shouted, then caught herself and cried out the name he had insisted she call him always. "Hugh!"

A faint groan brought her up short. Every sense alert, she yielded to instinct, turning off the trail among the thick stand of aspen. Breath seemed to explode from her lungs when she saw the bloody evidence of a battle staining the dirty snow beneath the trees.

"Hugh!" she called the name again. A sharp cry of fear broke from her throat as her eyes fell on the wounded grizzly sprawled across a fallen tree. The animal still breathed, still lived; if it had killed her own Shining Bear ... Without pausing to think, she tore the knife from her legging and leaped at the bear. Even when she saw the ragged hole Hugh's rifle had torn in the animal's side, she could not stop, plunging her knife into its heart again and again. Bloody froth bubbled from its mouth. It seemed to sigh and stopped breathing.

Gasping for breath, she stumbled back, staring around the grove. Her eyes searched frantically for the beloved man who had surely been this hideous creature's victim. Again, she heard a faint groan and her heart pounded as she ran toward the sound.

"Hugh!" At once she was on her knees beside him. There was a bloody trail in the snow where he had dragged himself toward home. He lay face down, his clothing shredded by the bear's claws. Blood seeped from his mauled and battered leg, congealing quickly in the cold darkness that was falling swiftly over the valley.

It was not given her to foresee the death of those she loved; Falling Star understood that at last. Fear choked her throat as she turned Hugh over and looked into his pale, unconscious face. Fate could not have given her this man only to take him from her now. She swore it would not be so.

Lifting him in her arms, she held his bloody head against her breast, fiercely, protectively. "Hugh . . . Hugh." She sobbed the name over and over, his warm breath like a blessing against her cheek.

Gently, she wiped the blood from his torn face with a handful of snow. His eyelids fluttered open, the blue eyes glazed and distant. Then he lapsed again into unconsciousness.

Cold air had stanched the bleeding, but the coldness that came with night was dangerous. She must get him back to the lodge and a warm fire at once.

Quickly, she spread her buffalo robe on the ground. Struggling to move his dead unconscious weight, she lost her balance and slipped on the snow. Even when she dropped him, Hugh did not rouse. At last she was able to heave him onto the robe. Now she could drag it over the swiftly freezing snow back to the lodge.

Nearly exhausted by the time she reached the lodge, Falling Star called to the boys to help her drag the inert body of their father inside. Reassuring them, Falling Star quickly undressed Hugh and cleaned his wounds. The two small boys sat side by side, watching with wide frightened eyes.

The claws of the grizzly had scratched his face and made deep incisions on his arms. But the leg was grievously wounded. Falling Star packed the shredded flesh in fresh moss over a mixture of healing herbs, and bound it tightly with soft deerskin. When she finished, he was still unconscious, shivering violently. Falling Star covered him with a warm blanket and a buffalo robe. She could not give way to the anguished fear growing inside her. His very life depended now on her strength.

By morning, he was awake and feverish, calling urgently and incoherently for water. From her medicine roll, Falling Star took the healing herbs she had gathered in the summer. While a mixture of them boiled, she cleaned and treated Hugh's red and angry wounds. After he drank the boiled mixture, he slept.

"Watch over your father," she said to her younger son, in the Nez Percé tongue. His dark eyes filled with tears of apprehension.

"No!" he wailed, and flung his arms about her legs.

"You are a big boy," she told him sternly. "You must stay with your father. Little Warrior will go with me to take what the wolves have left of the bear and bring in the mule with the beaver pelts."

Shaking as with a chill, the boy sat down beside the bed robes where Hugh slept a heavy drugged sleep. He did not look at his mother, or speak again.

The wolves had been at the dead bear until the meat was useless, but Falling Star took the skin from its back. A medicine robe, she thought, for Shining Bear, the brave warrior who had killed the terrible *hohots*. Beneath her sense of urgency, pride in her husband swelled warm inside her breast.

With Little Warrior's help, she captured the mule and led it back to the lodge, where she swiftly set to work preparing the pelts that must not be lost by neglect.

"Prime . . ." Hugh muttered, tossing feverishly beneath his blanket. "Prime now . . ."

Falling Star leaned over him, touching his burning face with a gentle hand. Even the willow bark tea she brewed for him had not cooled his fevered body. Smoothing the damp hair back from his forehead, she murmured softly, "Sleep now . . . sleep."

Blue eyes burned into hers as he struggled to form the words. "Prime pelts now . . . have to take . . . you do it."

"No!" She drew away, seized by an unreasonable fear.

Hugh's hot hand held her arm. "The bait . . ." His face was flushed and anxious. "I didn't lose it?"

"No." It was there with his bloody clothing. She hadn't touched it. Even though she'd grown used to the smell of it on him, she would never touch it. She always made him scrub his hands clean with sand after he had used it. Deep in her inner heart, she knew it was bad medicine for Falling Star.

"Please . . . you kin do it . . . take the pelts and bait the traps. Please." He was agitated now, beyond reason.

A strange word—please—she had never heard it before, but guessed its meaning. "Please." Falling Star saw that he would not be quiet, would not rest until she agreed. Reluctantly, she nodded. With a sigh, Hugh fell back and was at once asleep.

A gray and heavy sky hung over the valley, and the cold wind blew away yesterday's promise of spring. The creek, still high and swift, buffeted Falling Star as she waded in the waist-deep water to retrieve the trapped beaver.

A hundred times she'd watched Hugh take the beaver and rebait the traps, admiring the spare efficiency of his movements. For her, those same movements were painfully slow and awkward. Each time she spread the castoreum on a twig to bait the trap, she felt a surge of apprehension. Bad medicine.

At last she finished, skinned the beaver, and loaded the mule. By the time she reached the lodge and unloaded the pelts, her water-soaked gown and leggings were frozen stiff.

Ducking inside the lodge, she saw that the boys had kept the fire going. Wrapped in their blankets, they sat together beside it. Two pair of eyes . . . blue and brown, lifted to her, relief spreading across the small anxious faces.

"Good boys," she said, forcing a smile as she struggled out of her frozen clothing. Hugh slept heavily. When she touched his forehead, she let out a sigh of relief. The fever had broken.

After she had changed and eaten, she dressed the boys in their outdoor leggings and took them to help her with the skins. There would be a storm tomorrow, the pelts must be cleaned and stretched now.

In the brief respite inside the lodge, the fire had warmed her icy body and brought with its warmth a new and terrifying sensation—pain—deep inside.

With grim determination, she worked the skins, ignoring the pain clutching at her back. Inexorably, it grew, the fierce cramping in her abdomen almost doubling her over. She recognized the racking ebb and flow, for it was like no other pain in the world. Twice before, she had endured such agony for a great reward. Her glance turned to her sons, busy pounding stakes to stretch the pelts, and tears welled in her eyes. There would be no reward this time. It was too soon. The evil she had foreseen in the castoreum had been true. She was losing the baby, the girl-child she longed to hold.

Night lay about the lodge, heavy with the portent of the approaching storm. Across the banked fire, Falling Star saw her sons curled together, sound asleep beneath their warm buffalo robe. His fever broken, Hugh lay beside her in a deep, healing sleep.

Clenched fists pressed fiercely against her mouth, Falling Star stifled the cries of pain that rose to her lips. There was a rush of blood between her thighs and the pain ebbed. Rising on one elbow, she looked down at the bed of dry moss she had prepared. There on the bloody moss lay the perfect figure of her daughter, small enough to fit the palm of her hand as she lifted it.

Silent tears poured down her cheeks as Falling Star wrapped the tiny body in a piece of soft doeskin, laying it carefully in the basket that held her herbs and her medicine. Binding herself, she cleaned up the pallet, then lay again beside her sleeping husband.

Inside her head she fought against the shattering foreknowledge that kept the tears flowing. With deep and painful certainty, Falling Star knew she would never bear another child.

Hugh stirred and reached out an arm to draw her close.

"Hugh." She spoke through tears and his eyes flew open at once, clear of fever now.

"What?" Concern marked his face as Hugh gathered her close with his good arm.

"The baby . . . my girl-child . . ." Her voice broke with sorrow. "I lost her."

His arm tightened about her. "Ah, my Star . . . my woman, don't cry. There'll be more babies . . . your daughter . . . more sons."

"No," she answered, looking into his eyes. "No more children will come to us."

For a long moment, Hugh studied her face. Then he sighed resignedly and she knew he accepted her gift of sight. Gently he smoothed her hair and kissed her tear-filled eyes. "We got two strong sons," he told her in a low and loving voice. "They'll give you the daughter you want."

Star fell silent and the tears ceased. With a tremulous smile, she kissed her husband tenderly. "It will be so," she said and, pillowing her head against his shoulder, fell into exhausted sleep.

Chapter 8

1842

In the chill thin sunlight of early spring, Falling Star and her sons daubed chinking between the logs of the new cabin, a mixture of clay and pine needles. Above them, Hugh whistled as he worked willows into a tight mat between the rafters of the low roof. A misty veil of clouds drifted across the sky where a skein of geese beat northward.

Falling Star glanced up at him as she worked, aware of Hugh's pride in the cabin he had built.

Ever since he returned from the fall buffalo hunt, he'd kept busy, choosing lodgepole pines of the right size and height, notching them with his ax, and fitting them together like a puzzle atop the foundation of flat stones she and the boys had carried from the hillside. They had carried all the flat blocks of tawny sandstone that made up the fireplace wall at one end too.

"Reckon this is the best thing my pa taught me," he told Falling Star when she admired his work. "The old man was no shakes as a farmer, but he was plumb artistic with an ax. I helped him build two cabins, cussin' all the time." He grinned at her. "Now I'm mighty glad I larned how."

Jim Bridger had suggested it when he stayed with them on his way to Fort Laramie for the winter. "Build yerself a trading post like I done at Black's Fork," he told them. "Damn Injuns hang around yer place all the time anyways, usin' yer water an' good grass, killin' the game. Might as well put in some trade goods fer 'em . . . git yerself some buffalo robes t'sell."

Old Jim and Louie Vasquez, a partner he'd picked up in St. Louis, were building their own trading post, a big one, more of a fort like at Laramie. But their purpose wasn't just to trade with the Indians. They were dead on the route to Oregon, and ready to trade with the emigrants moving west along the Oregon Trail.

The trappers' annual rendezvous had died with the fur trade. Now the trappers hunted in small groups, coming out of the mountains to trade at the forts—Laramie, Bents, St. Vrain. Pierre Chouteau owned the fur company. There was no other, and he paid what he wished, except for the buffalo robes, which were in great demand.

"When we get the dirt roof on," Hugh said now, jumping down to go cut more willows, "we'll take us a trip down to see Ol' Jim's fort, and buy some trade goods frum the ol' coot." He hugged Star enthusiastically and the boys giggled. "Would ya like that?"

"Yes." Falling Star nodded, smiling. There would be Indian women to visit with at Bridger's place on Black's Fork. Jim had an Indian wife of his own. Once there had been the annual rendezvous to anticipate. Now only these occasional trading trips gave her the opportunity for company, gossip, visiting. And perhaps their beaver and buffalo would bring enough to buy some coffee and sugar again. "Will we sell horses too?"

"Reckon we could," Hugh answered dubiously. "Even though most of 'em aren't broken."

"When we get to Black's Fork, they'll be ready," she told him, and she bent to mix more pine needles into the wet clay.

Hugh gave her a surprised grin. Then he shrugged and went whistling off to the stand of willows along the creek, limping a little as he had ever since the battle with the bear.

"The Shoshone call you Horse Woman," Little Warrior told her with a grin. "Makes 'em mad they can't even steal our horses, 'cause they run away and come back to you."

Falling Star laughed at his obvious pride. "It's a gift, my son. Perhaps you will have it too." At once she knew that was not true. This boy had all the gifts necessary for the making of a great warrior. He needed no more.

Little Bear, watching this exchange, glared at his brother with jealous eyes. Filling his hand with the chinking mixture from the basket at his feet, he crowned Little Warrior with a gooey mess of clay and pine needles. At once, the two were wrestling on the wet spring grass, biting and kicking.

Falling Star sighed. Little Bear had been born with an envious heart. Even though she loved and praised him equally, he could not bear to hear her praise his bigger and stronger brother. Picking up the basket, she turned her back on the struggling boys and walked to the creek for more chinking clay. They could learn only by fighting their own battles.

"What if ya ain't bin t' Oregon territory fer a few years?" Jim Bridger growled, his sharp blue eyes peering at Hugh from beneath shaggy brows. They sat on a bench in front of the rough dirt-roofed log cabin that was Bridger's trading post. The summer day was hot. Hugh stretched out his gimpy leg, grateful for the soothing warmth of the sunlight.

"A mountain man worth the name never fergits a trail." Bridger spat into the dust and turned to eye the four-wheeled wagons sitting in the shade of the nearby cotton-wood trees.

The smith Bridger had hired was busy in his lean-to shop. Fire flared in his forge as an Indian boy worked the bellows. Metal rang against metal, making money for Jim Bridger repairing a wagon rim for the emigrants.

"Fitzpatrick brought them pilgrims from Fort Laramie through South Pass," Bridger continued laconically, "else they'd all be dead. The Sioux are on the warpath an' followed 'em all the way."

"Looks like they mean to stay," Hugh commented. The wagons carried household goods and plows and farm tools.

"Wagh!" Again Bridger spat into the dust. "Ain't gonna matter whether me, you, or the Injuns like it. That's jest the beginning. That's why me and Vasquez set up here. Mean to trade with them pilgrims. Look at those worn-out oxen. . . ." He pointed to the cattle grazing along the grassy banks of Black's Fork Creek. "I kin buy 'em fer near nothin' and sell 'em to the next emigrant train fer whatever the traffic'll bear."

"Seems like you're settlin' down, Jim," Hugh said with a laugh. His glance took in the twenty or more skin lodges among the cottonwoods. Smoke from cooking fires ascended in the cool summer air. Several women sat with Falling Star beside her fire. A band of Nez Percé had been collecting camas roots to dry and, hearing of Bridger's new trading post, crossed the Green to trade with him. Among them was Falling Star's brother, Looking Glass, and his family. There had been a joyful reunion, and now around the fire, an eager exchange of gossip.

She must be lonely sometimes, Hugh thought ruefully, catching the sweet sound of his wife's laughter on the breeze. Always had family, other women, and now she had only him and the boys.

"Fitz's got other fish to fry down south." Bridger interrupted his thoughts. "I tole Dr. White you could guide 'em to Fort Hall."

Hugh squinted into the hazy distance where the white-capped high Uinta mountains gleamed in the summer sun.

"Only a few weeks' work," Bridger urged. "An' these pilgrims pay well. They have to."

Silently Hugh contemplated the coffee and sugar, blankets, powder and lead, as well as the beads and looking glasses and pretty cloth that pay would buy. If he planned to do trade with the Injuns, he'd need such supplies. The horses they'd sold to the emigrants had brought enough for their own winter use, but the beaver was hardly worth the work of taking it, for the trade was now almost exclusively buffalo robes.

"My family—" Hugh began.

"Leave 'em here," Bridger interrupted. "The Sioux ain't through causin' trouble yet."

With a shrug, Hugh dismissed the angry Sioux, for it was

71

well known they never came so far west. "Let's talk," he said, and strolled with Bridger toward the wagons where the white men, puzzling over maps of an unknown land, sat about their blazing fire.

A woman of the Nez Percé did not weep and wail and beg her husband not to leave her. Stoically dry-eyed, Falling Star watched the emigrant train, horses and wagons and cattle, pull away from Fort Bridger. With the morning sun behind them, their shadows led as they headed northwest on the Oregon Trail.

Hugh Cameron, dressed in new buckskins she had sewed for him and mounted on his best horse, led the train. At the last sage-blue ridge, he rode to the back of the train, checking the movement of the wagons. There he paused, lifting a hand in farewell.

His sons shouted and waved in reply. With all her strength, Falling Star fought down the tide of fear rising within as her Shining Bear disappeared over a rise and the wagon train became only a cloud of dust on the blue-gray horizon. These men would pay in American money, he had told her. Money they needed for supplies, tools, knives, guns. They could do without those things, she knew, yet he would not listen to such words.

To her, those white men had smelled of disaster. Remembering the terror she had foreseen for Narcissa Whitman, she wondered if Shining Bear would be a part of it. Yet she could not call him back, nor change what was to be.

Looking Glass, her brother, and several of the Nez Percé wanted to ride with her back to the lush valley she had told them about. They would be company for her and the boys while Hugh was away. She had no desire to stay here where the crowds of emigrants and Indians had already made deep inroads into the forage and the game. Already, she had loaded the mules with the new supplies. Now they would go north.

"So yer goin'?" Bridger said, regarding her with a considering eye when she told him. "Might as well drive those cattle with you." With a wave of his arm, he indicated the gaunt, trail-worn oxen the emigrants had left behind. "More pilgrims show up an' need oxen, I'll send somebody fer 'em."

For a long moment, Falling Star stared at Bridger, seeing through his legendary guile. She was certain he had thought that with Hugh gone he could strike whatever bargain would most benefit himself.

Finally, he grew uneasy, his eyes sliding away from hers. "We'll run outa forage around here afore summer's over," he said defensively.

"They'll eat my grass," she stated. When he started to grin and wave a dismissive hand, she continued in a firm voice. "I'll take half."

"Half!" Bridger protested. "Good God, woman . . . what d'ya think you are?"

With a cool shrug, she smiled at him, sure of her victory. When he continued to sputter protests at such robbery, she turned away, walking back toward her lodge.

"Awright!" Bridger yelled after her. "Half. But ye'll take all of any ya lose or eat."

Smiling, she turned and held out her hand. Halting before her in surprise, Bridger slowly held out his hand and took hers, shaking it solemnly.

"I'm damned," he muttered. "What kinda woman has Cameron got hisself?"

The summer wore on and Shining Bear did not return. Falling Star knew there could be no certainties in the mountains. One waited. Perhaps he had gone on to Oregon, to the Columbia River, with the emigrants and not turned back at Fort Hall. And perhaps the still-angry Sioux had followed and taken their revenge. . . .

If the fear had not always been there, eating at the back of her mind, it would have been a happy summer for Falling Star. Her young sons hunted with their uncle Looking Glass and his warriors. She had the company and the help of his wife, Pretty Bird, and the other women. Together, they cured and tanned the skins the hunters brought, chattering at their work. Their lodges were pitched about the log cabin, which remained empty and unfinished, awaiting the return of its builder.

On a morning in August when the air had turned chill and the breeze held a scent of autumn, the Nez Percé struck their lodges and loaded their travois.

"We go to the Yellowstone for buffalo," Looking Glass told her in their own language. He was a tall, strong man with a proud face. "Then home to the Wallowa mountains before the first snow." Although his face was stern, she saw the affection in his dark eyes. "Your man has not returned. Will you come with us?"

"No." It required all her strength to conceal from him the shattering pain that had filled her being for days now. "I must wait for him."

It was not given her to know the death of those she loved, so she was certain Shining Bear still lived. But he lived amid death and danger. He would return. Of that she was certain.

Looking Glass nodded, accepting her decision. "You have fine sons, my sister. I have taught them to hunt, taught them the ways of the Nez Percé warrior."

"I thank you for that, my brother." She smiled, filled with love for this good, brave man who was her own blood, proud of his reputation as a warrior and leader among his people. He had made himself a second father to her sons this summer. They would not forget what he had taught them.

Little Bear wept, with his arms about Falling Star's legs, when the cavalcade moved north out of the valley. But Little Warrior did not weep. Instead, he leaped astride his pony and rode proudly beside his uncle to the top of the last hill. There he waited, watching until the moving train had faded into dust and blue distance.

The boys had ridden into the forest to hunt, vying with each other in their proficiency with the bow and arrows Looking Glass had made for them.

Beneath the brilliant summer sun, Falling Star worked quickly, cutting up the deer Looking Glass had left to spread on her drying racks. Winter food. In the cooking pot were two sage hens she had snared and perhaps the boys would actually bring back game . . . at least a rabbit or a squirrel.

Her heart had contracted in dismay this morning when she came out into the day. A quick thundershower had blown through the valley during the night and now the distant mountaintops were dusted with snow. Already, the aspen were turning to gold. An early winter, and Shining Bear still not safe at home.

Finishing the deer meat, a slow fire smoldering beneath her drying racks, Falling Star walked down to the creek to wash her hands. In the broad meadows, sleek oxen grazed along with the horses. Jim Bridger had not sent for them. Perhaps there was no profit to be made this year.

Something moved on the far ridge and Falling Star stiffened. Inside her heart a singing began, and she knew. . . .

Always, he came to her in the old vision . . . the Shining Bear riding toward her. Unaware of the sounds of the rippling creek, or the south-winging birds honking overhead, Falling Star waited, watching her man come home.

He led two pack mules, heavily loaded. When he came closer, she could see that his blond beard had grown long and beneath his wide-brimmed hat his hair hung about his shoulders.

A sudden sense of dread pierced her. Something was awry in the way he sat his horse, balanced almost awkwardly in the saddle. The Shining Bear who rode away from her at Fort Bridger would have raced his horse across the meadow and leaped from the saddle to seize her in his arms. This man never varied the even pace of his animals, except once to look at the horses and fat cattle feeding in the meadows.

Filled with longing and with fear, Star waited.

At last he crossed the creek to rein his horse before her; the mules were already plunging their muzzles into the water to drink. The intense blue eyes of Shining Bear burned into hers, red-rimmed, weary, and distant.

"I'm home." His voice was husky.

"Yes! Yes!" Falling Star went to him where he still sat on the horse, pressing her face against his thigh. Unashamed, she let the tears come as his big rough hand gently stroked her hair.

"Welcome, my husband." She stepped back and held her arms up to him.

"Home." He let the word out in a great weary sigh. Clasping the saddle horn, he dismounted with an unfamiliar awkwardness. It was then she saw his empty sleeve.

Chapter 9

1845

"He wuz drunk when he got here an' he's been drunk ever since," Jim Bridger growled. With one moccasined foot he nudged the inert body of the young man who lay curled unconscious in one corner of the trading post.

Dropping the bundle of beaver skins onto the dirt floor of the trading post, Falling Star wrinkled her nose at the vile sour stench emanating from the man and turned away. Hugh was just coming in the door carrying another bundle of furs and he grinned at her as he added it to the pile on the floor.

"Not too bad for a one-armed trapper," Hugh told Bridger, failing to conceal the gleam of pride in his eyes.

Bridger spat a stream of tobacco juice out the door. "Half the arms, half the furs, an' half the price," he replied with a grin. "Beaver ain't worth much no more."

"Fat oxen are, though, for certain." Hugh kicked the three bundles of furs toward the center of the room.

They'd come in to Fort Bridger only yesterday, bringing the trade horses and the herd of oxen they owned jointly with Bridger. Amazingly, the oxen seemed to fatten on dried bunch grass over the winter. They looked fine and sleek, fit to trade at a high price for the worn-out oxen of the emigrants moving west.

The trading post where they stood was the largest of the

three rough log buildings that made up Bridger's Fort. None of them, Star thought with pride, was as strong and well built as the log house Hugh Cameron had raised in what was now called Cameron Valley.

Her pride in the way Hugh had learned to compensate for the loss of an arm had deepened her love for him in a million ways. Watching him now as he haggled over prices with Jim Bridger, she remembered that shattering day three years ago when he had returned to her, fearful that he was less than a man.

The story he told her then only increased her dislike and distrust for the white emigrants flooding westward. Some breach of courtesy on the part of the wagon master had angered the Sioux who followed the train westward. East of Fort Hall, the Indians had worked up the fury to attack. Manning his rifle from within the circled wagons, Hugh had taken an arrow in the arm. Because the arrowhead was embedded in bone, the white doctor simply cut off the shaft after the attack had ended and the defeated Sioux headed east. But the wound festered. Ignorant of the cures for such things, the doctor had four men hold Hugh down while he cut off the infected arm.

Falling Star smiled inwardly now, remembering that first night when he came apprehensively to their bed robes. She had teased him, calling him by the silly, youthful nickname . . . Iron Tail. And he had come in to her, strong and vigorous, until she drowned in pleasure and he cried his triumph out with such fervor that he awakened the sleeping boys.

After that, he'd taken charge again, practicing with his rifle until he was as good a shot as most men with two arms. And he'd taught his sons to shoot, scorning their prized bows, ordering Henry rifles out from St. Louis for both of them.

The years had been good ones. The trade in horses and oxen prospered and grew, although their trade-goods business with the Indians was never brisk simply because Hugh refused to deal in liquor.

She was content, Falling Star thought. Her glance fell

again on the man passed out in the corner and something stirred in her. Reluctantly, she recognized the pain of foreknowledge.

"Who is he?" she asked Bridger, indicating the man.

Bridger grinned, marveling as he always did at her command of English. "Name's Charles Forester . . . not Charlie, by God, Charles. Came out last August with Fitzpatrick afore Fitz went to Santa Fe with General Kearney. To see the Wild West, he said. Fitz said he's a son of some friend of Cap'n Stewart." Once more Bridger nudged the man with a foot, none too gently. He stirred and groaned.

"Remittance man, they're called. Noble English family wants to git rid of a bad seed . . . pays 'em to stay away from home."

"A castoff son," Falling Star murmured, seized by an incomprehensible sadness. The young man's eyes fluttered open and looked directly into hers. Such strange eyes, and she stared at them in fascination . . . gray like the sky before an autumn storm. And empty, she thought sadly, empty of light as a pool of muddy water.

Charles Forester groaned, turned his face to the wall, and lapsed again into a stupor.

Bridger grimaced, spat tobacco juice on the cabin's dirt floor, and turned away to count the buffalo robes Hugh Cameron had brought to trade.

"Howdy." Jim Bridger sat down beside the cooking fire just as Falling Star was serving their evening meal. The hubbub of the fort quieted now as the blazing sun disappeared behind the high Uintas.

Both Hugh and Falling Star stared at him in astonishment. During the summer months of trade, Bridger seldom took time for visiting. The Jim Bridger of old, who loved to sit by the fire yarning and trying to top his companions' lies, was too busy nowadays making money from the emigrants and the trade-hungry Indians.

"I'd be mighty obliged if ye'd take Forester home with ya," he said without preamble.

"Jesus Christ, Bridger," Hugh protested. "You send all

your damn worn-out cattle home with us. Now you want us to take on a drunken Englishman whose own family kicked him out."

"They send money ever' quarter through Chouteau's fur company," Bridger said, a calculating look on his rugged whiskered face. "It's yers fer keepin' him."

"I don't have whiskey on my place," Hugh protested.

"All the better." Bridger nodded wisely. "He's educated . . . mebbe he could teach yer boys t'read and write."

"I taught 'em myself," Hugh said, failing to conceal a gleam of pride. "They can both write their names good as me. Jed Cameron and Alex Cameron . . . full out."

"Kin they read?" Bridger demanded.

Hugh's pride faded as he shook his head. The miller's wife long ago had taught him his ABCs and how to write his name, but reading was a slow and painful process for him.

"Only reason I kept this worthless critter around," Bridger continued. "He sure could read purty, an' he brought books with him. But it's got so he's passed out most of the time. Far as I'm concerned, he's no damn good to me. Not even got sense enuff to go outside to puke."

"I'll study on it," Hugh said reluctantly, carefully cutting off a chaw from the plug of tobacco Bridger offered him.

Covertly, Bridger slid a questioning look at Falling Star. With no change of expression, she nodded, and he relaxed visibly.

She had never seen this kind of sickness, Falling Star thought as she helped the Englishman to his bedrobes when they stopped to camp for the night. The Nez Percé were a temperate people, although she had seen her father and his friends groaning and complaining after a drunken spree at rendezvous. Her husband never touched whiskey, and although she did not understand his reasons, she was glad of it.

Charles Forester was thin to the point of emaciation. Beneath the buffalo robe she laid over him, he trembled as with a chill even though the night was warm and pleasant.

80

They were still in the low country, with sagebrush-covered hills stretching to the horizon. Twilight filled the sky as the last streaks of gold faded in the west. Pinprick stars began to appear in the darkening heavens. Forage around the spring was already trampled and thin from emigrant animals feeding on it. Hugh and the boys drove the horses and cattle farther on after they had watered, looking for a spot with more feed to bed for the night.

Quickly, Falling Star gathered dry greasewood to make a fire. At the spring, she cut willow branches, stripped the bark, and set it to steep in the kettle over the fire.

The Englishman slept noisily, groaning and muttering. All day he'd ridden beside her, following the cattle herd, never speaking. What had passed between him and Bridger, she could not guess, but she thought the man had been given no choices.

Filling a cup with willow bark tea, she roused him, lifting his head to make him drink. As soon as he tasted it, he spat it out.

"Whiskey," he groaned. "Please, get me some whiskey."

"No whiskey," she answered, putting the cup to his lips once more and forcing him to drink. The cadence of his voice was pleasant to her ears, each word as sharp as polished flint. Captain Stewart, who used to come to rendezvous, had been an Englishman and he spoke in much the same manner.

At her insistence, he drank it all. Falling back against his blankets, he muttered, "God damn Bridger," and fell asleep.

Soon her men would be coming into camp, hungry and tired, ready for their meal, yet Falling Star sat for a long time staring at the sleeping face of Charles Forester. Occasionally, he cried out, his expression tortured, his body shaken with tremors. Surely this man was of an age with Hugh Cameron, yet he seemed somehow unfinished. Even with one arm and a limp, Hugh was a complete man, sure of his skills, competent and comfortable in his world.

Charles Forester's skin was unnaturally pale, even for a white man, with a faintly yellow tinge. His brown hair and beard were dirty and unkempt and he stank, although Jim Bridger had outfitted him with new clothes. And then there were the lightless gray eyes . . . Star sighed.

This man was bound into the fabric of her life as surely as the Shining Bear. Hugh was not glad of his presence and had only agreed to take him at her urging, for the purpose of teaching his boys. It had begun to trouble her, wondering whether her sons would be prepared for a future that would surely have to be lived on the white man's terms. One day the emigrants would not go on to Oregon. They would settle here and build their cabins and plow the land. Her sons must be ready, and this man would show them the way. Beyond that, she told herself now, she would not look.

Charles Forester lifted another log into place on the new corral fence and grinned to himself. Two months ago he couldn't have raised that log off the ground. Hands that had once been white and aristocratic were now brown, scarred, and rough. I'm alive . . . by God, he thought, for the first time in my life, I'm really alive. Out here in the wilderness, a million miles from England, he'd been cured of a terrible sickness, and he'd found a home.

Thanks to her . . . and his eyes turned across the meadow from the new corral Hugh had decided they must build to protect the horses from marauding Blackfoot and Crow.

A band of Nez Percé had come east from the camas prairies to trade dried camas root. With the first chill of autumn frost in the air this morning they had struck their lodges, ready to move north to hunt the buffalo before heading west to their home mountains for the winter.

All talking at once as they said their farewells, they'd gathered in the clear early sunlight beside the log cabin. The cabin was home for his hosts as well as their trading post. Charles slept with the two boys in the skin lodge, and he'd found it a great improvement over the floor of Jim Bridger's stinking cabin.

Falling Star moved through the chattering crowd of Indians. Charles's heart quickened and he felt a stirring in his loins as he watched the slender figure embracing her sister-in-law, her brother, and her friends in farewell. Perhaps because she had borne only two children, her figure remained slender as a girl's. And because her husband cherished and protected her, she was not coarsened by overwork. The thought brought a start of guilt to Charles's mind.

He had no right to desire her in this way. Gruff and demanding Hugh Cameron might be, but he had proven himself a friend. Only a week after his arrival in Cameron Valley, desperate for whiskey, Charles had taken a horse and headed for Fort Bridger. Still weak and sick, he'd fallen. The horse had run away. He might have died there in the empty miles of sagebrush if Hugh Cameron and his wife had not come looking for him.

Now he wondered how she could have been so tender with a stinking drunk. She'd bathed his face through the fearsome agonies of withdrawal, dosed him with her bitter willow bark tea, forced him to eat the broth from her cooking pot. Without her, he might have died, and no one, including himself, would have cared.

It was as though out of those agonies had been born a new Charles Forester. This man had no noble lineage dating back to William the Conqueror, he had not grown up a lonely younger brother, motherless, with only nannies and servants to care for him, and he had never assuaged that loneliness with whiskey. That other Charles Forester, the wild young blood who had been booted out of Oxford, blackballed at all his London clubs for drunkenness, that Charles Forester had died here in the wilderness.

Watching from this safe distance, he could give in to his yearning for the dark and beautiful woman laughing there with her relatives. It was not that his bed had been empty. There had been eager and willing girls among this band who sneaked into the lodge and awakened him, leading him out to lie with them in the grassy meadow beneath the stars. But his heart and soul was filled with the woman who had brought him to rebirth.

Hugh Cameron joined the chattering group, shaking hands with the men. He was a strong and powerful figure of a man even with one empty sleeve. His golden hair and beard gleamed in the sunlight as he turned to place his arm about his wife.

A breeze lifted the dark fall of her black hair and the morning light blessed her face as, with eyes of love, she smiled up at her husband.

An ache settled in the heart of Charles Forester. With deep and painful certainty, he knew he must live always with this longing buried in the secret part of him.

Chapter 10

1848

A ripe odor of buffalo skins filled the log cabin. Robes for trade had been cleaned and stretched, dried, then folded and pressed into bundles and stacked in the lean-to built for storage behind the trading post.

Falling Star sat on a stool at the roughly built table before the fireplace wall. Early summer sunlight slanted through the open door, falling on the precious sheet of paper where she was writing the numbers as Charles took inventory of the buffalo robes. During the last year, they had taken many in trade from the Indians, a good business now that Hugh no longer rode to the hunt. When she and Charles had finished the counting, they would be packed in the parfleches, loaded on the mules, and traded at Fort Bridger for supplies.

"Five in this bundle," Charles called, heaving another into the stack growing on the hard earthen floor. A faint sheen of perspiration stood on his tanned face. He was dressed too warmly, Star thought, in the buckskin tunic she had made for him.

Seeing that he was waiting, Falling Star wrote the number neatly and precisely with her pen. Then she looked up at Charles and smiled.

Three years in Cameron Valley had wrought such a change in Charles Forester it would have been difficult to recognize the emaciated drunk in this tall broad-shouldered buckskin-clad man. There was a real strength about him now. The straight dark brown hair and his neat beard shone with vibrant health; the once-lightless gray eyes glowed with life.

Without pausing, Charles ducked back into the lean-to for another bundle of robes. For an instant, Falling Star was lost in admiration of the numbers she had written beneath the title: "Hugh Cameron." At first, Charles had been surprised when she insisted on joining in her sons' lessons. Her quickness to learn had surprised him too. Hugh's insistence that she speak English from the first had been for his own convenience, she knew. But now it seemed a part of the inexorable future, for it had helped open to her the world of knowledge Charles offered.

Charles had ordered reading primers from the east and she mastered those. Now he was teaching her and the boys to cipher. Today she would write down the numbers as he took inventory and he would show her how to add them.

"Are you sure we have enough mules to carry all these?" Charles joked as he added another bundle to the stack beside the cabin door. "Five in this bundle," he added, and she wrote the number down carefully before she replied.

"We grow rich in the buffalo trade?" Star asked, tilting her head to look inquiringly into his smiling face. The cadence of his speech delighted her, so that she tried to emulate his way of talking, much to Hugh's annoyance.

Charles laughed aloud, pausing to wipe the sweat from his face with the back of his hand. "Nobody gets rich trading with Jim Bridger," he said. A tin bucket of water sat on a bench beside the door, and Charles took a drink from the dipper. Leaning against the doorjamb, he grinned at Falling Star. "When that wagon train of Mormons came through last year, Jim told them they'd never grow crops in the valley of the Great Salt Lake. I think he wanted them to stay at Fort Bridger and make him rich."

Suddenly thoughtful, Falling Star frowned. "Those trappers last week said there are white-topped wagons all the way from here to the Missouri." Like a river in full flood, she thought, the tide of white men she had envisioned was moving west. Sometimes she wished for the power to turn it back, knowing its coming meant tumult and pain.

"It's the gold rush to California." Charles moved back toward the small trapdoor of the lean-to. "Greed is what's driving most of the western travelers this year."

He ducked into the lean-to, and Falling Star stared thoughtfully after him. Yes, she thought, gold brought greed and violence. And the United States was warring with Mexico, drawing their troops away from the west, where Tom Fitzpatrick, now Indian agent on the North Platte, was struggling to keep peace with the Sioux.

"Six here," Charles called, tossing a bundle of robes out into the room, his voice muffled. Falling Star marked the number down, then leaned her elbows on the table, her eyes surveying the log cabin that was her home. The walls were lined with pegs where traps and saddles and bridles were hung, as well as shelves for Charles's books. Other than the table, with the five stools Hugh had built, the only furniture was a low bed standing against the opposite wall. On the rawhide laced between poles were piled the bed robes of Hugh and Falling Star. Their sons and Charles Forester slept in the snug skin lodge nearby.

She had grown used to living enclosed by log walls because it was the home her husband preferred. All the iron cooking pots were hung beside the fireplace, with the boxes and sacks of supplies neatly arranged on shelves. The huge fireplace kept them comfortable in winter, and the sod roof cooled the rays of the summer sun.

Leaning back on her stool, she rubbed the taut muscles of her neck. They had been at this since breakfast. Hugh had gone to round up the oxen they would be driving to Fort Bridger, taking Jed to help him, for Alex had chosen this time to go on his vision quest. Another time would have been more convenient for all of them, but Falling Star dared not defy the forces that called her son.

"Six here." Charles's voice broke into her thoughts as he tossed another bundle of robes beside the door. "That's it," he added, brushing the cobwebs from his buckskin tunic.

"Now we add all the numbers?" she asked.

Charles nodded. Pausing for another drink from the water bucket, he crossed to the table. Standing beside her, he studied the figures she had written on the paper. "You do very well," he said in a low voice. "A fine hand."

"But I must learn to add," she interrupted, anxious to get on with her new lesson. She found a deep satisfaction in the learning Charles Forester had given her, and she was always eager to learn more. Fate had brought him to this place, for reasons not yet entirely clear to her, but certainly for the learning he could give to her and her sons.

That first year when they'd gone to Fort Bridger to trade, she'd been on edge, watching Charles, fearful that he would once more fall into the clutches of his sickness. But he never touched the whiskey. He collected his remittance, spent it on supplies, and rode back with them as though he had always been a part of their family. It had been the same in the two years since, so that now their family would have seemed incomplete without him.

From a shelf, Charles took the small willow basket filled with hard juniper berries that he used to teach the meaning of numbers. Drawing a stool up at the table beside her, he counted out six berries, the first number on her list. Then he had her count out five, the next number. Drawing a line beneath the two numbers, Charles explained how five and six make eleven. Understanding dawned in Star's mind and she laughed aloud in the joy knowledge always brought her.

Working quickly, they added the list: fifty-two buffalo robes to trade at Fort Bridger. A fine winter's profit.

Filled with pride in her work, Falling Star set aside the paper to show to Hugh when he returned. She reached to gather up the scattered berries just as Charles did, and their hands touched. Unexpectedly, his hand closed over hers, clasping tightly. Those slender, aristocratic hands were brown and hard now after three years in the mountains. Star kept her eyes fastened on them, unable to speak or move, for all the breath seemed to have gone out of her. Yet she could feel her heart beating furiously against her ribs.

"Star." Charles's voice was low, and she felt his other hand softly stroke her long, loose hair. Closing her eyes, Star fought against the rush of emotion that drew her to this man.

She had known for a long time that Charles loved her. But he was an honorable man. Hugh Cameron had rescued him from a degraded life and he would not betray that friendship.

Until this moment, she had been certain her feeling for him was only the grateful love one has for a beloved teacher, something akin to the way she had loved Old Grandmother. Inevitably, she raised her head and met Charles's gray eyes, dark now with emotion.

At once he turned away, composing his face into a calm, unemotional mask. Star stood up and walked to the open doorway, knowing she must defuse the moment. Shining Bear was her destiny. Nothing could change that.

Standing in the open door, Star looked out across the dusty yard. She was startled to see her elder son, for she'd been certain he'd gone with Hugh this morning. Jed sat on a stump near the corral, fitting feathers to the arrows Looking Glass had taught him to make. The boy had a knack for such things and his arrows flew straight and true. His eye was faultless, for his aim with the Henry rifle was just as unerring.

Far across the meadows she saw Hugh's figure, riding among the cattle, cutting out the animals they would take to Fort Bridger to trade. Yesterday he and Jed had gone into the forest to bring back a deer for meat for their journey south. Now she realized that this morning Jed must have refused to help Hugh round up the cattle and horses. Thirteen years old, Star thought, and already a proud and intractable warrior. Hugh was a stern but loving father who never touched his sons in anger. She was certain he would not know how to deal with Jed's growing rebellion.

Regretfully, she thought that his younger brother could never equal him, no matter how hard he tried. Lately, it seemed Alex had stopped trying, turning more and more to Charles, devoting himself to lessons in a way Jed refused to do.

But Jed must have the white man's knowledge in order to

survive the years ahead. The thought spurred her to call to her son.

"Running Buffalo." Carefully, she used his Indian name, the name he preferred. Last summer he had gone alone into the mountains seeking his vision and his medicine to become a man. The autumn before, Looking Glass had taken him along on the buffalo hunt, and Jed's dream vision had been a dramatic and significant one of great herds of buffalo running over vast plains.

"Come inside," she called now. "Charles is teaching me to add the figures. You can learn too."

Raising his head, Jed glared at her. "I don't need the white man's figures. Can he make an arrow like this?" And he held up the shaft, pure and straight . . . a work of art.

Falling Star shrugged and sighed. Sorrow touched her heart with the realization that it was impossible to give knowledge to those who did not wish it. Jed would choose his own path.

Turning back to the dim interior of the cabin, she caught the sympathy in Charles's warm gray eyes. He held the small basket of juniper berries in one hand. What had passed between them moments ago was gone now, carefully hidden.

"You'll never make a white man of him, Star." Charles's voice was low. She knew he guessed her sadness for this son, even though he could not know that his words only repeated what she had seen in the firelight long ago.

Summer sun lay warm on Jed's shoulders as he leaned back against the corral poles. Sitting cross-legged on the weathered stump of pine, he carefully slit an eagle feather with his knife, making it ready to fit to an arrow shaft. The vast arch of the sky above him was blue and empty of clouds. In the distance, he could hear his father shouting at the cattle.

Head down, he watched through half-closed eyes as his mother returned to the cabin . . . to Charles Forester and his white man's lesson. Had Charles ever ridden to the buffalo with the Nez Percé warriors? he asked himself with youthful arrogance. Perhaps even his brother Alex would never ride in that greatest hunt of all, where boys became warriors, and only the strong proved worthy. Fleetingly he thought of Alex out there in the forest now, seeking his vision. Too much a white man, he told himself, doubting that Alex would even find a vision. He'd been proud of his own dream of buffalo running to a distant horizon, bragging to his uncle and his cousin warriors of its clarity and strength. Looking Glass had been impressed enough to honor him with the gift of a fine buffalo horse.

Seeing his father riding homeward, Jed frowned. A buffalo horse could not be ridden among the fat dumb oxen his father fed and sold. He would not dishonor the horse, or himself, by such an action, even though his father had been angry at his refusal. Once he had thought his father a part of the mountains like the Nez Percé, but more and more he followed white man ways. Rebellion surged in Jed's heart.

Again, his eyes turned to the open doorway where his mother had disappeared. He hated the log cabin, its close and stinking confinement where all the light seemed shut out. A lodge was better shelter, and the open hunting camp even better.

Looking at Charles's reading primers made his head ache. He could write his name, and he learned his numbers so that traders could not cheat him. That was all he needed to know.

Lifting his chin proudly, Jed softly sang to himself the war chant Looking Glass had taught him. One day he would be as great a warrior as his uncle. One day, he would be all Nez Percé.

Alex Cameron lay on his back, staring into the vast blueness of the empty sky. The flat rock where he lay was warm against his back, and the breeze in the pines above his head was soothing. Yet he felt tense and uneasy. His head swam with hunger from the fast for his vision, and his stomach roiled.

"Give me a vision!" he cried despairingly at the empty sky, using the old language that was so difficult for him.

Three days he'd been alone in the mountains, already a day longer than his brother had been on his vision quest.

Nothing he ever did measured up to Jed . . . Running Buffalo, and despair fell over him. It was Jed who made fine bows and arrows, whose rifle shot drilled the great elk between the eyes. It was Jed who had been chosen by their fabled uncle, Looking Glass, to ride to the buffalo hunt. Jed, who'd come home with the robes he'd taken, demonstrating to the delight of his mother and father how Looking Glass had taught him to ride full gallop into the herd to the kill.

It was Jed who made Falling Star's eyes shine with pride when he spoke Nez Percé better than she did now. Alex found the words heavy on his tongue. There was no glory in the fact that he had learned to read and write far better than Jed, or that he found Charles's lessons a fascinating challenge. If only he could be as strong and competent, as good a Nez Percé as Jed, he would not care whether he could even write his own name.

Alex's stomach lurched violently, and he turned quickly to lean over the side of the rock, retching. Shaking, he lay back and stared up at the hot yellow summer sun. Jed would not have vomited from his fast, Alex was certain of that.

Jed's dream had been that of a great warrior. Now Alex could find no dream. When he fell into an uneasy slumber, the dreams were not vision dreams, but dreams of food, born in the growling depths of his uneasy stomach.

Something moved up there in the empty sky. With an arm across his forehead, Alex shielded his eyes from the brilliant sunlight and strained to see.

Slowly the creature circled, moving lower and lower with each revolution. At last he could perceive its form, and Alex let out the breath he had been holding.

A great red-tailed hawk rode the updrafts from the heated canyons, searching for prey. Endlessly . . . endlessly . . . it seemed to Alex, and in his agony of spirit he thought the creature sought him as its prey. A great and lonely hawk, alone in the empty sky. Tears poured down Alex's face as he lay inert, watching the wheeling bird.

Suddenly the hawk seemed to fold its wings and plunge

earthward, out of Alex's range of vision. A terrible weakness poured through Alex and he cried out in pain. For a long time afterward, he lay trembling in the vast silence of the forest.

At last, the sky faded to silver and the west blazed with sunset. Surely the hawk was his vision, Alex told himself as he struggled to a sitting position. There would be no other, of that he was certain. Lone Hawk was name enough for such a poor warrior as he.

His legs trembled as he stood, but he forced the strength to stumble homeward through the darkening forest.

Chapter 11

"Chouteau sent these letters out fer ya on the supply caravan," Jim Bridger said, handing the packet to Charles. He nodded at Hugh and Star. "All these here pilgrims headin' west means the mail comes through more'n oncet a year."

With a disinterested shrug, Hugh heaved a bundle of buffalo robes onto the trading post floor. The walls of the rough log cabin were lined with shelves and boxes of trade goods. A long table centered the room where Bridger stood to count the incoming robes and skins that filled the place with a rank odor. From his leather tunic, Hugh drew the inventory Star had made of their robes and offered it to Bridger. Intimidating Bridger, Star thought, with a smile, for he knew Old Gabe couldn't read.

Star's eyes followed Charles as he walked away from the building, leaning against a nearby cottonwood tree to read his letters. Yearly letters for Charles came with his remittance. They were written in cold, formal language by the secretary to his father, Lord Hedwick, and they always closed with the words, "God Save the Queen." A coldness filled Star's heart now, for she knew this year the letters would be different.

Leaving Hugh to haggle with Bridger over the price of buffalo robes, she stepped out into the glaring summer light.

White-topped Conestoga wagons were camped all around Fort Bridger . . . dozens of them, and hundreds of oxen, cattle, and horses. The ring of the blacksmith's anvil blended with the bellowing of the oxen, barking dogs, and the shrill voices of children at play. Around the buildings, the grass had been pounded into dust. So great was the migration westward this year that even the willows along the creek banks had been stripped for forage.

Bridger, grinning slyly over his profits, had told them of the many companies heading west to the gold fields in California or to make farms in Oregon. The Mormons heading for their promised land in Salt Lake Valley were another story. They hated trading with non-Mormons like Bridger and avoided his fort whenever possible. In a grumpy tone, Bridger insisted they were all skinflints anyway.

The tide Star had foreseen swept past the empty lands of Dakota territory, past the Laramie Plains and the high valleys of the Wind Rivers. One day they would stop here and then the greatest change of all would come.

Charles looked up from his letters as she approached, his gray eyes shadowed and his face grim.

"My father died." He spoke abruptly.

Star nodded sympathetically. Wondering how deeply such a loss would affect Charles, she waited for him to continue.

"I have to go back to England." The words, loaded with resentment, burst from him. "My older brother inherits the title and the estates, but he says they can't settle it without me."

"Then you must go," she said quietly, seeing clearly the bitterness he had so carefully concealed all these years.

Charles drew a deep breath. "Yes." His face twisted with such unhappiness that tears stung Star's eyes.

Carefully folding the letters, Charles tucked them inside the leather tunic she had made for him. His eyes met hers and for a moment all the longing he felt for her was revealed, naked and unashamed. Star turned her head, unable to look at it.

"Maybe it's best that I go," he said, tearing his eyes from her face as Hugh and Bridger came out of the trading post.

"But I think that if I do, I'll never come back and I can't bear it."

Yearning to touch him in some comforting way, she resisted the impulse. She was all too aware how carefully Hugh watched whenever she was with Charles. Circumspect as Charles had always been, Hugh could only guess at his true feelings toward Star. Jealousy was there inside her husband, for he was often testy and short with Charles. And as though he knew the reasons behind them, Charles was always tolerant of those outbursts.

Charles was her friend, her teacher. Star told herself she could never think of him as a lover. Only the Shining Bear, her true mate, could hold that place in her life. Yet she knew Hugh could never understand that. He saw those occasional admiring glances and heard Charles's praise for her progress at learning, and his resentment grew.

"You will return, Charles," she said hurriedly. "Believe it. This is where you belong now." She knew this with the certainty of her gift. Charles Forester was worked into the design of her life as surely as the Shining Bear.

"I'll be looking for a party heading east," Charles said, turning to Bridger with a businesslike air. "I've been called back to England."

"Black Harris'll be leavin' in a couple days to take my robes to St. Louis fer trade," Bridger replied. "Reckon you could ride along with him."

"Won't give you time to collect yer stuff from the valley," Hugh protested.

He wanted all of Charles Forester gone from his home, Star thought. Why couldn't he understand that what she felt for the Englishman was only gratitude? Or that a man of Charles's integrity would never violate his host's hospitality or his marriage.

"Your books . . ." Star began.

"They're yours," Charles answered with a smile. "You know enough now to practice your reading, writing, and arithmetic without me."

It would not be the same without his gentle guidance, she

knew. Yet she was grateful for the world he had opened to her. The things he had taught her would be needful to know in the years ahead.

Charles's remittance had been sent out from St. Louis and he spent it all, paying Hugh for the horses he would take with him to travel east with Black Harris. In addition to the gear he bought from Bridger for his own use en route, Charles purchased axes, awls, ammunition, coffee, sugar, and flour he insisted be taken back to Cameron Valley.

"A small payment for the three years' living," he said in answer to Hugh's protests. His gray eyes flicked past Star. "And for saving my life."

The caravan started in the cool gray summer dawn, when only the first streaks of pink light colored the eastern horizon. Rising from her bed robes in the temporary lodge she had erected, Star awakened Hugh and the boys.

As they walked together beyond the trading post where the caravan was assembling, Star struggled to conceal the sense of loss and sadness that filled her heart. She had told Charles he would return, and she knew the truth of the words. Yet she was certain the years would be long and difficult for Charles.

Alex seemed the most distraught at the departure of his teacher and friend. Watching her son's struggle to control his tears, Star understood his feelings for the man who had given him the self-esteem and a sense of accomplishment he had never found in the hard world his father and brother conquered so easily.

"Don't forget what I've taught you," Charles said seriously, shaking hands with the tall boy whose face worked painfully as he tried to conceal his emotions.

"I won't . . . not ever." Impulsively, Alex hurled himself against Charles, embracing him roughly. Embarrassed by his display of emotion, Alex fled down to the creek, where he stayed until the caravan had departed.

"Taz alago," Jed said, holding out his hand, very straight and solemn. "Good-bye, Charles Forester."

"Good-bye, Jed . . . Running Buffalo," Charles replied, grasping the hand of this boy he had never been able to truly touch or understand.

"Safe journey, Charles." Hugh took Charles's proffered hand, affable now that the man he had begun to see as a rival was departing. "Thanks fer teachin' my sons." He did not thank the Englishman for teaching his wife things he felt she needn't know. What need had a woman like Star for reading and writing? Her newfound learning had somehow put a barrier between them, and Hugh hated that.

"Kuse timine," Star told her friend. "Go with good heart."

The flame behind Charles's gray eyes was quickly suppressed. His friendly smile faded into sadness. "You have taught me more than I have taught you," he said to her. "I will never forget you."

"You will return," she said once more, in a voice so low the others could not hear.

Charles looked startled, but he said nothing. Mounting his horse, he raised a hand in farewell, kicked the animal into a gallop as he headed into the rising sun to join the caravan already disappearing on the horizon.

The cold wind smelled of autumn rain. Standing in the doorway of the log cabin, Star searched the hills and forest in vain for some sight of Jed returning from his hunt.

Beneath the gray and threatening sky lying low across the valley, she could see Alex bringing another bunch of cattle in to join those already bawling and milling inside the fenced holding pasture. It was hard and difficult work for a boy alone. She should have ridden with him, but she dared not leave Hugh's side until his fever subsided. The army doctor's vicious knife had done something to her husband's arm that defied all her medicine. At first, the stump seemed to have healed perfectly, but in the last year it flared in periodic infections, filling Hugh's body with fever, the stump racked with pain.

Inexplicably, Star found herself wishing for Charles Forester's comforting presence. There had been only one letter from him in the year since he had gone away. He had thanked them again for their hospitality and said nothing about his future plans.

This summer, through Tom Fitzpatrick, Hugh had contracted to furnish beef cattle to the Indian Agency at Fort Laramie. The herd should have been headed south long before now so that they would be safely back in Cameron Valley before the first snow.

Part of the herd would be the oxen they'd driven back from Fort Bridger, fattened already on Cameron Valley's thick rich grass. Star frowned, remembering how angry Hugh had been when Jed chose to go with his uncle from Fort Bridger, north to the Bitterroot mountains and the buffalo. They had needed his help driving the cattle to Cameron Valley. But after all, Hugh had been pleased with the buffalo robes Jed had brought back from his hunt.

A low groan from inside the cabin told her Hugh had awakened, the laudanum had worn off. It was a white man's medicine that Charles had left with her, and the only thing that eased her husband's pain at these times.

Quickly, she knelt beside him where he lay in the low bed. Stroking his forehead with a gentle hand, she let out a long breath of relief. The fever was gone.

"Star . . ." He reached out for her as he always did, and she looked tenderly into his face.

"I'm feelin' better," he told her, and she saw from his clear eyes that he spoke the truth. "Might be we kin start the cattle south tomorrow."

"Not tomorrow," she replied firmly, carefully removing the poultice from his stump. It smelled foul with the poison it had drawn from him.

He lay quiet, not arguing, his eyes following her as she renewed the poultice from the pot of herbs she kept on the coals at the side of the fireplace.

"I ain't much use," he finally said in a morose voice.

Tying the poultice with a deerskin thong, Star leaned close to look into his eyes, smoothing back the damp gray-blond hair from his forehead. "You are more man with one arm than any other with two," she told him, smiling when she realized she'd fallen into the old language as she sometimes did in moments of deep emotion. *"Uakos titokas,* strong as a giant."

Hugh cupped her head in one big hand and drew her down to meet his kiss. His lips were dry from fever, but his tongue was warm and moist and demanding. A hot pulsing rose deep inside her. "Come lie with me," he murmured, his mouth against her pulsing throat.

"You are better indeed!" Laughing, she moved away, knowing well that his desire far exceeded his physical strength at this moment. Stirring up her cooking fire, she glanced back at him and met the hunger in his intense blue eyes. "Soon, Iron Tail," she promised, teasing. "Soon."

Except for the startling blue eyes in his dark face, Star thought her oldest son might have been all Indian. Dressed in the fringed buckskins the warriors of Looking Glass's band wore, with his black hair in two long braids.

He had appeared suddenly in the doorway, silhouetted against the fading light. Behind him, in the distance, Star could hear Alex shouting at the bawling cattle. Jed held up a fresh joint of meat. "I killed a deer," he said.

Struggling to a sitting position, Hugh grinned at his son. "Fresh liver'll be mighty tasty. Give us all strength fer the cattle drive tomorrow."

Jed's face darkened, and he tossed the hind quarter on the table. "What cattle drive?" he asked, frowning at his father. A faint insistent pain began to grow inside Star's chest, for she was certain he knew the plans perfectly well.

Hugh lifted a quizzical eyebrow, forcing himself to speak in an even tone. "I told you, son. I contracted to furnish beef for the agency and the army at Fort Laramie this fall. We'll start the drive tomorrow."

"I won't help you furnish food for the blue-coat killers and their tame Indians." Jed's voice was low and bitter. "Have you forgotten how they killed and scattered the Cayuse tribe for taking revenge on the Whitman robbers?"

Star grasped the edge of the table, her eyes riveted on the two men. The pain inside grew and spread, holding her immobile. Narcissa Whitman had died the dreadful death Star had foreseen that long ago day at rendezvous. But even the massacre of the Whitmans in Oregon hadn't slowed the stream of settlers pouring westward.

"I'm yer pa, boy." Hugh's voice rose as he stared up at his tall son. "You'll do as I say."

Jed returned his stare, unflinching. His voice was quiet, and he spoke in Nez Percé. "Once I thought you were of the mountains too . . . a part of our world. Now I know the white man can never be anything but the white man . . . destroyers of the people and the land."

"You've been listenin' to yer crazy uncle," Hugh shouted. "You won't talk to yer pa like that."

"I am a man now," Jed replied steadily. "I must make a choice and I choose my mother's people. From now on I will be all Nez Percé." Hefting his rifle, he turned and walked out into the cold dusk.

"Damn yer hide," Hugh yelled after him. "Damn Looking Glass and damn all red bastards!" His eyes met Star's unhappy ones and he seemed to choke on his words. "Oh God! God . . . what's happening?" With an agonized face, he reached out for her, his eyes pleading. "Star . . . Star . . ."

She drew him close, his face buried in her hair, his heart pounding violently against her breasts. "It will be all right, Shining Bear," she murmured, caressing his back comfortingly with her hands. "We must let him go. It will be all right."

But the pain in her chest seemed overpowering, filling her whole being until she could scarcely breathe. With all her gift, she knew the future marched, inexorable and unchangeable, toward them.

Chapter 12

1850

Winter melted into spring, but Jed did not return, nor did Looking Glass's band come again to trade in Cameron Valley.

Summer bloomed and faded, autumn blazed on the mountain sides. The trees were bare once more before Hugh Cameron could speak of the son who had defied and rejected him.

When he had turned his horse into the corral, Hugh walked across the yard to pause before the cabin where Star was working skins. Staring up into the leaden sky where the season's first thin snowflakes drifted downward, he muttered, as though to himself, "Jed's dead . . . or he'd have come back."

The air was heavy and still, warning of the slow-moving storm coming down from the north. No time to finish the skins she had been working, Falling Star was thinking, barely hearing her husband's low-spoken words. When she realized what he had said, she stared at him, carefully letting out her breath, almost afraid to disturb the moment. She had waited so long for Hugh to speak the name of the lost son. Now he was ready to turn his grief at the boy's rebellion into grief at his death.

Quickly, she laid aside the skins she must gather into the safety of the cabin, and went to him. With her hand on his arm, she turned him to face her. For the first time he let her see, there in his eyes, the sadness he had kept inside.

"I would know if he was dead or in trouble," she said softly.

"Aye." Hugh looked down at her, searching her face. He put his arm about her, drawing her close to his side. "But you told me it weren't given you to know of the death of those you love."

"I know of Jed," she replied, her heart filled with pain for his hurt. "You were angry and I didn't dare speak of him."

Hugh's blue eyes looked deep into hers and she saw no anger, only a longing to have his son back again.

"He's with my brother, Looking Glass. Running Buffalo has found his home."

"How d'you know that?" Hugh demanded.

Falling Star smiled into her husband's face. "Long ago you stopped asking me how I knew. You believed. Can't you believe now?"

"He belongs here!" The old anger had flared again, fueled by his yearning for Jed.

"My father would say I belonged with him too," she answered quietly.

Hugh looked startled, then thoughtful. Suddenly he grinned. "Woman, I can't outsmart, nor outtalk you." His mouth covered hers then, and she responded with a passion that was forever new.

Slowly, he drew away, looking into her face, still holding her against him. "I believe," he said.

Alex swung the corral gate shut behind him. Across the yard, in front of the cabin, he saw his parents, holding each other, kissing with a fervor he would have thought their years denied. He grinned to himself, for he liked to see them loving like this. Such moments had become rare in the past year. His father had grown more and more gruff and taciturn, even with his mother.

A pain shot through him in the certainty that his father's behavior came of grieving for the favorite son who had rebelled and gone away. Resentment ate at Alex like a worm.

It was he who stayed, drove the cattle to market at the forts, cared for the horses, helped load the buffalo robes to trade for goods at Fort Bridger, and made the long trek there and back. Yet it was Jed who was always on his father's mind.

As he watched, Hugh cupped Falling Star's hip in his hand and pressed her against him, grinning lustily. Alex felt his manhood stir. He'd had Indian girls enough already . . . at the fort and among those who came to Cameron Valley to trade.

With a burst of anger, he thought of how the white emigrants at the fort spoke derisively of "squaw men." But Hugh Cameron's reputation among the traders and the army men was good, and Alex had to respect that, in spite of his anger at his father's feeling for Jed. He knew his mother had let Jed go, knew she loved him equally just as he returned her love. But the world was changing faster than his parents guessed. The army meant to subdue the Indians. This country would belong to the white men. Let his brother go backward, he meant to go forward into the world of the white men that was beginning to build already in Wyoming territory.

Brilliant spring sunlight nearly blinded Falling Star as she stepped out of the dim confines of the trading post. The band of Shoshones who had come to trade milled about the yard, gabbling, displaying the trade goods they had taken from her in exchange for their fine soft deerskins, their horses stirring up a dust.

A young man shouted, pointing to the further ridge where the mountains broke into low sage-grayed foothills. Falling Star shaded her eyes with a hand and turned to follow his pointing finger. A lone horseman rode toward them, trailing two pack mules.

It was not an unusual sight nowadays. Those who had failed to find riches in the California gold rush were spreading out all over the west, panning the streams for color where once only the beaver trappers had worked.

But she knew at once this man was not one of them. Even

though he was still only a silhouette against the gray sagebrush, Star felt a warmth pervade her being, a sense of welcoming. It was her friend, Charles Forester, come back to the west after four long years.

Hugh came out of the small cabin he'd built for a trading post, closing the latch behind him to keep out any light-fingered Indians. From the corner of her eye, Star watched his frown deepen as he recognized the new arrival. Careful-ly, she composed her own expression. She must not seem too happy to greet Charles, must not arouse Hugh's jeal-ousy.

Alex mounted a horse and rode bareback to meet Charles, shouting his greetings as he reached to clap his friend's shoulder. Indians crowded around as the two of them rode into the yard, jabbering to each other, poking at the mule packs, hoping the new arrival brought whiskey.

Star moved forward as Charles dismounted, holding out her hand. "Welcome home," she said simply.

His gray eyes filled with moisture, and he seemed unable to speak as he stared hungrily into her face, his hand clasping hers tightly.

"We never heard from you," Hugh said, coming up to slip his arm possessively about her waist. "Figured you planned to stay in England." His tone was friendly if not warm, and Star stepped away from Charles, her arm encircling Hugh's waist.

At once, Charles controlled his emotions, grinning at Hugh, hugging Alex roughly. "It's good to be back," he said heartily, "damn good."

"You've been ill," Star said to Charles. She stirred the cooking pot on the fireplace coals and turned to study his thin, hollow-eyed face. The mule's packs were safely inside the log trading post, the Shoshones had satisfied their curiosity about the newcomer and departed for their own camp.

"Yes." Charles's gray glance moved quickly over them— Star, Hugh, and Alex. Then he fell silent, staring down at his crossed legs where he sat on the skin-covered woven willow backrest beside the fireplace, so much more comfortable than the hard stools. "The old sickness," he finally added. Drawing a deep breath, he raised his head and met her eyes.

"I thought I was cured of it when I left here. At my father's . . . brother's . . . estate at Weststone there was brandy and port and whiskey. Before long I was exactly as you found me that day at Fort Bridger . . ." His voice trailed off and his eyes fell, dark with shame.

"For some there is no cure," Star told him quietly.

"I know that now," Charles answered without looking up. "But I'll never go back to England. I've come west to get well and find myself again."

"You're welcome to stay here as long as you want," Alex said, his happiness in his old friend's presence glowing in his dark eyes. "Isn't that right, Pa?"

With only the briefest hesitation Hugh replied, "Why sure . . . sure . . ."

His eyes met Star's and she saw the old fear in their depths. An ache filled her chest with the knowledge that this man she loved so dearly could never understand the feeling that bound her to Charles Forester. Charles was her first real friend since Old Grandmother. Why was her gratitude and love for a teacher beyond his comprehension when he still held that feeling toward Tom Fitzpatrick?

Since he'd lost the arm and become One Arm Cameron to the Indians, he'd also lost the adventurous spirit that seeks new things . . . the very spirit that had sent him west and made him steal a young Nez Percé girl from her father.

This man, her man . . . the Shining Bear was as precious to her as the air she breathed. His pain was her pain. She felt it even as he struggled to hide his jealousy of Charles Forester.

She rose to pour more coffee for the men.

"We don't get a lot of Indian trade on account of not stocking whiskey," Alex was telling Charles.

"Don't have drunken bucks tearin' the place apart neither," Hugh muttered with a hostile glance at Alex.

"But we've done well tradin' oxen with the emigrants,"

Alex continued as though he had not heard his father. The boy's eyes were intent on Forester, seeking his approval.

Seeing that eagerness, Star sighed. Hugh's yearning after Jed seemed a rejection to Alex. Now he sought approval and understanding from Charles to replace what his father never gave.

"We sell the weak stock to the army for beef," Alex continued. "They'd buy more if we had 'em."

Charles nodded approval. "I heard in St. Louis and all the way west how scarce game has become with all the emigrants coming across the plains and living off the land."

"Did they tell you how the army kills the buffalo so they can drive the Indians out of the country?" Hugh growled.

Charles's face grew somber. "There were white-topped wagons as far as the eye could see all the way out from Independence."

"If they keep comin', the Indians don't stand a chance. The army'll round 'em up an' herd 'em out jest like Alex herds the cattle." Standing up, Hugh walked to the fireplace and spat into the fire. "Dumb pilgrims don't know the first thing about livin' in the mountains. They'll ruin the country."

"Likely you're right," Charles agreed. "Maybe you should be prepared for that."

"I'm prepared," Hugh exploded. "Long as I've got my rifle, I'm prepared to keep 'em out of my valley."

"Some settlers come into the south valley last year," Alex explained to Charles. "Planned to build a farm, but me and Pa invited them to move on."

"Damn right!" Hugh's voice was harsh. "This here's Cameron Valley and it belongs to me and the Indians."

Leaning against the backrest, Charles studied Hugh's bitter face. "I stayed awhile with Chouteau in St. Louis and had a chance to talk to some lawyers about land laws. People are heading west looking for land, Hugh. You'd better make sure Cameron Valley belongs to you by law . . . not just by your gun."

"Damn the rotten pilgrims!" Hugh stood up abruptly, his face stormy. "They ain't welcome here and I don't need help from you to keep 'em out." With that he stomped across the room and out into the night, leaving the plank door swinging behind him.

An embarrassed silence fell. At last, Charles cleared his throat and shrugged. "Maybe I'm interfering in things that are none of my business. But you've helped me . . . and this is coming no matter how much we might hate it."

"Pa lives in the past a lot nowadays," Alex replied. His allegiance would be with Charles now, Star saw, and against the father who had loved him second best. Sadly, she knew Charles was right. Yet even if her son's rebellion had logic on its side, she could not go against her husband.

"Star?" Charles's eyes were on her, questioning. "I brought the papers that'll be necessary. I know how to run a survey if Alex can help me." He paused to smile at Alex. "Have you remembered the mathematics I taught you?"

"You can bet I have," Alex answered proudly. Smiling at Star, he added, "I want you to take a look at Ma's bookkeeping. Bet there ain't a white woman could do better."

Charles's eyes hardened and he frowned at Alex. His voice was reproachful. "Does your mother's race concern you, Alex?" His face softened as he turned to Star. "I can assure you, she's unique in all the world."

For one brief flaring moment, she saw longing burn in his gray eyes. Then it was gone, like a doused campfire. A sense of unease filled her heart. The tall Englishman loved and desired her still. Even though her own feelings were simply affection and gratitude, she knew how bitterly her husband resented Charles's love for her. It would not end well, she thought sadly.

"We can start the survey tomorrow," Alex was saying eagerly. "If you say it needs to be done, then it needs to be done. Pa'll come around, you wait and see."

Winter had descended early on the Wind River country in 1854 and stayed late into the spring of 1855. The residents of Cameron Valley kept close to their log cabin and the adjacent skin lodge, leaving only to hunt for meat or care for the horses and cattle. To pass the time, Charles renewed his lessons and read to them from the new books he had brought. Hugh fought through another bout of infection in his stump. With all Star's attention centered on her husband, Alex and Charles were left to fend for themselves. Eager, Alex began to learn the rudiments of bookkeeping and of the surveying they would begin with the coming of spring.

Spring thaw had come at last. From where he stood on the top of a rolling sagebrush hill, Alex watched a skein of geese honk their way northward through a sky as clear as blue glass. Grinning up at them, he stretched, glad to be free of the confines of winter. This morning he and Charles left the ranch early, riding to the stone cairn they'd built to mark the southeast boundary of the land Charles intended they claim. From here they would survey a line westward, scouting the parameters, Charles measuring with his instruments, Alex writing down the figures he dictated.

"The way cattle winter here," Charles said, "it seems to me you ought to raise your own. That way you'd be free of Bridger."

Startled by the words, Alex glanced up from the figures he had just written carefully on the map Charles had made of Cameron Valley. "Pa sells the heifers to the army," Alex replied, watching Charles adjust the transit. "And Bridger's done right by us so far."

Charles shrugged. "I didn't say anything before, but those prospectors who came through last week said Bridger was still back east. There are rumors Vasquez is making a deal to sell out to the Mormons."

"Jim Bridger ain't no Mormon lover," Alex replied with a laugh. "He figures they gouge him at every turn. He won't sell."

"He's not here." Charles's answer was filled with meaning.

"You're sayin' if we depend on Bridger for animals, we're likely to be up the creek without a paddle?"

"That's what I'm saying."

Alex stared off at the horizon where the infinite blue of the Wind Rivers pierced the pale morning sky. "There's cattle in Oregon, so they say," he mused. "More'n a plenty . . . and cheap."

"Might be the place for a man to go and buy a herd," Charles said carefully, certain that Hugh would flare up at the suggestion if he knew its origin.

Studying his map, he avoided Alex's eyes. The boy was only eighteen, inexperienced and naive. He could scarcely guess at the passion for Falling Star that gave Charles no peace. He'd thought he'd drowned that longing for her during those painful months in England, but the moment he saw her lovely face again the passion surged through him, grown more powerful in denial.

If Alex were too young to understand, Charles was certain Hugh guessed. Surely it was more than his recurring illness that caused his shortness of temper, his irascibility. And he had a way of never letting Star be alone with Charles.

Charles sighed. He had seen the fear Hugh's illness brought to Star's eyes, and seen Hugh's own anger at his incapacity. The news the prospectors brought had depressed him deeply. Tom Fitzpatrick had died, far away in Washington, D.C., still fighting to make sense of the government's Indian policy.

Today, as he had in all the three weeks they had been working on the survey, Hugh had found an excuse not to join them. "We need meat," he'd said, and gone hunting by himself.

"Would you ride to Oregon with me?" Alex asked, interrupting Charles's thoughts with youthful urgency. "We'd have to leave right away if we want to get back before snow."

Charles grinned and nodded, concealing the aching certainty that it was best he go away. "I've always had a desire to see that country."

"It's that crazy Englishman fillin' your head with wild ideas!" Hugh shouted. "Be damned if ye'll take my money to Oregon to buy cows." He paced the length of the cabin, pausing beside the glowing fireplace to rub his arm stump.

"Pa, listen . . ." Alex tried to interrupt his father's tirade.

Charles had discreetly absented himself from a confrontation he was certain would come.

Star stood with her back to the two men, carefully arranging the rolled, tanned deerskins on the shelves. Her fingers were cold with apprehension, but she could not speak. What would come must be between her son and his father.

"The damn drunk . . ." Hugh raged. "Comes here and tries to tell me how to run my life. Crazy idiot . . . sayin' I need to pay the government for the land that's already mine."

"Pa," Alex managed to interject, desperate now to convince his father. "The world is changing."

"Not here!" Hugh cried vehemently. "I won't have it changed here." He glared at his son. "Listen, boy." Blue eyes blazing with anger, Hugh stood toe to toe with Alex in the dim log room. "I ain't sellin' no more beef to the army. Let the bastards starve! And we don't need no cattle. We still got plenty deer and elk and buffalo."

"I'm going to Oregon, Pa," Alex answered in measured tones, his mouth set with determination. "Ma thinks it's the right thing too."

Hugh whirled on Falling Star, his face twisted with fury. "The son-of-a-bitch got to you too, huh? In how many ways?"

Falling Star winced, hoping Alex had not caught his father's bitter implication. Her heart ached for the pain and frustration in Hugh's expression. To him, Charles was a rival . . . a rival with two strong arms and a head full of knowledge Hugh Cameron had never acquired.

"You know the truth of it, my husband," she replied in a soft voice. Instantly, Hugh looked shamed and turned his face from her piercing look. "My heart is for the Shining Bear alone," she added with quiet certainty, saying the words in Nez Percé for his ears.

"Ah, Star," he said, the words almost a cry of relief. Quickly, he moved across the room, to draw her into his embrace. His rugged face, lined now with pain and years, looked into hers, flooded with love.

"Let the boy go," she whispered. "He must prove himself a man."

Hugh buried his face in her hair. She felt him trembling and fear shot through her. The stub of his arm was hot inside his deerskin tunic, and Star steeled herself, knowing the sickness was returning. They must make the journey north to the sinks of the Popo Agie River where a Shoshone medicine man had, last fall, told her there were seeps of thick black liquid with healing power. Although she was a Nez Percé medicine woman, the wisdom of other tribes was not to be scorned.

"You can go," Hugh said, looking at Alex. His arm tightened about Star, holding her possessively. "You can go if the Englishman goes too and don't come back."

"Pa!" Alex protested, outraged. "Charles is our friend. How can you say somethin' like that?"

Hugh turned furiously on his son. "I said it and I meant it. You can bring back the cows, but not Charles Forester."

"Ma?" Frustrated, Alex turned to his mother, appealing for her support.

Through the arm she held tightly about Hugh's waist, Star felt only weakness and pain. This man was the center of her life, her destiny. She could not fault him that his great frailty lay in his inflexibility and his dislike of change, or that he could not bear it that another man desired his wife. She had known from the beginning it would come to this choice.

"It is best," she said, pained for the flaring anger in Alex's eyes. "This life isn't for him. He's taught and helped you, Alex. Now he needs to make his own life . . . away from Cameron Valley."

Chapter 13

It began to rain in the night, a soft spring rain with no wind. Awakened by the rhythm of raindrops on the sod roof, Falling Star lay still, listening to Hugh mutter in his sleep. The banked cooking fire sizzled as a few drops fell through the chimney.

Turning on her side, she looked into Hugh's face, which was frowning even as he slept. It had been a hard day for him, she thought, his last son leaving him in rebellion almost like the first one had left him. But Alex would return, she told herself. In her mind she followed him along the desert trail to Fort Bridger, where he and Charles would deliver the fresh oxen to be sold to emigrants. From there they would take the old Oregon Trail to Fort Hall and beyond.

She wondered what Charles would do afterward. He had spoken of California and of St. Louis, and promised her that Cameron Valley would be legally filed on at the territorial land office. Repressing a sigh, Star eased out of the bed robes. A blanket about her shoulders, she stirred the fire, adding twigs until it blazed into life. Hugh still slept heavily. Last night she'd added to his willow bark tea a few drops of laudanum from the medicine kit Charles had brought. A pain killer, Charles reminded her, more powerful than any of your medicine and to be used with care.

Unwilling to risk waking Hugh with her movements, she settled against the willow backrest, drawing the blanket close about her. In the dim light of the fire, her eyes surveyed the cabin walls, the shelves filled now with all the things Charles had brought last year. The two pack mules had been laden with gifts and supplies. There were axes and knives, saws and shovels, hammers and nails, and a new repeating rifle for Hugh. For herself, he had brought scissors, sharp knives, needles and awls, a length of bright plum-colored silk as soft and smooth as baby skin. There was a box of white queensware dishes, knives and forks and spoons of silver. She'd thanked him and stored the dishes and silver away in the trading post, certain they had no place in a skin lodge, and perhaps not even in a log house.

Smiling to herself as she gazed into the flickering fire, Star remembered how Charles had waited several days, until they were alone in the trading post, to give her the beads. It was dim and quiet in the cabin, the only sound the distant bawling of oxen. Alex had insisted Hugh join him in the hunt to try out their new repeating rifles.

Strangely diffident, now that they were alone, Charles turned from storing supplies on the shelves of the trading post. Drawing a small black velvet bag from his pocket, he said, "These were my mother's. I want you to have them."

Opening the bag, he poured the long strand of pale opalescent spheres into her palm. Star stared at the jewels in awed silence as they lay glowing against her work-hardened skin. They seemed to have a light from within, unlike any jewelry she'd ever seen. Unthinking, she touched the deer-skin locket about her neck where Old Grandmother's blue stone lay.

"They're pearls," Charles murmured in a choked voice. "From China." His hand still cupped hers where he had held it to empty the jewels into her palm.

She nodded and, looking up to meet his intense gaze, knew that he had dreamed of those pearls lying against her dark and naked breast. Quickly, she drew her hand away from his burning touch. "Yes," she managed to say. "I remember when we read about China . . . a strange land on the other side of the earth."

The longing in his eyes was more than she could bear, and Star looked away, dropping the pearl necklace back into its velvet bag. Hugh would guess the meaning behind the gift, she knew. For the first time in their lives together, she must deceive him. He must never see Charles's gift.

They did not speak of the pearls again, she and Charles. She wondered if he guessed they were hidden now, beneath the box of queensware in the storeroom of the trading post.

"Star?" Hugh's voice was soft, but it startled her from her thoughts. "How long you been up?"

His hair was rumpled, but the blue eyes were clear in the pale morning light. She smiled, reaching out to touch the gray-blond beard she had trimmed short with her scissors.

"Come back to bed," he said, grinning, pulling her toward him. "I think ol' Iron Tail's come home again."

Star slid between the blankets, peeling off her doeskin gown as she did. It was the first time in many weeks he had been able to seek her loving. She thought Hugh winced as he turned toward her, lying on his stub. But the expression was quickly stifled as his good arm embraced her, his mouth hot and hungry against hers.

Slowly, Star's hands moved down his body, dismayed at how prominent his ribs were. Since Hugh's injury they often made love with her atop him, but tonight she sensed his need to be dominant. Turning on her back, she smiled up into the eyes that were still as blue as the most distant Wind River mountain.

"Star, my woman . . ." he murmured, bending his head to press his lips against the pulse pounding at the base of her throat. "My own Star . . ."

Hugh rolled over on top of her and she bore his weight gladly, wanting him inside her as urgently as she had long ago on a moonlit night at the Green River rendezvous.

"So good . . ." he murmured, his eyes closed tight as he reveled in the sensation of being enclosed in her silky warmth. "So good . . . always . . ."

Clasping his hips in her hands, Star moved against him and he groaned with pleasure. Her flesh seemed to take flame. Fiercely, she embraced him with arms and legs, answering his movements with frenzied need until at last she heard her own exuberant cry above the harsh sound of his breathing.

Hugh laughed aloud, a wild triumphant sound, then flung back his head as his cry of fulfillment fell on the echoes of her own.

"My woman," he murmured against her throat, his head pillowed on her shoulder as they drifted into fulfilled euphoria.

"My own Shining Bear," she answered, smiling at him as her hand caressed his damp hair and down his back, which was drenched with sweat. "My husband . . . my love."

With a soft chuckle, Hugh drew her close, holding her with a leg over her hip. "Shining Bear . . ." he said. "You ain't called me that in a long time."

He winced and drew in a sharp breath as she turned toward him, the weight of her shoulder pressing against his stub. Moving carefully so as not to touch him there, Star leaned to kiss his mouth.

"Tell me again," he said, his blue eyes dark with love. "Tell me about the first time you saw me, comin' to you in a vision on the Night of Falling Stars."

When the story was finished, Hugh had fallen asleep, his head on a soft beaver pelt, his cheek pressed against her shoulder. Studying his face by the gray dawn light, Star felt pain clutch at her throat and her eyes burned with unshed tears. Dark circles shadowed the beloved blue eyes. The bones of his skull seemed sharply defined beneath skin that was strangely gray under his dark tan. The naked stub of his arm lay against the blanket, red and swollen. For the first time she was aware of an odor emanating from him. Not the odor of the old Hugh Cameron . . . castoreum, sweat, worn leather, and woodsmoke. It was the odor of death.

Snow still lay on the high reaches of the Blue Mountains of Oregon.

"She was one damn hard winter," the stationmaster at the stage station told them. Alex and Charles listened to the garrulous old fellow who talked from sheer loneliness. He'd served them whiskey from the makeshift bar in one corner of the log cabin, then joined them at the scarred and stained table by the fireplace.

"Reckon if you want to buy cattle, you'll find plenty folks anxious to git out of the business." The old man spat at the nearby spittoon, adding to the stains that testified to his poor marksmanship.

With a straight face, Charles cast a triumphant look at Alex. "Seems you picked a good year to be buying."

"I'm lookin' for breedin' stock," Alex told the old man.

"Might try the Barnes spread" was the reply.

Following the stationmaster's directions, they rode across the Barnes place. In the cold late spring the grass had barely started. The cattle were skin and bones, but Charles said they were good stock . . . Durham, like his father's tenants raised back in England.

"You got the cash money?" Barnes asked when they were drinking coffee in his cabin.

"That's right," Alex told him. Glancing at Charles, he sensed that he was being left on his own to negotiate the deal. At once, he felt his palms grow sweaty. Charles was a lot smarter than he was and knew the ways of the world. Maybe he should just turn it over to him.

Barnes gave a grunt of pleasure as Charles drew cigars from his pocket and passed them out. Lighting his cigar, Charles leaned back in his chair, still silent, his eyes on Alex.

"What you askin'?" Alex began, hoping he was making the right moves, but unable to gain a clue from Charles.

Barnes glanced at his wife, who was watching intently from her station beside the kitchen stove. "Ten dollar a head," he said. But Alex caught the falling inflection in his voice, and was certain Barnes was trying to conceal his eagerness to sell.

Shaking his head sadly, Alex sighed. "That's more'n I can afford."

A dismayed expression on her face, the woman crossed to

lay a hand on Barnes's shoulder. "I might cut the price," Barnes muttered reluctantly.

Once more Alex looked to Charles for a clue. None was forthcoming. Taking a puff on the cigar, Alex blew smoke at the ceiling, deliberately avoiding Barnes's stare. "Make me an offer," he said coolly.

In the end, Alex paid in gold, five dollars a head including a good bull, and some of the cows with calf. Eighty head, by count as he and Charles and Barnes rounded them up. An Indian with a seamed, hard face was Barnes's only hand, and likely to be out of a job now Barnes was selling out.

"I call him Magpie," Barnes told them with a grin, "'cause he never stops talkin'."

Alex looked across the clearing where the Indian was expertly bunching the cattle. "Reckon I could trust him to ride with me to Wyoming?" he asked Barnes.

"Hell," Barnes replied. "I'd trust that old bastard afore I'd trust a white man. And I'll bet he kin find water holes nobody else ever heard of."

He'd need the help, Alex thought. Charles planned to join a wagon train to California at Fort Hall. "Does he speak English?"

"Sure." Barnes waved the Indian over to them and explained quickly what Alex wanted.

The old man's black eyes took Alex's measure shrewdly. With a dubious expression he began speaking in an incomprehensible mixture of tongues. Unexpectedly Alex picked out familiar words.

"Kaiziyeuyeu," he said with a grin. "Greetings."

For a moment the old man stared, then he recovered with a shout, "Eeeagh!" His black eyes gleamed. "Nez Percé," he said. *"Uako ues timine . . .* I go with you."

August sun lay hot and bright over the valley. In front of the cabin, Hugh leaned against the backrest Star had made for him padded with soft furs. He liked being out in the sun like this, for he was always cold now.

"Where d'ya suppose he is now?"

Startled, Falling Star looked up from grinding coffee in

the new coffee grinder Charles had brought. Which of his sons did he mean? she wondered, feeling the pain rise in her as she looked at Hugh's wasted face. It had surprised her how fast his disease progressed . . . almost as fast as summer had gone, fading already. Sheer strength of will had carried him for longer than even she knew. But now he'd given up trying to hunt or work with the horses and the cattle. When the Indians, or trappers or gold seekers came by to trade, he ignored them, enclosed in his illness and his pain.

She was afraid to leave him alone, and she'd even slaughtered one of the oxen rather than go into the forest to hunt for meat. Then a band of Shoshones arrived to trade. One of their young men helped her with the horses and the cattle. He was an orphan, she learned, poor and raised by an uncle. His story made her think of Jed. When the band made ready to move on, she asked Little Knife if he'd like to stay and work for her.

"Where is who?" she asked now, dumping the ground coffee into the water boiling in the iron coffeepot.

"Alex, of course," he growled with an impatience born of his illness. "Should be back with his cattle any day now."

"You'll be glad to see him?" she asked, sitting down beside him, reaching out to touch his worn face.

"Aye," he answered, and added with a sheepish grin, "My boys both fought against me. Guess that's what it takes to make a man. I never knew . . ." His voice trailed off wearily.

"They chose different ways," Star said softly. "Who knows which was right."

"I wanna see 'em again," he said fiercely. "Once more." He stared at her as though imploring her to say that it would be so.

Certain that he would not see his sons again in this world, Star rose and hurried to the fire so that he could not see the tears filling her eyes. Struggling for control, she poured the coffee and took a cup to him.

"Sure good coffee," he said, making a valiant effort to hold the cup without trembling.

"Yes," she answered. It was good because this time she had not blended it with dried berries.

"Alex's letter said Charles is going to California." It was less a statement than a question.

She met his blue gaze then, straight on. He could not, even now, forgive Charles for wanting her. Laying her palm softly against his sunken cheek, she answered, "Yes, Shining Bear. It is so."

His eyes shifted away from her, looking out across the wide green valley she knew he loved as though it were another child. A long sigh shook his emaciated body. But when he looked up at her, he was smiling. Taking her hand from his face, he pressed it to his lips, then held her palm lovingly to his cheek.

Leaning back against the backrest, he sighed again. "It's been good, Star," he said, his voice quiet and strong and certain. "It's been all a man could ever ask."

Falling Star washed the body that had been Hugh Cameron, the Shining Bear, from which the spirit had departed. Then she dressed it in the new buckskins she had made for him, with soft moccasins on his feet. She did not weep, competently doing what must be done, holding herself in for the mourning that would come later.

Laying his emaciated body on a fine buffalo robe, she went to call Little Knife, the Shoshone boy. In silence, the two of them carried the body to the hillside where Hugh Cameron had liked to sit, smoking his pipe and looking over the valley of which he was the king and which he loved so dearly. With the new shovels Charles had brought, they dug a hole for the body to lie in. Then she sent Little Knife away.

Kneeling beside the grave, she looked for the last time on the beloved face. Carefully, she laid the medicine bearskin she had taken long ago from the *hohots* killed by the brave warrior, Shining Bear, over his face so that the dirt would not touch it. After the blanket of earth covered him, she carried the stones to build a cairn so that all that was mortal of Shining Bear would remain untouched. On the hillside

above her, the wind moaned softly through the pine trees
. . . *hattia tinukin,* the death wind.

It was dusk when she left her vigil on the hillside. Little
Knife had put on the cooking pot and made a meal for
himself, but when he saw her coming, he stole away in
silence. She did not look at the food, but went inside the
empty cabin where she dressed in her Nez Percé ceremonial
clothes. Taking up a warm buffalo robe, she walked back to
the hillside. Beside the grave, she sat cross-legged on the
robe. Falling Star closed her eyes, lifted her head to the
heavens, and gave herself over to grief.

Little Knife sucked in his breath and covered his ears
against the terrible wail of sorrow that filled the valley in the
silence of the night.

Book II

❌❌❌❌❌❌❌❌❌

Lone Hawk

Chapter 14

1855

The evening campfire had burned down to red coals. Alex drew on his pipe, letting the pale smoke drift upward into the starlit sky. From the darkness beyond he could hear the low mutter of grazing cattle settling for the night.

When he'd bought fifty more head of cattle from the ranch of Sam Hartley on the Snake River where it divided Oregon and Idaho, the man had offered his two sons as cattle drovers. They seemed honest and competent enough and it was obvious the family needed the money. Magpie and Tom Hartley were with the herd tonight. Fred Hartley, barely thirteen and doing a man's work, slept heavily in his blankets.

Magpie, the ancient Nez Percé, had been sheer luck. The old man seemed to have a nose for water and feed and had proved invaluable in bringing the herd this far with a minimum of losses.

Two days' drive and they'd cross the Green near Fort Bridger. Idly, Alex wondered whether he should stop by the fort now that Jim Bridger was selling out to the Mormons.

From out of the blackness, he heard the high lonesome call of a nighthawk. Alex tensed, waiting. When no answering call came, he relaxed, certain it was a nighthawk . . . not Indians. A lone nighthawk, he thought wryly. Like old Lone Hawk Cameron, who had never managed to fit in anywhere.

He couldn't make himself into an Indian like his brother had, and he was still only half a white man.

A pang of homesickness surprised him as he thought of his mother and father waiting back in Cameron Valley. Had the old man been a loner too . . . before he met Falling Star? An old and unacknowledged resentment clogged his throat. His parents had made him a misfit simply by producing him, and yet the fault was not really theirs. The world had changed and moved on past their time. It was he who would have to fit into that new world.

He missed Charles's good company, and thought with nostalgia of his friend heading for California on a wagon train out of Fort Hall.

Alex sighed, the loneliness like an empty space inside him. Maybe he needed a woman, but he'd had a girl just a few days ago at Fort Hall. An Indian girl, he thought with a dismissive shrug. If he was going to be a white man, he would have to find a white wife. Someday . . . somewhere . . .

The last of the sun glinted off the eternal snows of the high Uintas as Alex and Fred rode into the wagon train circled for the night. Magpie had spotted the white Conestogas from far off and they'd bedded the cattle down well away from the emigrant camp.

A huge fire blazed in the center of the circle, shedding warmth and light in the gathering dusk. Alex reined up his horse as a tall, stooped man with long hair and beard came to meet them, his rifle loose in the crook of his arm.

"Who be ye?" he asked by way of greeting.

"Drovers," Alex answered, undaunted by the man's unfriendly air. "Takin' a herd of cattle from Oregon back to Wyoming."

When the man only grunted in reply, Alex continued. "Where you folks headed?"

"We're Mormons." The man's voice was like a trumpet proclaiming the news. "Gatherin' to Zion in Great Salt Lake valley."

Over the man's head, Alex could see the women in their

126

travel-worn clothes working at the cooking fires, glancing covertly at the strangers in their midst. The wagons, he could tell, had been patched and repaired many times.

"Your stock looks poor," he told the man, seeing the bony oxen grazing alongside. "You should've traded 'em back at Fort Bridger."

"Couldn't afford it," the man snapped, turning a questioning face to the fat, red-faced man who had joined them.

"Brother Hickman," the man burst out. "The hunters are back and they're empty-handed."

Dismay flitted across the tall man's face. Then he composed his features and resorted to his stentorian tones. "This here will be a meatless day . . . good fer the Saints."

There seemed to be children running everywhere, and Alex felt a twinge at the thought of meatless supper for them and for the weary-looking women.

"I could let you have a beef to butcher . . ." he began.

The tall Mormon started, and stared at him, demanding, "How much?"

"Nothing," Alex replied, chagrined by the man's belligerence. "I got a footsore cow that'll likely never make it to Wyoming. She's yours to feed the women and kids."

The man's weathered face broke into a grin. He clapped his stout companion on the shoulder. "See, Brother Martin, I done tole you the Lord would provide."

Katrin Jensen could not take her eyes from the tall young stranger who had provided the beef for tonight's feast. He was not a Mormon, that was certain. The way he walked, the way he held his well-shaped sandy head, the easy grin on his clean-shaven handsome face, all proclaimed a confidence that was almost arrogant. She wondered if Brother Rasmussen would play his fiddle for dancing tonight after services, and her heart gave a bound inside her chest with the hope that the young stranger might choose her for a partner.

"Katrin!" The sharp tones of Sister Martin made her aware that she was staring. "A bold woman is the devil's own." The woman gave her a hard, bitter look.

Chastened, Katrin busied herself with cleaning the dishes

and packing them away for tomorrow's journey. Liza Martin hated her, just as she hated Cora, her husband's second wife.

Katrin's heart seemed to sink into her shoes when she thought how near they were to Salt Lake. When her mother and father died of the cholera in St. Louis, President Snow had found the Martin family to bring her to Zion. Before long, she became aware of Brother Martin's lustful eyes, and by the time they reached South Pass, it was acknowledged in the family: in the valley of the Great Salt Lake, Katrin would become Brother Martin's third wife.

Desperation seized her at the thought of such a hateful life. She'd gone along, doing her work, trying to ignore the sly pinches of Brother Martin. Salt Lake valley was only a few days' journey ahead. If she meant to escape, she must do it now.

Again, her eyes turned to the young man talking with the elders on the far side of the big campfire. Surely he wasn't married. She guessed him to be only a couple of years older than she . . . not more than eighteen.

The lustful glances of many a man in the wagon train had made Katrin doubly aware of her soft pale blond beauty. She knew very well that if she had been old and ugly, Brother Martin would have found a way to abandon her in Missouri, or refuse to take her into his household.

Ducking behind the wagon, she found her hairbrush and smoothed her hair, pinching her cheeks and biting her lips to make them glow.

The communal campfire blazed high, the fiddle sang, and the caller's voice rang out above the laughter and talk. Alex leaned against a wagon wheel, watching in amazement as these travel-weary, poverty-stricken people forgot their troubles in music and dance.

He'd noticed the girl the first time he rode into camp. Her hair was the color of moonlight, worn in a coronet of braids that gleamed like a pale halo around her young face. His loins stirred and he fought against it, his face flushed. After all, he'd had a woman at Fort Hall, he wasn't that needful.

As his eyes met hers, she smiled invitingly and Alex felt the heat rise in him. She stood sedately beside an older woman, watching the dancers. Magpie had stayed with the cattle, but Alex had brought the two Hartley boys with him. Already, they had chosen partners and were cavorting happily among the dancers.

Although he'd never danced, it looked easy enough. The thought of holding the golden girl by the waist, touching her, drew him around the circle of dancers to her side.

"Ma'am," he said with more confidence than he felt, "I'm Alex Cameron and I'd take it fine if you'd dance with me." It came out wrong. He was as red-faced and stammering as the simplest fool.

Close up, he saw that her eyes were the pale gray blue of a morning sky, her lips soft and full in a round, young face. Her gown was of faded calico with a patched skirt, but her breasts filled the bodice, tapering down to a slender waist. Again, he felt the heat in his loins, and took her hand quickly to lead her among dancers before he shamed himself.

"My name is Katrin Jensen," she told him as they stood waiting for the set to end and a new one to begin. "Both my mother and father died in Missouri of cholera. We came from Denmark after we joined the church. I learned English on the ship because my parents couldn't seem to learn it." She allowed herself a small prideful smile. "We were supposed to travel with this wagon train, so Brother Martin and his wives brought me along in their wagon."

"You're an orphan," he said, filled with quick sympathy as he studied her vulnerable, confiding young face. "How old are you?"

"Sixteen," she answered, then glanced fearfully around to see if anyone was listening. "Brother Martin means to make me his third wife when we get to Salt Lake." Tears glistened in her eyes, turned imploringly on him. "I can't bear to think of it."

Before he could answer, someone pulled them into the set for a reel and he was occupied with trying to follow the pattern of movement. Katrin smiled at him, helping to lead him, but her moist eyes still glistened in the firelight.

Alex Cameron was so strong, Katrin thought, her eyes never leaving him as they danced. She liked the hard young touch of his hands on her waist, the way the fringed buckskin shirt accentuated the movements of his lithe body. Firelight glistened on his sandy curls, and the dark brown eyes were intent on her face each time they held hands to promenade.

Breathless from more than dancing, her heart pounding, Katrin let her hand stay in his when the dancing ended.

"There's water in the barrel there," she told him and led him to the wagon, drawing a tin cup full for him.

Brother Martin was dancing with Cora, but Katrin could feel his angry eyes on her. Revulsion clogged her throat, hot and bitter tasting. She would not be his wife. This stranger staring at her with adoring eyes would be her escape.

Women, she had observed, were always at the mercy of men. Her own dear mother had been heartbroken to leave family and friends and the snug cottage near Aarhus. But she'd had no choice. She must follow her husband into the new religion and to their Zion in faraway America. To her death . . . Katrin thought, and felt her whole body burn with bitter grief. All the good life they might have had in Denmark gone because her father had been convinced this religion could lead him to his own personal godhood.

She thought of the Salt Lake valley ahead of them, and of living in the same house with the resentful Cora and Liza and all their children . . . of sleeping in the same bed with Brother Martin while he grunted and rutted against her as she had heard him in the nights with the other wives.

"I have to get away," she said to Alex, desperation mirrored in her face. "Help me." Alex Cameron was a man of substance; she knew from the size of his cattle herd and the fine horses he rode. With him, she would not live in poverty and repression.

"You'll dance with me now." Brother Martin's demanding voice interrupted them. His florid face was streaked with sweat from his exertions, and there were dark, wet stains under the arms of his cotton shirt. He barely managed to control the fury blazing in his small eyes. "Ain't seemly for you to spend so much time with a Gentile stranger." Clasping her hand roughly, he dragged her into the circle of dancers.

Meeting a party of Mormon horsemen next morning, Alex allowed himself a wry grin. They were searching for strayed oxen. The wagon train would be delayed until the animals were found. He'd sent Magpie on an errand last night and the old man had performed admirably.

What was it that Katrin feared so, he wondered as he rode toward the Mormon camp. Magpie and the two boys were already pushing the cattle herd eastward, but he could not leave behind this girl, so desperate and afraid. The thought of her shimmered, pale gold, in his mind. God, she was a pretty thing, and he cursed when he realized the havoc his thoughts had caused in his loins.

Alex had himself under control by the time he rode up to the Martin wagon where the women were packing for the day's journey. Brother Martin had gone with the oxen-hunting party. Alex tethered his horse to a wagon wheel and looked around for Katrin.

Suddenly she was there beside him, slipping her hand in his, saying, "Let's walk out from camp a bit."

He was aware of the scandalized looks that followed them, and spoke quickly, fearing they would be interrupted as they had been last night. "Why can't you just say you want to go back east? I'd offer to take you to Fort Laramie and find transportation for you."

"No . . . No . . ." Her breath came quick and panicked. The hand on his arm clutched desperately, and her eyes shone with fear. "Don't you see . . . they'd never let me go with a Gentile. I've been promised to Brother Martin . . . and he wants me. He'd never consent."

Any man would want her, Alex thought, looking down

into her pleading face, wanting to enfold her in his arms, feel her softness against his own hard body. "Then what—" he began.

"You have to help me," she interrupted, glancing back toward the camp as though afraid someone would come after her. "Help me run away . . . please, oh God, please say you'll do it."

"I'll jest take you on my horse and ride out of here," he said firmly, clasping her by the shoulders.

He felt the tremor that shook her as she cried out in protest. "They'd kill you first." Her eyes narrowed and darkened, giving her a calculating look.

"What can I do?" he asked, longing to help her but at a loss to know how it could be done.

"I'll run away tonight after they're asleep. Will you meet me?"

When he hesitated, she moved so close to him he could feel the softness of her breasts pressing against his chest. Something melted inside him. With an effort, he restrained the impulse to seize her in his arms, hold her against him, and kiss her trembling mouth. "All right," he spoke quickly, aware that a tall bearded man was walking purposefully toward them, a cluster of women watching from beside the wagons.

"You follow the trail." He spoke quickly. "It's a clear one. I'll go on with the cattle today, and ride back when we bed them down."

The joy that suffused her face almost staggered him. "You're my savior, Alex Cameron," she said in a husky voice, glancing at the frowning brother bearing down on them. "I'll never be able to repay you."

The black night was like a living menace hanging over her. Katrin stumbled along the ruts of the almost invisible trail, clutching the tiny bundle of clothes containing Mama's wedding ring and fine lace collar . . . all that was left of the old life. Coyotes wailing in the distance made her flesh creep. When a hunting night owl swooped near her, she cried aloud in terror.

Tears of desperation coursed hot down her face, blinding her. She had placed her life in Alex Cameron's hands and now it seemed he had failed her as all the men in her life had failed. Papa had promised a new and better life in America, then he died beside the fetid banks of the Missouri and Mama followed him. Brother Martin had promised her safe passage to Great Salt Lake, only to turn lustful eyes on her, determined to force her to marry him.

Stumbling from weariness, she fell into the sagebrush, scratching her face painfully. Lying there exhausted, Katrin gave herself over to abandoned sobbing. Worn out with weeping, she turned on her back and stared up at the inky sky, clutching her bundle of keepsakes. What did it matter if she died now? She felt alone on the earth, abandoned by every living thing. Tears welled in her eyes once more.

A faint sound penetrated her pain. Was it horses' hooves on the sandy trail? Hope welled in her and she struggled to her feet, calling without thought that it might be the Mormon brethren pursuing her. "Alex . . . Alex . . ."

The hoofbeats quickened, then he was beside her, leaping down from the horse to seize her in his arms. "Oh God," he cried. "I thought I'd missed you in the dark. Are you all right?"

Katrin couldn't speak. Clutching Alex, she rained grateful kisses on his stubbled face, clinging to him with every ounce of her strength. Alex's mouth captured hers and she felt the hunger in him. Out of gratitude, she yielded to his fierce embrace, returning his hot kisses.

At last, he broke away from her, breathing heavily. "God, Katrin," he said in a choked voice. "I could kiss you forever, but we'd better get outa here."

Cradled in front of Alex on the saddle, Katrin dozed fitfully. She awakened with a start as the horse came to a halt and Alex dismounted. In the dark distance she could hear water running in the Green River, and the snorts of the bedded cattle.

A shape melted out of the night and Katrin almost screamed. The dark face of an Indian peered up at her, his gray hair wild beneath an old slouch hat.

133

"Stake my horse, Magpie," Alex said, handing the reins to the old man. "This little gal's plumb wore out." Reaching up, Alex lifted her down into his arms, steadying her against him.

She was trembling uncontrollably by the time he had his bedroll laid out, and she slipped gratefully between the blankets. The last thing she saw before she fell into exhausted slumber were the silhouettes of Alex and the Indian talking beside the dying coals of the campfire.

False dawn streaked the sky with gray light when Alex came full awake. All night he'd held her, soothing her when she cried out in her sleep, giving her his warmth. Now he looked on her sleeping face, her pale hair mussed, her mouth soft and slightly open. Desire poured through him with such violence his whole body shuddered.

As though she felt it, Katrin murmured softly, turning so that her thigh brushed against his throbbing erection. "Oh God!" he muttered. Unable to restrain himself, Alex drew her into his embrace, cupping her hips tight against him, then pushing open her gown to take her warm, soft breasts in his hand.

Suddenly she stiffened. Her eyes flew open, staring into his in frightened dismay. His mouth covered hers, sucking, seeking, and he felt her relax against him, murmuring something against his lips.

He kissed her throat and she smiled. Lifting her breast, he fitted it to his mouth, running his tongue over the nipple, tasting the sweetness of her. Katrin moaned softly, her arms about his neck now, her hands stroking his hair, then moving down his back, pressing him against her warmth.

Frantic to possess her, Alex pulled at her underclothing roughly, shoving it aside until his fingers found the soft moist center of her. She gave a soft cry of protest, recoiling from his searching touch. Blind with his need, Alex opened his trousers. He crushed her mouth beneath his, spreading her legs as he moved on top of her. With a cry of utter abandonment, he plunged into the silken depths of her body.

Katrin stifled the scream that rose in her throat. She felt

torn apart, wounded and bleeding. Pain radiated through her whole body. Instinctively, she pushed at his shoulders, but he was too strong, too heavy, and he seemed not even to be aware of her. Just when she could bear no more, a cry of agony bursting inside her chest, Alex's whole body shuddered violently. A wild guttural moan broke from him, and then he was still. It was over.

Katrin lay rigid beneath him, tears pouring from under her closed eyelids. This was what her mother had meant when, red-faced and embarrassed, she'd tried to speak of men and women and marriage. "It's woman's duty to submit to her husband," Mama had said. This was what "submit" meant . . . this painful and revolting violation of her body. Alex Cameron had rescued her, he was handsome, and he was kind. She had liked his kisses, the touches, the embraces. But she could not bear the thought of "submitting" ever again.

Alex lay beside her, holding her close, her head pillowed on his arm. He seemed not to notice that her cheeks were wet with tears. When he spoke, his voice was thick, sleepily contented.

"There's a missionary stayin' at Pacific Springs," he said. "We'll go that way and get married before I take you home."

Burying her tearstained face against his shoulder, Katrin nodded.

Chapter 15

On the high peaks, the aspen were already blazing with autumn gold. The buffalo grass had ripened, and the wind had a bite to it. Alex paused on the high south ridge, looking down into Cameron Valley. A strange uneasiness settled over him. Horses and oxen grazed in the meadows, but there seemed no other sign of life. No smoke rose from the cabin chimney. With a shrug, he dismissed the feeling. Perhaps his parents had gone hunting for winter meat.

The girl in his arms stirred, and Alex drew her closer. His heart swelled with pride as he looked down at the golden head sleeping against his shoulder. On Katrin's finger was the thin gold wedding ring that had been her mother's. She was his wife now . . . truly his wife, with the words said by the Episcopal father at Pacific Springs . . . a wife as pale and golden as he had always dreamed. Now he would never be lonely again.

All the way, he'd carried her in front of him on the saddle, cradled in his arms. She wasn't used to horses and was even a bit afraid of them. When he tried to seat her astride his saddle, she'd cried out with pain. The Hartley boys exchanged wickedly significant glances. He'd felt himself flush, knowing they weren't ignorant of the reasons he and Katrin took their nooning rest apart from the drovers and slept a distance from the camp.

Looking down at the weary little face, Alex felt his heart squeeze with contrition. God knew she had reason to be sore, the number of times he'd taken her since that first night. But he couldn't seem to help himself. It was like a madness in him and the more he had of her, the more he wanted. She didn't thrash about, clutching and moaning like the Indian girls he'd had; she simply lay quiet until he had finished. Maybe that was the way of white women. He didn't have anyone to ask about it except Charles and he was far away in California. But, God . . . it was good. Even now, he felt himself hardening against her soft thigh where it rested in front of him on the saddle.

Lovingly, he pressed his mouth against her forehead, careful not to awaken her. Desire was a thunder in his veins, but he steeled himself, waiting for darkness and the incredible joy he found in her yielding body.

Below them in the valley, Magpie and the two boys were following his orders, spreading the newly arrived cattle out on the meadows, circling them in. They'd hold them until the critters were used to being here, not up and ready to move every morning. He'd pay off the boys and they'd head back to Oregon before winter set in. If Magpie would stay, he'd make a valuable hand with the cattle.

His grin widened. He'd done it . . . proved himself a man at eighteen. He'd gone to Oregon and back before the first snow. And he'd brought himself back a wife, he thought triumphantly, squeezing Katrin so that she protested sleepily and came awake.

"We're home, Mrs. Cameron," he told her, leaning to kiss her hard on the lips. "This here's your new home." With an expansive gesture, he gave her all of Cameron Valley.

Katrin stiffened against him as her gaze swept the rolling sagebrush-covered hills, the wide meadows with the pine-clad foothills rising beyond them into the distant icy blue of the Wind River mountains.

"There's only one house," she said in a small voice.

"Yes," he answered, filled with a sense of homecoming, proud of the log house his father had built. Now they would build another beside it, a home for himself and Katrin.

"We're the only ones here. This valley belongs to the Camerons."

Silent tears slid down Katrin's pale face. Alex bent to kiss them away, certain in his own happiness that she wept with joy to be home.

Exhausted from her long mourning, Falling Star sat slumped beside the dead fire in the cabin. From the enveloping haze of weariness that lay like a blanket over her, she heard Little Knife shouting in the distance. She drew in a long, shaky breath and lifted her head, waiting. Lone Hawk had come home.

Alex stood in the open doorway staring at her. She watched the dark eyes so like her own take in the cold emptiness of the cabin, the ceremonial gown she wore, and the grief that surely filled her face. Understanding dawned in those eyes, and his voice was hoarse when he spoke. "Pa?"

Taking off his wide-brimmed Oregon hat, Alex sat down opposite her on the willow backrest that had been his father's. "When?"

"Two days," she answered softly, and felt a surge of pain in her heart at the anguish in his young face.

"I could have been here. . . ." His voice fell to a whisper. "I could have made it, if only . . ." Guilt washed his features, and he bowed his head.

A profound sense of loss welled through Alex, made more painful by the knowledge that he had parted from his father in anger and rebellion. A part of his life was gone forever, and he found he could not imagine a world without Hugh Cameron. A kaleidoscope of memories poured through his mind, happy and unhappy mixed together so that he scarcely understood his own feelings.

"You're makin' too damn much noise, Alex!" The words sprang from out of the past, recreating with agonizing clarity a day from long ago . . . a day when his father had taken his sons to hunt for deer.

As though he were once more a small boy burdened with a heavy rifle, Alex seemed to stand in the shadowed depths of the forest, watching Hugh and Jed moving on silent moccasined feet as they stalked the elusive deer.

A magnificent antlered buck broke from the scrub oak cover beyond them. Jed lifted his rifle, steady as a rock. The shot reverberated among the trees as the creature fell thrashing into the underbrush. Then Hugh's rifle sounded. His shot penetrated the stag's head and the animal lay still.

Eyes gleaming with triumph, Jed turned to his father for approval. "Good shot, boy." Hugh grinned, clapping the boy's shoulder. Together they walked forward to inspect their kill.

His loaded rifle seemed an immense burden to the boy who watched. Alex had not even got off a shot. Never even had his rifle in position. His shoulders sagged in defeat as his own inadequacy seemed to bear him down. He stood quite still, staring at the ground while his eyes burned with shame.

Suddenly Hugh stood beside him, moving so quietly Alex hadn't heard his approach. Ashamed, he dared not look at his father.

Seeming not to see Alex's pain, Hugh clasped the boy's shoulder. "C'mon," he said in a gruff tone. "There'll likely be a herd over yonder ridge."

Trailing behind his father, Alex scarcely glanced at his brother, who was struggling to gut and skin the stag he had killed. Silently, he followed Hugh through the stand of lodgepole pines and scrub oak, up the hill until, at the top, Hugh suddenly dropped to his knees behind a fallen log.

"Here, son." His voice was low and patient as he drew Alex down beside him. "Rest yer rifle on the log to keep 'er steady." He pointed. "There's a doe comin' down that side hill."

With trembling hands, Alex held the gun, finally catching the deer in his sights where her pale brown hide blended with the tree trunks.

"Now!" Hugh said, and Alex squeezed the trigger. The doe made one wild leap and fell, sliding among the fallen pine needles until she was still.

The cry of triumph that broke from Hugh's throat made

Alex stare, for his father was always quiet in the forest. "Ya did it!" he cried, pounding Alex on the back.

His heart still in his throat, Alex broke into a grin. "I did, Pa," he said, still amazed at his own success.

"Right in the heart," Hugh told him, looking at him with such pride in his expression that Alex felt his own heart soar. "You're a damn good shot, boy." Abruptly, he hugged Alex against him, and the boy's eyes stung with joy. He knew then, and truly, that his father loved him.

How often I forgot that, Alex thought now as tears of grief for his father poured hot down his face. Hugh Cameron, the warrior Shining Bear, had only wanted to give his sons the skills to survive in this hard world. If he was harsh with them, it was because that world would be more harsh. That he could not accept the truth that his world was gone, nor accept the new order of things, had brought conflict between them.

Alex drew in a deep painful breath, covering his face with his hands. If only he could have seen his father once more, if somehow he could have let him know that in spite of their differences he loved him.

Star watched her son's grieving in silence. The sight of that bright head with its crown of dark golden curls, exactly like Shining Bear, brought her own grief sharply back. Tears spilled from her eyes and she caught back a sob.

Alex looked up, his sun-darkened cheeks wet. "Ma . . ." he began.

Falling Star held up her hand to still him. "Do you remember the old songs I taught you, Lone Hawk?" She spoke in Nez Percé now and he strained to understand. "The song of mourning cleanses the heart of grief, and it sends the departed spirit, free and happy, into the other world."

Alex nodded again, the tears still flowing from his unhappy eyes.

"Sing with me, then," she said. "For the spirit of Shining Bear." And she began in a low voice, the ancient words, in the old haunting rhythm. Alex followed, watching her face, for he was uncertain of the words. His deep voice blended with hers as the mourning song lifted into the infinite sky with the spirit of Shining Bear.

Katrin huddled on the stone step at the door of the log cabin. A young Indian boy, with black unfathomable eyes, had led Alex's horse away to the nearby corral and log stable. Old Magpie and the Hartley boys were still working the cattle in the meadows. Alex, her husband, had told her to wait, then gone into the cabin with no explanation.

Now she listened in horror to the sounds coming from the inside. Alex's voice and a woman's voice joined in a kind of song, a primitive, savage kind of song, mournful in its rising wail. Dear God, what kind of heathen ritual was being performed by this man she had married? She drew in her breath painfully as tears flooded her eyes. When she begged Alex to help her run away, how could she have guessed he would bring her to this place at the end of the earth? The sacrifices her parents had made to send her to school in Denmark seemed pitifully ironic now. Of what use would an education be in this isolated valley where civilization seemed nonexistent?

Covering her ears against the rising rhythmic wailing, Katrin buried her face against her knees and wept. She had escaped the trap of polygamy, but now she found herself in a far worse trap. An old saying of her mother's came into her head: "Better the devil you know than the devil you don't know." The longing for her sturdy, sensible mother was so intense, Katrin wished she could die too, and be done with it.

The long silence after the mourning song ended as Alex rose stiffly and reached out to embrace Falling Star. Looking down at her, he said, almost shame-faced, "I've brought back a wife, Ma. That's why I didn't get here before Pa . . ." His voice choked. "We could have made it up . . . me and him."

Falling Star touched his cheek comfortingly. "It has been

141

made up, my son." She rose and took his hand in hers. Mourning was ended now, life must go on. Briskly, she said, "A sad welcome for your wife. We must change that now."

Katrin stood up as they moved toward her, shrinking back against the log wall, staring with wide horror-stricken eyes. Alex looked down at his mother, suddenly seeing her as Katrin must see her . . . a savage woman dressed in a fringed doeskin gown and moccasins, her long black hair flowing about her shoulders, dark-eyed, dark-skinned. Oh God, he thought miserably, what have I done?

Determinedly, he grasped his wife's shoulder, forcing her to stand straight before Falling Star. "This is Katrin, Ma," he said. "Father Burke at Pacific Springs married us two days ago. And this is my mother, Falling Star," he added, his voice hard and demanding.

"Welcome." Falling Star held out her hand.

The girl cringed away as though she feared her touch. "What were you doing in there?" Her eyes clung to Alex and her voice wavered.

"My pa died, two days past. We sang for him." His voice was harsh with unreconciled grief.

Suddenly Katrin began to weep wildly. Alex gathered her into his arms, holding her as she clung to him. Over her head, he said to Falling Star, "She's awful tired and scared. If you'll help me, we'll make up a bed in the cabin and she can rest."

Without speaking, Falling Star stepped past her son and his wife, into the dim cabin. As Star padded the rawhide-laced bed with furs and spread the blankets, she fought against the foreknowledge welling painfully from the depths of her soul.

She guessed truly that Alex had meant to do only good in rescuing this lost girl, and that perhaps his youthful need for a woman had a part in his impulsive action. It was done now. Falling Star raised her head, closing her eyes against the pain, mumbling an old petition to *Hunyewat* for ease. But it could not be changed. The coming of this bright-haired woman would carry sorrow for the Camerons through undreamed-of generations.

Chapter 16

1858

Dim and golden, the first rays of the sun illuminated the skins of the lodge. Star lay in her bed robes, watching the light grow stronger. It was pleasant living in her own lodge, in the old way, free of the constant tension in the cabin. Soon after Alex brought his wife home, Star had understood that the cabin was too small for three people. She understood the constraint the young couple felt, making love with her sleeping across the room. And Katrin was not companionable. In the two and a half years she had lived in Cameron Valley, she had made the log cabin her own, throwing out the things that irritated her, constantly scrubbing the walls and sweeping the hard-packed earthen floor. Even though they shared meals, including Magpie and Little Knife, Katrin insisted on cooking in her own way.

With a sigh, Star sat up now, reaching for her doeskin gown. The only thing she had been able to share with Katrin was the girl's desire to learn to read in English. As soon as she had mastered the words, she spent her leisure hours devouring their few books. Now when Alex went to Fort Laramie, he always carried an order to be sent east for books for Katrin.

It was an uneasy household, Star thought, and sighed again. Perhaps if Katrin had conceived a child, she would have been more loving, less short-tempered and cold. Perhaps.

Coming out of the lodge into the silvery morning air, Star saw two strange Palouse horses staked farther down the creek, munching the dew-wet spring grass. Nowadays there were always strangers passing through: gold seekers, nesters looking for a place to settle, and stray bands of Indians. But as the horses lifted their heads to stare at her, she knew their owner.

Even as she ran toward him through the dewy grass, Jed rose from his sleeping robes and held out his arms. Falling Star clasped her oldest son in her arms and wept. She had sensed his coming, longed for it, and at the same time feared it.

Finally, Jed released her from his fierce embrace, looking down with a somber face. "I was trading at Fort Hall when I heard it said that the mountain man, Hugh Cameron, was dead these past three years." He spoke in Nez Percé, the language that was his now.

Star had thought she'd shed all her tears long ago, but they overflowed now. Grief pierced her heart and she could not speak.

Jed's features twisted with pain. "I can't forget that I parted from my father in anger."

"It is often so with fathers and sons," she told him, brushing away her tears, knowing that now she must comfort her son. Taking his arm, she led him across the creek, along the worn path to the stone cairn beneath the pines.

"He had a great pride in you, Running Buffalo," she told him as he stood beside his father's grave, tears streaking his dark face. "You are a man of the mountains, just as he was. All his skills are yours . . . and more. Don't blame yourself for the quarrel. He did not, for he came to understand that you did what you must do."

"Stay with me, Mother," he said.

They sat in silence beside the grave and Falling Star felt the strong presence of the Shining Bear holding them together in love. Jed lifted his head and smiled at her. She sighed in relief, knowing he felt the presence too.

The sun had risen, bright and hot, above the eastern hills before they stirred.

Alex came from the log cabin, shouting at Magpie and Little Knife, who slept in a skin lodge Falling Star had made for them. Now the day's work would begin. They would ride the meadows and the hills, turning back any cattle or horses that had strayed from the natural boundaries of Cameron Valley. Afternoons were spent training the horses Falling Star had already gentled, to be sold to the army or the emigrant trains.

At once, Alex's eyes fell on the strange horses. His searching eyes caught sight of Star and Jed beneath the pines on the hillside. With a shout, he ran toward them, ignoring Katrin's questioning cry from the doorway of the cabin. Already, she was busy sweeping the floor.

The two brothers clasped each other in a fierce bear hug. Alex stepped back, searching Jed's face. "Welcome home, Jed." His voice was choked with emotion. "I hope you've come back to stay."

Without answering, Jed looked past him at the golden-haired woman standing on the stone stoop of the cabin staring up at them. "At Fort Hall it was said you'd taken a wife . . . a white woman." He shook his head as though amazed and still unbelieving.

"There she stands," Alex replied, grinning with pride. "Ain't she a pretty sight?"

A cloud drifted across the sun, and Star shivered. She looked at her two tall sons . . . so alike and yet so different. Jed, in his worn buckskins, his black hair braided in two plaits, his blue eyes brilliant in his finely chiseled tawny face. And Alex, with his sandy hair gleaming in the morning light, his dark eyes gleaming with joy at Jed's homecoming, and filled with pride in the golden-haired wife shading her face as she stared at them.

An inward battle filled Star with pain and she closed her eyes against the scene, longing for the power to change the things she foresaw.

Sitting on the stoop after they had eaten, Katrin covertly watched the two men as Alex proudly showed his brother the improvements he had made, walking from the new corral to the log stable, the enclosed spring, the stout bridge across the creek.

Alex had told her of the brother who had gone away to join the Nez Percé. The story had dismayed her nearly as much as the original knowledge that her mother-in-law was a full-blood Indian, and that the man she had wed was a half-breed. She had adapted to her life, grateful that at least she was never cold or hungry. Alex was an indulgent husband, always bringing gifts and books from the fort. And she thought proudly that she'd made a snug home of their cabin, glad that her mother-in-law had moved out.

Katrin saw a similarity in the brothers, in the high cheekbones, the dusky shade of their skin in spite of the striking difference in hair color. Yet as she watched them now, a more subtle difference communicated itself to her.

Jed Cameron moved with a grace and power that made something ache inside her. She thought of the mountain lion staring back at her one morning when she walked to the spring. Menacing, yet fascinating.

Beside Jed, Alex seemed almost awkward in his long, purposeful strides. Like one of his damn bulls, she told herself. Resentment clogged her throat as she carried the comparison back in her mind to the way he mounted her and satisfied himself, leaving her filled with longing for something she could only guess at vaguely.

The men came back toward her, Jed's face quiet as he listened to Alex's plans. Katrin knew she was staring, but she could not seem to stop watching Jed. His blue eyes met hers and something flared between them, almost painful in its intensity. All the breath seemed to go out of her. Katrin hugged her skirt about her knees, unable to look away, and a hot ache grew between her thighs.

Thunderheads stair-stepped across the wide sky above the valley. Indigo smudges of rain squalls appeared on the eastern horizon and the wind had the smell of distant rain. Hurrying to finish cleaning a deerskin, Star sat in front of her lodge watching as Jed saddled his horse. All morning he had helped Alex drag up the cut logs for the new corral. When they ate at midday, he announced he would hunt this afternoon. Now as he mounted his fine Palouse horse, his rifle in front of him on the saddle, Star saw Katrin come out of the cabin.

She stood utterly still, devouring Jed with her wide blue eyes. Star wanted to cry out in protest. There was a madness in the girl; some kind of warped and evil spirit surely possessed her. Her obsession with Jed was strange, for he was so totally an Indian and Katrin had called Falling Star a savage, and screamed recriminations at Alex more than once for his ancestry.

Katrin stood there, unmoving and silent, until Jed's figure disappeared into the forest. Then she went back into the cabin.

How could Alex not be aware of the tension between his wife and his brother? Falling Star wondered. In spite of the old rivalry he felt toward Jed, Alex seemed truly happy for his brother's company now, even blithely assuming that Jed meant to stay in Cameron Valley.

Clutching the tiny doeskin bag about her neck, Star fought down the sense of dread. She must call on her *wyakin,* spirit of the blue stone, for strength. Drawing a deep purposeful breath, she stood up and walked toward Alex, who was notching logs for the corral.

"This'll make it easier for you to take care of the horses while me and the boys are gone to drive the cattle south to the army."

Last year, the President back in Washington had sent an army west to subdue the Mormons in Salt Lake valley, for they had refused to accept government-appointed officials. The troops had taken over Fort Bridger and provided a lucrative market. Alex grinned at her, pausing to wipe the sweat from his face with a sleeve of his cotton shirt.

"We are rich in horses," she said in Nez Percé.

Alex looked startled. "I figured on taking some of the gentled ones to sell."

"If Running Buffalo took those horses back to the Wallowa mountains, he would be a rich man," she went on, ignoring his use of English, persisting in using her own tongue.

He frowned, familiar glints of stubbornness gleaming in his brown eyes. With an expansive wave of his hand, he indicated the meadows of Cameron Valley dotted with fat cattle and fine horses. "Part of all this belongs to Jed." He said it in English, defiantly. "Out there, with the Nez Percé, he has nothing."

"He's found a home," Star answered quietly. "Because his way is not yours doesn't make it wrong. Let him go."

"He'll die out there," Alex cried in protest. From his pain-filled face Star saw that in spite of their differences, his love for his brother was deep and abiding.

Filled with anguish by words she knew to be true, Star managed to speak. "It is his choice, Alex . . . his life."

"Then I'll give him the choice," Alex replied stubbornly. "Let him make up his own mind." He turned away and picked up his ax. "Anyway, he's promised to stay with you and Katrin while I'm gone."

Defeated, Star stood for a moment, watching as Alex concentrated on his work. With a long sigh, she walked away. Drops of warm summer rain spattered in the dusty yard as she ducked into her lodge, her refuge.

A week now since Alex and Magpie and Little Knife had disappeared over the southern ridges with the cattle herd. And a week, Katrin thought, since she'd witnessed the argument between her husband and his mother. She'd been too far away to hear them, but the result had been that the finest of the horses were cut out from the market herd and left behind in the new corral.

A week in which Jed had carefully kept his distance from her, although she caught him watching her with eyes that reflected the same hunger that was eating at her.

Now, she lifted the stew pot from the fireplace and set it on the table. They ate together, at her insistence, from the white queensware plates Alex had told her were a gift from

Charles Forester. Tonight there was company for supper—two prospectors, combing the mountain streams for color as so many did since the great gold rush to California in '49.

She didn't like the two grizzled strangers, with their sly looks and hot eyes. The thought of sleeping alone in the cabin while two such men slept outside nearby made her hands tremble as she returned to the fireplace to lift the coffeepot from the coals.

Bending to pour the coffee in the queensware cups, she let her full breasts brush against Jed's shoulder and sensed the way he stiffened at the contact. Perhaps he would stay in the cabin tonight to protect her. She would ask . . . no, she would insist, with tears as she did with Alex when she wanted something.

Resignedly, Star closed the cabin door and made her silent-footed way to her lodge. After Jed gave in to Katrin's tearful pleading, he'd suggested Star sleep in the cabin too. Too weary now to fight the inevitable any longer, Star refused. The two rough prospectors would not bother her, she knew, for she had seen them warily eyeing the big skinning knife she wore at her belt.

"Sepekuse," she murmured to herself. "So be it . . ." She could not change the tides of destiny any more than her husband could hold back the tides of change in the land he loved.

Katrin blew out the candle. Watching Jed's lithe figure bend to roll his bed out on the floor before the fireplace, she began unbuttoning her bodice. Her fingers were stiff and awkward, trembling with the pounding pulse that beat through her whole body. In some blind, wild way, everything in her yearned toward this strange, savage man. When he straightened and his eyes met hers, she could have screamed with the urgent need that tore through her.

Like a sleepwalker, she moved toward him, untying her skirt so that it fell to the floor with her discarded blouse.

"Katrin," he said. It was half protest and half resignation. When she touched him, he seized her violently, pressing his hips against hers so that she felt the hot hardness of him through his buckskin trousers. His mouth covered hers, and she returned the kiss with such passion she tasted blood inside her lip.

"Katrin," he said again, as they broke apart, gasping for breath. "Oh . . . my God, Katrin!"

Impatiently, she pulled off her underclothing, taking the pins from her hair so that it fell about her shoulders, glimmering softly gold in the firelight.

Jed stood before her, the fire casting a ruddy glow over his lustful face. The passion blazing in his eyes triggered a kind of explosion inside her. Katrin cried out and threw herself against him, tugging at his clothing. It would hurt as it always did, and she would lie awake restless and unsatisfied, but the need that drove her took no thought of that.

"Please," she whimpered as his big hands slid over her body, cupping her breasts, stroking between her thighs. Discarding his own clothing, Jed pulled her down with him onto the buffalo robe spread beside the dying fire.

Lying beside her, he began to kiss her eyelids, her ears, her throat, moving down to caress her breasts with his warm tongue. Katrin moaned softly. She felt a moistness between her thighs and a hot driving ache settled there.

"Please . . ." she moaned again, not knowing what it was she begged for. Her hands smoothed the dark head bent to kiss her breasts and moved down his hard muscled back, fingers tingling at the touch of him.

Jed covered her body with his, and she drew in her breath, suddenly afraid. Gently he penetrated her, his mouth sucking hot at hers, his hands caressing her breasts.

Katrin lay still and waited for it to be over, feeling sad and cheated. A moment later, he swore softly in her ear.

"Dammit, woman . . . are you dead?"

He lifted his head to look into her dismayed face. Slowly understanding dawned in his puzzled eyes and he grinned. "You move too."

"How?" she asked in a small, frightened voice.

"Like this." Jed cupped her hips in his hands and lifted her against him, demonstrating.

Tentatively, Katrin moved against him. She gasped at the shaft of pleasure that shot through her body. Jed chuckled softly, thrusting against her.

Katrin answered his movements, lost in new sensations throbbing, pulsing, growing through her body. The pleasure deepened in intensity as her movements grew more abandoned. She was lost in a wild and savage joy that grew and expanded within her until it seemed she was lifted up into the burning heat of a sun that suddenly exploded.

She cried out, a long deep cry torn from the very depths of her being. Throwing her legs about his hips, she held him, wanting to prolong this ecstasy. Then Jed burst within her and she soared again into the exploding sun, echoing his cry of fulfillment.

It was a madness in him, Jed told himself. A madness that had made him betray his own brother, and a madness that moved him through the days in a kind of daze. He was scarcely aware of his mother's silent presence. The prospectors had moved on, but he stayed in the cabin at night, he and Katrin making love beside the fire, for he could not bear to lie in Alex's bed.

Katrin was even more caught up in madness, for she could not seem to get enough of him. The nights were not enough. She followed him into the forest where they took each other beneath the pine trees on a high ridge . . . into the meadows where they lay in the grass with the wind blowing over them and the meadowlarks calling.

A part of his mind protested and yet he could not stop. This woman sent his senses reeling, and she fulfilled him in a wildly primitive way he'd never known before. That Alex had never given her the joy she found with him filled Jed with a sense of triumph . . . a victory over the brother who was so much smarter and wiser in the ways of the white man.

Riding in with the deer he had killed that morning on a distant ridge, he dumped the gutted carcass in front of Star's lodge. Without thought, he found himself looking eagerly for Katrin's pale bright head.

Star came out of the lodge, glanced at the deer and nodded, then looked up at him, grim-faced. "Come to the corral with me," she said, and walked away, not waiting for his reply.

Katrin stood on the cabin stoop, watching. Riding past, Jed gave her a small salute with his hand, warning her away. He could feel her lust for him across the space between them, a physical thing drawing him to her. His loins stirred in answer and he cursed himself.

"These are the finest of our horses." Star spoke abruptly in Nez Percé. She watched him unsaddle and turn the horse loose to roll in the dust of the corral. "You will take them as your inheritance from your father since you do not wish to stay in Cameron Valley."

Jed stared at her. He had never meant to stay. His home was with the Nez Percé, but now the thought of leaving Katrin tore through him with physical pain.

"You wish me to go, Mother?" he asked.

Star's lips trembled, but she tightened her mouth and lifted her chin proudly. "Lone Hawk will return very soon. It is best you go before then."

Across the yard, Jed saw the bright-haired woman watching them apprehensively. The heat of his need for her poured through him, so intense he could scarcely speak. "I cannot leave her."

"Then ask her to go with you." Star's voice was harsh, her eyes hard and accusing. Quickly, she turned and walked back to her lodge, unsheathing her skinning knife to begin work on the deer carcass.

With one fearful glance at him, Katrin rushed back into the cabin. Jed followed, closing the door behind him. At once, she flung herself into his arms, straining against him, kissing his face until he could think of nothing but his need for her.

"Take me now," she whispered, pulling away her clothes. "I've been nearly crazy all day with needing you. Please, Jed . . . now . . ."

It was violent and quick. Afterward they lay together on

the bed he had sworn he would not violate, exhausted and drained of passion.

Falling Star knew, Jed thought, wondering now how he could have been so blind as to think she would not know. Alex would know too, at once, that his wife and his brother had betrayed him. For such a betrayal, someone must pay with death. He did not wish to die, nor did he wish to kill the brother he loved. Yet he could not give up this woman who obsessed him.

"I'm leaving, Katrin," he said suddenly, decisively. "West . . . back to the Wallowa mountains. Come with me."

Her face was soft, filled with the contentment he had brought to her. "Where would we live?" she asked in a faintly drowsy voice.

"With my people . . . the Nez Percé." He said the words and waited, holding his breath.

The pale blue eyes widened. Katrin lifted herself on her elbow to stare at him in disbelief. Her shining golden hair moved across his shoulder like a caress, and Jed trembled.

"To live like your mother lives . . . in a tepee." Her voice rose. "You're asking me to be your squaw?"

A coldness came over Jed as he watched the spark of anger grow in her eyes. "To be my wife," he answered gently, "among my people."

"You know that's impossible," Katrin cried, sitting up on the side of the bed. "I gave up a decent life in Great Salt Lake to come here with Alex . . . and now you . . . you want me to sink even lower than this." Tears coursed down her flushed face. She stared at him, waiting for him to give in to those tears.

Silently, Jed rose and pulled on his clothes. Then he crossed to pick up his bedroll from the corner, taking up his rifle in the other hand.

"Don't go," Katrin cried, leaping to her feet and seizing his arm. "I can't live without you . . . don't you see, I can't bear to have Alex touch me now. I need you so. . . ."

Jed looked coldly down at her pleading, tearstained face. The truth was a burden on his heart. What he had felt for this woman was lust, not love . . . and even that was dead now. He had betrayed his brother for the pleasure of her body, so sunk in madness he would even have stolen her away. With a rush of relief he realized he was free now, and he felt a sadness for Alex, still in the trap of this white bitch.

"Good-bye, Katrin," he said, and did not look back.

Long after the sounds of the moving horse herd faded in the dusk, Falling Star sat in silence beside her fire. From the cabin, the sounds of agonized weeping went on and on.

Chapter 17

Alex knew Katrin had not cleaned the cabin just for his homecoming. Every day she scrubbed the new whip-sawed plank floor until it was white and smooth, dusted the shelves and the inside logs. She'd even scrubbed the fireplace rocks. And at least once a month, she took down the muslin ceiling she'd tacked up beneath the dirt roof, washed it, and rehung it.

"I sure am hungry," he said, kissing her cheek. "Could you rustle up some grub, honey?"

Unresponsive to his touch, without a word, Katrin went to the fireplace, where she stirred the coals into life. Setting the stew pot over the flames, she took down the flour tin and began to mix biscuits.

Alex let out a sigh. He'd been home a half hour and things were still the same. Now he wondered why he'd let himself hope Katrin had missed him, that she'd welcome him. Well, he told himself with a shrug, she'd welcome the gifts he'd brought when the pack mules were unloaded.

If only she'd caught a baby, he thought sadly, that would give her a real interest in life, maybe even bring them closer to each other.

Feeling his mother's penetrating gaze, Alex composed his face carefully. She sat in a chair near the door to catch the light, reading Charles's letters in chronological order.

"So Charles has married at last," she said, smiling at Alex. He had read the letters back at Fort Bridger, glad that the new Butterfield Stage Line from St. Louis to San Francisco brought the mail more often. But he'd wanted Star to learn the news from the letters.

The news of the marriage had taken him by surprise, although when he thought it over, it seemed logical. The bride's name was Monique Chartrand, daughter of a prominent St. Louis family who had made their money in the western trade and in river shipping. Now they were investing heavily in railroads, Charles wrote.

Star laughed aloud. "He says he heard old Jim Bridger has gone to farming somewhere near Independence." She looked up at Alex. "He made a pile of money selling the fort to the Mormons, but I can't believe he'll ever make a farmer."

"Only a garrison left at Fort Bridger," Alex said glumly. "Johnston's army marched into Salt Lake City and made peace with the Mormons. That little war's over, but it means there won't be much market for cattle at Fort Bridger from now on."

When the United States Army marched west to subdue the Mormons for President Buchanan and his rabble-rousers, it had proven a gold mine for Alex. The cagey Mormons stole or ran off the army horses and cattle. Desperate to replace them, General Johnston paid premium prices for Alex's livestock.

"Charles thinks they'll build a railroad all the way to California soon—if there isn't a war," Alex commented. "Can you imagine a railroad through Cameron Valley?" He addressed the question to Katrin, crossing the room and hugging her in a vain attempt to bring her into the conversation. Busy rolling out biscuits, she ignored him.

Uneasy, Alex returned to stand beside his mother, looking down at the letters. The tension between the two women had begun to communicate itself to him. There had never been any affection between them, only labored courtesy. But they had not spoken directly to each other since his arrival.

156

Suddenly he wondered if it had anything to do with Jed's leaving so abruptly. He'd been disappointed to find his brother gone from Cameron Valley, but not really surprised. When he'd invited him to stay, Jed had made it clear he intended to return to the Nez Percé.

"All the talk at the fort is that there'll be a war," he said, addressing his remarks to the room at large. Whatever the quarrel between his women, he wished they'd mend it. He didn't like feeling this way in his own cabin.

"Between the slave states and the free north, so Charles says." Star sighed. "White men's madness." Then she gave Alex a wan smile. "Perhaps if they're fighting each other, they won't have to kill Indians."

It was a sore point, the escalating war between the Indians and the emigrants . . . and the army's attempts to force Indians onto reservations. "It won't get better," Alex replied morosely. "That gold strike at Cherry Creek in Colorado Territory is bringing a whole lot of white folks west."

"Trash folks," his mother answered succinctly, her eyes on Charles's letter.

"Charles sent more papers to be signed for land." He reached past his mother to open a large envelope lying on the table. "Every time the government thinks of a new way to give away their land, he takes advantage of it for all of us." He grinned at Katrin, who was watching him with cool eyes. "Now that I've got me a wife, he's filing on land for her too."

Silent, Katrin dusted the flour from her hands and set the dutch oven of biscuits in the coals. Alex felt a burst of irritation. Frowning, he announced, "I'll see if the boys have finished unloading the mules. Little Knife wants to leave tomorrow to go home for the winter." He gave Katrin a stern look. "I expect supper'll be ready by the time we're through."

As he stepped out into the hot late afternoon light where Little Knife and Magpie were taking the packs from the weary mules, Alex shrugged resignedly. Tonight he'd give Katrin the lengths of fine merino wool and sprigged muslin, the ribbons, and the pretty straw bonnet he'd brought for her. When they were alone in the dark cabin, she'd let him hold her and drown himself in the soft warmth of her body.

Gathering Charles's precious letters into a neat pile on the table, Star stood up and crossed to the fireplace. Pain like a lead weight lay on her heart . . . a sadness for Alex and his elusive dream of happiness. What had happened could not be changed any more than it could have been prevented. But this ugly thing between Katrin and herself must be settled now. She should not have delayed the confrontation so long.

"It would break his heart to know the truth," she said to Katrin's stiff back. She saw a tremor shake the girl's body. Katrin did not turn around, but continued to stir the pot of boiling meat in silence.

With a cautious glance out the open door to where Alex was helping unload the pack mules, Star continued in a low voice. "For his sake, I will not speak of it, but you must make me a promise in return."

Katrin drew in a sharp, fearful breath, turning to stare at Star with wide tear-filled eyes. "A promise?" There was nothing submissive in her tone, and anger bubbled beneath the words.

Only with an effort could Star restrain herself from grabbing Katrin by the throat, physically forcing her into some realization of the wrong she had done and the need to make retribution.

"Alex has been a good husband to you," she said, dropping all pretense at friendliness, her tone hard and uncompromising. "He gave you a home when you had nowhere to go." Star glared into Katrin's suddenly frightened face. "From this day on," she said in low measured tones, "you will be a good wife to him. If you cannot love him, you will be kind to him."

"Yes, yes . . . whatever you say." Katrin said the words impatiently, as though anxious to be finished with this exchange.

"I would not wish to hurt my son by telling him of his wife's betrayal," Star went on, fighting down her anger at the girl's lack of remorse. "But neither will I allow you to hurt him. I'd rather see him cast you aside than live without love forever."

"Supper ready?" Alex called, his tall figure filling the cabin doorway. In his hand he carried a lacy bonnet trimmed with velvet ribbons and silk flowers.

With one searing glance at Star, Katrin crossed the room. Pausing in front of Alex, she took the bonnet from him, her eyes glowing with delight as she stroked the soft velvet ribbon. "It's lovely, Alex," she said, kissing his cheek. With a malicious smile at Star, she hurried to the mirror to try on her new bonnet.

Katrin moaned softly, her body still sore from the long travail of birth. She'd begged Alex to bring a white woman from Fort Laramie to be with her through the birth. "My mother will take care of you," he'd said, seeming surprised and annoyed at her request.

Alex had been wild with delight at the news that she was pregnant. And she'd never lied to him once . . . never told him the child was his. But that was her secret, a secret her mother-in-law seemed sure to keep now.

Across the room, Star was changing the baby beside the fireplace. Allowing herself a small smile of triumph, Katrin watched her mother-in-law adjust the cotton didy on her granddaughter. To think Star had wanted to put the baby in a cradle board, packed in clean moss instead of in civilized didies.

Laying her hands on her flat stomach, Katrin felt the emptiness inside her. Closing her eyes, she drifted in exhaustion, conjuring up an image of the father of her child, her only true lover . . . Jed Cameron.

She'd known from the timing of her flow that the baby was Jed's. And why not? she thought now. She'd opened herself to him completely and he had given her the child Alex hadn't in three years of marriage. Surely it must be that a child was conceived only in that wild and rapturous moment when the world exploded between two bodies.

Once or twice with Alex she'd been able to achieve that moment . . . but only by closing her eyes tightly and pretending that the male body joined with hers was that of Jed.

"You all right, honey?" The words, and the touch of Alex's big rough hand, jolted her back into reality. He sat beside the bed, watching her with concern.

"I guess you're disappointed it wasn't a boy." Her tone was accusing, her eyes cool on his suddenly abashed face.

"Don't say that, honey," he pleaded, stroking her hand. "We'll have a son one day; you can bet on it. And a girl will be company for you."

Katrin closed her eyes, wishing it were Jed's face there looking down at her. Oh God, she thought, why hadn't she gone with him? Even now, the memory of his loving sent flames racing through her body. Surely she could have endured any kind of life to have him . . . and yet, she hadn't the courage to risk it.

Withdrawing her hand from Alex's clasp, she thought resentfully that there would not be a son, nor any other child. Alex wasn't the man his brother was, not even man enough to father a child.

Opening her eyes, Katrin looked across the room to where Star stood beside the fireplace, cradling the baby in her arms and crooning softly to it. Resentment flamed through Katrin. Her daughter would not be Indian, or even half Indian like the man she would call father. She would be all white.

"Bring her to me," she ordered in a firm voice. If she shared her daughter too much with this Indian woman, she might lose some of her control over the child and that was the only thing in her life she could control.

A strange sort of baby, Star thought, trying to cuddle the child to her breast. It did not respond to loving touches and sounds as her sons had. At the sound of Katrin's demanding voice, it stiffened and wailed. This baby seemed to be a piece torn from her mother, bearing the same cold shell about her tiny being.

Carrying the baby across the room to Katrin's outstretched arms, Star looked down at the dark-haired infant.

Long ago, in her grief for her lost daughter, Shining Bear had promised that her sons would give her the girl-child she longed for . . . a child to bear her gift of sight. A stab of sorrow went through Star now, for she knew this was not that child. A child conceived in sin and born in falsehood.

"A pretty child." She managed a smile for Alex's sake as she laid the baby in Katrin's eager arms.

Gazing fondly at the mewling infant, Katrin said, "Her name will be Hannah Maria . . . for my mother. And you're right, Alex." She gave him a hard, determined look. "She will be company for me . . . my daughter . . . all mine."

Chapter 18

1858

"Your heart is sick since your return, my nephew." Looking Glass spoke quietly, his wise old eyes studying Jed's face.

Jed let the pipe smoke drift from his lips into the cool autumn darkness. One of the women brought more wood for the fire burning in front of his uncle's lodge. He nodded gravely at her, grateful for the added warmth.

His uncle was waiting for an answer. Jed gazed into the leaping flames, knowing he could not speak the truth. He could never tell Looking Glass how he had betrayed his brother and lay with a woman of evil. Instead he said, "I return to find my grandfather, Many Horses, has become a reservation Indian . . . gone to live at Lapwai in a log cabin." He drew a deep breath. "Everything is changing. White settlers turned their pigs onto the camas prairies so that the Nez Percé can no longer go to dig the camas roots for winter food. I'm glad now I did not ask my mother to return with me."

Looking Glass's expression grew even more somber as he replied, "I hoped she would return to her people now that Shining Bear is dead."

Perhaps he could have persuaded her, Jed thought. But his madness for Katrin, the way he had left Cameron Valley, all that had denied her the chance. Another stain on his conscience.

"I have talked with Tall Bear, the medicine man," Looking Glass interrupted Jed's gloomy thoughts. "He says you have lost your *wyakin,* the guardian of your spirit."

"It is true." With those words, Jed clearly saw the reasons for his emptiness and despair. He looked up at his uncle. "Will Tall Bear tell me what I must do?"

Out of the darkness, the medicine man appeared. Squatting before the fire, he let his black eyes bore into Jed's. "Go alone into the mountains," he said in a stern voice. "Go as you did when you first became a man. Wait for the vision that will make you whole again."

Weak from fasting, Jed leaned against the sun-warmed rocks on the south side of the cliff. Below him, rolling away into blue distance, were the endless forests of the Nez Percé country, the dark green of the pines broken by frost-gilded aspens. Shivering in the cold air, he pulled the buffalo robe closer about him.

The distant forests and hills swam in a haze before him and he seemed to sleep. Yet he was no longer in the forest, but on the plains far to the east where he had hunted the buffalo with Looking Glass. The dream was familiar, for as he watched, a dark thundering cloud poured over the horizon . . . a herd of running buffalo. The vision shifted and changed. The plains were deep with winter snow. In his dream, he drew closer to the buffalo, seeming to see them from above. His heart grew faint within him, for the buffalo were gaunt and weary, staggering through the deep snow, rushing toward some impending doom beyond the horizon where he could not see.

It was dark when he awakened and very cold. The stars gleamed, brilliant pinpoints of light in the autumn sky. At once, he felt overcome by longing for his mother, for Falling Star . . . the magic woman, his father had called her. He was certain only she could interpret the true meaning of his vision. She was far away, across tall mountains, volcanic deserts, and deep rivers, yet he felt now her loving presence.

There was forgiveness in that presence, and Jed wrapped the buffalo robe about him, falling into a healing sleep, knowing he had made peace with his family and found his *wyakin* once more.

Around the fire in Looking Glass's warm lodge, Jed could not tell all his vision. He did not understand why himself, but the words did not come.

"I dreamed again of the running buffalo . . . many of them, streaming across wide plains," he told his listeners.

Tall Bear nodded wisely. Looking Glass looked proud, drawing himself up as he pronounced, "Your name is again Running Buffalo. Now you are Nez Percé. You will not go from your people again for you are to be as my son, in my lodge."

1859

The first tender grass of spring speckled the black earth. Water ran everywhere, melting rivulets from beneath the snowbanks. The Nez Percé village of Looking Glass was busy with preparations for the move from winter camp.

"You are a fine hunter," Looking Glass's wife said as she helped Running Buffalo unload the deer carcass from his horse. She giggled, adding with a sly sidelong glance from her bright eyes, "You will make a fine husband . . . rich with horses, a brave warrior, and a mighty hunter." She giggled again in spite of the stony glare he gave her.

Seating himself on a stump nearby, he began cleaning his rifle. Silly woman, he thought, wondering why Looking Glass thought it necessary to take a second wife. For himself, he'd not had a woman all through the winter. Perhaps that long denial had cleansed him of the bright-haired woman who filled his veins with madness.

Looking Glass sat down beside him, nodding toward the chattering women cutting up the deer carcass. "My family has eaten well this winter," he said, smiling.

Running Buffalo accepted the implied compliment with

grave silence. Sensing that his uncle had something more on his mind, he waited.

"You are of an age to take a wife," Looking Glass began sternly. "Yet you do not court the young girls." Frowning, he looked into Running Buffalo's face. "Soon they will begin to say you are a *berdache,* the woman-man, soon if you do not marry."

"It is of no interest to me what is said about me," Running Buffalo answered in a harsh voice.

"That is not my concern either," said Looking Glass, attempting now to smooth over his joke that had not gone well. "I wish the best for you, my son. It is time you had your own lodge and your own woman." He paused portentously. "Since you will not make a choice, I have chosen for you."

Running Buffalo stared at his uncle in amazement. How could he think to force him into a marriage? he asked himself. Then he sighed, seeing the women watching covertly. Perhaps they were tired of doing for him in their lodge, even though he brought meat. He could not remain a son forever. All men must grow into warriors and hunters and husbands.

Drawing in a deep breath, he nodded. "As you wish, my uncle."

What strange spirit had moved his uncle to choose this child to give him for a wife? Running Buffalo wondered. Perhaps because Snow Flower was slight and small-boned, she could be bought from her father for few horses. An Indian wife must be strong and sturdy.

Seated beside his fire, eating the stew she had served from her cooking pot, Running Buffalo pretended not to watch his wife at her work. All the women in the village had come to help her raise their lodge, but now this child must play the part of wife and do her own work.

Just now, she was working tallow into a deerskin, a little away from the fire, her small hands working the knife with surprising strength. The moccasins she had made for him were the best he'd worn since his mother's hands had sewn for him.

As though aware of his scrutiny, she glanced up at him, dark shy eyes gleaming through the curtain of black hair fallen about her slender face. Quickly, she looked away, her cheeks coloring.

They have married her too soon, Running Buffalo thought sadly. He could not feel more for her than he felt for the small daughters of Looking Glass.

In the bright spring air about the village, mating birds called raucously. Dogs howled and chased the females in heat. Even in the meadows, the horses rutted in the mating rituals of the year's blossoming.

Running Buffalo moved to ease himself, for his loins felt heavy and congested. He could not bring himself to take the small, shy creature who was his wife, and yet his need grew with every passing day.

The ache persisted and he stood up abruptly, reaching for his rifle. "I will go out to hunt now," he told Snow Flower. Riding to the kill would ease him, though she need not know that.

Peering up at him, Snow Flower brushed back her fall of black hair. Her dark eyes were filled with apprehension, and her young face fell into lines of sadness as he turned away from her.

With quick efficiency, Snow Flower built up the low fire inside their lodge, for the spring nights were still cold. The village was quiet now, with only the distant howling of coyotes to break the silence of the night.

Seating herself across the fire from her husband, she stared at him accusingly. "We have been wed for two moons now," she said.

Startled, Running Buffalo looked up from the arrows he had been fashioning to please himself.

"I am fourteen summers," she continued, her voice determined even though her soft lips trembled. "Old enough to be a wife."

Seated on his bed robes, across the fire from where he had instructed her to make her own bed, Running Buffalo stared at his wife. Tears swam in her dark eyes, and he was assailed by guilt. Reaching across the fire, he stroked her small hand. "You are a child, Snow Flower."

"No!" She jerked her hand away, resentment gleaming in her damp eyes. Her voice was accusing. "You didn't want me because I am small. You only took me because Looking Glass said you must." Lifting her chin, she continued with pride. "You see how well I can work. I am not ugly. Why will you not take me as your wife?" Tears spilled from her eyes, streaking the soft cheeks, as she asked bitterly, "Did you want a warrior woman like Eagle Wing to ride with you to the hunt?"

"No," Running Buffalo protested, filled with guilt that he had hurt her by his neglect. "You are a good wife."

"Then make me truly yours," she demanded. With a determined look on her young face, she rose and crossed the space between them, throwing off her gown as she moved. Falling to her knees beside him on his bed robes, Snow Flower pulled him down onto the soft furs. Clasping his face in her hands, she pressed her mouth to his with fierce passion.

Fire leaped within him as her slender naked body covered his. The firm young breasts seemed to burn through the soft leather of his shirt and he felt himself harden with urgent need. Involuntarily, his arms tightened about her as his mouth answered hers.

With a soft triumphant laugh, Snow Flower drew away, tugging at his clothes until he lay naked in the bed robes beside her. Gently, he stroked her soft young body, memorizing every sweet curve of her, while she sighed, and kissed and caressed with sure instinct.

Running Buffalo took her carefully, aware of the size of his body above her childish slenderness. Snow Flower cried out joyfully at their joining, arching against him with wild eagerness. He was lost in her, drowned in the warm silken sweetness of her.

When she stiffened beneath him, a wild guttural cry burst from her throat at the moment of fulfillment. Running

Buffalo let himself go then, bursting deep within her, his cry echoing hers, his whole being pervaded by a kind of joy he had never known.

"My husband," she murmured sleepily, content against his shoulder.

Running Buffalo smiled, tucking the blankets about her shoulders. "My wife," he answered softly, kissing her forehead.

Coals of the fire gleamed in the dark lodge as the first drops of spring rain spattered against the sturdy skin walls. Running Buffalo sighed and drew his wife closer, knowing he had truly come home at last.

Chapter 19

Star drew the door of the trading post shut and locked it, turning to glance after the three prospectors riding north. They had stopped to buy tobacco and coffee. Luxuries, she thought, knowing they were greenhorns, and certain this country would defeat them.

An old ache touched Star's heart as she saw her four-year-old granddaughter come out of the cabin. Dressed like a miniature of her mother, the golden-haired little girl sat down on the wide porch Alex had built, cuddling her rag doll.

"Good morning, Maria," she called, forcing her voice into pleasant tones. The child glanced up, her face turned sullen, and she did not reply.

Star sighed. Even though she knew this child was not her gifted heir, she had tried to love her, and tried to win her affection in a hundred ways. Katrin stood like a wall between them, as she did between Alex and the little girl.

"She's Mama's girl . . . Mama's girl . . ." The words echoed in Star's mind and her heart grew heavy with the knowledge that Katrin's selfishness could only bring harm.

She did not glance again at the child as she walked past the house toward her own skin lodge beside the creek. Idly, she wondered whether Hugh Cameron would approve all the changes that had taken place here in the last six years.

Star's eyes surveyed the cabin where a thin trail of smoke lifted from the chimney into the cool spring air. The cabin Hugh Cameron had built as sturdy as himself had two new rooms added on, a shingle roof, and a planed-board floor now. Charles had sent the sawmill equipment out from St. Louis, along with the miller to run it. Strange, she mused, this talent Charles seemed to have to guess the future and grab the opportunity to profit by it. He was even profiting from the War Between the States.

As soon as the sawmill was in operation, Alex had begun to add buildings to the ranch. The stables were large enough to hold a dozen horses, as well as the milk cow Katrin had insisted upon. There was a bunkhouse and cookhouse for the men he hired, since Katrin refused to cook for them or even have them in her house. Now he was building a barn. He'd have it filled with wild hay scythed from the meadows, he'd told her, to see them through the hard winters.

The whole mountain west had changed, Star thought as she stirred the coals and built up her cooking fire. Nearly every year there had been a gold strike somewhere in the mountains: first at Cherry Creek, where the city of Denver was growing now, on the Comstock Lode far away in Utah territory, in the Snake River country of the Nez Percé, where the whites had built a place called Lewiston, and now to the north in Montana. In every one of those towns there was a market for Alex's beef, and for the cordwood he hired men to cut and haul from the nearby forests.

The first wagon road into Cameron Valley had been cut by men bringing in Charles's sawmill equipment. She was glad the road was one way . . . into the valley, and back out. Isolated as they were, they were seldom troubled by the trashy humans flooding westward.

For now, the west was nearly free of the army presence, for they all fought against each other in something called a civil war.

A cloud of dust raised by horsemen coming along the road caught her eye. At once, she knew it was Alex and let her breath out in relief. He was gone so much these days, delivering cattle and lumber, making deals with the butcher shops and merchants and builders in all the boom towns within traveling distance.

As she watched the horses moving toward her through the hot midday light, Old Magpie came out of the stables, shading his eyes as he strained to see. Star smiled. While he was away from the ranch, Alex left the old Indian in charge and he took his duties seriously. With a pistol holstered at his waist, a long knife in a scabbard, and his rifle in the crook of his arm, Old Magpie commanded the respect of any ruffian in the west.

Alex rode directly across the ranch yard to where she stood waiting beside her lodge. "I'm back, Ma," he said, reining in his horse and dismounting. The cow hands riding with him were unsaddling their horses to turn them into the fenced pasture.

With a grin, Alex took off his hat to beat the dust from it against his leg. Then he glanced briefly toward his own house, where his daughter had run indoors at his approach. Star saw his face harden, a flash of pain in his dark eyes.

With a shrug, he continued, smiling at her. "Got a good price. Them miners sure go through the beef."

"They go through the game too," she told him. "And the Indians grow angry when they must go hungry because of white man's greed."

Looking grim, Alex replied, "They raided an Overland Stage station last week. Blackfoot, they say. Ben Holladay says he's movin' the stage line south to get away from the Indians."

"How far south?" There was a sarcastic edge to Star's question.

"Can't go further than the Gulf of Mexico, I reckon," Alex replied with an ironic laugh. "He says once the war is over the army will take care of the Indians."

"Like they did at Sand Creek?" Star asked. "A massacre, slaughtering women and children."

"Oh God, Ma," he said, turning away. "Don't talk about it." After a silence, he changed the subject decisively. "Everything all right here while I was gone?"

"I did a little business at the trading post," she replied,

and he laughed. How seldom he laughed anymore, she thought, watching how his face was transformed, and made younger. He looked older than his twenty-six years, with squint lines at the corners of his eyes, his face leather brown from the sun. And always there was that taut, wary look behind his eyes, a tension in his tall, lean body that never seemed to find ease.

"Charles would be proud of your bookkeeping, Ma," he said, reaching out to squeeze her shoulder. His face fell into moody lines. "If the damn war hadn't come along, he'd have been back here."

"Yes." She nodded, knowing that Charles Forester had left his heart in the mountain country and would never be truly happy anywhere else. "But he has a wife and a son in St. Louis now, and he is growing rich."

"Mostly on railroads." Alex looked thoughtful. "There's going to be a transcontinental railroad built after the war. Charles means to make money on it, and so do I."

"You could have told me you were back." Katrin's strident voice broke in. She came across the dusty ranch yard toward them, holding her daughter's hand.

Alex's eyes softened for a moment as they rested on his wife and child. Although Katrin had never become pregnant again, she had gained weight through the years. Her pale face was full and round, her breasts heavy and ripe beneath the calico gown. The pale gold hair gleamed like a halo in the brilliant light.

"What did you bring me, Papa?" Maria demanded, her small delicate face lifted to his, dark eyes filled with expectation.

Alex stooped to lift the little girl in his arms. She squeezed him about the neck and kissed his cheek, then leaned away to look into his face. "Where is it?"

A kiss bought and paid for, Star thought sadly, but Alex grinned, hugged his daughter close, and kissed her forehead.

"Right here, honey," he said indulgently. Untying his saddlebags, he turned to shout, "Here, Magpie . . . take my horse, will you?"

From the depths of his saddlebag, Alex drew a package

wrapped carefully in a soft piece of muslin. Maria seized it, and cried out at the sight of the brightly colored music box. Looking pleased, Alex bent to show her how to wind it. The painted figurines of a peasant boy and girl twirled to the tinkly music.

"What about my present?" Katrin asked, looking at Alex with cool, appraising eyes.

His eyes were even colder, and his voice held an edge of bitterness. "You'll get your present in the morning," he said.

"Whatever it costs," Katrin snapped. Seizing the child's hand, she flounced away toward the house. Fury glittered in her eyes, and the look she gave Star was filled with hatred.

Morning light lay clear and golden over the meadows as Alex crossed the ranch yard next day. Rolling a cigarette, he lit it and leaned back against the rail fence of the corral. It was a habit he'd picked up in the mining camps. He'd never liked chewing tobacco, but somehow he found the cigarette between his lips and the sight of blue smoke drifting upward soothed the tension in him.

In the distance, he could hear the whine of the sawmill, the ring of axes. Cattle bawled from the high meadows to the north where he had pushed them to summer pasture. It was more than his father had ever dreamed, he told himself, wondering if Hugh Cameron would approve all the changes, certain he would not.

He took a long drag on the cigarette, watching as Katrin set up her washtubs beside the house, making ready to launder the dirty clothes he'd brought back from his trip.

Damn her, he thought, the banked fire of anger burning inside him. She was no better than the whores he'd bought in Virginia City. He had to buy her body too, and she was his wife. This morning she'd smiled and exclaimed happily over the bolt of blue silk he'd brought her, and he'd felt cheated. Cheated by a wife who lay as though dead while he loved her.

Maybe . . . always there was the maybe that if he did something more, she would truly love him, truly give herself. Next trip, he'd take her to Fort Laramie, she could wear her new blue silk gown and visit with the officers' wives. Perhaps that was all she needed . . . other white women. Maybe.

Crushing out the cigarette with the toe of his boot, Alex turned toward the stables and the day's work. A lone horseman was riding across the south meadow, and he paused to peer into the distance.

"Good Lord," Alex swore to himself. It was his mother, riding alone. What was she doing out this early? Magpie and Little Knife did all the hunting for the ranch and the horses she tamed were brought into the corrals for her.

In the empty sky above her, he saw a lone hawk circling slowly, and his heart contracted painfully.

Star had explored every corner of Cameron Valley, and when she found this place, it had seemed familiar. The steep hillside, with an outcropping of red sandstone rising abruptly from the meadows, was very like the one she had climbed with Old Grandmother long ago. There was a grove of tall cottonwoods surrounding the cold clear spring, and a swift-running creek teeming with trout. The wide meadows would feed her horses.

This would be home now, she told herself, standing before her lodge pitched beneath the cottonwood trees and gazing up at the midsummer sky where thunderheads built in the west, portents of a coming storm.

For a long time, Star had known she must leave the home she and Shining Bear had made together. With every passing year it had become less her home, and more the home of the bright-haired woman her son had married. Now the time had come to go away so that she no longer had to look on her son's loneliness, a loneliness she had no power to assuage. She needed to distance herself from the cold hatred of her daughter-in-law, a hatred she knew grew out of her knowledge of Katrin's guilty secret.

Sounds of sawing and hammering echoed in the heavy air, for when Alex saw she was adamant about this move, he had been equally adamant in his insistence that she have a comfortable log house, corrals and stables for the horses she

174

intended to raise and train here. He sent his own men, with wagon loads of logs and sawed lumber, to do the job.

Now, Star studied the smoothed piece of pine in her hand on which she still kept books as Charles Forester had taught her. She had marked down three wagon loads of sawed lumber, far more than Alex needed to order for this job. And far more, she thought, than had been used.

Walking past the log stables and the corral to the log cabin, she winced at the sloppiness of the construction. She had watched Hugh Cameron build a cabin straight and true and she knew good workmanship. With a piece of charcoal, she marked down the sawed lumber used . . . in the roof and in the floor of the cabin. Adding it, she knew she had not been wrong. There had been a loaded wagon driving away in the middle of the night.

"Mr. Fraser," she called in a commanding tone to the man Alex had put in charge of the building.

"Yeah?" The man sauntered over to her, spitting tobacco juice as he did.

Watching the way his eyes never met hers, Star thought how much she disliked him, as she disliked so many of the failed prospectors and drifters Alex hired.

"Did I hear a wagon leaving in the night?" she asked.

Fraser spat again, his eyes on the horizon. "Yeah. Sent some boys to the mill fer more sawed lumber to finish the roof and fer shingles."

"What happened to the three loads of sawed lumber Alex sent already?" she demanded, watching his face.

She saw him start in surprise. Then a slow grin spread across his stubbled face. With rising anger, she sensed his contempt for her.

"Twarn't three," he said carelessly. "Reckon you never learned to count."

"You ignorant thief," she replied in a low, hard voice. "I can count a lot better than you." There was a sudden silence as the workmen paused to listen apprehensively. "You're stealing the lumber, aren't you?" she demanded. "Sending it up to Virginia City to sell?"

"Now, you ain't got no call to say sech a thing," he

protested slyly. "Yer jest an Injun squaw who don't know nothing about sellin' lumber nor countin' wagon loads." Laughing, he glanced up at his workmen, swaggering a bit in what he saw as his triumph over her.

"Nobody cheats Star Cameron," she told him in a voice like ice. Turning on her heel, she walked back to her lodge, scarcely hearing his jeering voice behind her. Carefully, she loaded the old Hawken rifle, just as Shining Bear had taught her.

With the heavy rifle cradled in her arm, she confronted Fraser. "I know how to use this," she said in a loud, clear voice. "If you aren't on your horse and out of here right now, Fraser . . . you're a dead man."

His face blanched, and when she cocked the rifle, he ran, stumbling across to the stables to saddle his horse.

Slowly, Star turned to face the silent, staring workmen, the rifle still in her hands. "Anyone else want to join him?" she demanded. The silence grew uneasy.

"If you want to stay and work for me," she went on, "you'll work for me and no one else. Now pull down those logs and start over. If I'm going to build a house, I'll have it built right. The way Hugh Cameron showed me."

Chapter 20

1865, the summer the War Between the States ended, Charles Forester came back to the mountains. Ten years he'd been away, and he'd never dreamed it would be so long. Nor did it seem to have been that many years with the constant flow of letters and business between himself and the Camerons.

With the wise investment of his money and that of his wife, he'd grown rich from the war. A fortune made on the misery of others, he knew, and felt the need to somehow cleanse himself of that knowledge. Yet even as he traveled west, he found himself looking for new opportunities, as addicted now to making money as he had once been to liquor.

In St. Louis, he had a beautiful wife. Monique was learned in the social mores, if not in books, and moved through the salons and dinners with elegant composure. Even his family in England had been impressed by her graces when they had visited there two years ago. And he had a son . . . William Chartrand Forester, a strong, bright child whose very existence filled Charles with joy. But even there, amid the trappings of his success, he felt empty. There was a great void inside him that could be filled only by a horizon looming with mountains and the sight of a beautiful, dark-skinned woman.

The whole world had changed, Charles told himself as his caravan descended the wagon road into Cameron Valley. Why had he expected this place to stay the same? Where there had been a single log cabin and a rough corral, he now saw a substantial, shingle-roofed log house with half-grown trees beside it, extensive corrals and stables, and a huge barn, half log and half sawed lumber. Other outbuildings surrounded the main house, quarters for the workmen, Charles surmised, for there were cattle and horses feeding in the meadows. The Wind River mountains loomed against a blue cloud-mottled sky in exactly the way he remembered.

Then he realized what was most lacking . . . the skin lodges of the trading Indians that had almost always been pitched along the creek. He shook his head, saddened by the knowledge that the Indians were being herded onto reservations, the recalcitrant, roaming bands slaughtered by the army.

A tall figure came from one of the small buildings carrying a saddle on his hip. Spotting the approaching caravan, he dropped the saddle in the ranch yard, waving both arms and shouting incoherent greetings.

Impulsively, Charles spurred his horse forward, leaving behind the wagons and horsemen accompanying him. As the clean, sweet air rushed past his face, his eyes riveted on Alex's welcoming figure, a joyous sense of homecoming filled Charles's heart. This boy . . . Alex, grown now to a man . . . was his true son, the child of his heart. There was over forty years in age between himself and the son back in St. Louis. Sometimes it seemed an insurmountable barrier.

"Ten years, damn you," Alex exclaimed, releasing Charles from the fierce bear hug in which they'd seized each other as soon as Charles dismounted. "How could you stay away for ten years?"

"Not because I wanted to," Charles answered, overcome by a rush of affection for this tall, strong man who, ten years ago, had been a gangly, unsure boy. He sensed a hardness to Alex now, a reserve surrounding him like an invisible wall.

A rustle of silk fell incongruously on his ear, and Charles

turned to see a woman in a blue silk gown coming toward them.

"This is Katrin, my wife, Charles," Alex said. His face broke into a smile as he glimpsed the little girl hiding behind her mother's skirts, her blue silk gown a replica of Katrin's. "And this is my daughter, Maria." He drew the reluctant child close to him, looking down at her with unabashed adoration.

She'll be a beauty, Charles thought, kissing her hand as gravely as he had kissed her mother's. Her dark eyes met his, unblinking and unsmiling. After a moment, she broke away from her father, returning to hug her mother about the waist.

"We're glad you're here, Charles," Katrin said, her petulant face breaking into a smile, her pale blue eyes eager. "I've fixed a big dinner for you and your men. I hope you'll like it."

"But how did you know we'd be here today?" Charles asked in surprise. The woman and child were dressed in their company best, and tantalizing odors of cooking food drifted from the open door of the log house.

"Star knew," Alex answered, his eyes carefully avoiding Katrin's.

Yes, Charles remembered now . . . she always knew. And his heart leaped against his ribs just as it had that first long ago summer. "Where is she?" he asked, his eyes searching, eager to behold her, yet half afraid of the changes ten years might have wrought.

Katrin broke the short, stiff silence. "Tell the men to wash up. I'll get dinner on the table." Whirling about, she seized the child's hand and marched toward the house.

Frowning, Charles turned his inquiring look on Alex, who stood staring at the ground, scuffing the dirt with the toe of his boot. At last Alex raised his eyes, his expression half ashamed, a grim set to his mouth.

"Ma's at her place. Said she'd see you later on." Once more, Alex studied the toe of his boot, then drew a deep breath. "Her and Katrin never quite hit it off."

"That's why she moved to her own place?" Charles prompted.

Alex nodded. "I reckon . . . even though she claimed it was because she wanted to raise horses, and train them her own way." Reaching out, he laid a tentative hand on Charles's shoulder, searching his face as though fearful of finding condemnation there. "We'll ride down there this afternoon . . . you and me."

The colt was a fine one, Star thought, stroking his muzzle, certain he would grow into a great stud. Hands Down, Alex had named him for the white Palouse markings on his hip in the shape of a man's hand. She was proud of the way she'd upgraded the herd since she'd moved here and could manage the animals in her own way . . . with only Magpie and Little Knife to help. Blowing softly in the animal's nostrils, she smiled and handed the halter reins to Little Knife.

The horsemen she had been expecting had just cleared the ridge. Their figures blurred and wavered in the cloud shadows cast by the afternoon sun. Hands Down snorted and shied as Little Knife led him away. One hand resting on the top corral pole, Star waited.

Charles reined in his horse and sat frozen in the saddle, staring at her as though she were a ghost.

"Welcome home, my friend," she said, holding out her arms. She had dressed in her best white doeskin gown, beaded with medicine signs, her finest moccasins and leggings. About her neck she wore the Forester pearls, gleaming softly against the pale doeskin.

"Star . . ." Charles answered in an awed voice. Sliding from the saddle, he seized her in a long embrace, her face pressed against his shoulder. After a time, Charles held her away, looking at her in wonder. "How can it be," he asked, "that everything in the world changes except you?"

She laughed at him, knowing how terribly she had changed. But he shook his head, reaching out to stroke her dark hair. "Not a gray hair," he mused, "while I . . ." And he smoothed the wings of silver hair above his ears. "And you're still slender as a girl."

Studying his face, Star saw the lines the years had etched around his eyes, around his mouth, hidden now by the full mustache he wore. But his eyes were still a warm gray, still filled with youthful enthusiasm. As she looked into them, she moved quickly out of his embrace, at once aware that Charles's old passion for her still burned within him.

Alex stood watching them, a puzzled line between his brows. Star wondered if he had guessed at the depth of emotion flowing between her and Charles.

A wagon that had come around by the road rattled into the ranch yard. Two men sat on the spring seat, the driver pulling the stout horses to a halt with harnesses jingling. "What's this?" Star asked.

Alex laughed. "Charles always comes loaded with gifts, Ma. Don't you remember?"

They watched as Charles directed the two men in the unloading of the wagon. "He brought the iron stove Katrin wanted," Alex told her, then grimaced. "She's acting like he's a little tin god, bowing and scraping. Makes Charles nervous, I think."

"I'm sure it does." Star smiled to herself, imagining Katrin catering to Charles . . . the rich man with noble ancestors.

Charles was scarcely able to contain his delight in the act of giving as the gifts were unloaded and spread out on the wide porch of Star's cabin. There was a fine new saddle for Star, the latest repeating rifle with a finely carved stock, a set of oak table and chairs, knocked down and tied in bundles for transporting, a feather bed wrapped in canvas, pots and pans and knives and tools for trading . . . bags of coffee and sugar . . . bacon, powder and shot, blankets . . . a crate of books. The last thing unloaded was a large trunk. Charles had it carried inside, unopened.

"You're far too generous, Charles," Star said, almost overwhelmed by the plethora of goods.

His gray eyes met hers, dark and intense. "You saved my life," he told her gravely. "I can never repay you for that."

Smiling, she touched his arm. "It was a life worth saving," she murmured. "That is payment enough."

A long silence stretched between them as he looked into her face. She saw there the war of desire and honor she had seen there years ago when they were young and she could feel only sympathy for him because she loved another man.

"What'll we do with the wagon, Mr. Forester?" one of the workmen interrupted them.

"Leave it here and ride the horses back," Charles commanded. Turning to Star, he grinned. "Reckon you could find use for a wagon?"

She began to shake her head, but Alex interrupted. "Sure, we'll need wagons to haul out railroad ties next year, Ma."

"Then the railroad is really coming west?" she asked Charles.

"It certainly is," he answered, looking pleased with himself. "And by the time they get here, you and me and Alex are going to own all the land south of here and they'll have to pay us to build through."

During the following weeks, the small canvas-topped wagon carrying Charles's surveying instruments and his crew crossed and recrossed the sagebrush plains south of Cameron Valley. The teamsters who'd driven the big wagons had gone to work for Alex, cutting ties in anticipation of the coming of the railroad.

Charles surveyed and mapped, then filled out the government papers for land preemptions. He rode into Star's ranch yard late one summer afternoon, alone and carrying his leather portfolio.

The papers were spread out on the reassembled oak table, which stood in the center of Star's cabin. Katrin had been furious to learn of its existence and the four chairs that went with it. She was placated only by Alex's promise that Charles would bring a load of furniture for her when he returned next year, and she'd already made out a list.

The books Charles had brought were carefully arranged on a shelf Star had built, and below them was the brass-bound trunk. It contained gowns of silk and fine wool, underclothing of soft linen trimmed with rich lace . . . white women's clothing. Star had left it all untouched, although she had placed the Forester pearls on top of them.

"Sign here . . . and here . . . and here," Charles was saying, marking each paper with an *X* where she wrote her name, "Star Cameron," as he had taught her. There were other papers for land claims in Alex's name, and Katrin's.

"It seems very greedy, Charles," she said doubtfully, leaning back to watch him as he stacked the papers neatly and placed them in the portfolio.

Cocking an eyebrow, Charles gave her an amused look. "You can't be generous when you're dealing with railroads. They're the ultimate in greed." Chuckling, he reached across to squeeze her hand. "I'll make a rich woman of you, Star Cameron."

"What more do I need?" she asked, waving a hand to take in her comfortable cabin. It had been built as she wished, a duplicate of the one Hugh Cameron had built except for the shingled roof and the board floor. The red sandstone fireplace filled one wall, and on the opposite wall stood a laced rawhide bed.

His face changed then, and she saw the fires leap in his gray eyes as his hand tightened on hers. Withdrawing her hand, Star stood up, astonished to find that she was trembling.

Forcing her voice to remain steady, she asked, "Do you want something to eat, Charles? I have stew on the fire, but I thought you might be going on to spend the night with Alex."

Charles leaned back in his chair, his face calm and under control now. He smiled. "I suppose I should go on. Alex tells me he traded a cow for a bottle of sourdough starter from an emigrant woman. Katrin is baking bread every day in her new oven."

"She'll be out of flour before fall comes," Star said as she stirred the stew.

Charles's grin widened at the tinge of resentment in Star's voice. "Fresh bread or not," he said. "I've never tasted anything better than your stew, so if you've got plenty . . ."

"You've never gone through the trunk I brought, have you?" Charles asked as he helped her scrape and wash the graniteware plates from their supper.

"Everything is very beautiful," she told him, hoping she hadn't hurt his feelings. "But they are for white women."

"Nonsense," he replied briskly, crossing the room to tug open the trunk lid. "I picked these out myself because I thought you'd look wonderful in them." He drew out a plum-colored silk gown with jet-trim on its ruffled yoke. "Try this on for me," he commanded.

"But, Charles . . ." she tried to protest.

"And these . . ." He drew out the underclothing, holding it out toward her with a mock-stern look. "The country is moving west, Star. You'll have to live among white people. Dress like them. I can teach you to do that just as I taught you to read and write and cipher."

"You're mad to think you can make a white woman of me, Charles," she said in a low unhappy voice. In one painful flash, she was transported back across the years . . . hurrying to cut a bolt of bright calico into an imitation of white women's long skirts, wanting to please Hugh Cameron, the white trapper she had married. She could hear his laughter, then the warmth of his reassurance, and felt her loss as keenly as though Shining Bear had left her only yesterday.

Charles seized her shoulders in his hands, looking into her face. The years rushed into now, to the comforting presence of this man who loved her. "I don't want to change you, Star." His voice was thick and choked with emotion. "I only want to teach you to survive in this changing world. I couldn't bear to see you defeated by it. . . ."

"As Hugh was," she finished for him, and turned away.

He was there between them, as he had always been . . . Hugh Cameron, the Shining Bear. Charles swallowed hard, a sick hot feeling in the pit of his stomach. Even now, he wasn't sure what he'd expected when he returned to Cameron Valley. Falling Star was the beautiful, unattainable dream he'd carried in his mind for ten long years. He'd simply wanted to behold the dream again. And she was the same, incredibly the same, the quick girlish turn of her head when she looked up at him, the way her dark eyes gleamed when he made her laugh. . . . Desire poured through him and he could not believe that ten years ago he had wanted her any more intensely than he wanted her now.

Dropping the plum silk dress over the back of a chair, he drew her into his arms. Cupping her face in one hand, he turned her to meet his kiss. As his mouth covered hers, the years fled. All the pent-up longing poured from him as his mouth devoured hers. His arms tightened about her, pressing her close as his body hardened with desire. Joy leaped through him as he felt the answering pressure of her lips against his, her arms about his shoulders, clinging, her hands stroking.

"Star . . ." he murmured breathlessly against her ear. "I've wanted you for so long."

It was so unexpected, she could scarcely catch her breath. Not just Charles's kiss, but her own reaction. All these years she had thought of him as a beloved friend, her teacher and mentor even though she knew the reality of his feelings for her. But now, to her surprise, she felt within herself the stirrings of half-forgotten desire.

The years alone had been long, and they had been lonely. When Charles's mouth sought hers once more, Star responded instinctively, her flesh quickening in answer to his passionate kiss and the pressure of his aroused body against hers.

His mouth was gentle on her eyelids, but his voice was hot and urgent. "Let me love you, Star," he said. "You want it just as much as I do."

Almost stunned by the rush of desire that poured through her body, Star caught her breath. In one last valiant attempt to deny her body's longing, she protested softly, "Dear Charles . . . we aren't young anymore."

Charles looked down at her, unsmiling, his gray eyes dark. "Where is it written that passion is the exclusive province of the young?" he asked, and suddenly the corner of his mouth lifted in a smile. "You and I know more about love than when we first met . . . and I wanted you then . . . nearly as much as I want you now."

All her will to resist fled beneath the passionate onslaught of his kisses. A flame she had thought dead forever leaped inside her body, and her blood pounded hot through her veins.

There before the softly muttering fire, with a purple mountain dusk falling outside the cabin, they undressed each other, every movement punctuated by kisses and caresses. Star marveled to see how flat and hard his body was, though not as slender as it had once been. His hands moved over her body, setting her skin afire until she ached with her need for him.

As Charles drew her with him toward the bed adorned by her new feather bed, Star reached into the trunk. Picking up the rope of pearls, she put them about her neck, where they gleamed against her dusky breasts.

Charles laughed aloud, hugging her fiercely against him. "You knew," he said, kissing her. "You knew what I dreamed when I gave those to you. . . ."

He was a gentle, caring lover, arousing her to fever pitch, holding back when his first penetration stung her as though she were a virgin. Her body, denied love for so long, throbbed and demanded, opened to him. And she moved against him, gently at first and then with frenzied need until she was lost in rapture and cried her joy into the quiet room.

Chapter 21

1868

Last winter when Charles headed for St. Louis, the end of the rails had already been built to a booming town they'd named Cheyenne. "I'll bring you a railroad when I come back in the spring," he'd promised Star as they said good-bye. By summer, the end of the rails had come to the sagebrush plains south of Cameron Valley. The town building there was called Helltown at first, as all rail-end towns were called unless they proved to be permanent settlements. Now the sign above the railroad loading dock read CAMERON CITY.

The railroad wasn't all Charles had brought, Star thought today as she looked along the rutted, muddy street strewn with horse droppings. Raw new buildings lined the street, all facing the railroad tracks on the south. Hammers and saws resounded in the late summer air from the permanent three-story hotel being built to replace the ramshackle shanty next door.

Horses lined the hitching racks, and the wooden side-walks teemed with men . . . railroad workers, drifters, gamblers, traders. In every other one of the shacks and tents down the street, a saloon was doing a booming business. There was a busy livery stable and a barber shop advertising baths for twenty-five cents.

Cameron Lumber Company had provided the lumber to

build this town . . . the ties to lay the tracks already leading westward beyond the horizon . . . the shanties where the railroad workers and hangers-on lived, the makeshift saloons, even the hitching rails in front of the board sidewalk.

The whole town had a kind of tumult and disorder Star found offensive. As she stepped from the muddy street to the board sidewalk in front of the Cameron City General Store, she nearly stumbled over a drunk passed out beside the water trough. Cameron City was filled with gamblers and whores and drunks, rough uncouth men and worn-out, hard-eyed women. She had already told Charles she did not like this new world he was building.

Seizing every opportunity, Charles had opened a bank in one corner of the general store he and Alex owned. As Star entered the dim interior of the building, Charles rose from his desk and came to greet her.

Smiling, he took her hand. "If the ladies in St. Louis could see you, they'd start a whole new fashion." He gazed admiringly at the outfit he'd had made for her back east.

The divided riding skirt was of the fine doeskin she'd traded from the Shoshone. She wore a blouse of pale blue silk beneath a jacket of doeskin with a soft beaver collar. On her feet were the fine leather boots Charles had chosen. Perhaps it was too grand for the half day's horseback ride into town from her Red Hill Ranch, but it was comfortable.

"Howdy, Miz Cameron," Dave Billings called from behind the store's long counter. He was a broad-faced man, bald and running to flesh. Charles and Alex had hired him to run the store. Because he was to share in the profits, he'd run it honestly.

Businessmen like Dave were bringing their families west to settle in Cameron City. A street of homes was growing beyond the main street that faced the railroad. Next to the Billings's neat two-story frame house, the Dutchman who owned the livery stable had built a cottage for his family. Even a couple of the saloon owners were building family homes on Second Street.

"Good morning, Dave," Star said politely, and he grinned. She knew it amused him, as it did all the newcomers, to see her dressed up, her hair braided and wound in a dark coronet about her head.

What others thought of her was of little importance to Star. Their values were not hers, and unlike white women she did not have to hook herself into constraints of behavior as they hooked themselves into corsets.

A smile curved her lips and her dark eyes gleamed as she remembered the summer night when Charles had insisted she finally try on his gifts.

They had been lovers for two summers then, and they'd come to feel easy with each other, comfortable and companionable. At the supper table, Charles had looked at her gravely and said, "It's time you prepared for the new world that's coming west, Star. You can't ignore those clothes I've brought you any longer."

Humoring him, Star watched as he laid the clothing out on the bed: the chemise and drawers, the corset and the petticoats, the plum silk gown he'd brought the first year.

"I'll show you how it all goes together," he promised, but when she pulled her doeskin gown over her head, revealing her slender nakedness, Charles drew in his breath and groaned. "This may not be as easy as I thought."

"It was your idea." Star laughed, teasing, all too aware of the desire flaming in his gray eyes. She watched with amusement his struggle to control himself as he pulled the chemise over her head and tied it beneath her bosom. Then came the underdrawers and she cried out in protest as he wrapped the stiff, boned corset about her torso.

"Take it off—hurry," she demanded, gasping, almost as soon as he finished hooking it up. "I told you I couldn't be a white woman, Charles."

With a chagrined look, he quickly unhooked the corset. "You don't really have to wear a corset, you know."

"I don't intend to," she stated, glaring at him.

Suddenly, Charles burst into laughter. Drawing her into his arms, he kissed her long and lovingly. "I'll burn the damn thing tomorrow," he said, and paused. In a coaxing voice, he added, "But please try on the gown."

Without the corset, the gown was a bit tight, but Star

loved the silken feel of it against her skin, the soft whisper of the material when she moved, whirling about the room for Charles's admiration.

Firelight gleamed on the high cheekbones of his aristocratic face, the heat reflected in his eyes. "You're beautiful," he murmured in a choked voice. "Dear God, you are so beautiful."

Smiling, she paused before him. "I'll wear the gown whenever you want me to, Charles, but this"—and she picked up her discarded doeskin gown—"is much more practical for the life I lead."

"The time will come," he said, his gray eyes burning into hers. With a trembling hand, he stroked her long black hair, carefully pulling it back from her face. "Another time, I'll show you how to do your hair up." His hand cupped her head as he bent toward her, the heat of his desire pulsating so that she felt it when he drew her close into his arms.

As he helped her out of the gown, his hands awkward with haste on the buttons, Star laughed aloud. "It must be very difficult to make love to a white woman with all this clothing to cool your heat."

She felt him stiffen, his hands perfectly still on the buttons at the back of the gown. He let out a long sigh, then carefully continued unbuttoning her gown. In that sigh, Star heard all the unhappiness he kept concealed . . . the wife he never spoke of, and his other life during the winters in St. Louis.

Slipping the gown from her shoulders, Charles drew her back against him. His hands cupped her breasts and he bent to kiss the curve of her shoulder. "My love," he murmured as his lips caressed her ear. Then he turned her in his arms, his eyes devouring her face. "The best of my life is here with you," he said. Gathering her close against his body throbbing with passion, he whispered, "You are my only love."

The touch of Charles's hand on her arm brought her swiftly back to the present. He led her to a chair beside his rolltop oak desk, the Cameron City Bank. The desk was shoved against the wall opposite the counter and was surrounded by sacks of grain and flour and sugar and coffee. Everything smelled new and raw, from the leather boots stacked on the shelves to the green lumber already shrinking on the floor.

Star sat down, her eyes on Charles's face. A flame leaped behind his gray eyes, but his face was composed. Charles was always circumspect. He was married to another, a vague distant creature, and he lived two separate lives. She had no idea whether Alex, or anyone, suspected they were lovers, and simply felt it was of no concern to anyone else.

"Now that Wyoming's a territory, we'll have to get a bit more civilized," Charles said, sorting through the contracts she had come into town to sign today. "Government's even trying to improve the mail delivery." With a grin, he spread the contract on his desk. "Cameron Freight Lines is going to carry the mail to South Pass City . . . for a start." Gold had been discovered in the mountains near South Pass. Prospectors were flooding into the area and a boom town was growing.

"Why do you need to be involved in everything that goes on, Charles?" she asked, shaking her head as she signed the contract.

Leaning back in his chair, he smiled at her. "Cameron City won't be like other railhead helltowns. This town will last. Lots of settlers moving in, taking up ranches. This is the natural trading center for all the country south of the Wind Rivers." He leaned toward her, his gray eyes intense. "We were here first, Star. Why shouldn't it be our country? Why shouldn't we get rich on it?"

"I'm not sure I like this new world you're building," she replied quietly.

"It's inevitable, Star," he replied. "Either we build with it or we go under." He gave her an amiable smile. "The only thing certain in this world is change."

The swivel chair squeaked as he leaned forward to pick up a telegram lying in the confusion of papers on his desk. "Talk about change . . . I just got this from a friend of mine in the legislature in Cheyenne. Seems they've decided to give women the vote in Wyoming territory. How do you like that?"

Star laughed. "What difference does that make? You and Alex will tell me how to vote anyway."

Charles studied her with speculative eyes. "I wonder how much we can tell you." They laughed together. He shuffled papers and handed her another to sign. "You're an officer of the Cameron City Bank, you know. We started the building without your signature, but this makes it legal."

"Think about that," she said with a small smile. "It makes what I said about voting sound reasonable."

Chuckling, Charles rose from the chair. He looked impressive in his dark gray frock coat and trousers, a white linen stock at his throat. Picking his black silk hat from the top of the desk, he smiled down at her. "Let me buy dinner for you at the hotel. We can argue there."

"Do we have more to argue about?" she asked, with a laugh.

"Beef contracts," he said, suddenly sobering. "You won't like it, but the government is buying beef to feed the Shoshones at the Wind River Reservation."

"Now that they've killed all the game," she murmured, an edge of bitterness in her voice.

"I've got another herd of Texas longhorns coming in to my ranch this next week."

"And you'll sell them to the government at a fat profit," she said, pursing her lips and shaking her head. Charles had taken up a ranch south of Cameron City on the open plains, part of the land-grant sections he'd bought cheaply from the government. He'd built a rough log cabin to house his cow hands and the cook and never stayed there. He did keep a room at the hotel for when he was in Cameron City on business.

Charles's eyes were sparkling as he linked her arm through his. "It's an adventure, Star, building a civilization on a wild frontier . . . a great adventure. And you're part of it."

* * *

Alex turned his horse into the corral, throwing his saddle on the top rail. It was already full dark, and the autumn air bit like a cold knife. Hunching his shoulders inside the leather jacket, he turned toward his mother's house where the yellow gleam of a coal-oil lamp illuminated the windows.

He'd left Katrin and Maria in town at the hotel, where Katrin had insisted on going to recuperate from her miscarriage. She needed a woman to look after her, she said, and Dave Billings's wife would help. And women to gossip with, Alex thought bitterly.

Last spring, when he returned from Virginia City, he'd been amazed at his wife's passionate greeting. He'd told himself not to question it, to just enjoy her suddenly insatiable need for loving. Then she'd become pregnant and the loving stopped abruptly. Alex shrugged. His wife's erratic behavior no longer surprised him, although her anger when she lost the baby seemed misplaced, directed at him, at Star, at life on an isolated ranch.

Star had heard him ride in and she was waiting in the lighted doorway, smiling at him. He wondered whether she had known he was coming, and if her perception extended to what was on his mind.

"I'll stay the night, Ma," he said, giving her a quick embrace. "Katrin's still in town and it's damn dark out there."

As she set supper on the table for him, Alex looked around the cabin. A twinge went through him as he realized there were signs of Charles everywhere. The new iron stove, smaller than Katrin's, the comfortable leather chairs on either side of the fireplace, the rugs, the books on the wall shelves . . . and the addition. Two doors led from the original cabin into two bedrooms that had been added on with a bath between. In there, he knew, was a long tin tub and the small potbellied stove for heating water. Each bedroom had been furnished with a tall carved wood bed and a bureau.

"How is Katrin?" Star asked as they settled into the chairs beside the sandstone fireplace.

Concentrating on rolling a cigarette, Alex nodded. "Doing fine, far as I can tell. But you know how she complains." He lit the cigarette and drew the soothing smoke deep into his lungs. "She's talking about moving into town. Some of the women are trying to get a schoolmaster out here to start a school."

Star nodded, sensing Alex's uneasiness, a discomfort that had nothing to do with Katrin. "Maria should have an education," she agreed. "Katrin can only begin to teach her what she needs."

"There's talk in town," he said, rising abruptly. He walked to the fireplace, flipped his cigarette butt into the flickering flames. The kind of talk he meant, the talk of Katrin and the town women, was as foreign to his mother as this very room would have been twenty years ago.

Star did not speak. The silence seemed to grow, filling the room, roaring in his ears. It had to be said. He had to know the truth. Avoiding her eyes, he half turned, his whole posture reflecting his discomfort.

"It's being said you're Charles's mistress, Ma, that he lives with you here . . . sleeps with you." He strangled on the last words, turning to concentrate once more on the fire.

He heard her sigh. Her voice was low, but with no hesitation.

"Your father has been dead a long time, Alex. I've often been lonely. Even though I chose to live here alone, it's difficult to be without a loving companion. Lonely."

The last word fell on his heart like freezing rain . . . lonely. God knows, he knew the meaning of the word. The wife who should have been his companion was a woman of wildly fluctuating affections. And the daughter he adored, loved him only in return for his gifts.

"Lonely," he repeated in a choked voice, suddenly envying his mother . . . envying Charles. He knew Charles's marriage had been one of convenience . . . his wife's money and his noble forebears traded in the bargain. Even though Charles never spoke openly of the situation, it was evident to Alex that he found no love and little comfort in St. Louis.

Silence deepened between them again. After a moment,

he heard her rise and felt her hand on his arm in loving supplication. Alex drew a deep breath and looked into his mother's questioning face.

"I respect whatever is between you and Charles," he told her. Impulsively hugging her against his side, he added, "We won't speak of it again . . . ever."

Chapter 22

1869

Running Buffalo felt himself become Jed Cameron again as he drew rein at the high ridge overlooking Cameron Valley. Overwhelmed by the flood of memories, he sat his horse in silence, staring at the rolling, sagebrush-covered hills, the wide green meadows dotted now with cattle, the pine-clad foothills rising into the distant blue of the Wind River mountains. And above it all the summer sky filled with towering thunderheads.

He had grown to manhood here, and he had gone away in anger and in pain. Lost in the past, Jed was scarcely aware of the uneasy scrutiny of his companions. Beside him, his treasured seven-year-old son watched with questioning eyes. Shifting his position on the back of his own spotted horse, Red Moon turned to his mother.

Snow Flower gave the boy a reassuring smile, moving uncomfortably in the saddle Jed had padded with fur for her. Pregnancy made her ride uncomfortable and she feared for the child because she had lost so many babies.

At last, Jed met her look and his face softened. With a grin, he turned to the five young warriors who had accompanied them because they wanted to see the land east of the Wallowas, and they hoped to hunt the fast-disappearing buffalo.

Waving his arm, Jed urged them forward, down the rocky

ridge, through the sagebrush where grasshoppers whirred and leaped at their approach . . . home to Cameron Valley.

To the small boy riding beside him, Jed said, *"Aikit palojami . . . fair land."* The child nodded, his great dark eyes brimming with all the strangeness he had seen in the past weeks.

They had traveled light, with no lodge, the provisions and bed robes strapped to the packhorses. And they traveled fast, careful to avoid the settlements where there might be soldiers looking for Indians to drive to the nearest reservation.

Home again, Jed thought, in the land of his birth. "For the last time," he said the words aloud and in English so that his companions did not understand. Nor would they understand that he had come to say good-bye to his mother, and to somehow repair his betrayal of his brother.

When he found a remembered stand of cottonwoods beside a small stream that flowed down the eastern edge of the valley, he halted again. "We will camp here," he told them, sadly aware of the relief in Snow Flower's weary face. He would ask his mother, the medicine woman, for herbs to help his wife carry her children to term. Of all her pregnancies, only one had brought them a living child, this fine boy, born on a night when the full moon was painted red by forest fires.

Late afternoon shadows lay across the dusty yard when Jed rode alone into the old ranch yard. He'd left his wife and companions resting at their camp, not quite sure what welcome he would find here.

Dismounting, he tied his horse to the hitching rack, taken aback by all the changes. This place was unfamiliar now with all the outbuildings, the extensive corrals, and the large log house, the cottonwood trees rustling in the summer wind. The Camerons had prospered in the manner of the white man, he told himself.

Smoke rose from the chimney of the large log cabin, and the smell of food cooking drifted in the cooling air. He glimpsed men working in the stables and the barn. As he turned toward the main house, he searched for the sight of his mother's skin lodge, the home she had returned to after Alex's marriage. Its old place was empty and a sense of cold fear clutched Jed's heart. What if he had come too late and his mother lay beside Shining Bear on the rocky hillside?

The little girl who answered his knock on the open door stared at him with wide dark eyes for a brief moment. With a horrified shriek, she turned and ran back into the house, her long golden ringlets bobbing wildly.

"Mama!" she cried. "An Injun! A wild Injun!"

Jed stepped inside and looked around at the neatly furnished house, the tables and chairs, the huge iron stove. . . .

Katrin straightened up, the pan of biscuits she had just taken from the oven still in her hand.

"Jed!" The word was a cry wrung from deep in her wounded being. She was not even aware she had dropped the pan. Hot biscuits rolled across the braided rug.

"Mama?" Frightened, Maria tugged at her mother's skirts. But for Katrin there was no reality beyond the tall man who stood in the middle of her cabin, watching her. His image was engraved so deeply on her heart, she would have recognized him anywhere in spite of the changes the years had wrought.

He seemed taller and more muscular than she remembered, and he wore his black hair in two braids. The stained fringed buckskins and scuffed moccasins were not so different from the way he dressed when she first knew him. His beloved face was older, harder, yet somehow softer too, as though the years had made him less angry and impatient.

Quickly gaining control of herself, Katrin smoothed back her bright hair and patted her clinging daughter. "Pick up the biscuits, Maria." With a shaky laugh, she added, "I've made such a mess."

Then she moved toward the man, holding out both hands, her pale face soft and smiling. "Oh, Jed . . . you've come back."

Jed tensed when she touched his arm, and moved away. "Where is my brother and Falling Star?" he demanded.

"Alex is driving a herd of beef to Conrad Kohrs in

Virginia City," she said, unable to take her eyes from his face. "He won't be back for weeks."

He made a disappointed grimace, then his face was impassive once more. "Where is Falling Star?"

Why did he have to ask about the old squaw, Katrin thought impatiently. She reached out again and succeeded in taking hold of his arm.

"Where is she?" he asked again, and Katrin drew a deep breath.

"She has her own ranch now," she told him, trying not to let resentment color her voice. "South of here, next to the red hills."

"You drove her away." It was not a question. In spite of herself, Katrin flinched. Her hand tightened on Jed's arm.

"Star didn't like it here after Alex hired all those men to work for him," Katrin replied defensively. "We tried to get her to stay, but she wanted her own place. And . . ." Her voice fell. She didn't want to speak of Star.

The hard muscled arm she held in her clutching hand tightened. That movement sent such a rush of hot emotion through her, Katrin reeled. There was moisture between her thighs, and a throbbing flame that rose through her whole body, beating insistently.

"Oh Jed," she said again, slipping her arms about his waist and lifting her face to his. She felt his body stiffen against her taut breasts, but she clung, wanting him with a blind madness.

"Katrin!" His voice was sharp, his hands hard and bruising on her shoulders as he pushed her away. "Stop! Your child is watching."

"Our child!" she cried, struggling against his grasp, desperately needing to feel his body against hers once more.

"We made her." Her voice was low and urgent. "You and me, Jed . . . we made that child in love. She's yours."

"Tananisa!" he choked. "Damn you, Katrin. You're a mad woman."

"Yes, I'm mad," she cried wildly. Maria stood as though petrified beside the stove where her mother had shoved her aside.

Katrin flung herself against Jed, clinging, her mouth hot and seeking against his. "I'm mad for wanting you," she cried when he held her away. "I've never stopped wanting you. Your brother's touch makes me sick. Why do you think I have no child except yours?"

"Kapsis itu," Jed groaned, forgetting his English in his distraction. "This is a bad thing, Katrin. The child is my brother's; you are his wife." He shoved her away from him and turned toward the door. "I will not come here again," he said.

"Go!" she screamed, torn with pain. "Go to your mother, the old bitch. She's nothing but Charles Forester's whore."

Jed whirled on her, eyes blazing. "Beware, Katrin. Already I would see you dead. Don't speak of my mother."

"Everyone knows!" she cried, out of control now in her need for him. "It's common gossip among the townfolk and the ranch women. Charles lives with her every summer. She's nothing but a whore!"

Jed's hand flashed out so quickly, she could not avoid the blow. He struck her full across the face, one powerful blow that sent her off balance, staggering across the room and against the oak table. Struggling to regain her feet, she rushed to the doorway, but he was already mounted, his horse pounding along the trail southward.

With one long cry of despair, Katrin turned and flung herself into a chair, her head in her arms on the tabletop as she wept with total abandon.

On the rug before the iron stove, the little girl sat carefully rearranging the biscuits in their pan. Her small face was tight with fear and she did not look at her mother.

"I've been expecting you," Star said in the old language as she stepped down from her porch into the embrace of her older son. A lavender haze of twilight lay over the valley as the last rays of the sun gilded the thunderheads building in the western sky.

"You knew I was coming then?" Jed held her away to look intently in her face. She smiled and nodded, hugging him to her again. Joy and dread had battled within her as she

200

awaited his arrival, for the heart of a seer is never at rest. Deep knowledge is a painful burden.

"I went to the old place first," he told her, and his voice fell, reluctant to share what had transpired there.

"Alex is away," Star said, watching his face. Sensing his inner turmoil, she guessed that he had seen Katrin alone and she feared for the anguish that meeting might have brought him. Urging him into the house, she called Little Knife to take his horse.

Jed paused inside the doorway, his face mirroring his disbelief. "You live as a white woman now?" he asked. "I saw the lodge and looked for you there."

Star smiled. "The lodge comforts me when I'm lonely, and it's cool on hot summer nights. But this is my home." With a laugh, she moved toward the stove, adding, "I still cook in the old way; the stew on the stove is the same."

"Then I'll have some," he announced, sitting down at the table. A sense of relief flooded through her. He seemed at ease and completely self-possessed.

Dishing up the stew for him, Star regarded him quizzically. "Where is the rest of your party?"

"Camped at Cottonwood Creek," Jed replied, not questioning that she would know he rode with a party. "I'll go back for them tomorrow."

"Do you have news of Charles Forester?" he asked, sniffing the dish of stew she set before him appreciatively.

The question was natural enough, but Star knew he had spoken with Katrin. In a low steady voice, she said, "Charles is in Denver now. They're building a railroad to connect Denver with the Union Pacific at Cheyenne. He's heavily invested in the Denver-Pacific." She paused, but Jed did not speak. He seemed to be waiting for her to say more.

Drawing a deep breath, she went on. "Charles stays here with me when he is in Cameron Valley. He has been very kind and generous as you can see." With one hand she indicated the furnishings of the cabin.

"What is he to you, my mother?" Jed asked in a low voice.

Star met his gaze steadily. "Among the Nez Percé, it is the custom, when a warrior dies, for his brother to take the wife into his own lodge. Charles was brother to Shining Bear. That is all, my son."

Jed grinned and began eating heartily, obviously relieved by her explanation. "My brother is married to a mad woman," he said.

Sitting at the table, Star watched her son's face as he ate and talked, memorizing the look of him for all time. He told her that her father, Many Horses, had died in his cabin at the reservation; that her brother, Looking Glass, was growing old, but still the leader of the rebellious Nez Percé who had refused to move to the reservation.

"We move further and further north, pushed out of our country by the white settlers. Game grows scarcer every year and we cannot travel to the Big River to trade for salmon. Even the camas prairies are no more, gone to feed settlers' pigs."

Staring sadly out the open door into the deepening dusk, Star asked, "What will you do?"

"We'll never be penned up like animals on a reservation," he growled between bites. "Not if we have to fight to the last man."

Drawing in a long, shaky breath, she fought against the knowledge of what lay ahead for her son. If he knew, perhaps his courage would waver, and he was too brave a man to be diminished in that way. Tonight her gift of sight was a burden she would have wished to be free of, yet it was her burden and not to be shared by another.

Old Magpie was delighted by the arrival of the Nez Percé warriors, chattering away to them in rusty Nez Percé as he showed them where to turn their horses to graze.

It was the small boy who held Star's full attention. Jed lifted him down from his pony, standing him in front of Star with a proud grin. "This is my son, Red Moon. And this is your honored *nakaz*, your grandmother, my son."

The boy stared at her, unsmiling, his eyes wary as he regarded this strange woman standing before her white-man log house.

The burden she carried in her heart seemed too heavy to

bear as she looked into the small handsome face. Stooping, she brought her eyes level with the boy's. "You will be a great warrior, Red Moon," she told him, amazed at the words coming from her mouth. "A leader among your people, honored and respected."

Involuntarily, the child stepped toward her, and with heart overflowing, Falling Star took him into her arms.

"Did you hear?" Jed was almost shouting as he reached out to draw Snow Flower close. Hugging her against him, he looked down into her face. "My mother is a medicine woman given to know the future. Did you hear what she said of our son?"

Snow Flower nodded, tears glimmering in her huge dark eyes as she regarded her husband's mother. Slowly, Star released the boy and stood, holding both hands out to her daughter-in-law.

"Welcome, Snow Flower," she said, clasping the younger woman's hands tightly. "Welcome."

"He is a fine boy," Star said, smiling toward the sleeping child lying in his own bed robes on the floor of the cabin. Outside the promised spring storm roared in full fury, sweeping through the cottonwoods, streaking the darkness with brilliant lightning, shaking the sky with thunder. The young men slept snug in the skin lodge; Jed and his wife and child in the cabin with Star.

Snow Flower turned a grave face to Star. "You spoke the truth of him today?" she asked.

"Yes." Star's voice was low, her being suffused with such pain she struggled against the threatening tears. "He will be a great and honored warrior."

"I carry another child," Snow Flower said, placing her hands on her belly in a significant gesture. Tears welled in her eyes. "I have lost all the others. . . ." Her voice trailed into a sob and she glanced at Jed, who placed a comforting hand on her small shoulder.

"It is a great sorrow to her," Jed told Star, gently stroking his wife's back. "Surely you know some medicine that will help her carry this child to full time."

Star smiled. "Is that why you came . . . for my medicine?"

"No." Jed drew in a long breath, his brilliant blue eyes darkened with sadness. "I fear the Nez Percé will soon have to leave this country. Perhaps we will move north, into Canada where the forests are still free." With Hugh Cameron's eyes, he looked steadily into Star's face. "It may be that we will never meet again, my mother."

All her being cried out in protest at the injustice of it. Yet she knew he spoke truth. Slowly, she nodded. "No, my son . . . we will not meet again."

The young warriors longed to hunt the buffalo, knowing they might be the last of their people to achieve that honor. In only two weeks the nights had already turned chill. If they were to hunt and return home in time to make winter camp, Jed said they must go now. It was a long trek back to the Wallowa mountains.

With a somber face, Falling Star watched Jed and the men herding the horses she had given him into the holding pasture. Red Moon rode proudly beside his father, doing a man's work.

"We are sad to leave you," Snow Flower said. She stood beside Star at the corral fence.

Concealing her own sadness at this parting, Falling Star turned to smile at the girl. "My son has married well," she answered. "It comforts my heart to know that."

Snow Flower's dark eyes glowed as she returned the smile gravely. Touching her belly, she said, "This child will live because of the counsel you gave me. And there will be other children after."

"You and Running Buffalo have been blessed with an extraordinary son," Falling Star replied, nodding toward the boy racing his horse toward them. "Do not despair if *Hunyewat* does not see fit to bless you more."

A shadow crossed the girl's face at the words, and Star's heart contracted painfully in sympathy. She knew too well the sorrow of the children who were never born. The child Snow Flower carried would live, but after that . . .

"Someone coming!" Red Moon called as he reined his horse recklessly beside them, sending a flurry of dust into the still summer air.

Star shaded her eyes against the sunlight glaring down on the sagebrush hills. It was Alex. As she recognized the tall straight-backed figure on the stout roan horse, her throat clogged with apprehension. Jed had said no more of his meeting with Katrin on his arrival two weeks ago, but Star was certain that confrontation had been painful. Now, she could only hope Katrin had not said something to Alex that might cause trouble between the brothers.

Warmth filled her inner being and her eyes filled with tears as Jed rode quickly to meet Alex. The two men leaned from their saddles to give each other a hearty embrace. With a quick clasp of hands, they turned their horses and rode toward the corral where Falling Star and Snow Flower waited. Red Moon spurred his horse to meet them.

"I just got back yesterday," Alex said as he dismounted and hugged his mother. "Katrin said Jed had been there and gone on to Red Hill." Jed had dismounted too, and Alex clasped his brother's shoulder with warm affection. "I was afraid I'd missed you."

"We leave tomorrow," Jed replied in rusty English. Snow Flower and Red Moon frowned as they tried to follow the conversation.

"This is my wife," Jed added, drawing the girl close to his side. *"Inepne"*—he switched to the old language. "And my son, Red Moon." Pride glowed on his face as he indicated the boy watching from horseback.

Some of the pleasure faded from Alex's expression and his eyes were shadowed. Then he grinned, reaching up to shake the boy's hand, taking off his hat and nodding to Snow Flower.

"When I heard you were here, I hoped you'd come back to stay," Alex said, his voice tinged with disappointment. He looked directly into Jed's eyes. "Won't you think about it?"

Jed shook his head, his mouth firm. "My home is with the Nez Percé. We leave tomorrow to hunt the buffalo and travel back to the Wallowa mountains."

The silence was filled with tension as the brothers looked long into each other's eyes. Shouts of the cow hands and their Indian helpers faded into distance. Falling Star waited, aware that she could scarcely breathe for wanting Alex to accept Jed's decision with love and respect.

"Then I'll stay the night." Alex broke the silence, managing a tight grin. "It's a long time between visits and who knows when I'll see you again." He glanced at Star. "Right, Ma?"

"Yes," she answered in a low voice. "It may be a long time."

Stooping to add a stick of wood to the low fire in the stone fireplace, Falling Star was aware of the dark eyes of Red Moon watching her intently. The boy was curled up in his bed robes beside the fireplace. Alex sat slumped in one of the leather chairs, staring into the flames while a cup of coffee grew cold in his hand.

Star reached out a hand to gently smooth the boy's cheek. In the short time he had been here, she had come to love him dearly and the possibility that they might never meet again seemed too much to bear.

"He should stay here," Alex's gloomy voice broke into her thoughts.

Star sighed. Red Moon smiled at her and snuggled down into his blankets. Turning to Alex, Star looked down into his glum face. "No, Alex," she told him. "Jed has made his decision. Give him that right."

It had been a joy to her to be seated at the supper table with her two grown sons and Jed's family. A kind of bonus she hadn't expected. But the conversation soon faltered, for the brothers had little in the way of common interests. Alex had told of the towns growing to the north, of a small herd of buffalo he'd seen along the trail. But his business interests meant little to Jed, just as Jed's concerns for the Nez Percé held little meaning for Alex. Despite the tenuous affection between her sons, it was best that each go his own way.

Laughing voices came from the darkness as the door swung open on Jed and Snow Flower. They had gone to the creek to bathe after supper in spite of the chill air, refusing Star's offer of her warm bathroom. Water dripping from his wet black hair stained Jed's buckskin shirt as he closed the door and looked down into his wife's shining dark eyes.

Star's heart contracted in sweet pain. They had been making love, she knew . . . out there in the dark grass beside the creek. As Jed crossed to the fireplace, rubbing his hands before its warmth, she heard a strangled sound from Alex, who shifted in his chair. He had seen it too, Star guessed from the pained expression on his face, that open, glowing love between Jed and his wife. Without a word, Alex rose and went outside into the darkness.

He might have gone out merely to relieve himself, Star told herself, yet she knew in her heart he had gone from them to hide his pain and envy.

"You'll have good traveling weather," Alex said when he returned sometime later. "The stars are out, clear as a bell."

Pouring himself another cup of coffee, he came to sit opposite Star in the other leather chair. Jed and Snow Flower sat on a blanket folded on the sandstone hearth. With loving hands, Snow Flower combed her husband's long dark hair, braiding it into two tight plaits.

"A good omen," Jed said, smiling at Alex. With one hand he reached to stroke his son's hair where Red Moon had moved to lay his head on his father's thigh. "A good omen," Jed repeated, and his eyes were on his son's drowsy face.

Everything changed, Star thought sadly, watching Alex's expression . . . and yet nothing changed. All the old envy Little Bear had felt toward his brother, Little Warrior, was there in Alex's dark eyes. It was of no consequence that he had succeeded in making a place for himself in the white man's world. His brother, who had turned his back on that world and become an Indian in every way, had what Alex longed for most in all the world: a loving wife and a son.

Chapter 23

1870

Star hung the dishpan behind the stove and stepped out onto the porch. The spring air was warm, sweet with the scent of new grass. Catkins from the cottonwoods littered the ground and newly arrived robins sang lustily. In the fenced pastures, new foals frolicked behind the staid mares. Beyond the corrals and stables, she could see Old Magpie sitting in front of the bunkhouse mending bridles.

With a sigh of contentment, Star sat on the steps between Alex and Charles, pulling the skirt of her doeskin gown down over her legs. On the red hill above the ranch house, long-needle pine trees sighed in the spring breeze.

Charles puffed on his pipe, his eyes surveying the ranch. Alex ground out the butt of his cigarette and immediately began making another.

Despite his usual pleasure in Charles's return to Wyoming, Alex had seemed ill at ease ever since the two men arrived from town. Star knew when he smoked this much, something was bothering him. Since the first thaw, she had known this summer would change their lives.

"I told you Cameron City would grow," Charles was saying. "It's in the right location to serve the ranches, the farmers, and the mines. One day it'll rival Cheyenne, you can bet on that."

"I have bet," Alex answered wryly. "Just about everything I own."

With a chuckle, Charles said to him, "Money loves you, Alex. I've told you that before."

Lighting his cigarette, Alex shrugged and did not reply.

Turning to Star, Charles continued. "If you haven't been to town since last fall," he said, "you're in for a surprise. There's a new dry-goods store, a saddlery, even a millinery." With a grimace, he added, "And of course, a couple more saloons."

"And more trail herds coming up from Texas," Alex broke in. "We're buying more cattle, Ma. There's plenty of open range and there's money to be made in beef." He flipped his cigarette butt into the dust of the ranch yard, staring gloomily after it. "Like Charles says . . . money loves me." He gave them a strained smile. "And I guess I've learned to love money too."

For lack of anything else to love, Star thought sadly, knowing how little love Alex found at home.

Alex rose, stretching. "I'd better make tracks if I plan to get home before dark." He held out a hand as Charles stood up. "Good to have you back with us, Charles . . . and good to know you're going to stay." Alex broke off, looking uneasy as Star rose to kiss his cheek.

Alex strode across the ranch yard to where his horse stood tied to a corral rail. Nearby stood the new surrey Charles had shipped west by train, its red paint shining in the late sun. Standing side by side in silence, Charles and Star watched him ride away. As horse and rider blended into the shadows lying long across the green meadows of the valley, she felt Charles's arm steal about her waist.

Gently, he turned her to face him, his gray eyes warm. "God, how I've missed you, Star."

Over his shoulder she could see her ranch hands riding in for supper. The cook yelled something at Old Magpie, who rose reluctantly at the summons. Taking Charles's hand in hers, she led him inside the house.

With the door closed behind them, Star surrendered to his embrace, to the urgency of his mouth against hers. The long and lonely winter seemed to dissipate from memory as her body warmed in response to his.

"Ah, my beautiful Star," Charles murmured, smoothing her long dark hair back from her face. "You're never more beautiful than dressed as you are now, so much like the girl who saved my life all those years ago."

"Then why do you keep bringing me all those white-woman clothes?" she teased, moving away from him, indicating the new trunk standing beside the fireplace.

His expression grew serious. "Because Cameron City is growing up and becoming civilized. Someday you'll have to take your place among its citizens . . . and I want you to be ready."

"Why must I take a place there?" Star demanded. "This is my home." With a sweeping gesture, she indicated the house and all the land around it.

"Red Hill Ranch is not the world, Star," he protested, taking her shoulders in his hands and looking lovingly into her face.

"It is my world," she replied, a bit annoyed with him. The annoyance melted beneath his warm kiss, as his strong arms gathered her close.

With a shaky sigh, she stepped out of his embrace. It was not yet dark. She dared not let things go too far when one of the ranch hands might still come to the house for some reason.

Trying to defuse the moment, she asked lightly, "What was Alex saying about your staying in Wyoming? Does that mean permanently?"

Charles bent to strike a match and light the fire already laid in the fireplace, for with sundown the air cooled quickly. To her surprise, he remained there, on one knee, his arm resting on the other knee as he gazed into the rising flames. A long ragged sigh escaped him.

At last, he stood up, his face earnest. "I hadn't meant to tell you right away," he began. "But then Alex . . ." He cleared his throat, reaching into the pocket of his gray corduroy jacket for the cold pipe he had placed there. "I'm building a house in Cameron City this summer."

"Why?" she asked, and felt her heart sink. She had known

this summer would bring momentous changes in her life, now she was certain Charles would tell her exactly what her foresight had only hinted.

Charles cleared his throat and turned back to stare into the fire. "Monique . . . my wife . . . has decided to move to Cameron City when the house is built." Almost apologetically, he continued. "She's grown dissatisfied with life in St. Louis, and then there's the boy. . . ."

"Your son—Will?" Star asked.

Charles nodded. "He's spoiled and rebellious. Monique can't handle him and she thinks he needs the full-time attention of a father."

"Perhaps she's right," Star said softly to his stiff back, a posture reflecting his misery. The years of companionship and love she had shared with Charles had been a transient gift. Now her heart ached with the knowledge that it must end.

"About that . . . she is right," Charles agreed. There was a moment's silence before he whirled and seized her in his arms. Looking deep into her eyes, he pleaded, "Tell me this won't change things between us, Star. I couldn't bear to lose you."

Gently, Star laid her hand against his cheek, meeting his look with loving eyes. "Oh, my dear friend," she said sadly, wondering how she could comfort him for what must be.

"Not friend," Charles protested vehemently. "My love, we aren't just friends."

"No," she answered softly. "We are dear companions, Charles, as well as lovers and friends." Postponing what must be said, she turned from his imploring eyes to add more wood to the flickering fire. Drawing a deep breath, she faced him squarely, knowing for a certainty now how her life would change.

Trying desperately not to let him see the deep sense of loss twisting her heart, she went on. "We will always be friends, my love. But we can't be lovers when your wife and child are in Cameron City." A long sigh escaped her. "When your wife was far away, I could make myself forget her existence. Now that she'll be here, I won't betray her."

Charles reached out and drew her gently into the circle of his arms. Smoothing back her hair, he kissed her forehead.

"Dear love," he said sadly. "I suppose I could have guessed you'd say just that." His arms tightened about her. "As much as it breaks my heart to let go, I won't ask you to betray your own principles. I suppose that's part of the reason I love you so . . . you'd never deliberately hurt anyone."

"She would be hurt, Charles . . . and so would the boy."

"Yes." His voice was low and strangled. For a moment, he held her so close she could feel his heart pounding against her breast. With loving hands, she stroked his hair and kissed his cheek. Only now did she realize how deeply she loved Charles. It was a love totally unlike that between herself and Hugh Cameron, without the mad rush of youth and passion. Yet it was equally precious to her.

Straightening, he looked gravely at her. "I want my son back, Star. Above everything . . . I want that."

"You shall have him," she promised, understanding his need and certain she spoke truth. Placing her mouth against his, she yielded to his passionate kiss.

Drawing a deep shaky breath, reluctantly holding her away, Charles looked at her with fierce possessiveness. "Will we have this summer then, Star?"

"Yes, Charles," she promised, unbuttoning his shirt in the old familiar way. "We will have this last summer together."

Closing the pasture gate behind his horse, Alex picked up the saddle and carried it to the tack shed. A violet-colored spring dusk lay over the ranch and the valley. In the meadows beyond, he could hear the bawling cattle gathered for the shove-up to high mountain pasture for the summer. Light gleamed from the cookhouse and the bunkhouse. Sounds of the talk and laughter of the ranch hands drifted out into the darkness.

Home. Standing beside the tack shed, Alex rolled a

cigarette and lit it. Light from the coal-oil lamps gleamed inside the house where he could see Katrin moving about her work. A pang shot through him when he recalled how his mother had greeted Charles, circumspectly of course, but with obvious affection. He would find no such greeting here. Fleetingly, he wondered how Star and Charles would resolve their relationship now that Charles's wife was determined to live in Wyoming.

Charles had asked about Jed, and Star had told of his visit last year . . . of his beautiful wife and fine son. At first, Alex had been sorry Jed wouldn't stay in Cameron Valley. Only later did he realize that the envy he felt toward his brother would have ruined their relationship. Even now, in some secret part of his heart, he guessed Katrin was drawn to his brother in a way she had never felt toward him. And Star . . . he was certain she still longed for the lost son.

With a bitter oath, Alex threw his cigarette to the ground and scrubbed it out with his boot. Jed was an anachronism, left over from the old life that had died with Hugh Cameron. It was Alex who belonged to the new world he was helping to build. He would be everything his brother was not . . . rich and powerful.

"What did you bring for me, Papa?" Maria greeted him as he entered the warm kitchen. Clasping his hand, she gave him a beguiling smile.

"Charles will bring the presents out tomorrow," he said, longing to hug his daughter and knowing she would simply stiffen and push him away. She frowned, pouting her lips at his reply, and dropped his hand.

"I suppose Charles is staying at Red Hill Ranch," Katrin said, her lips set in a thin disapproving line.

"Yes." Alex's reply was short. He would not discuss Charles and his mother's relationship with Katrin.

"Set a place for Papa," Katrin ordered her still-pouting daughter. To Alex, she added, "You could have brought her something from Cameron City."

"She doesn't need a present every time I go to town," Alex snapped. He sat down heavily at the table, suddenly depressed after the exhilarating day spent with Charles. It occurred to him that he had to buy his daughter's love, and his wife's love, just as he paid for the whores he slept with in Cameron City.

Katrin served his plate with a slab of juicy roast beef, creamy mashed potatoes and gravy, and carrots cooked with onions. Whatever her other shortcomings, she was an excellent cook, and a formidable housekeeper.

Looking as sulky as her daughter, she sat down at the table opposite Alex. "I would have liked to go into town with you," she said, her eyes accusing. "Mrs. Hamlin, the doctor's wife, asked me to call on her. She wants me to join the Ladies Literary Club she's organizing."

Alex concentrated on his supper, certain that whatever was on Katrin's mind was about to surface.

"The lumber mill foreman came by today with a load of lumber," she went on in a tight voice. "He said it was for the new house Charles is building in Cameron City. Is that true?"

"Yes," Alex answered. "Charles is building a house so that he can bring his wife and son to Wyoming to live." As soon as he said the words, he knew he was in for a scene.

Katrin's face contorted with fury. "You're as rich as Charles," she cried. "Why do I have to go on living in a log cabin so far from town I hardly ever see another woman? Why can't our daughter go to school with other children? Why, Alex?" Her voice rose, harsh and strident. "I'm your wife, Alex . . . why can't you give me the things Charles gives his wife?"

All the years of emotional loneliness, all the times she had rejected his need for love, boiled up inside Alex. He glared at her across the table. "Maybe Charles's wife is really a wife," he said in a hard flat voice.

Katrin recoiled, then quickly recovered her poise. "So that's it," she hissed, glancing at Maria, who was reading beside the fireplace. "That's always it, isn't it? You never think of anything else."

Breaking off a slice of bread, Alex mopped up the last of

the gravy from his plate. Just as he had so many times before, he tried to contain the anger and bitterness he felt toward his wife. It was hopeless. She could never understand what he really needed from her: not the physical act, but true loving.

The silence went on and on, until Maria glanced up curiously at them. When neither of her parents responded, the child shrugged and returned to her picture book.

At last Katrin broke the silence, her voice low and tense. "I'll give you what you want, Alex, whenever you want it. I'll be the wife you think I should be. But you'll have to give me a house in Cameron City, a house as fine as Monique Forester's."

For a long moment, Alex stared at her. She was still a pretty woman, with her round face, the pale skin jealously guarded from the sun, her full breasts and hips, the golden halo of hair as bright as ever. Yet he wondered now if he really wanted her.

"I'm not sure it's worth it," he said cruelly, and was pleased when she winced.

Watching her, he felt a flicker of ironic amusement as she changed her tactic. Smiling, she reached across the table to stroke his hand. Her voice was wheedling. "I've pleasured you, haven't I, Alex?"

Silent, he shrugged, nodding reluctantly.

"Tonight I'll show you I mean it. I'll do anything you want." She tilted her head in a coquettish manner.

"We'll see," he replied. With a wry smile, he thought he would let her worry for a while. The house would be built, if only for his daughter.

"Take off the damn nightgown," Alex growled later when Katrin came to the bed where they usually slept stiffly apart.

She hesitated for a moment, then meekly pulled the gown over her head and dropped it on the floor. Her pale nude body gleamed softly in the dark bedroom and Alex felt himself harden with desire.

Roughly, he pulled her down beside him and covered her

mouth with his. Katrin held her breath and stiffened beneath him. After a moment, Alex turned on his side, staring out the window into the pale starlit night.

Damn! he thought. He didn't want to love her. He wanted to take her brutally, hurt her, and somehow repay her for all the years of his own hurts. It was what she expected, he knew, as he listened to her quick, shallow breathing.

An ironic smile twisted his lips and he remembered the whore in Virginia City who had protested, "You make love like a damn bull." Because he had paid her for the whole night, she undertook to educate him in the arts of lovemaking. It pleased him to recall that by morning he'd even made her cry out with unexpected rapture.

Katrin lay tense beside him, waiting for him to mount her. Instead, Alex leaned over her, his mouth gentle and moist against her eyelids, gently tracing the curve of her cheek, nuzzling her throat, while his hands slid over her body in soft caresses. Lifting her full breasts in his big hands, he teased them with his tongue until the nipples hardened and he heard her draw in a quick breath.

His mouth and tongue traced the lines of her belly, her hipbones, his hands gentle. Alex felt her relax with a long sigh. Then he parted her thighs and she tensed again, protesting, "Alex . . ." With probing fingers, he caressed the most sensitive part of her, a sense of triumph flooding through him as her breathing quickened.

When he covered her body with his, her arms were tight around him, her mouth searching for his. He insinuated his tongue between her lips, probing the hot warmth of her mouth. Katrin moaned, deep in her throat.

Her body stiffened again when he entered her, but only for a moment. Alex cupped her hips in his hands, lifting her into the rhythm of his own movements. . . . Suddenly, she arched against him, her cry of fulfillment echoing with reckless abandon. Alex thrust deep into her, groaning aloud in the joy of release as he spilled his seed in her body.

Katrin lay deeply asleep beside him, but Alex stared, sleepless, into the darkness. For one rapturous moment they'd shared the ecstasy that is the heart of love. Then Katrin murmured, "The house, Alex?"

A shaft of pain shot through him. He sighed, knowing nothing had changed. "Yes," he answered. She turned on her pillow and fell asleep.

Beyond the window, he heard the nighthawk's lonesome call echoing beneath the sighing of the wind in the pine trees.

Chapter 24

1871

"You look very beautiful." Charles fastened the pearls at Star's throat and turned her to face him.

She looked down at the deep blue silk gown he had bought for her in St. Louis, amazed as always at how he knew the exact size of her slender figure. In the mirror above the dresser she saw her image reflected. Her pale copper skin was lightly touched with rice powder. The black hair worn in a braided coronet about her head had only a few strands of silver.

Seeing Charles's image reflected beside her, she sighed. He had grown so gray in the past year, and he'd lost weight so that the finely tailored black formal suit did not quite fit. Affection for him suffused her heart and she turned to cup his face in her hands.

"Dear Charles," she said. "Are you sure this isn't a terrible mistake?"

He kissed the palm of her hand lingeringly, then smiled down at her. "Nonsense, Star. You own half the town of Cameron City. When my wife gives a housewarming for all the leading citizens, you should certainly be there."

She stepped away from him, glancing around the hotel room. "Perhaps you shouldn't have come here. Did you just want to make certain I looked presentable?"

"I came here because I love you, Star," he said in a tired

218

voice. "If we can't have a life together, I intend to see that your life is a good one."

"Everything is changed now, Charles," she murmured. "Your family is here in Cameron City . . . and you must be discreet."

"You've forced me to be that," he answered with a wry smile. With a quick kiss on her cheek, he turned to pick up his silk hat from the bed. "I may be almost sixty, Star," he added, giving her a wink, "but the fire still burns."

"Charles . . ." she chided softly, knowing he wanted her and knowing that part of their life must be ended.

Settling the hat on his thick gray hair, Charles nodded. "Alex will come for you then, and I'll see you at the party."

When the hotel room door closed behind him, Star let out a long breath of relief. At least she hadn't revealed to him how terrified she was of this evening.

Charles's mansion had been completed this spring. With the coming of summer, his wife and son had arrived along with two box cars filled with furnishings for the house. Tonight was the housewarming to which all the substantial citizens of Cameron City, as well as the big ranchers living nearby, had been invited.

Star's invitation had been hand-delivered by Charles, although she had seen the engraved invitation Alex and Katrin had received through the mail. Somehow, Charles had contrived that she never meet Monique . . . until tonight. And Star smiled a bit sadly as she realized she had abetted Charles, for she had not been in Cameron City this summer . . . until tonight.

Again, Star's eyes turned to the mirror. For a moment she was startled by the sight of the strange woman looking back at her. This dark-haired woman dressed in elegant silk was surely not Falling Star, the Nez Percé girl who had run away with the white trapper, Hugh Cameron.

Ah, Shining Bear, she thought. If you had lived, perhaps it would have been different . . . better. We would have had our life together, living in the old way. I would never have been drawn into this white world where I will never be comfortable. I need you, Shining Bear . . . and tears burned her eyes.

Quickly, she dashed them away with her hand. Life went on, she told herself firmly, and there was no time for self-pity. Tonight was to please Charles, who had led her into the new world while the old one was dying.

Alex touched the whip lightly to the horse as their buggy rounded a bend and came in sight of the Forester mansion. He heard Katrin and Maria draw in their breath at the sight. Through the first dark of summer evening, lights gleamed from every window of the huge three-story house. Set on a rise at the edge of town, it dominated the surroundings . . . a huge, elegant house with two round towers, bay windows, and vast covered porches, all painted a pristine white.

"I stopped by to look at our house today," Katrin said as they passed the acreage at the foot of the hill where construction was under way.

Alex groaned. "God, Katrin, I wish you'd stay away. Every time you go over there, half the workmen quit."

"Well," she huffed. "If they were doing the job right, I wouldn't have anything to criticize."

"If you want the house finished," he growled, "leave them alone."

As the buggy entered the wide circular driveway lighted by torches, coming under the pillared portico, Alex caught Katrin's glare. Dismissing her with a shrug, he pulled up the horse and waited as a uniformed black man helped his wife and daughter descend from the buggy.

A young man took the horses' reins and Alex spoke quickly to him, telling him he would need the buggy in a few minutes. How much simpler it would have been to bring his mother with them, but he hadn't mentioned it, knowing what Katrin's reaction would be.

A crystal chandelier shed brilliant light over the mahogany-paneled foyer where Charles and his wife stood to greet their guests. Monique wore an elegant ivory satin gown with a bustled train trimmed by lace ruffles. At her throat was a three-strand choker of pearls and diamonds, and a diamond clip held an ostrich feather to her dark elegantly coiffed hair. She was a stately woman, full-figured, with a kind of aristocratic elegance that is gained only through a life of wealth and ease.

Civilization has really come to Wyoming, Alex thought. He had been in fine homes in Denver and Cheyenne, the homes of men he did business with, but this mansion Charles had built for his wife surpassed anything he had yet seen.

Amused, he saw that Katrin was struggling to conceal her awe at the opulent surroundings, smiling and nodding to Monique and Charles. Dressed in a rose-colored brocade gown, her pale hair elaborately curled, Katrin looked the part, even though her unease was obvious.

"Please go on in," Monique was saying in her cool, well-modulated voice. "There's champagne and a buffet waiting for you." Piano music drifted out to them, punctuated by voices and laughter.

"William!" Alex took the hand of the formally dressed boy standing beside the father he so strikingly resembled. The same thick brown hair and gray eyes, the same finely chiseled bone structure. "When are you coming out to the ranch again? We've missed you."

"Very soon, I hope, sir," Will replied politely. He shifted his feet, glancing at Maria, who was studying him with open admiration.

Frowning slightly, Alex watched his daughter. Dressed in a soft blue silk that accentuated the loveliness of her coloring, she seemed far more at ease than her mother. She opened her fan, giving Will a flirtatious backward look as they moved into the parlor. Alex drew in his breath. He hadn't noticed before tonight how tall she'd grown, or that her breasts were already budding. It made him feel suddenly old to be the father of a young woman.

"You look wonderful tonight, Ma," Alex said as the buggy entered the circular driveway once again.

"And so do you, Alex . . . as much like a nobleman as Charles."

He chuckled. "Who would ever guess that you and I grew up in moccasins?"

"Perhaps we should have stayed in them," she answered hurriedly, her voice wavering.

"The world moves on, Ma," he said, choosing to ignore her nervousness. "And we're moving with it."

The black man helped her down from the carriage and Alex took her hand, placing it in the crook of his arm. His smile was encouraging. Star took a deep breath, raised her chin proudly, and swept through the wide carved mahogany doors into the Forester mansion.

Already, the buffet was being served and the Foresters had joined their guests. Alex led her across the room toward Charles. Star could scarcely breathe for the multitude of impressions crowding in on her. Rooms filled with ornate mahogany furniture, thick brilliantly colored oriental rugs, gilt-framed paintings on the walls, heavy wine-colored brocade draperies at the windows, and crystal chandeliers glittering everywhere.

"You're here at last," Charles said, smiling, taking her hand in his. "Welcome to my home, Star."

He beckoned to his wife, who was standing nearby, chatting with a stout, bearded man. Flipping open her fan as she murmured her excuses, Monique moved slowly to join them, her face a cool mask.

Looking pleased with himself, Charles took his wife's arm, drawing the two women toward each other. "This is Star Cameron," he said. "I've told you how she saved my life."

"Oh yes," Monique's voice was like shards of ice falling. "The Indian woman." Ignoring Star's outstretched hand, she grasped Charles's arm. "Come, dear. I want you to meet Mr. Stanford. He's a railroad man from San Francisco."

With a dumbfounded expression on his face, Charles allowed her to lead him away.

"Bitch," Alex muttered under his breath, taking Star's hand in his.

Gathering all her defenses to present a calm exterior, Star drew a deep breath. "It's all right, son," she said in a low voice. "In this new world of yours, I expect we will have to grow used to such things."

From across the room, she caught Katrin's hostile glance. It was all a terrible mistake, Star knew. She'd allowed her affection for Charles to lead her to do something she had known was wrong. She did not belong here.

Alex's hand tightened on her arm as he watched her apprehensively. Now Star became aware of the covert glances of other women in the room. The air was filled with their animosity. Monique Forester was studiously ignoring her. Clinging possessively to Charles's arm, she chatted with Mr. Stanford. Charles looked distracted, his eyes straying to Star.

"She knows," Star said to Alex. It was evident that the good ladies of the town had wasted no time in informing Monique of her husband's Indian mistress. The price for the happy summers she and Charles had shared must now be paid.

"Oh God, Ma!" Alex groaned softly. "What are you gonna do?"

"Go talk to Mr. Stanford," she told him firmly, taking her hand from his grasp. "He's in railroads too." She managed a reassuring smile. "Let me handle this . . . please."

With a doubtful face, he moved slowly away from her. Chin up, a false smile on her face, Star walked calmly through the crowd of guests, and out the front door.

It was a long walk back to the hotel, she thought, ignoring the questions of the surprised black man. No doubt her fine kid shoes and the silk gown would be ruined by the gravel and dust. But that was of little consequence. After tonight, it seemed quite likely she would never wear her white-woman clothes again.

Chapter 25

"I was naive to think no one guessed at our relationship, Star." Charles paced before the ranch house fireplace, puffing angrily on his pipe. He paused beside the table where Star sat quietly drinking coffee and watching him. "God forgive me for placing you in such an untenable position." One hand stroked her shoulder gently. "Can you forgive me?" he asked.

"I should have told you," she replied. "Alex said there had been talk."

"Damn!" he snorted, and resumed his pacing.

For the past two days, she'd kept busy at the ranch, all the time wondering whether she had truly lost her one friend. Today Charles arrived, still filled with fury that the town gossips had gone to his wife almost as soon as she arrived in Cameron City.

"Like a true Frenchwoman, she planned to keep silent about it," Charles told Star.

"Until you brought me into her house," Star said grimly. She had lost the world of her girlhood, the world she had shared with Shining Bear, but she'd created her own world here in the shadow of the red hill, in sight of the towering Wind River mountains. It was wrong of her to seek to be a part of this other world that had come to Cameron Valley.

Suddenly Charles dropped into the chair beside her,

seizing her hand in his. With sorrowful eyes, he looked into her face. "I can't bear it that I've caused you pain, Star."

"Dear Charles," she answered, covering his hand with hers. "It was my fault. Never again will I deny my instincts. I knew I shouldn't go, but I wanted to please you."

He sighed. "You were right and I was wrong."

Squeezing his hand, Star rose and went to the stove to fill a cup of coffee for him. Somehow they would work out a new kind of relationship now . . . business partners, friends, no longer lovers.

Turning in his chair to watch her, Charles said, "Alex's house will be finished by fall. I suppose Katrin will be happy to live in town."

"If anything can make Katrin happy." Star gave him a wry smile, setting the coffee cup in front of him.

"There's a nice piece of property next to Alex," Charles continued, studying his steaming coffee. "Forester Creek runs through the back of it. I talked to Hansen, the builder, about putting up a house there."

"Why would you need another house, Charles?" Star asked, looking at him in surprise.

"Not my house," he said, looking self-satisfied. "Yours."

"You're mad, Charles." Her eyes widened in disbelief. When he smiled and shook his head, she protested quickly. "I don't plan to ever leave this ranch again. This is my place and I'll stay here."

The gray eyes regarded her steadily. "You've forgotten the one immutable rule of life, Star . . . change. You mustn't spend the rest of your life fighting against it as Hugh did." Taking a sip of coffee, he leaned back in his chair, smiling. "You're my business partner, Star. I need to have you in town to help run the businesses we own. Besides," he added in a teasing tone, "the people who own the town should be willing to live in it."

She could only shake her head doubtfully, remembering the animosity she'd felt from the women at Monique's party. Charles continued. "I've seen you do business with white men, and best them in their self-conceit. Now it isn't as though you can't afford a fine house. . . ."

Star smiled, conceding. "I'll admit you've made me a rich woman, Charles. But perhaps it's time to quit."

"Never say quit to Charles Forester," he said, then laughed at his own pompous tones. Once more his hand covered hers, his eyes pleading. "I'll see to the building, Star. You won't even have to look at the house until it's finished. Please . . ." He lifted her hand to his lips, his gray eyes dark with love. "Let me do this for you. You've given me so much."

She had not foreseen this, or even expected it. Now it seemed a logical progression. And how could she deny this man who had loved her for so long, who would never feel he had done enough to repay her for the life she had given back to him.

"All right, Charles," she said reluctantly. "Build the house."

It was a far more modest house than the Forester mansion, or even Alex's house which stood between the two. Two stories high, it had a square tower on the north side. At the front were matching square bays set with arched glass windows. The wide roofed porch between was supported by round pillars. Clapboard siding was painted a light cream color and now the painters were adding a deep blue trim around the windows and doors.

"Do you like it?" Charles asked anxiously.

"It's a beautiful house," Star replied, adding wryly, "but much too grand for a squaw." She had known that work continued on the house during the winter when the weather was open. But she had refused to come into town and look at it. Now Charles was back from the winter in St. Louis, where Monique had insisted they return so that Will could continue in school. As soon as his family was settled in Cameron City for the summer, Charles had come to the ranch for Star, insisting she must see the house.

"Don't say that," he snapped. "You're a princess, my dear, and you deserve the finest." Glancing with distaste at Alex's house nearby, where two gardeners were busy planting lawn and flowers, he added, "Breeding always shows."

Star smiled, for even her untrained eye had been offended by the plethora of gingerbread, curlicues, round and square towers, fish-scale and square shingle siding that Katrin had insisted on adding to her home. It was as though since she could not compete with the Forester mansion in size, she meant to outdo it in ornate decoration.

"Come inside," Charles said, pushing open the carved oak front door. "You'll have to start choosing furnishings so we can order them."

He seemed unaware of the sly smiles of the workmen. Star lifted her chin and ignored them. Since Charles meant to continue their friendship openly, in spite of the town gossips, she could be as strong and bold as he.

Following him through the spacious rooms, she marveled at his fine taste. Downstairs there were five high-ceilinged rooms with woodwork of hand-carved cherry. Each fireplace, one in the dining room and one in the sitting room, had a mantelpiece carved of black walnut, the opening framed in Dresden tiles. A wide staircase, its banister of the same black walnut, curved upward to the second floor, where there were four bedrooms and a bath.

"We'll have to build stables and a corral in back," Charles told her. "I've ordered a wrought-iron fence from Colby, the blacksmith. He's quite an artist, you know."

"I'm afraid it's more than I can handle," she said in a low voice. "A white woman's dwelling . . . while I belong in a skin lodge."

"Nonsense!" Charles turned on her, his gray eyes hot with anger. "It's the house of a princess; don't forget it."

Star drew a deep breath, looking down at the shining oak floors. There was something about the house that spoke to her, some intimate quality that made her comfortable here. Perhaps it was because Charles had put so much love into the place.

"I won't object anymore, Charles," she said, smiling as she touched his arm lightly. "It's a beautiful home and I'll always be proud of it."

"Good!" He gave her a relieved grin. "Now let me tell you what else is needed. I've ordered all the kitchen equipment

—stove, pump, sink—and it should be here soon. But you'll need really good furnishings . . . rugs, and crystal chandeliers."

Seeing how much he enjoyed the planning for the house, Star laughed softly. "Do I really have a choice, Charles . . . other than to pay for all this?"

"Of course," he replied. "The chandeliers are only a thousand dollars, more or less, and the rugs . . ."

Star gasped. "That's far too much. I'd rather use my coal-oil lamps."

"In this house?" He looked offended. Taking her arm, he led her back outside, through the carpenter and painter litter to the road where his horse and buggy waited.

When they were seated in the buggy, Charles cocked an inquiring eyebrow at her and gave her a teasing grin. "I can show you those very chandeliers, Star, and I know you'll agree they're worth the money."

Her eyes turned up the hill toward his white mansion gleaming through the cottonwood trees. "In your house?" she asked coolly.

Charles cleared his throat, looking a bit chagrined. "Not my house . . . Augusta's."

Amazed, Star gave him a level glance. "Don't tell me you resort to the whorehouse, Charles?"

Refusing to meet her eyes, but apparently undismayed by her disapproval, he replied lightly, "Monique is terrified of conceiving a menopausal child and she was never eager. We've slept apart for a long time. And you . . ." His voice fell. "You are too ethical to allow me your bed. What else am I to do?"

With a stab of pain, she felt his loneliness, deeper than hers because aloneness was part of her life. But their friendship endured, and she gave him a conspiratorial smile. "Are you going to take me to meet Augusta?"

After she had eaten supper in the hotel dining room, Star walked alone down the board sidewalk to the new brick building of the Cameron City Bank. Charles had set aside an office there for her private use, and she had her own key.

Charles was waiting in his office, the only light the oil lamp on his desk.

He grinned when he saw her, and winked. "We'll go out the back way." With a chuckle, he added, "What a scandal if the town gossips saw the two of us go in the back door of Augusta's."

A plump Negro maid with improbably red hair admitted them. From the front of the house came the sounds of raucous laughter, voices, the tinkle of a piano. Down a long, dim, thickly carpeted hall the maid opened a door and announced, "They's here."

Augusta was a tall, large-boned woman elegantly dressed in mauve silk with lace ruffles at her throat and wrists. Her light brown hair was piled in an elaborate pompadour, diamond teardrop earrings her only jewelry. The blue eyes looking Star over were sharp and discerning. With surprising grace, she crossed the room, holding out a hand in welcome.

"Miz Cameron," she said in a soft southern drawl. "You wanted to see my house." The emphasis was carefully placed on the word "house."

Charles chuckled. "Gussie," he said, and there was a chiding note in his voice. "Star just wanted to see your famous chandeliers."

"Any friend of yours, Charlie, is a friend of mine." Gussie chortled, opening the door to lead them toward the front of the house.

In the front parlor, three bored-looking young women in revealing gowns lounged on a red velvet sofa. At the piano a skinny sallow-faced man stroked the keys with lackadaisical fingers. There were no customers in the room.

Gussie proudly showed off the glittering chandeliers in the parlor and the foyer. "Austrian cut crystal," she said, eyes gleaming possessively. Charles pointed out the thick oriental rugs in deep glowing colors. "Turkish," Gussie corrected him. "They're the finest."

The front bell rang and Gussie abruptly hurried them back down the hallway. Tea had been laid in her private sitting room in their absence.

Holding the thin china cup of tea Gussie poured for her, Star tried to contain her amazement. Obviously, Charles had discussed her with this woman, yet he hadn't indicated that he knew Gussie this well. Perfectly at ease, he sat in the chair next to Gussie, sipping tea and making polite conversation.

"Gussie is from Atlanta," he said to Star. "Of the Atlanta Beauforts."

With a throaty laugh, Gussie said, "That don't mean much in Cameron City," she said. Sighing, she settled back in her chair. "Before the War Between the States, my daddy owned the biggest plantation in Georgia. After the war . . . nothing: no land, no slaves." Her heavy features tightened. "Daddy shot himself, poor man; no guts either."

After a moment's silence she continued. "I was all alone with no way to make my living, so I went into the business. Didn't like it much, so me and Lydie, my maid who's been with me my whole life, set up our own house." She gave Star a deprecating grin. "It's been right profitable, and I figure it fills a real need."

Charles laughed. "Seems to me a well-bred southern lady makes the best madam."

"Long as we have well-bred customers like you," Gussie replied in spirited tones, with a sidelong glance at Star.

"You're a survivor in a changing world, Gussie," Charles said affectionately. "Just like Star." And he reached over to briefly squeeze Star's hand.

Gussie smiled at Star. "Charlie's told me about you and I've got to say, you're a gutsy lady, doin' what you've done alone."

"I wasn't really alone," Star answered mildly. "I had Charles to help me." She met his fond glance with a smile.

Gussie's laughter boomed out. "We're an unlikely trio, ain't we? An Indian princess, an English nobleman, and a southern belle."

Star felt herself warm toward the big, hearty woman whose past surely contained horrors of which she would not speak. Gussie had survived and prospered. If her life was not one polite society approved, she had made the best of it.

They were alike in that. The sense of kinship grew as Gussie turned her friendly eyes on Star.

"I hope you'll come to see my house when it's finished," Star said as she rose to leave.

Gussie's face mirrored her astonishment. "Me? Come to visit in a house on Forester Creek? My God, Star Cameron, you don't know what you're saying."

Aware that Charles was regarding the two of them with unconcealed amusement, Star lifted her chin stubbornly. "I don't suppose you have any more friends than I do, Gussie. Maybe the two of us can be friends.

"I'll send you an invitation," she added as Charles held the door open for her, chuckling quietly to himself.

Gussie did not answer, simply staring after them in astounded silence.

Chapter 26

Sometimes it happened like this in late August . . . a cold rain filled with portents of the autumn to come. Star drew back the lace curtain of the parlor and looked out into the gray, drizzly day. Down the street she saw Augusta's black umbrella, and beneath it, moving with her usual purposeful stride, Gussie herself.

She glanced back to where she had set tea before the fireplace. It was all exactly as Gussie had taught her, the shining silver service on the marble-topped tea table, the cakes from Grossman's Bakery. In a way, Gussie had taught her almost as much as Charles, not about business, but about the little niceties of life.

Just as Gussie paused to open the gate in the iron fence Charles had ordered made with arrow-shaped posts, a black-haired child accosted her. Begging . . . and Star sighed as she watched Gussie fumble in her purse and place a coin in the outstretched hand. For some time now, she'd been aware of the half-breed children who ran wild in the streets of Cameron City, fatherless, neglected by the hapless Indian women who had borne them, and abandoned by the white men who had brought them here. Some of the women lived by begging, most by selling their bodies cheaply. What chance had those children, Star wondered, when there was no Indian village to offer them security, and they were outcasts in the white man's world?

"Miserable day." Gussie propped her umbrella on the porch and stomped the mud from her boots. She warmed her hands at the fire before sitting down to sip the steaming tea Star poured.

It had become a weekly ritual with them, and their conversation was comfortable and desultory. Star mentioned the new Masonic Hall just being built, and Gussie told an amusing story about a group of Masons who had reveled at her house recently.

"Funny thing," Gussie said, breaking the easy silence. "I had a young woman come to me the other day looking for a job. No experience, either." She pursed her lips, frowning. "Now that don't happen often."

At once, Star thought of the abandoned Indian women. "Who was she?"

"That's a funny thing too," Gussie replied. "She looked so pale and skinny, I had her come in and drink some tea, and Lydie fixed her a meal. We got to talking. . . ."

Star smiled, knowing Gussie's talent for easing information out of people.

"She's from Boston—a wealthy family. But she ran away with a low-class Irishman named Hanrahan. He came west to work on the railroad and dragged her along. By then, her family had disowned her and I could tell she's the kind that's too proud to go back." Gussie sighed. "Anyway, the damned Irishman up and died on her. She don't know how to do nothing to earn her way. Right now she's scrubbing floors at the hotel."

Stirring sugar into her tea, Star felt something leap within her. Lately, she had begun to think she'd lost her gift in her preoccupation with the ways of the whites. Now she felt its power possess her. The girl was important.

"Did she think prostitution would be easier?" she asked bluntly.

"She's not the kind," Gussie said decisively, reaching for another cake. "The life would destroy her. I told her no."

"What will she do then?" Star's voice was low, a sense of urgency flowing through her.

"I offered to loan her train fare back to Boston," Gussie replied. "She wouldn't hear of it." She sighed. "I guess she's back at the hotel."

"Send her to me." Gussie looked startled and Star realized her voice had been unnecessarily sharp.

"You can't save the world, Star," Gussie said with a wry smile. "Even though I know the power you wield in this town."

"What's her name?" Star interrupted.

"Caroline Hanrahan," Gussie replied. "The damned Irishman did marry her."

"Stop at the hotel on your way home and send her over here." Star's voice was urgent.

"Sure," Gussie agreed, studying her with puzzled eyes.

"Don't look so scared," Star told the frightened girl sitting on the edge of her chair. "I won't scalp you."

Caroline looked up, startled, and laughed nervously when she met Star's friendly smile. She was a slight girl, and too thin. Her dark brown hair was pulled back in a tight, unbecoming bun so that her cheekbones seemed to protrude from what could be a pretty, patrician face. The hazel eyes were tired, and wary. Star saw that the small hands clasped in the lap of the faded calico gown were raw and red.

"Miz Beaufort thought you might have work for me," she said in a faint voice.

"Tell me about yourself," Star said, pouring a cup of fresh tea for the girl and offering the plate of cakes left from the tea she'd shared with Gussie. They were accepted eagerly.

"I come from Boston," Caroline began hesitantly. Tears glistened in her eyes as she added, "But I can never go back there."

With gentle prompting, the story Gussie had told was repeated: the handsome, feckless Irishman who had caught her up in a whirlwind of passion such as girls from proper Boston homes seldom know, her family's wrathful disowning of her, the struggle to survive in the harsh environment of the railroad towns, and then her husband's death in a saloon brawl.

"It was all a terrible mistake," she ended in a low, shamed voice. "He wasn't a good husband, and I was a silly little fool who could only see his handsome face and listen to his wheedling."

Feeling the burden of the girl's misery, Star walked slowly to the window. In the cold, wet dusk of the muddy street, two children ran heedlessly . . . two of the black-haired half-breeds she had seen earlier. Their misery struck another chord in her heart. They could not pay to attend the local school, nor was there any way for them to learn to better their pitiful lives. Without a mentor like Charles, her life might have taken such a turn.

Struck by sudden inspiration, she turned back to Caroline. "Are you well educated, Mrs. Hanrahan?" she asked, certain from the girl's precise speech that she was.

Pride filled the thin, young face. "Yes, I am, Mrs. Cameron." Then her voice fell. "For all the good it will do me."

"I want to start a school," Star said firmly, the plan forming strong in her mind now. "For the half-breed children who can't afford the town school." She looked into Caroline's startled eyes. "Would you be willing to teach half-breeds? Here, in my house?"

"Oh, Mr. Cameron! Mr. Cameron!"

Alex groaned inwardly as Elizabeth Billings scurried across the bank in pursuit of him. Why Dave had married such a gossipy wasp of a woman, he couldn't imagine. But it was because of her pushiness that Dave had prospered since their marriage. He had borrowed from the bank to open his own dry-goods store and built a fine new house in the Forester Creek section of town.

"Good morning, Mrs. Billings," he said politely, lifting the rim of his wide-brimmed hat to her.

"I told the ladies I'd talk to you about it," she began at once, pursing her mouth, her gimlet eyes piercing him.

"And what's that, ma'am?" he asked tolerantly, knowing he could not escape her.

"Dave said you'd been away, delivering allotment cattle to the Indians at Fort Washakie, or we'd have come to you before now." She paused, self-importantly.

Seeing no need to reply, Alex waited for her to continue.

The words came in a rush, Elizabeth's face growing red with resentment as she spoke in bitter tones. "Nothing but ragamuffins. We can't have it in our neighborhood. It's simply beyond bearing and you must do something about it immediately."

"Ma'am, I don't even know what you're talking about." Alex tried to control his exasperation.

"Your"—she choked slightly—"your mother is running a school in her house for those half-breed hoodlums. The neighbors expect you to put a stop to it."

"What my mother does in her own house is her own business," Alex replied coolly, frowning at her.

"Go see!" she cried in self-righteous wrath. "See for yourself!" Tossing her head, she walked away, pausing to call over her shoulder, "Your wife will have something to say about it when she gets back, you can bet."

Alex shrugged and stepped up to the teller's cage to deposit the government draft he'd brought from Fort Washakie. Stupid woman, he thought as he walked out of the bank. Just the same, maybe he should go by Star's house and see what was going on.

The warm September day closed around him, the air filled already with the dry scents of autumn. The cottonwoods along the street hung lifeless in the unseasonable heat, their summer gloss fading. Mounting his horse, Alex rode slowly toward Forester Creek Road.

When your wife gets back, the blasted woman had said, and a faint misery struck deep inside him. Katrin and Bertha Hamlin had gone to Denver, where they would enroll Maria in that city's most expensive boarding school. Because she and Dr. Hamlin were childless, Bertha took a proprietary interest in Maria. The two women planned to stay and shop in Denver's fancy stores and see the musical shows at the opera house.

Katrin had made another of her demeaning bargains with him: give me this trip, give Maria this expensive school, and you can share my bed again. She considered the house paid for long ago. He'd taken her brutally, because he didn't care anymore. Afterward, she wept and he left the bedroom, cursing her and cursing himself. He felt soiled and ugly and empty. It was the last time he would lower himself to this. There were whores to take care of his needs. He would never touch Katrin again.

Now, he tied the horse at the iron hitching rack, smiling at Charles's fancy that had created the iron fence in Indian motifs. The surrey was gone from the stables in back of the house. Perhaps Star was at Red Hill Ranch, he thought, pushing open the front door.

Childish voices came from the dining room, intermingled with the low tones of a woman. Was this the school? he wondered, and paused in the dining-room door, surveying the scene with amazement.

Seven black-haired children of assorted ages were clustered around Star's fine mahogany dining table. At the head of the table sat a young woman, her dark brown hair in a soft pompadour framing the pale slender face intent now on the lesson. She was teaching the children numbers, with dried juniper berries as counters.

"If one plus one equals two," she was saying in a low, warm voice as she placed the correct number of berries on the numerals written on a sheet of paper. "What comes next, Ross?"

The boy hesitated, then reached for the juniper berries. As he did, the woman raised her head and her eyes locked with Alex's.

Something tugged his heart painfully, for in the soft depths of those hazel eyes, Alex sensed a loneliness as deep as his own. For a long, breathless moment, their eyes held, then she tore her gaze from his. He saw her slender hand tremble as she reached to correct Ross's sums.

"Dinner time."

Astounded, Alex stared at the plump black woman with bright red hair standing in the kitchen door, her dark gray silk gown covered by a voluminous calico apron. In the few weeks he'd been away, his mother had made some amazing changes in her household.

"You mus' be Mr. Alex," the black woman said as the children began pushing and shoving to form a line at the kitchen doorway. "I'm Lydie an' I come ever' day to make dinner for the chillun. You hungry?"

"No, thanks," he managed to say, watching in amused disbelief as the young woman marched the children into the kitchen, admonishing them to remember their manners.

In a moment, she returned, smoothing her hair, looking at him with wary eyes. Alex studied her, admiring the curve of her slender figure, the softly rounded breasts covered by a blue silk gown he seemed to recall his mother wearing.

"I'm Caroline Hanrahan," she said, holding out her hand. "The teacher . . ."

Alex enfolded the small warm hand in his, and felt his pulse leap in response to her touch. Caroline drew in her breath and pulled her hand away as though stung.

"Alex Cameron," he told her. Nodding toward the children chattering at their meal in the kitchen, he added, "If this is what the neighbors are complaining about, they can go to hell."

She laughed, and the hazel eyes were warm. "Maybe they're more upset about this. . . ." Moving gracefully, Caroline walked past him, through the sitting room to the tall windows looking out on the side yard. Smiling, she pointed out the half-finished skin lodge standing there beneath the trees.

"The children are helping Star build it," she explained. "She thinks it's important they know about their Indian heritage too."

"Umm." Alex shook his head in wonderment. The sight of the skin lodge brought back memories he had thought lost in the rush of the years.

"Your mother is a wonderful woman." Caroline turned to

look up into his face. "She helped me when I was desperate, gave me a place to live and a chance to earn my own way." Her voice grew defensive. "And she's helping the children too, no matter what the neighbors may think."

"I'm afraid I don't give a damn what the neighbors think," Alex said, his eyes devouring the earnest young face lifted to his. Her mouth was soft and vulnerable and he found himself wondering how it would taste beneath his own.

As though she guessed his train of thought, Caroline lowered her eyes. "Will you stay for supper?" she asked politely. "I'll ask Lydie to fix something before she leaves. Ordinarily, she works for . . ." Her voice fell and her face colored.

Alex chuckled. "I know where Lydie works."

"Oh." The flush on her cheeks deepened. Enchanted, Alex could not look away.

"I'll stay," he finally managed to say, his throat so clogged by a strange new yearning he could scarcely speak. He thought of the cold, empty house up the street where only Mrs. Schrader, the surly housekeeper, awaited him. "I'll stay, if you'll have supper with me."

Chapter 27

Lighting his cigarette, Alex leaned back in the chair and blew smoke at the ceiling. A blustery early fall wind rattled the windows, but here by the fireside it was pleasantly warm. He had never felt so relaxed, so completely at ease.

On the other side of the fireplace, Caroline bent over the table, preparing the lessons for tomorrow. Alex's eyes rested on her dark hair, shining in the firelight. His hand moved involuntarily, longing to touch her. When he sighed, she looked up and smiled, her eyes warm.

"When will Star be back, do you suppose?" she asked, stacking her papers neatly to one side.

"Depends on whether they run into trouble bringing the horses down from summer pasture," he replied. "A week . . . ten days, maybe two weeks."

With a nod, Caroline rose to take the papers into the dining-room schoolroom. Alex's eyes followed her graceful movements and a hot ache stirred in his loins. He should have been at his ranch, taking care of business just as Star was doing. But somehow he found excuses to stay in town. Buck Webster, his foreman, was a good man, a man to be trusted with the cattle. Still, a man who didn't look after his own business soon didn't have one and he couldn't go on neglecting his duties. He would have to ride to the ranch in the morning. It couldn't be postponed any longer.

After that first night he'd spent every evening here with Caroline, unable to make himself stay away. Lydie left a meal to be warmed for supper, for Caroline laughingly admitted she was no cook. Whether or not she could cook, Alex didn't care. She made him laugh, she listened to him with admiring eyes. She was warm and sweet and smelled like summer roses. After supper she played the piano for him while he sat by the fire, surrendering to an unfamiliar sense of contentment.

When she came back into the room carrying a tray with coffee and cake, he thought his heart would burst with wanting her.

"What is it, Alex?" she asked, staring at him.

Quickly, he leaned to flip his cigarette stub into the fire, wondering whether she had seen the naked desire on his face. Something about her remained appealingly innocent, even though she had been married and widowed.

"I'll have to go to the ranch tomorrow," he said, not meeting her eyes. "They're driving the cattle to winter pasture."

"Oh . . ." Her voice fell in disappointment. "How long . . ." She let the words trail away, her eyes holding his.

Elation made his heart pound. Did he only imagine the yearning in those brief words, the desire in her warm hazel eyes. Had she come to feel as he did in the past few days . . . that something was drawing them to each other inexorably?

When she sat down and began pouring coffee, the moment slipped away. Alex wondered if he had dreamed it for wanting her so.

Piano music, faint and far away, drifted in the cold September dusk. Walking down the creek bank path that led to his mother's house, Alex smiled. Charles had insisted on buying the piano for Star, but it had never been used until now . . . until Caroline came into their lives.

He'd slept badly last night at the ranch, hating the dusty, deserted air of the place that had once been home, and unable to put this longing from his mind. The drive was going well, the calf count was good. With a few peremptory instructions, he'd left this afternoon, riding hard to get back to Cameron City.

When he opened the kitchen door, he could smell Lydie's stew simmering on the stove. Music flowed through the house, drawing him like a magnet.

Caroline sat on the piano stool, her straight, elegant back turned to him, her slender white hands moving gracefully over the keys. She did not even seem startled when he gently placed his hands on her shoulders, merely lifted her head to smile at him.

"I've never heard that before," he said in a low voice. "It's beautiful."

"It's Mozart," she answered, and let the music trail away, unfinished, as she rose to face him.

"Caroline . . ." His voice was thick with longing. Then she was in his arms, her body pressed fiercely against his, her soft mouth responding eagerly to his kiss. Her lips parted beneath his and the sweet musky taste of her tongue filled his mouth.

Gasping for breath, they broke apart. "Darling . . . darling," she murmured against his throat, her arms tight about his shoulders. "I didn't guess I could miss someone so much in just one day."

"Neither did I," he choked. Alex slid his hands down the curves of her back, cupping her hips to press her against the hot hardness of him, wanting her with such intensity he could have taken her that moment . . . fully clothed and standing up. "Oh God, Caroline," he groaned, pressing his face against her soft hair. "I need you . . . want you."

The hot moistness of her lips teased at his ear, moved along the curve of his chin to pause, a breath from his own mouth. "I love you, Alex," she murmured breathlessly, "love you so, darling, darling . . ."

His mouth took hers in a devouring kiss, and his whole body seemed to take flame.

Tearing her mouth from his, Caroline cupped his face in her hands. Her lovely eyes were grave and steadfast as they looked deep into his. He sensed that she had made a decision. Unspoken consent passed between them. Without a word, she took his hand and they mounted the stairs together.

No word was spoken until she had closed the bedroom door and turned down the covers. With a shyly loving smile, she stood before him, unbuttoning her shirtwaist with trembling fingers. Carefully, Alex took the pins from her hair, letting it fall in a dark cloud about her shoulders, his fingers reveling in its soft warmth. Bending, he began to kiss her face . . . her eyes, her ears.

"Alex," she protested with a soft laugh. "Help me undress."

Never taking his eyes from her face, he undid the button of her skirt. When it fell to the floor, he pushed the petticoat down over her hips. Then he pulled the straps of her chemise down, kissing her pale bare shoulders, pulling the garment down about her waist so that he could bury his face against the sweet warmth of her breasts.

Her clothing in a heap beside the bed, Caroline lay against the white sheets. There was no hesitation in the way she held her arms up to him, her eyes dark with longing. Tugging off his own clothes, Alex lay beside her, seizing her in his arms, filled with a wild urgency to possess her.

Their mouths melded, hot and moist. He felt her soft hands caressing his back, stroking his hair. Then she broke away from his kiss. "Wait, darling," she murmured. "I want to look at you."

Forcing himself under control, Alex lay on his back, watching with devouring eyes as her lips and hands moved over his face. Her hot tongue moved along his ear, teased at the pulse pounding in his throat, caressed his nipples. Her own taut nipples made a trail of fire across his chest as she moved downward, hands and lips exploring his body. Gentle, stroking fingers lifted his passion to almost unbearable need.

"I love you, Alex," she said softly, leaning across his chest and looking into his eyes. "I didn't know I could want someone so terribly. . . . I love you."

He turned her on her back, wanting with all his being to

take her now and assuage this pounding need. But he kissed her as she had kissed him . . . the hot pulse at the base of her throat, the full erect breasts thrusting against his tongue, and at last the sweet moist core of her being where his gentle stroking fingers made her gasp and lift her hips into his touch.

"Alex!" Her voice was urgent, her hands hot on his back.

He entered her with gentleness, but she lifted her hips to take him deep inside her.

"Caroline," he groaned as their mouths joined. "My love . . . my love."

Her movements answered his in frenzied passion, building, building . . . until he felt her stiffen beneath him and cry his name in wild abandon. His cry answered hers as his body exploded in rapture.

Twilight filled the room with lavender shadows, and Alex pulled the blankets over them against the cooling air. Utterly drained, they lay in close embrace, Caroline's head pillowed on his shoulder. Stroking her soft hair, Alex pressed his mouth against her forehead.

"I love you," he said, and the words were filled with wonder at this miracle that had happened to him. "I love you, beautiful Caroline," he repeated, amazed at the reality.

"Darling Alex," she murmured against his throat. "I think I must have run away from home just so I could find you."

Alex laid his hand against her cheek, his whole being overflowing with gratitude. "Dear love," he said in a low choked voice, "I've been looking for you all my life."

They had scarcely slept that first night in their insatiable desire for each other. And all the nights of the week since, Alex thought, and the days broken only by the necessary presence of the children and Lydie.

Lydie knew, he was sure of it, and it seemed to please her as she went her blithe, unassuming way. And so, of course, she must have told Gussie. Perhaps everyone in town knew . . . and Alex didn't care. He intended to marry Caroline as soon as a divorce could be arranged. Nothing could stop him from having her in his arms every night for the rest of his life. He had found his mate, his home, at last.

Business occupied his days while the school was in session: the lumber yard, the store, the bank. He and Charles were working out a new business venture: shipping cattle by railroad to the slaughterhouses in Omaha. If the market worked, the cattle business would boom and they would make another fortune. Charles would be leaving for St. Louis late this year. Monique had delayed their departure to complete the ballroom she'd added on to the mansion.

Alex had gone home to change clothes, and walked now along the creek-side trail as he had done every evening since that first night together. As he opened the back corral gate, he saw his mother's surrey, her matched team munching hay being forked down to them by Clint, the stableman.

"Damn!" he said aloud, then grinned at his own reaction. It was the first time in his life he remembered not being glad to see Star. But he couldn't stay with Caroline when his mother was in the house, nor could he take her to his own place.

"Damn!" he said again as frustration burgeoned in him. He'd been thinking about her all afternoon, and just now on the path, wondering if she'd want to make love before they had supper.

The door banged shut behind Alex and Star looked up, closing the oven door on the pan of baking-powder biscuits she'd made to go with the chicken Lydie had left simmering.

"Hello, Ma," he said, looking at her almost as though she were a stranger.

Touching his arm, she gave him a quick peck on the cheek. "You must have been busy in town," she said, pulling the coffeepot to the front of the stove. "I went by your place and pointed out to Buck a few chores he'd been neglecting."

Puzzled, she watched his face, for he seemed not to hear her, his eyes on the doorway leading into the dining room. "Caroline here?" he asked.

"In the sitting room," Star answered, turning as he walked past her. "There's whiskey on the sideboard if you want a drink," she called after him. "And you might as well stay for supper."

Alex paused to splash whiskey in a heavy crystal glass. Star followed him into the sitting room, where the air seemed suddenly as charged as in the midst of an electrical storm. Caroline and Alex did not speak, simply looked at each other with fevered, yearning eyes.

Drawing a long breath, Star thought: So it has happened. She had known these two were fated, known it from the time she first heard Caroline's name. But she hadn't guessed it would be so soon.

After a moment, Alex crossed in front of the fireplace to where Caroline sat with the mending on her lap. As though he had been doing this forever, he laid his hand on her shoulder in a way that seemed an act of love. Without looking at Star, Caroline covered his hand with hers and leaned her cheek against his arm, her face suffused with tenderness.

"Alex is staying for supper." Star broke the tense silence.

"Shall I set the table?" Caroline asked unsteadily, forcing herself under control as she folded the mending neatly into her basket.

"Please," Star replied, watching as Alex's hungry eyes followed the girl from the room.

With an uneasy glance at her, he sat down in the chair Caroline had vacated, gulping his whiskey.

"So . . ." Star began abruptly. "What are you going to do now?"

He finished the whiskey and set the glass on the table. Star knew he would not protest or pretend not to understand. He knew her too well and knew the depth of her insight, something he had always respected.

Standing up, Alex went to the fireplace, where he bent to add a log to the fire. Then he turned to face her squarely. "I'm going to divorce Katrin," he said in a hard voice. "I should have left her long ago."

"Divorce is not so easy, Alex," Star said softly. "It takes a long time. What will Caroline do until you're free?"

"Are you going to throw her out?" he demanded, glaring at her.

"Don't be a fool," she said impatiently. Her eyes slid away from his. "Do you think I'd condemn you for something I've done myself?"

His face colored and he did not reply. Star waited. At last the words burst from him. "I love her, Ma . . . like I've never loved anyone or anything."

"I know," she said softly, staring thoughtfully into the flickering flames. From the dining room came the sound of Caroline's quick footsteps, the soft clink of china and cutlery. "She's very easy to love," Star added with an affectionate glance toward the sounds. Alex's face softened at the words.

"That Dutchman Vanderpool came to see me today," Star said in a deliberate voice. "He wants to sell the cottage he built on Second Street. He's moving to Rock Springs."

Alex frowned, puzzled by the abrupt change of subject.

"I'm going to buy it," she finished decisively. "I'll sign it over to Caroline."

Moisture gleamed in his dark eyes as Alex looked down at her, his face filled with loving gratitude. Her heart aching for all the lonely years he had lived without love, Star reached up to lay her hand tenderly against his cheek.

"Every woman should have something of her own," she told him.

Chapter 28

"You could have been there to meet my train," Katrin's vituperative voice was not diminished by the fact that she was lying in her bed, staring up at Alex. Her pale hair hung in two long braids against the pink satin pillows. In the light from the tinted glass globes of the bedside lamps, her full breasts strained the white silk and lace of her nightgown.

"I was at the ranch," he replied reasonably, "and you didn't let me know when you were coming back." He'd expected to change from his ranch clothes and walk to his mother's where Caroline was staying until the cottage was repainted and furnished.

"Have you seen Bertha?" Katrin demanded in querulous tones. "Have you talked to anyone?"

"Only Mrs. Schrader, who greeted me in her usual sweet manner," Alex replied sarcastically. The housekeeper had never bothered to conceal her dislike of him. When he met her on the stairs just now, her scrawny face twisted in disapproval and she mumbled something about "Men are such beasts."

"Then you don't know," Katrin cried, tears overflowing.

"Know what?" he said impatiently. "And for God's sake, what are you doing in bed in the middle of the afternoon?"

"You bastard!" Katrin screamed, flinging one of the satin and lace pillows at him. Alex ducked and heard something glass fall and shatter behind him.

Her face contorted with fury, Katrin heaved herself to a

sitting position, glaring at him. With every word she spoke, the strident tone of her voice rose higher. "You never think of anything but your own pleasure, Alex. You made me pay for the trip to Denver, and now—" She broke off, sobbing, struggled for control, and continued in a high angry voice. "You selfish bastard, you've got me pregnant."

All the strength seemed to pour out of him. Dear God, he thought, surely that miserable joining hadn't resulted in a child. "You're nearly forty, Katrin," he said, in a low controlled voice. "You couldn't be pregnant. It's probably menopause."

Another pillow flew past his head, landing harmlessly against the ivory damask draperies. "What do you know?" she screamed. "All you care about is satisfying your disgusting needs." Tears poured down her face as she pounded her fists futilely on the pink satin comforter. "I started with morning sickness in Denver. Dr. Hamlin examined me as soon as we got home. I'm pregnant!" She shouted the last words at the top of her voice. Covering her face with her hands, she burst into wild sobbing.

Sickness poured through Alex. Sweet Caroline, he thought painfully . . . dear God, sweet Caroline . . . what will this mean to us? He felt immobilized, trapped as Katrin had trapped him again and again since the very beginning when, in his ignorance, he had believed she loved him.

"Get out!" she screamed, searching for another pillow to throw. "I can't bear the sight of you."

Moving mechanically, stunned and heartsick, Alex opened the door to Star's kitchen. From the sitting room he could hear the sound of the piano and he had an irrational urge to weep. Music was one of the joys Caroline had brought to his life, and now, for one stupid act done in anger and revenge he would lose her. No court in Wyoming would grant him a divorce while Katrin was carrying his child.

For a moment, he paused in the doorway, surveying the pleasant scene before him: Caroline, intent on her playing, her slender fingers flying over the keys, and Star leaning back in her easy chair beside the low fire, eyes closed, caught up in the music.

When he stepped into the room, Caroline whirled on the piano stool. At once, she rose and came toward him, her hands outstretched, her face aglow with love. Something painful clutched at Alex's throat as he seized her in his arms and held her close, his lips against her soft hair. With all his heart he wished this moment might last forever.

Then he heard his mother stir, and met her eyes over Caroline's head. In the depths of her dark eyes, he saw apprehension, and heard it in her low voice as she said, "Katrin's home. We saw her go past in the Hamlins' carriage."

"Yes." His voice sounded strangled with the effort to hold back his pain and anger.

Something flickered in her eyes, some deep sorrow. Alex felt his eyes sting with the certainty that she knew. But her voice was brisk when she spoke. "We didn't know you'd be here tonight. Caroline and I have had supper, but I'll warm something up for you."

Without waiting for his reply, she walked out of the room, carefully closing the door behind her.

Alex's mouth sought Caroline's as though to draw comfort from her kiss. She responded passionately, holding nothing back. At last, she drew away from him. When she looked earnestly into his face, he saw that he had not concealed his tension from her.

"What's wrong, Alex?" she murmured, cupping his face tenderly in both hands.

Forcing himself to turn away from her, Alex shoved his hands in his pockets and stared blindly at the fire. There was no easy way to say it. "Katrin's pregnant."

"Oh . . ."

Alex's heart twisted painfully. He thought how often she used that one simple word, and how effectively. It had told him that she loved him, and now he heard it in accents of despair.

Unable to refrain from touching her, Alex took her by the shoulders, looking intently into her face. "It happened before she went to Denver . . . before I ever met you, Caroline. Now, I wouldn't touch her. . . ."

His voice fell as she placed her fingers gently against his lips. "She's your wife, Alex. It's not . . . not . . ." Her control broke then and she flung herself against him, holding him fiercely as she wept against his shoulder.

Damn Katrin . . . damn her, Alex cursed silently as he held Caroline's weeping figure close, gently stroking her back. Drawing a deep breath, he lifted her chin in his fingers and kissed away the tears.

"It won't make any difference to us, my sweet love," he said decisively. "Only that I won't be able to get a divorce until after the baby is born."

"What if it's the son you've always wanted?" Caroline asked.

For one brief, unspeakable moment, Alex hesitated, then he said firmly, "I love you, Caroline. You're the only thing that matters to me."

Slowly, she drew away from him, taking a handkerchief from her sleeve to wipe her tear-wet face. Silence grew as she stared into the flames in the fireplace, studying them as though an answer lay there.

"You can't leave her," she said, in a voice so low he strained to hear the words. "Not while she's pregnant . . . not ever if she gives you a son."

"No!" Alex protested, reaching out to touch her slim shoulders.

Turning, Caroline looked up into his unhappy face with a tremulous smile. "I love you with all my heart, Alex," she told him. "I would die rather than lose you." He drew a deep painful breath as she interlaced her fingers with his, lifting his hand to caress it with warm, loving lips.

Love for her filled him with a bitter mixture of pain and joy as Alex drew her into his arms. Caroline's lips trembled, but she managed a teasing smile. Looking into his eyes, she asked softly, "Will you have me for your mistress, Alex?"

With a sigh, Star closed the ledger and turned to look out the study window at the yellow cottonwood leaves drifting on the wind. Years might have passed, so much had happened in such a short time. In August, Caroline had come to her and now, as October drew to an end, she had gone to live with Alex in the Dutchman's cottage.

An ironic smile touched Star's lips with the thought that in a Nez Percé village the situation would have been accepted without comment. If a warrior's first wife proved unsuitable, he was free to take another as long as he provided for the wife he set aside. But Alex was not a Nez Percé warrior.

And Cameron City was not an Indian village. Its inhabitants had even forgotten that it was once a railhead hell-town. Nearly three thousand people lived here now, Charles had told her, adding that already they were divided into classes almost as rigid as those he'd known in England. The merchants and the wealthy cattlemen, the bank manager and the railroad superintendent—all built fine homes along Forester Creek Road. Shop clerks, married railroad men and small businessmen lived in the houses on Second Street. Then there were the itinerant cow hands, the emigrants passing through, the gamblers and harlots who plied their trade in the saloons. Four saloons in the town now, two general merchandise stores and a dry goods, as well as a feed and farm equipment. The Methodists had built a church and the Baptists met in an empty storefront. A Catholic priest came out from Cheyenne once a month to celebrate Mass in the borrowed Methodist church.

Star kept aloof from the society of the town, content with her life divided between Red Hill Ranch and the encircled world she'd made of her town house. But she guessed how difficult it must be for Caroline to choose to live openly with another woman's husband, and she knew how lonely the girl must be.

Yet Caroline had settled happily into the cottage, making it into a snug home. Star had the piano moved there, thinking it would be a comfort to Caroline, even though she missed the music herself.

School went on as before, with Caroline coming each day

to teach the children. Lydie came to do the cooking still, staying longer now, cleaning up through the house where she felt the weekly cleaning woman had not done an adequate job.

Everyone in Cameron City knew Alex Cameron, the man who owned half the town: the bank, the lumberyard, the general store, the hotel. He was a cattle king who lived in one of the biggest houses in town. He wore tailor-made suits and hand-sewn boots when he went to town. His pearl-gray Stetson would have cost an ordinary cow hand a month's wages. People spoke in sly whispers of the mistress he kept in the cottage on the street behind the bank. He went to the big house on Forester Creek now only to change clothes and make sure the servants were performing their duties and the bills were being paid. His horse was turned into the small stable behind the cottage, and stayed there through the nights.

"Miss Augusta said to tell you she's comin' over this afternoon," Lydie said as Star walked into the kitchen where she was washing the children's lunch dishes. A reading lesson was under way in the dining room with each pupil taking a turn reading aloud. Caroline's soft voice prompted them when they stumbled over the words.

"Good," Star replied, smiling. "She hasn't been to visit for quite a while."

"She thought maybe you had enough scandal to deal with right now." Lydie inclined her head toward the dining room with a significant look in her black eyes.

Star shrugged. "What would the town talk about if not the Camerons?"

Lydie drew a deep ominous sigh, her face suddenly grim. "Miss Augusta got somethin' important to tell you," she announced, then unable to keep the secret, burst out: "She's fixin' to leave Wyoming."

Surprised, Star studied Lydie's sorrowful face. "Where will she go?"

"Back to Georgia, she says." Lydie's eyes glistened and

her words grew shaky. "Buy back the ol' plantation with all the money she's made." For a moment, Lydie stared mournfully into the pan of dishwater, then burst out once more, "I cain't go back there, Miz Star. The war ain't truly changed things, an' I cain't be a slave agin."

"But you're free, Lydie," Star protested. "You've always been free."

"Not in Georgia," Lydie said. "Miss Gussie offered me the house if I wanted it, but I cain't do that neither, not alone." She seemed to gather her courage before she turned her black eyes full on Star. "Kin I stay here with you, Miz Cameron?"

"Would Gussie mind?" Star asked, and with those words realized how much she had come to depend on this woman, how much she would miss her company. Lydie was even a part of this house Charles had built, for it was she who had seen to the planting of the lilacs and the roses in the yard, organized the kitchen, and instructed the cleaning woman.

"She sez I'm to please myself," Lydie replied defiantly.

Star hugged her impulsively. "I'd be proud to have you stay with me, Lydie."

When the children were leaving for the day, Caroline lingered. With a wry smile, she asked Star, "Could I stay for supper? The Foresters are having a farewell party tonight before they leave for St. Louis. Katrin threw a fit and insisted Alex go with her. I guess he's going so as not to offend Charles."

"I'm sorry, Caroline," Star said, squeezing the girl's arm. So Monique's extravagant ballroom was finished. Its building had kept Charles in Cameron City far past the usual time and Will had traveled alone to his uncle in order to enter school. "Please stay," she told Caroline. "Gussie's coming over."

"I made my choice, Star," Caroline mused, looking out the kitchen door reflectively, down the path where Alex used to come to her. Golden leaves drifted from the cottonwoods, and the willows along the creek were russet. "But sometimes it's a lonesome one."

Sliding her arm around the girl's slender shoulders, Star hugged her briefly. I made the same kind of choice once, she thought . . . to leave my people and their ways, to make my life with the white trapper, Hugh Cameron . . . and for me too sometimes it was a lonesome one.

Just then, Gussie's driver, a moon-faced old fellow with less than all his wits, appeared at the kitchen door carrying a large box. "Miss 'Gusta says put this on ice," he told them, adding with a quizzical expression, "I got the ice in the buggy."

Lydie bent over to look in the box and laughed heartily. "Champagne! That's my Gussie. She likes to go in style."

The driver struggled back in with a gunnysack of ice and another box, this one of tinned oysters.

Lydie laughed again. "Reckon she wants one of Lydie's good oyster stews . . . for the last time."

"We'll have a party of our own," Caroline announced when told of Gussie's plans. "A farewell party."

With a knowing wink, Lydie told her, "I figger that's what Gussie had in mind."

Gussie's carriage arrived at dusk, driving up Forester Creek Road in the midst of all the fine carriages bringing the cream of Cameron City society to Monique's ball. From the open windows of the great house on the hill, the sound of the orchestra hired from Denver poured out in the unseasonably warm autumn dusk.

"We didn't even have to pay for the orchestra." Gussie's laughter boomed out as they sat down to begin their supper.

Caroline had set the table with the Irish linens, the Spode china, and the heavy silver Charles had purchased and Star seldom used. From the garden, she'd managed to gather a few late roses and some fading chrysanthemums, arranging them with golden cottonwood leaves into a colorful centerpiece. Candles glowed in the tall silver candelabra, casting a warm golden light over the four women at the table. From the kitchen came the tantalizing odor of Lydie's oyster stew, thick with butter and canned milk.

Filling their thin crystal glasses with champagne, Augusta

looked around the table. "A toast," she said, raising her glass. "To us . . . the untouchables." Taking a sip, she sat down her glass, surveying the puzzled faces watching her. "In my long and checkered career," she said with a throaty chuckle, "I never sat down at a table with three finer ladies, and not one of us would be welcome at the big house on snob hill."

"I've been to parties like that one," Caroline said, smiling at Gussie, "and I'd rather be here." In spite of being denied Alex's company, Star thought Caroline looked relaxed and happy, and the champagne had brought a flattering glow to her young face. Everything about Caroline seemed softer and fuller now.

"I wouldn't be settin' at no table up there." Lydie chuckled as she rose to bring the china tureen of oyster stew from the kitchen.

While Lydie served the food, Gussie refilled the champagne glasses. Her face grew thoughtful, and she sighed, emptying her glass in one gulp. "I'm a liar, ain't I, Lydie?" she burst out. "I wouldn't be goin' back to Atlanta to flaunt my money if I didn't want to be invited to places like the Foresters'."

"It's your home, Miz Augusta," Lydie said, but her face was doubtful and she kept her eyes on the thick rich stew she was serving into china bowls.

"That's right," Gussie agreed, pouring more champagne. She began to regale them with hilarious stories about her adventures in what she called "the trade."

Laughing with the others, Star still felt a wrenching sense of loss. This friend would soon be far away, and she'd had so few friends in her life. The world Gussie was returning to was so foreign to her, she could not guess what the outcome would be. If the women in Atlanta were like Monique Forester, all Gussie's money would not buy their acceptance. But tonight was not for sadness, or fear of the future; tonight was for laughter and friendship and happy farewells.

"Mr. Cameron!" The pounding on his bedroom door grew louder, and Alex groaned. Sitting up, he clasped his head. That damn champagne! It always gave him a head-ache.

"Mr. Cameron . . . come quick!" Mrs. Schrader's frantic voice finally penetrated his consciousness. Reaching for his robe, he opened the door of his bedroom.

"For God's sake," he grunted. "What's the matter with you?"

"It's your wife, you fool." The woman glared at him. "She's taken sick."

"No wonder," he growled unsympathetically. "She tried to drink all the champagne at the Foresters' party." And she had made a fool of herself dancing endlessly with that foppish cousin of Monique's. He'd felt like slapping her and dragging her home. She was three months pregnant, but no one was aware of it because of the cleverly concealing gown she'd chosen. That sappy Louis Chartrand had fawned over her all night as though he had a chance at more than an evening's flirtation.

"She's having labor pains," Mrs. Schrader said, glaring at him. "I've sent the stableman to bring Dr. Hamlin."

Pulling on his pants after the housekeeper had gone back to Katrin's bedroom, Alex cursed softly to himself. All he had put Caroline through because of this baby—postponing a divorce, making her an outcast, an object of scandal—and now Katrin was likely to miscarry just as she'd done so many times before.

There was nothing he could do. Katrin did not want him in the room. The doctor arrived; the door was closed and the screams went on and on. Alex lit the fire in the front sitting room and poured himself a whiskey to ease his headache. Depression settled over him like a dark cloud. Watching dawn fill the sky, he wondered whether any other man had made such a mess of his life. But he had Caroline, and he loved her, more than he would have believed himself capable of loving. When this was over . . . he'd make it up to her.

"Sorry, Alex," Dr. Hamlin said, pulling his frock coat about his rotund figure. "She lost the baby . . . a boy."

"A boy," Alex repeated, torn by a sense of irreparable

loss. The son he had longed for all these years, lost because his wife danced half the night and drank too much champagne.

"She's always had difficulty carrying to term," the doctor continued in a consoling voice. Clearing his throat, he added diffidently, "She shouldn't have another child."

Giving him an ironic glance, Alex growled, "I can assure you of that, doctor."

Embarrassed, Dr. Hamlin quickly took his leave. He knew all about them, Alex thought, through Bertha, all about Caroline, and all about his and Katrin's constant battles.

"Aren't you at least going up to see her?" Mrs. Schrader demanded, pausing at the foot of the stairs to fix her hostile eyes on him.

"Sure," Alex said wearily.

"You're not going to put me through that again," Katrin spat the words at him as soon as he opened the bedroom door.

"You can count on it," he replied sarcastically.

Propped on her satin pillows, she glared at him. "I suppose I can." She sneered. "Now that you have your whore."

"You rotten bitch," he said in a low hard voice. "You're not fit to say her name. You're the one who behaved like a whore last night, drinking and dancing and flirting." His voice rose. "Did you mean to lose that baby, to kill my son?"

"Damn you!" Katrin's voice rose to a screech. "You aren't man enough to father a living child. You've never done it . . . and you never will now."

"What?" Alex stared at her in horror, the ugly meaning of her words spreading like acid in his mind.

"Maria isn't yours," she cried bitterly. "She's Jed's child. Your brother was my lover and there's nothing of you in her." Triumph glittered in her eyes.

She had her revenge, Alex thought, transfixed by the expression on her face. All the years she'd kept Maria from him, spoiling her, imprinting her own selfish coldness on the child. Sickness washed through him and he hated her in that moment as he would not have believed himself capable of hate. If he stayed in this room . . . if she shouted another vile word at him . . . he would kill her.

"Good-bye, Katrin," he said, and closed the door behind him.

Chapter 29

The winy scent of ripe chokecherries hung in the still afternoon air. Aspens on the high ridges clung to the last vestige of golden leaves and the scrub oak was brilliant in a thousand shades of scarlet. Here beneath the tall pines, the air smelled pungent and heavy in the Indian summer heat. Unusual weather for so late in October, like a day stolen from summer.

Untying a blanket from his saddle, Alex spread it on a thick mat of fallen pine needles beneath the trees. With an amused smile, he watched as Caroline picked a chokecherry and tentatively tasted it. When she grimaced and spat it out, he laughed aloud.

"Why do you think they're called chokecherries?" he asked.

She came toward him, holding out her hand for the canteen of water he was untying from his saddle. As it always did at the sight of her, his heart seemed to tighten in sweet pain. How beautiful she was, her slender figure dressed in a dark blue riding skirt and a shirtwaist of some sheer pink material. A few strands of dark brown hair had blown loose in their ride up from the ranch house and curled enticingly about her pale face.

Rinsing the chokecherry taste from her mouth, she tilted her head. Laughing hazel eyes met his, and Alex could resist no longer. Drawing her into his arms, he covered her mouth with his.

He never tired of looking at her, touching her, loving her. This was the first time he'd brought her to the ranch since they'd been together. He wanted Caroline to see his first home, wanted to share that part of his life with her as he'd come to share everything else. No doubt he was, as Bertha Hamlin put it, "flaunting that woman," but he no longer cared about public opinion.

Furious at the gossip, Katrin chose to pretend outwardly that nothing had changed. All the respectable town women clustered about her sympathetically, and Alex thought she reveled in it. "It's so beautiful here, Alex," Caroline said as he reluctantly released her. "How can you bear to leave it for Cameron City?"

"Because *you* are in Cameron City." He grinned and attempted to kiss her again. With a teasing laugh, she whirled away from him, dropping down to sit on the blanket he had spread beneath the trees. Tethering the horses to the frost-yellowed chokecherry bush, Alex sat beside her.

Watching him make a cigarette, Caroline pressed her cheek against his shoulder. Thoughtfully, she mused, "I hope all the students will come back after this little vacation."

Alex gave her a sidelong glance as he lit his cigarette. "I thought Ma was going to pay for some of them to go to town school."

"Ross is the only one who wanted to go," Caroline replied, her voice subdued. "It's difficult for them, you know. The white kids tease them terribly."

"It's difficult for you too, love," he said, putting his arm about her shoulders and drawing her close. He thought of the sly looks, the cruel remarks, the loneliness she endured in order to be with him. "I'm going to hire a lawyer in Cheyenne," he told her. "Harry Thomas seems to be working for Katrin, not me, and I heard about a guy who specializes in divorces." Burying the ugly memory, he had never repeated to anyone what Katrin had said about Jed being Maria's father. He'd told himself it didn't matter now that he had Caroline, and he'd half convinced himself that Katrin had lied in her need to hurt him.

Without answering, Caroline moved closer, cuddling her head against his shoulder. She had never asked him to get a divorce and marry her. Since she became his mistress, she had never looked back on that decision with regret or recrimination.

"I love you, Alex Cameron," she murmured, and kissed his chin.

His arm tightened, his cheek pressed against her soft hair. "I know," he said. "Almost as much as I love you."

Through the thick stand of pine trees, Alex could see the tumbled rocks on the hillside below. A curious feeling came over him, as though time had circled back upon him.

"See that rock . . . the wide flat one," he said. "That's where I had my vision." His voice fell. "So long ago."

"Tell me about it?" she prompted, her wonderful shining eyes looking into his face.

The years seemed to crowd in on him as he recalled the unhappy boy he had been. "My brother did everything well," he heard himself telling her. "He was bigger, stronger, smarter. He even had a true warrior's vision . . . of running buffalo. When my turn came, I fasted three days and there was still no vision." Meeting her intent eyes, he went on. "I thought perhaps I didn't deserve a vision, that I would never be a man. Then I saw a lone hawk soaring over the canyons, plunging to take its prey."

Suddenly realizing how much of himself he had revealed, Alex gave an embarrassed laugh. "I didn't tell you my other name is Lone Hawk, did I?"

"Lone Hawk," she repeated softly, taking his face in her two hands. In the depths of her hazel eyes, Alex saw sorrow and compassion for the lonely boy he had been.

Scrubbing his cigarette out in the dirt, he drew her into his arms, laying her back on the blanket so that he looked down into her face.

Her mouth curved softly as she whispered, "Now Lone Hawk has a mate." She pulled his head down to hers, kissing him gently at first, then with growing fervor.

Heat rose in his loins. Sliding his hand down her back, he drew her body close against his. The beating of her heart leaped and surged as his hand covered her breast.

Breathlessly breaking their kiss, Caroline looked at him with smoldering eyes. "Will you make love to me here . . . now . . . Lone Hawk? Then I'll be part of your vision too."

"Already you're part of my heart," he told her, his lips a breath from hers. Her mouth claimed his and he was lost in the soaring joy of loving her, giving, taking, until the pulsing need between them rose to a crescendo of utter fulfillment.

Afterward Alex lay completely sated, staring up at the tall pines, stirring softly now in the late afternoon wind. Straightening her clothing, Caroline leaned to look down into his face.

"Do I make you happy, Alex?" she asked.

Sensing something behind that question, Alex embraced her slender shoulders. "You've given me the greatest happiness I've ever known, my beautiful love," he murmured. Kissing her face softly, he added, "You must know that without asking."

In their lovemaking, her hair had fallen loose and it lay soft as silk across his throat as Caroline cuddled her head against his shoulder. Drowsily, Alex stroked her smooth bare shoulders, gradually becoming aware of her tension.

"What is it, sweetheart?" he asked, puzzled.

"I didn't know how to tell you." Her voice was low and hesitant. "Oh, Alex . . ." Her arms tightened convulsively about him. "I don't want anything to make a difference between us. I love you so."

"Nothing could make me stop loving you," he protested, frowning.

"I've been so careful," she continued as though he hadn't spoken. "And now . . . now." Her voice broke as she cried out the words. "Oh, Alex . . . I'm going to have a baby."

It was a moment before full realization broke over him. With a shout of pure joy, Alex sat up, taking her with him, lifting her chin to cover her tearful face with kisses.

"A son . . ." he said, looking into her eyes. "Yours and

mine." And he kissed her with all the passionate gratitude overflowing from his heart.

"I won't wait until next month now," he said. "I'll get Max Guthrie on the divorce right away. We'll need a bigger house . . . or would you like to live at the ranch for a while?"

When she laughed joyously, Alex realized he was babbling. Yielding to her arms, he lay back on the blanket, looking up into her glowing face.

Smoothing back his hair with a gentle hand, Caroline looked down at him with loving eyes. A teasing smile played about her soft lips. "A little while ago, I asked if I made you happy," she began.

Alex's arms tightened about her as he interrupted. "I wouldn't have believed it was possible to be happier than I was at that moment." Gently, he kissed her eyelids. "But I am, dear love, and happier than I have any right to be."

Lying contentedly in each other's arms, they talked desultorily, making tentative plans. Katrin was already fighting the divorce with every legal resource she could muster. Surely now she would give way, Alex thought.

After a while, Caroline dozed against his shoulder while he daydreamed of a future filled with limitless joy. Far across the tumbled rocks of the hillside below them, soaring against the intense blue of the afternoon sky, two hawks moved in graceful precision.

"Two hawks," he murmured softly, contented and certain now that the vision was good and true.

"I'll see you in hell first!" Katrin shouted.

Alex was glad he'd closed the doors of the parlor against the prying ears of Mrs. Schrader and the other servants. Determined to keep his temper, he spoke in a reasonable tone.

"You don't give a damn about me, Katrin. When you miscarried my son, our marriage was over. Why keep up the pretense?"

Her face twisted and ugly with hate, Katrin glared at him. "I'll never give all this up." A wave of her hand took in the elaborate house, the carriages, and the servants in a telling gesture. "I've earned everything I have . . . and I won't give up anything."

With an effort, Alex managed to control his rising anger. "I'm not asking you to give it up. The house is yours. You'll have plenty of money—"

"But not your name . . ." Katrin's wrathful voice rose to a screech. Tossing her head, she continued in a low menacing tone. "I promise you, Alex . . . your whore can give you a dozen bastards and none of them will have your name."

A red film colored Alex's vision and he clenched his fists against the murderous rage that filled his heart. He should have known better, should have guessed that Caroline's pregnancy would only enrage Katrin when he asked her again to consent to the divorce.

"Damn you, Katrin," he said, his voice harsh. "You can't keep me in this trap forever. I'll divorce you if I have to drag all our dirty linen through the courts." When Katrin only sneered in reply, Alex felt himself engulfed by fury. "Go to hell, you bitch!" he shouted.

Turning on his heel, he stalked from the room, slamming the door behind him.

April 1873

Alex flipped his cigarette butt into the low flames burning in the small brick fireplace. This was home . . . this cottage so different from the rustic ranch house, or the mansion on Forester Creek. A bright braided rug lay on the gleaming plank floor. White ruffled curtains hung at the windows, and the chairs beside the fireplace were soft and comfortable. The home Caroline had created.

The months they'd been together had been the happiest of his life. For the first time he realized all these years he'd lived on a knife edge of tension. All that drained away in Caroline's presence. She could make him laugh, and forget a day of harassing business. Together, they shared their delight and anticipation of the child growing within her. When winter locked in the countryside, Alex felt he had been locked into paradise.

Now, his glance fell on the piano against the far wall as mute and forlorn as himself. Restlessly, he crossed to the window to look out at the slow drip of late April rain from the eaves of the Dutchman's cottage.

At the sound of the door opening, Alex whirled from the window to confront the stout figure of Dr. Hamlin. The doctor had scarcely closed the bedroom door when Alex seized his arm.

"How is she?" he demanded. Beyond the door he could hear Caroline, her cries diminished now to mere animal whimpers of pain.

Shaking his head as he rolled down his shirt-sleeves, the doctor refused to meet his eyes. "She's small, Alex, and she hasn't dilated properly. It could be a long time yet."

"It's been all day and all night," Alex cried. Unable to control himself in his distraction, he grabbed the doctor's shoulders and shook him. "She can't stand any more. Do something, you incompetent fool!"

"I'm doing all that can be done," the doctor replied reproachfully, pushing Alex's grasping hands from his shoulder. "I've got to have some rest. I'll be back in the morning."

"No!" Alex shouted, spinning the man around to face him. "You can't leave her. Do something. It doesn't matter about the baby . . . just save my Caroline." His voice broke and he struggled against the anguished fear that threatened to destroy his composure totally.

"Try to rest, Alex," the doctor advised. Picking up his bag and opening the front door, he was gone.

In the bedroom, Lydie sat beside the bed, gently wiping the sweat from Caroline's drawn pale face with a cold cloth.

Crossing the room to look down at her, Alex felt his inner self shatter with pain. It was his child in there, tearing her apart, and the sense of guilt made his chest ache.

"Darling . . ." Caroline murmured, weakly lifting a hand toward him. On his knees beside the bed, Alex pressed her hot fingers to his lips. She managed a smile, her eyes loving.

Tenderly, she caressed his cheek, smoothed back his hair. Alex swallowed the sob rising in his throat.

"I'm sorry, dear love," he whispered. "So sorry."

"Sorry you gave me a child?" she asked, her pale lips forming the words carefully. "Don't be sorry for anything we've had, darling Alex. You've made me so happy—" The words broke off as her face twisted in pain and her swollen body heaved. "Go," she gasped. "Don't watch this."

Alex met Lydie's fearful eyes across the bed. Taking Caroline's hand tight in his, he kissed her sweaty face. "Hang on to me, sweetheart," he managed to say. "Maybe that'll help."

All through the night, he held her, sharing her agony. When the first gray stormy light seeped into the bedroom, Caroline slept in exhaustion. Reluctantly, Alex left her side. Pulling on his coat, he told Lydie, "I'm gonna send for Ma. She'll know what to do."

Somber black eyes met his, but Lydie did not reply.

Head down against the fine cold rain, Alex cursed softly to himself as he walked toward town. If Ma were here, she'd know the right thing to do, he told himself. Why in God's name had that horse buyer from Cheyenne come in when he did . . . and why did Ma have to go with him to the ranch? She'd gone before Caroline started labor, and Caroline was certain she wasn't due for weeks, or Ma would have stayed by her side. Ma loved Caroline too. He should have sent a messenger yesterday to bring her back, but he hadn't guessed it would be like this.

Charles was unlocking his office door when Alex came down Main Street. He'd come back to Wyoming early this year, eager as always to be back in the mountains. When he turned his questioning gaze on Alex, the words tumbled out, broken with emotion.

"I'll send Clint," Charles said, relocking the door. His gray eyes dark with sympathy, he patted Alex's shoulder. "Go back to her, Alex. I'll take care of this."

By the time Alex got back to the cottage, Dr. Hamlin had returned. "I sent for Ma," Alex managed to whisper to Caroline, and kissed her before the doctor sent him out of the room. Lydie carried a basin of boiling water from the kitchen. In reply to Alex's questioning look, she said, "He's gonna try forceps. It's all he kin do now."

Pacing before the fireplace, Alex tried to control the hot tears that kept welling in his aching eyes. At the sound of a long, agonized scream Alex burst into the bedroom. He did not even glance at the small, mewling creature Dr. Hamlin handed to Lydie. He had only eyes for his love, who lay unconscious and gray as death in the bloody bed.

Kneeling beside her, Alex seized her in his arms, staring into her silent face. "Caroline," he begged. "Open your eyes, love. Speak to me." Beneath his hand, he felt the faint beat of her heart, and tears flooded from his eyes.

"It's all right, Alex." Dr. Hamlin laid a hand on his shoulder. "She passed out from the pain. She'll come around soon. Now let Lydie clean up in here."

Caroline drifted in and out of consciousness as the morning wore on. Immobilized by fear, Alex stayed beside her on the chair Lydie brought for him. He was only vaguely aware of Lydie moving busily about in the front room arranging the cradle Caroline had purchased with such anticipation, bustling into the room to check on Caroline. . . . His eyes were only for the pale beloved face on the pillow, and each time her lovely eyes opened his heart quickened with hope.

Toward noon, Lydie came into the bedroom carrying a small whimpering bundle. "I'll be back right soon, Mr. Alex," she said. "This chile's gotta be fed."

The words might have fallen on deaf ears, for Alex did not raise his head or turn his eyes from Caroline's face.

He was not even aware that Lydie had returned until he heard her greet the doctor at the door. "She's bleedin' awful bad," Lydie was saying as she led Dr. Hamlin into the bedroom. In reply, he merely shook his head resignedly.

Dusk fell early in the gray rainy weather. Water dripped from the eaves of the cottage in a slow mournful cadence. Standing in the bedroom doorway, Lydie held the bowl of soup Alex had just refused. He had scarcely left Caroline's side all day and his face was nearly as gray and sick as hers.

The slight figure on the bed stirred, turning her head to look into Alex's watchful face. With an effort, Caroline lifted a hand to touch his cheek. "So happy . . ." she said, smiling, and closed her eyes.

A cry of agony tore from Alex's throat as he gathered the still figure into his arms. Lydie felt her heart turn to ice.

The cottage was spotless and empty with all the fires out. Its coldness seemed to enter Star's very being in the certain knowledge that tragedy had taken place here.

She shouldn't have gone to the ranch with that horse buyer, she told herself now. But there were so few nowadays interested in the real Appaloosa horse. And Caroline had seemed well.

The horses had been scattered and hard to gather in the rain. Then a day had been spent cutting out those the buyer wanted. She'd left Little Knife to oversee the drive into the railroad shipping pens and come on ahead. The feeling of urgency that had oppressed her all through the day came into painful focus when she met Clint on the road and heard his message.

Whipping the horses now as she drove the surrey toward her own house, Star felt sorrow pour over her like the cold April rain. Caroline had almost been the daughter she'd always longed for. Even while she turned the horses over to Clint and ran toward the house, the sense of loss grew in her.

Light from the kitchen window lay across the blooming lilac bush. Its purple spikes were weighted with raindrops, gleaming like tears. Lydie turned from the kitchen stove. Star met her sorrowful eyes and knew. With a cry of pain, she went to Lydie, glad for the comfort of another woman as they held each other and wept for their loss.

"Is Alex here?" Star asked at last.

The question brought a new burst of weeping from Lydie. "Oh, Star . . . he was like a madman, plumb out of his mind. Mr. Charles had to come and take him away 'fore the undertaker could even get in the house."

"Then he's with Charles now?" Everything in her ached

for her son's loss, for the love he had found so late and lost so soon. Thank God, Charles had returned early from St. Louis.

"At the hotel," Lydie replied, wiping her eyes. "Dead drunk, Mr. Charles told me. It's the only way he could handle Mr. Alex."

"Yes . . ." Star replied absently. "Charles will look after him." Restlessly, she wandered into the dining room, where Caroline's presence filled the room with memories of her gentle teaching, into the sitting room which she had filled with music.

Star drew a deep painful breath. Once she would have known the future, once she would have stayed and used her knowledge to help Caroline . . . and perhaps saved her. But she had lost herself in the white man's world. Her gifts had withered with neglect and her heritage seemed as distant as the Big River she had known as a child.

It was time to go back, she told herself. Mounting the stairs to her bedroom, she searched out the old basket where she kept the medicinal herbs she gathered. From it she took a bundle of sweet grass, dry and crumbling with age.

When she came downstairs again, she ignored Lydie's gasp of surprise, passing her in silence as she went out into the rain to the skin lodge she had built for the half-breed children. She wore her beaded ceremonial doeskin gown, packed away for so long, a beaded band around her head that held the dark gray-streaked hair flowing about her shoulders, and moccasins.

Inside the lodge, she built a low fire in the old way, so that the smoke rose through the smoke hole opened in the top. From about her neck she took the blue stone, her strongest medicine. Long ago, when she and Charles had been lovers, she had told him of its import. The next year he had brought a gold chain with an open-work gold locket to hold the stone. Holding it now in one hand, she reached to lay the sweet grass on the fire. Its scent filled the lodge.

Falling Star lifted her head toward the heavens . . . toward the gods she had forgotten. The aching sound of the Nez Percé mourning song rose into the damp night air.

Book III

✖✖✖✖✖✖✖✖✖

Gray Dove

Chapter 30

Through the front windows, Star watched Katrin descend from her buggy, holding her fur cape about her, the cold wind tugging at her still-bright hair. Under the low gray skies, she flung open the front gate and stalked toward the house. The only time Katrin had been here was when Alex brought her to see the house soon after Star moved in. That had been curiosity. Star was certain this visit meant trouble.

Catching Star's eye, Lydie hurried to open the door at Katrin's knock. "Mornin', Miz Cameron," she drawled, putting on her best southern maid act.

Star glanced in the mirror hanging above the fireplace, smoothing her hair, amused that she felt stronger because of the elegant gray silk gown she wore . . . as though that white woman's gown was armor against Katrin.

"You have to stop him," Katrin announced without preamble.

In spite of the warmth of the fireplace where she stood to face Katrin, Star felt a chill of apprehension. Alex, of course, she thought, and waited. In the days since Caroline's death, Alex had kept to himself at the cottage, alternately drinking and weeping until she couldn't bear to visit him anymore.

"It isn't enough that he disgraced the family with that whore," Katrin continued, trembling with anger. Her hands in their fine kid gloves writhed together, and her eyes glittered venomously. "Now he's raising a monument to her, right out there in the town cemetery."

"That's his right, Katrin." Concealing her surprise, Star managed to keep her voice calm, although Katrin's words had kindled an inner rage at Katrin herself.

"Not when he gives her his name!" Katrin's voice rose, harsh and strident. "Caroline Cameron, it is . . . *carved in stone.*" She raised her voice to emphasize the last words, then paused, staring expectantly at Star.

And carved in his heart, Star thought, stifling the urge to strangle this bitchy woman. Unable to frame a reply, she kept silent.

"You're the only one who can stop him!" Katrin cried, her eyes wide with impotent fury in the face of Star's calm demeanor. "He's disgracing your name too!" With a toss of her bright head, she glared at Star, turned, and swept from the room.

Cameron City had built its graveyard on a low sage-covered hill south of town. In spite of the short history of this place there were many graves: railroad workers, drifters, town dwellers, children dead of diphtheria, young women dead in childbirth. Star pulled the horse and buggy to a halt on the muddy road at the edge of the cemetery.

Pain filled her heart at the sight of the tall man silhouetted against the cloudy spring sky. Everyone needed to mourn, she thought, but Alex's grief had an edge of madness to it.

Securing the horse, she walked among the gravestones and the wooden crosses. Wind blowing ahead of the coming storm lifted the sharp-sweet scent of sage into the air.

Alex looked at her with bleak eyes when she stood across the fresh mound of earth that was Caroline's grave. Tears stung her eyes as she read the words on the granite monument, the largest in the cemetery. Colby, the blacksmith, kept a supply of headstones, carving the letters himself with a certain artistry. CAROLINE CAMERON it said, with the dates below, 1847–1873, and below that the single word, BELOVED.

"She'll have my name now," Alex said, his chin jutting defiantly. He had shaved this morning and she saw with sadness how sunken his cheeks were, his dark eyes hollow and empty.

"Yes," Star said. Aching for him, she walked around the grave to lay a gentle hand on his unyielding arm. "No one can deny you that, my son."

A sob broke from his throat, and he covered his face with his hands. Stroking his shoulder sympathetically, Star waited, her eyes on the words carved in stone.

Something clicked inside her head, an intuition, and she thought how painfully difficult it was to gain back the gift she had put by for so long.

When his grieving quieted, she asked in a low voice, "Isn't the child buried with her?"

Alex's face hardened; his voice was harsh and bitter. "It killed her. I'll never forgive that." Turning on his heel, he walked across the cemetery to where his horse was tethered, moving like a man pursued by demons.

"Why didn't you tell me?" Star demanded furiously. She had raced the horse and buggy back to the house to confront Lydie.

Tears filled Lydie's eyes. "I tole you, Star," she protested. "More'n once, but you wouldn't hear. You was so busy gettin' Miz Caroline buried and tryin' to look after Mr. Alex, an' shippin' them horses." Her voice broke. "I thought you didn't care no more than he does."

"Where is that baby?"

"The poor lil' thing had to be fed," Lydie said defensively. "There's a family livin' in their wagon box east of town. They was headed for Idaho when the wagon broke down and the woman had a baby. She's wet-nursin' our baby."

"Take me there!" How could she have been so absorbed in her own grief and so shaken by Alex's reaction that she'd been deaf and dumb and blind for three days? Mentally berating herself, Star walked out to the buggy, with Lydie scurrying behind her.

Ragged, dirty-faced children clustered in front of the Conestoga wagon. Its running gears gone, its bed sat on the muddy ground in a sagebrush flat near the road east from town. Jumping down from the buggy, Star flung aside the canvas door flap and stopped so suddenly Lydie bumped into her.

The canvas top of the dim, crowded wagon flapped eerily in the wind. Seated on a quilt-covered bed, a scrawny woman with light brown hair nursed a baby. She stared at Star in dismay, but smiled when she saw Lydie.

"She's doin' real fine," the woman said cheerily. "Gainin' ever day. And she's a mighty purty little thing."

"Oh, Lydie . . ." The words burst from Star's overflowing heart. "How could I not know about her?" She held out her arms, but the woman looked to Lydie for consent before she surrendered the child.

The baby gurgled as Star cradled her against her breast and blew a milk bubble with her perfect little mouth. Dark fuzz covered her softly pulsing head, and her dark eyes stared solemnly into Star's.

Laying the child's head against her shoulder, Star pressed her lips against the soft baby cheek. Closing her eyes, she surrendered to the sense of mystery flowing through her. It was as though a healing hand had been laid upon her own head. She had waited so long for the gifted one who would follow her . . . waited and despaired so that she nearly lost her own gift. Now she held that girl-child in her arms . . . hers to keep and to teach, a last gift of the beloved Caroline.

"I called her Julie," Lydie said hesitantly beside her. "It was my mama's name and I allus thought it was so purty."

"Julie . . ." Star repeated, holding the child away to look into her face. "At last . . . at last."

Everything was quickly arranged. Clint would come four times a day for Mrs. Haskins, bringing her to Star's house to feed the baby. There would be new clothes for the ragged children peering curiously through the doorway, and groceries delivered from the general store. The blacksmith would be paid to fix the wagon so that the Haskins's journey to Idaho could be completed.

Within days, the house on Forester Creek Road had been

reorganized around Julie. A nursery was furnished, a milk cow purchased to eventually replace Mrs. Haskins. When Star hired a carter to bring the piano back from the cottage, Lydie chided her.

"That chile ain't gonna play that thing like Miss Caroline for a lot of years."

"But it will be here for her," Star answered, happier than she had been in a very long time. Her life had purpose now, and a focus in Julie.

Determined that this baby's birth be registered as Julie Cameron, daughter of Alex Cameron, whatever else that silly Dr. Hamlin might have written on the birth certificate, Star sent for Charles.

"I'll see to it," Charles promised, sipping his coffee and smiling down at the winsome creature in the cradle beside the fire, playing with the hands she had recently discovered. "She'll be a beauty, Star," he added.

"I've sent word to Alex at the ranch that I wanted to see him." Star smiled as Julie grasped Charles's finger and he looked utterly enchanted. "He should know what arrangements I've made for his daughter."

Charles straightened in his chair, his face suddenly tight, his eyes avoiding hers. "I don't know, Star," he said in a subdued tone. "It's crazy, of course, but he blames the child for Caroline's death. Refused to even look at her from the first."

Watching his unhappy face, the way he toyed with his coffee cup, Star waited, certain there was more to be said.

"Alex's foreman, Buck Webster, was in town yesterday for supplies," he began. With a long sigh, he looked into Star's eyes. "Mostly whiskey."

"So that's how Alex has chosen to deal with grief," she murmured sadly, shaking her head in dismay. "I'd hoped he'd keep busy at the ranch, and come to terms with his loss."

"Liquor kills the pain," Charles replied, adding with a wry smile, "I should know. I tried it, if you remember."

Looking at the elegant, gray-haired man sitting opposite

her, Star could scarcely believe she had first seen him lying drunk in his own vomit in the corner of Jim Bridger's trading post.

"I remember," she said at last, acutely aware of the changes the years had wrought.

Reaching across the low, marble-topped table, Charles covered her hand with his comforting one. "Alex isn't just my friend and business partner, Star. He's been like a son to me all these years . . . closer than Will, my own son. Even though it caused a scandal, I was glad he'd found Caroline."

She nodded, tears filling her eyes for her heartbroken son, and his short-lived happiness.

"You saved my life back then," Charles went on. "Maybe the two of us can save Alex." With a fond glance at the cooing baby, he asked, "Can you leave this darling long enough to come out to the Old Ranch with me?"

In the distance beyond the ranch, Star could see the scarred gash of a timbered-off mountainside. Alongside the dusty road, the bunch grass seemed thinner, the land marked by the passage of too many hooves. There was no game for the Indians now, no way to live off the land as they had done in her youth. Now the government herded the people onto reservations, buying cattle from the white ranchers to feed them.

Somehow, she thought, it had all gone wrong. Greed had destroyed the life made so rich by closeness to the earth. Now the earth was being destroyed by thousands of cattle, by settlers tearing that earth with their plows. She was as guilty as any of the white men, she told herself now, reaching for the soft life, and for the money to live that life. There must be a way to stop the destruction and save the real riches of the earth for her granddaughter, the new medicine woman.

"Jesus, I'm glad you're here," Buck said, helping Star descend from the surrey. He seemed to have been waiting for them when they drove into the ranch yard in the afternoon's cold light. "It's gettin' to be more'n I can take."

278

An overpowering stench assailed her as she opened the door of the old ranch house, and she understood Buck's anger. Food rotted on the table, and everywhere there were empty whiskey bottles. Dried vomit was caked on the braided rug in one bedroom. In the other, Alex lay across the bed, unconscious and snoring loudly.

"Good Lord," Charles muttered, staring at him in disgust. "Was I that bad?"

When Star nodded, his face colored and he groaned with embarrassment.

"Leave him," she ordered, closing the bedroom door. "Bring in some water, Buck, and we'll get this mess cleaned up."

By nightfall, the house was clean, a stew simmering on the stove along with a pot of willow bark tea. Star changed back into her skirt and shirtwaist from the shirt and pants of Alex's she had worn while cleaning. Charles had ferreted out all the whiskey bottles and methodically broken every one, seeming to take a vicious delight in the chore.

They were seated at the table drinking coffee together when Alex stumbled from the bedroom, holding his head, his unshaven face gray and sick. Staring at them in surprise, he growled, "What the hell are you doing here?"

"Trying to save your life," Star replied mildly, concealing the pain his wretched condition caused her.

"Where's my whiskey?" Alex demanded, looking around the room, ineffectively trying to tuck in his filthy shirt.

"It's time to stop drowning in liquor and face reality," Star began. Charles shook his head at her. Puzzled because she was only saying what must be said, she fell silent.

Rising from the table, he took Alex's arm. "Sit down here," he directed. Alex sat, his shaking hands lying on the table before him. When Charles set a mug of steaming willow bark tea in front of him, he grimaced with distaste.

"You want something to drink," Charles commanded. "Drink that." With an anxious face, he watched Alex struggle to down the pungent tea. Placing one hand on Alex's drooping shoulders, he spoke in a low emotional voice. "I value you greatly, my son, and I won't let you destroy someone I love." He drew a long, shaky breath. "I've been where you are, and I can help you find the way back."

It was three days before Alex stopped shaking. Buck kept the men busy rounding up the cattle for spring branding. Star was aware that the ranch hands watched apprehensively as their boss, who had made such a sorry spectacle of himself, began to return to normal. He and Charles took long rides together. Star thought perhaps Charles shared with him that long-ago time when he had lived in depraved slavery to alcohol. While they were gone, she occupied herself with gathering the herbs she had neglected for too long.

That first night, Charles had offered to sleep on the sofa in the front room. Smiling, Star said, "We've shared a bed before, Charles. Would it be so terrible now that we're old?"

It was pleasant to lie together with comforting arms about each other, and talk quietly in the darkness, sharing concerns other than the immediate one of Alex. Monique had accepted this friendship between them, even though she scarcely acknowledged Star's existence when they met in Cameron City. Charles spoke with pride of his son, Will, fourteen now and becoming a man. He was a good student, although Charles had been obliged to rescue him from the consequences of a few schoolboy pranks the two of them kept secret from Monique. Someday, Charles said, someday his son would come to live in Wyoming for good, to learn his father's business.

As she sank into quiet sleep, gratitude filled Star's heart for the abiding love and friendship between herself and Charles . . . a rare and wonderful treasure.

Every day, Star walked alone to the rocky hillside where Alex had set up a granite monument above his father's grave. The carved words said simply, HUGH CAMERON, DIED 1855, for they did not know the year of Hugh's birth. It was a low stone, comfortable to sit on. But as much as her spirit longed for his company, the Shining Bear was not there.

They had been at the ranch nearly a week the late afternoon when Alex joined her there beside the grave. Dust rose from the sagebrush flats in the distance where the cattle were gathered for branding. On the cool spring breeze, Star thought she could smell the harsh odor of burning hair. The bawling of the cattle and the shouts of the cow hands came faintly to her ears.

Meeting Alex's clear dark eyes, Star felt relief wash through her. Surely now he would be whole again.

"Does the pain ever end?" he asked in a low voice, staring down at the pile of stones that was his father's grave.

"It ends, Alex," she answered, aching for him, "because life goes on. Part of Hugh lives in his sons, just as part of Caroline lives in your daughter."

A strangled cry broke from his throat, and he covered his face with his hands. Star could barely hear his words.

"My fault . . . my child . . . killed her." He looked at her and quickly away, his face agonized. "I can't bear to look at that baby and know it's the reason I lost Caroline."

Star touched his arm gently. "You can't blame an innocent baby, Alex." Staring into the distance, his face wet with tears, Alex did not reply. Star continued in a soft voice. "What you had with Caroline was rare and wonderful, something few people are privileged to know. Surely this baby could only remind you of that happiness."

"I can't, Ma!" The words seemed torn from him. "God forgive me, I can't." His voice fell as he looked away. "Will you keep her?"

"I planned to keep her . . . always," Star answered.

Silence fell between them as their eyes held for a long moment. Wind swept through the pine trees on the hillside . . . a low, sad sound.

"Do you mourn him still, Ma?" Alex spoke at last, his eyes on his father's headstone.

"You mourned with me, Alex," she said. "Long ago, do you remember?"

"I remember," he replied morosely, still staring at the grave.

Star's heart quickened, for she knew now the cure for her son's grief-sickness. "Sometimes we forget our heritage," she began softly. "We forget the great truths of the past in our greed for today. It's good to mourn in the Nez Percé way. It cleanses the heart of pain and leaves only the image of love."

Alex lifted his troubled face to look at her with moist eyes. "Will you show me the way? I've forgotten."

Clouds in the western sky were purple gray and edged with gold when the two of them rode away from the ranch house. Charles watched them go, for he knew this was something he could not share. They rode in silence broken only by the soft sound of horses' hooves on the forest floor, the sighing of the cold spring wind in the pines, and Alex felt a healing begin.

Star did not ask why he chose this place to stop. Perhaps she knew this was his vision place where he had seen the lone hawk so many years ago, where the second vision had come in the arms of his love . . . two hawks together. That vision, he knew now, was false.

While he tethered the horses, Star gathered stones into a circle, piling twigs and small dead pine branches for their fire. Oncoming darkness filled the glade with deep shadows. Flames flickered softly from the glowing fire, casting a warm light on Star's intent face. She wore her beaded ceremonial gown and moccasins. Dressed in the doeskin shirt his mother had brought for him, Alex sat down across the fire. Watching her, he longed for the serenity he saw in her calm face.

In silence, she opened the small leather pouch she carried and drew out something, holding it out to him across the fire. Alex opened his hand and drew in his breath painfully. Two feathers from a red-tailed hawk lay on his palm . . . gray and black and splashed with crimson. Grief clogged his throat, and his eyes burned as he clutched the feathers and he held them to his breast, imitating Star's gesture as she held her own *wyakin,* the blue stone on its gold chain, against her breast.

Ceremoniously, she took a handful of sweet grass from the leather pouch and laid it on the low fire. Its perfumed smoke rose toward the stars along with the rising wail of an ancient Nez Percé mourning song.

Chapter 31

1878

She had black hair, thick and straight as her grandmother's, and dark eyes that almost always brimmed with laughter. Julie Cameron was five years old now, in a world bounded by the arrowhead iron fence of the house on Forester Creek Road, a world of which she was the focus.

Sometimes she watched the town children pass by that fence, and longed to join their play . . . but it was forbidden. Her grandmother was teaching her to read and write and her numbers. The schoolmaster had come and argued with Grandmother about sending Julie to school. It was the only time she ever saw fear in Grandmother's eyes.

Now that spring had come again, her favorite play spot was the skin lodge in the side yard. It was cool and dim in there, and peopled with creations of her fantasies. Cradling the soft doeskin doll her grandmother had made, Julie crooned to it just as Grandmother crooned to her at night before she tucked her into bed. Lydie had named the doll "Sweetie."

Her stomach growled, and Julie thought she would go to the kitchen where Lydie would laugh and give her a cookie. There was no hurt in the world that could not be made better cuddled against Lydie's ample breast in the kitchen rocking chair, listening to one of her deep, sad songs.

Brushing off the skirt of her gingham dress as she came out of the lodge, Julie paused to stare at the strange horse tethered to the hitching rack in front of the house. It was not her beloved Charles, because he walked to the house, swinging his cane and ruffling her hair when she ran to meet him. When he was seated in the parlor with Grandmother and Lydie bringing him coffee and cake, she could climb on his lap, certain of a loving squeeze and a pleasantly bristly kiss.

With a sigh, she paused by the back steps, wondering if it might be the tall man named Alex, who sometimes came to see her grandmother. She liked to watch him . . . the way his grave face broke into a smile as he bent to greet Grandmother, and the way the firelight played on his sandy hair. But once she had climbed on his lap just as she did on Charles's. Immediately, he stiffened, his hands gripping the arms of the chair tightly. Julie was aware that Grandmother was watching intently. Sensing the tension, the lack of welcome in Alex's stiff posture, Julie slid down from his lap and went to her grandmother, turning to stare at the man's set face with wondering eyes.

"Whose horse, Grandmother?" she asked, coming into the kitchen where Star and Lydie were working. Julie hoped it was only one of the men who came to see her grandmother on business. They seldom stayed long, and she wanted Grandmother to ask Clint to saddle her spotted pony so that they could ride together this afternoon.

With a questioning frown, Star walked through the dining room to look out the bay window at the front of the house. At her grandmother's sudden indrawn breath, Julie felt a pain strike inside her. Suddenly frightened, she ran to Star and flung her arms about Grandmother's waist.

Struggling to remain calm, Star opened the front door. The tall boy standing there wore a threadbare wool shirt, torn jeans, and a battered slouch hat. The black hair had been trimmed short like a white man's. The deep-set black eyes in his thin copper-skinned face were not the eyes of a boy. They were old eyes, filled with horrors.

"*Nakaz* . . . Grandmother?" he asked in an uncertain voice.

A sense of tragedy roared through Star, turning her knees to water so that she had to reach out to the doorjamb for support. She was scarcely aware of the big-eyed child clinging to her skirt, staring at the strange boy.

"Red Moon," Star said, and opened her arms to him.

"After the Sioux won the great battle over Yellow Hair Custer at the Little Big Horn, the white soldiers could not rest," Red Moon said.

Seated in front of the sitting-room fireplace, Red Moon sipped the coffee Lydie had brought, thick with sugar. Star sent Julie to tell Clint to care for their visitor's horse. She had asked the boy if he were cold, for he looked so thin and drawn. When he said no, she did not bother to light the fire.

They spoke in Nez Percé, for Red Moon's English was poor. Her own speech was rusty, but Star thought she must learn it well again, if only for Julie's sake. A medicine woman must know the language of her heritage.

"We heard how General Howard and General Miles trapped the Nez Percé at Eagle Creek, and how Chief Joseph surrendered his people there," she told him. "All this winter, I have longed to know of your father, Running Buffalo." One could not let fear rule one's life, but it had been there nibbling at the back of her mind. Now she was certain that what she had seen in the fire beside her father's lodge when Running Buffalo lay in her womb had come to pass.

For a moment Red Moon's face twisted with pain. With an effort, he composed himself. Taking another sip of the coffee, he sat straight in the chair, looking at her. There was pride in the young voice, deepening into tones of manhood. "I will tell you now of Running Buffalo, my grandmother."

In the spring Chief Joseph told the people they must gather their animals and their belongings and cross the Snake River to settle on the Lapwai Reservation. No longer could they resist the white man's soldiers. After the Sioux's great victory over Yellow Hair Custer at the Little Big Horn, the leaders in Washington were afraid. New troops came west with orders to subdue or exterminate the Indians.

Some white settlers took advantage of the confusion of the Nez Percé move to steal several hundred of the valued Appaloosa horses. Already heartsick at leaving their homeland, the people were enraged, for they had done nothing but good to the white settlers. A few of the bold young men could not be restrained. They took vengeance, murdering white settlers and driving back the stolen horses.

Chief Joseph knew then it was too late. There would be war. The people were ready to move. Instead of Lapwai, they would go to Canada, where the Sioux of Sitting Bull had found refuge after the battle of the Little Big Horn.

"Joseph led the people," Red Moon continued. "All of them, men, women, and children, sick and wounded and old. We crossed the mountains many times, running from soldiers. And always there were more soldiers, with more guns.

"The great warriors were killed . . . Looking Glass and Ollikut and the others. It was October and it began to snow. There was no food for the women and children except the dead horses."

Red Moon paused, his eyes unseeing except for the tragedy playing again in his mind. Falling Star listened in silence, tears flowing unheeded down her face. In her heart she was certain her beloved brother, Looking Glass, was not the only loss in Red Moon's tale of death.

"At Eagle Creek, the soldiers of General Miles came down to meet the soldiers of General Howard. We were surrounded. The women dug all through the wet cold night, making rifle pits where our warriors might hold back the troops."

"That night my father came to me where he had sent me to watch over my mother." Red Moon lifted his thin face, pride and love intermixed there. "'My son,' he said. 'You are of an age now to go on your vision quest and find your new name. When we are safe in Canada, it will be so.'"

Silence fell and Star looked anxiously at the boy who

seemed to have fallen into a dreaming sleep. But in a moment, he continued his tale.

"My father, Running Buffalo, kissed my mother and my little sister farewell and sent them with the pack train heading north into Canada. He would stay and fight. In the end, I would not go even though he told me I must. He left the war council of the chiefs and stayed with me that night."

Pausing, he looked directly at Star. "My father said you have the gift. That you foretold I would be a great warrior and a leader of my people. Is that true, my grandmother?"

Wiping the tears from her face, she met his questioning eyes. "You are already a great man, my grandson."

Red Moon nearly smiled. Straightening his shoulders, he continued his tale. "It was a gray dawn, with the sky spitting sleet." He drew a deep, shaky breath. "They had brought up a cannon and fired it into our camp. It killed a woman and her four children, and it killed our hearts. Joseph sent out the white flag.

"My father and I watched the parley from a rifle pit. Joseph returned and said we must surrender. We must return to the reservation. He would talk with the generals tomorrow. During the night old Chief White Bird took some followers and slipped away to the north.

"My father and I stayed in the rifle pit that night. We talked long and he told me of you, my grandmother." He looked up and met her eyes. "And of my white grandfather who had a Nez Percé heart. He said I must be proud of my heritage."

"It is so," Falling Star replied gently. Sorrow ran through her like the pain of a fever. For the boy's sake, she held herself in control.

Red Moon drew a deep painful breath, his face agonized now with what he must tell. "Chief Joseph spoke with the white generals the next day. We heard him surrender, and we heard when he turned to his own chiefs and said, 'My heart is sick and sad. From where the sun now stands, I will fight no more forever.'

"My father wept at the words. When the soldiers said the

warriors must come forward and give up their weapons, he made me hide in the pit. He would not surrender his rifle."

Red Moon covered his face with his hands, his scrawny shoulders heaving. Falling Star waited, letting him have his grief, her own face wet with silent tears.

Julie came into the room and leaned on the arm of Star's chair, staring at her with frightened eyes. She has never seen me weep before, Star thought, and gathered the child into her arms.

"The soldiers shot him then!" The boy's voice broke, high and thin and drenched in sorrow. "He fell back into the rifle pit, covering me. I lay very still while the soldiers took the rifle from his dying hands, but when they had gone I held him in my arms and tried to stop the bleeding."

Again, he covered his face, struggling for control. When he spoke again, his voice was weary. "My father said I must follow the pack train, find my mother, and run away into Canada. She would need a man to help her.

"When night came, I buried my father and sang his death song. Then I slipped away to follow White Bird's trail north.

"I remembered what my father had said about my vision quest that night when I saw the moon was great and round, and red. Not the red of fire as it was on the night of my birth, but"—his voice choked and fell—"red with the blood of the Nez Percé people.

"That is the name I have taken, Grandmother." And he looked directly into her eyes. "Blood Moon."

The stern control he had maintained through his harrowing tale broke at last, and Blood Moon wept noisily into his hands.

So it had happened as she had known it would. Her eldest son, brave and strong and handsome, was dead at the hands of the white men. Because she had always known Running Buffalo would not grow old, her grief had been spread over many years. Yet now it was done, and she felt a burst of wild, unreasoning hatred toward the whites who had destroyed the world her son struggled to preserve.

Nothing is inevitable except change . . . Charles's words

flooded into her mind. True words, yet they did not diminish the suffering of those who refuse to change.

With a sad face, Julie slid down from Star's lap and went to lay her face against Blood Moon's shoulder, gently stroking his cheek.

Brushing away the tears, the boy gave her a wavering smile. With a gentle hand, he smoothed the child's dark hair. He looked at Star. "She is very much like my sister, Sweet Bird."

Glad to know there had been another child, the child Jed had hoped for when last she saw him, Star nodded.

"Where is your mother now?" she asked, refilling his forgotten coffee cup.

Julie leaned on the arm of his chair, studying him intently as he sipped the hot sweet coffee. "She is in Canada with my sister and the other Nez Percé who escaped. She wanted me to come here, to tell you of Running Buffalo, for she knew your love for him."

"She is safe and well then?" Star asked, relieved.

"Yes," he answered, "but it was a terrible journey. We had thought the Sioux would help us fight the white men. Instead, they attacked our camp and stole our horses." He looked into the dark depths of the cup he held. "The Indians have too many tribes. White men have only one and they fight together."

Star sighed, knowing the bitter truth of his words. She held out her hand to Julie, who returned to climb on her lap. "Could you not bring your mother and sister here to live with me?" she ventured.

"No!" His voice was sharp and decisive. "We will make a home now with our own people in Canada."

Aware that this young man, barely sixteen as she had counted, was wise beyond his years, she could only nod assent. A great warrior and a leader of his people, she had foretold. And so it would be.

"Tonight in my lodge," she said, "we will sing for your father."

* * *

Morning sun filtered through the budding trees and nesting robins sang. Across the yard littered with cottonwood catkins, Julie watched with a mournful face as Star and Blood Moon loaded the surrey. His horse was tied to the tailgate, both boy and horse recuperated and fattened in the two weeks he had stayed here.

Catching sight of the small, unhappy face, Star smiled at Julie. "I'll be back soon, little love. I'm only going to the ranch to help your cousin pick out the horses he will take back to Canada with him."

"But why are you taking all those things?" Julie asked doubtfully, peering into the bed of the surrey.

There were warm blankets and clothes, boots, buffalo robes, tools, dried fruit and coffee . . . whatever Star could think of that might make life easier in the Canadian wilderness. If only Old Magpie were still alive, she would send him along to help Blood Moon.

"Blood Moon will load them on packhorses and take them to his mother and his little sister in Canada," Star answered, patting Julie's head. "He's told you about his sister."

Julie gave an exaggerated sigh. "I wish he would stay and be my brother."

With an absent smile, Star patted the small head again, her mind busy with the details of her grandson's departure. She would have chosen to have him stay too, but Blood Moon must go now and be the man of his family. She could see that he was rich in horses when he returned to Canada, fine horses descended from the great stud, Hands Down, but she could ease his life in no other way.

All through Blood Moon's visit, she had hoped Alex would return from Cheyenne, to have a chance to know his brother's son. But he stayed away for long periods now, on business, cattle buying, cattle selling, or at the ranch. Even though he had moved back into the mansion up the street, he kept the Dutchman's cottage as it was and she knew he often went there alone.

Perhaps it was best he'd not been here, Star told herself

now. Alex had always had an envious heart toward his brother . . . and that brother had a son, the thing Alex desired most in the world. She wondered if Julie had been a boy, whether Alex would have treated her differently.

His other daughter, Maria, was a spoiled and unloving girl. Her mother's daughter, Star reminded herself, knowing that Katrin and Alex seldom even spoke to each other. At Bertha Hamlin's urging, Maria had been enrolled in a fancy and expensive finishing school in Philadelphia. Katrin and Bertha traveled east with the girl each spring and fall, spending a month or more visiting Bertha's relatives in the east.

If only Alex wouldn't hold himself aloof from Julie, he might have had the love she was so eager to give. But it seemed Alex could never break that barrier, even though he greeted the child kindly when he came to the house, and he had set up a bank account in her name.

Without Caroline, the school for the half-breed children had never been revived. But it was known in the town that Star Cameron would pay for any Indian or half-breed child who wished to attend the town school.

"*Taz alago,* little sister." With a grin, Blood Moon lifted Julie into his arms and hugged her tight. Star smiled, pleased with the affection between these two. They had become warm friends in the past two weeks, communicating in a comical mixture of English and Nez Percé.

Tears poured from the little girl's wide dark eyes, and she hugged the tall young man fiercely about the neck. "Don't go," she begged.

"I must go," he said, and kissed her forehead. "Tell me *taz alago* now."

She managed to mutter the words through her tears. "*Taz alago.*"

Seated in the driver's seat of the surrey, Star beckoned to Lydie, who was watching from the back porch. She hadn't guessed Julie would be so broken up by Blood Moon's departure. Lydie would hold her and comfort her. But Julie broke from Blood Moon's embrace and raced to the skin lodge beside the house.

"Miss Julie . . ." Lydie chided, hurrying after her.

Again the little girl eluded Lydie, running back to Blood Moon, who was climbing into the surrey. "Look! Her name is Sweetie." Julie's voice was choked with sobs. Holding up the well-worn beloved doeskin doll, she said, "Give her to your other sister, Sweet Bird."

Blood Moon jumped down from the surrey. With a grave face, he ceremoniously accepted the doll. *"Imene kaiziyenyen,"* he said, stooping to look into the small, tearful face. "Thank you, little sister." She hugged him tight about the neck and he held her close for a moment before he climbed back into the surrey.

"Kuse timine," he said, smiling fondly at Julie. "I go with good heart."

Chapter 32

1880

The schoolmaster, Mr. Bergman, was a stern unbending old man, who did not hesitate to rap misbehaving students across the knuckles with his ruler. He had even thrashed two of the older boys soundly. Now he unbent enough to smile at Julie as he told her, "You've done very well this winter, Miss Cameron. Already you've passed the other students your age." Frowning, he added, "It wasn't right of your grandmother to keep you out of school until you were seven years old."

It wasn't Grandmother who had sent her at all, Julie thought as she gravely shook his hand and took the report card marked with *E*'s for excellent. Lydie had protested, "You cain't keep the child penned up here forever, Star. She needs other children."

When Alex and Charles agreed with Lydie, Grandmother had given in and sent her to the town school. Julie knew now that Alex was her father, but she had never dared call him by that title. He was never unkind to her, merely distant, and it had pleased her immensely that he had cared enough to insist she go to school. Grandmother told her often of her beautiful dead mother, Caroline, but never when Alex was there. Instinctively, Julie knew better than to ask about her mother in front of Alex.

Hefting the canvas bag of books and clutching the report

card she knew would bring a glow of pride to Grandmother and to Lydie, Julie started down the schoolhouse steps.

Already, the boys had run from the big frame one-room schoolhouse built in a clearing among the sagebrush, shouting their joy at freedom from school. Intoxicated by the warm spring sunshine, they were shoving each other, wrestling and laughing. Several girls clustered on the small porch of the plain clapboard building, giggling and comparing report cards. Without a glance at them, Julie started her lonesome walk down the dusty street toward home.

Last fall, when she first began school, some of the girls had been friendly. Then Dorena Billings had brought the story from home. Ugly words were hurled at Julie during recess, words that Lydie had to explain.

"Bastard is a word only low-class folks use, Julie," Lydie had told her, holding her close as she wept.

"But what does it mean?" Julie insisted through her sobs.

Lydie sighed, answering reluctantly, "It means your mama and daddy wasn't married, honey." She lifted Julie's chin and looked lovingly into her tear-filled eyes. "It don't mean they didn't love each other. Alex would've married your mama if he could've." She hugged Julie tightly. "Jest don't forget, Julie honey, your sweet mama loved you, and Alex loves you too, in his way. An' nobody could be loved more'n me an your grandma loves you."

But it was hard to remember she was loved at home, when she had been a loner the whole winter, eating lunch by herself, watching the other children's recess games from a distance.

The scent of lilacs filled the warm spring air and Julie's heart lifted. She would not think about the dreadful winter behind her, or the possibility of another such winter ahead. Now Grandmother would take her to the ranch where they could ride together every day . . . where all the ranch hands were kind and loving.

"Nigger lover!" At the sound of the taunting voice behind her, Julie felt a chill. She had been cautioned by Lydie and by Grandmother to walk away and never reply to such ignorant remarks.

295

"Dirty bastard squaw!" It was Dorena's voice . . . the ringleader in Julie's long winter of torment.

"Your ugly old grandma is a bastard too!" Dorena shouted, strutting as the other girls giggled at her daring.

A moment ago, Julie had been surrounded by the scent of lilacs, and the warmth of the spring sun. Now the day seemed dark and ugly.

"Your pa's a fornicater!" The girl stumbled over the word, then looked to her companions for approval of her insult. The laughter had an ugly edge to it.

"And your mother was a whore!" Dorena shouted, determined not to be outdone.

It was too much. Rage laid a red sheen over the sun. All the anger repressed through the long and painful winter burst violently in Julie. Dropping her book bag, she whirled about and leaped at Dorena.

The two girls tumbled into the dust of the road, clawing at each other. Julie doubled her fists and struck at Dorena's astonished face. Pain stabbed her as Dorena's fingernails raked down her cheek. Pounding her fists against Dorena's shoulders, Julie cried out as her opponent grabbed a handful of hair and pulled with all her might.

"What's going on here?" a male voice demanded. Julie felt herself dragged away from the screeching Dorena and set on her feet. As Dorena struggled to rise, the tall young man said sharply, "That's no way for ladies to behave."

"She ain't no lady." Dorena sneered at Julie. "She's nothing but a dirty Injun."

Julie lunged at the girl, fists flailing, only to be restrained by the young man's strong hand. Dorena's cohorts were easing away from the scene, looking apprehensive.

"Go on home before I hit you myself," he growled, glaring at the suddenly abashed Dorena. For the first time, Julie looked up into his face. It was Will Forester. She knew he was the son of her beloved Charles, but he never came to their house and she had seen him only at a distance. He was nearly as tall as his father and every bit as handsome. She'd heard Charles tell Grandmother about his son, his voice filled with pride as he recounted Will's accomplishments at school and his acceptance at some important place called Harvard.

Glancing at the three girls who were hastily retreating, Will picked up her book bag and the battered report card. With his other hand he tried to help her brush the dirt from the sprigged muslin gown she had donned so proudly this morning. Now it was torn and soiled.

"You're Star's girl, aren't you?" His voice was gentle. After the miserable day and the degrading fight, such gentleness broke the dam. Julie burst into tears.

Will picked her up in his arms, sweaty and bedraggled, her dusty face streaked with tears. Clinging to him, Julie gave herself up to misery and weeping while he carried her all the way home to her grandmother's house.

While Lydie bathed Julie and changed her clothes, Will sat with Star at the kitchen table and told her the story. Sipping his coffee, he watched her sad, silent face when he had finished. Outside the open kitchen window, lilacs perfumed the air. The low mumble of bees among the flowers was the only sound in the warm and pleasant room.

Will knew this woman had been his father's mistress once. They were business partners and friends still, a fact that Charles never tried to conceal. It rankled his mother, Will knew, even though Monique's cold sense of propriety did not allow discussion of such things.

By her dress, Star might have been any other Cameron City housewife, except for the coppery skin, the thin, high-cheeked face, and the blackness of her hair and eyes. She was still beautiful, with only a few lines about her eyes and mouth. An amazing woman, he thought, aware from the stories he'd heard that she'd adapted as few people ever had . . . making the transition from primitive life into civilization. There was about her such a sense of strength and serenity, Will began to understand why his father loved her.

"Thank you for what you did," she said in a low voice as she refilled his coffee cup. "It's been very hard for Julie this winter, harder than I guessed because she's kept it all to herself."

Will thought of the little girl's angry and determined face, and smiled. "She got even today."

Star sighed. "That won't be the end of it." Studying him, she changed the subject abruptly. "I'm pleased to know you at last, Will. Your father often talks about you and he's so proud of you."

Will flushed and looked down at his coffee cup. "Father and I have just started to become friends." He looked up and met her eyes. "That's why I hate to go away again this fall, when I know he isn't well."

"He wants you to go," Star began, and stopped as Lydie and Julie returned.

"You look quite beautiful, Julie," Will said, grinning and lifting the girl to his knee. She wore a clean pink muslin gown that accentuated the dark eyes and the long dark hair hanging loose and wet about her shoulders.

The eyes fastened adoringly on his face. "Lydie says you're a hero," she told him earnestly, "and I must thank you properly for rescuing me." With that, she pressed her warm moist lips against his cheek. Then, blushing furiously, she jumped down from his knee and ran to Star's outstretched arms.

Will laid his hand against his cheek, where the touch of her childish mouth lingered still. With a teasing smile, he winked at Julie. "I have never been kissed by a prettier lady."

Julie hid her scarlet face against Star's shoulder.

All the hurts of the long unhappy winter had poured out of Julie the next day as they rode together in the surrey to Red Hill Ranch. Listening, Star searched for the words to explain the vision quest to this small girl. Old Grandmother would have thought Julie too young to seek her vision, but Star knew Julie was old beyond her years. She had grown up in the company of adults who treated her as a companion. It was not like the girls growing up in the Nez Percé village, enjoying childhood with other children. Her age didn't matter, Star told herself, what mattered was that now, this day, she needed the reinforcement of pride in her Indian heritage.

Memories of the vision quests of her sons filled Star's mind as the mountains above Cameron Valley came into view. So long ago, she thought sadly, recalling Jed's elation at his strong warrior's vision, and Alex's disappointment that he had seen only a hawk. Prophetic visions, for Jed had told her of his second dream of the doomed buffalo . . . and Alex was still, as he had always been, a loner.

"I knew he'd die if he went back with the Indians!" Alex had cried out when she told him of Jed's death. Then he buried his face in his hands and wept openly for the brother he'd lost long ago. It was good he could weep, Star knew, for tears cleanse and assuage grief. Yet even now, she guessed that Alex somehow blamed himself for what had been Jed's destiny. And as she watched Alex going about his work, moving through the business life of Cameron City, always aloof, she feared for the pain his loneliness was certain to bring.

At the ranch, Star led Julie to the red hill, explaining to her the meaning of the vision quest. "Remember your cousin, Blood Moon?" she asked. "He told us of his vision. But yours will not be sad like his."

Julie nodded, her dark eyes fixed on Star's face. "I wish he would come to see us again."

He would not, Star knew. In the two years since her grandson had brought his tragic story, she had received one letter from him. Written with the assistance of the mission priest, it told of Red Moon's safe return to Canada. All the horses had survived and would make him wealthy by the tribe's standards. His sister attended the mission school and his mother, Snow Flower, was well. If all were not well, Star was certain she would know. Now she was content to let him be.

As she and Julie climbed the red hill together, Star thought of another starlit night long ago when she climbed a hill with Old Grandmother to find her own vision. There it had all begun, she thought, and sighed for the years gone so swiftly.

"Are you afraid?" she asked as they reached the crest of the hill.

"No." Julie glanced around in the gathering dusk, and set her lips determinedly. She wore a beaded doeskin gown Star had made for her and moccasins. Because she was so young, not yet into womanhood, Star thought *Hunyewat* would forgive the concession of one blanket against the cold air of early spring.

Shivering with apprehension, Julie watched her grand-mother descend the hill and disappear around the rock slide toward the ranch house. She had been here many times before, for it was a favorite spot of Grandmother's, over-looking as it did the far reaches of the ranch . . . the wide, stream-laced meadows; the distant rolling sage-covered hills; and far to the north the towering blue of the Wind River mountains.

The sun was gone now. In the violet sky, the evening star gleamed brightly above the eastern horizon. Shaking out the blanket, Julie wrapped it about her and lay down in the protected rocky crevice she had chosen. Night was a friend. She would not be afraid. Grandmother had told her she had the gift . . . of sight and of healing. When she was older, it would be there and she would be a medicine woman like Grandmother. It made her feel proud.

Clouds covered the half-moon and only a few pale stars shone. In the distance, a coyote howled and another an-swered, high and mournful. Wrapped close in the blanket, Julie turned on the hard ground and fell into a doze.

It seemed long after that she awakened, aware of another presence. She was very cold, shivering uncontrollably. Vi-sion cleared and the presence resolved into a gray dove perched on the rock above her. Trembling with cold and fear, she tried to speak. The dream shifted and changed, until the gray dove's wings seemed to enfold her into their comforting warmth. She saw that the dove's eyes were gray too, warm and loving, not sharp like birds' eyes. Safe and secure, she fell asleep.

"A gray dove," Julie told Grandmother as she sat at the table in the long room that served as both kitchen and sitting room for the ranch house. "It was big, I think, big as a person because it wrapped its wings about me and warmed me."

"Then you will take Gray Dove as your woman name?" Star asked, smiling at her.

Julie's empty stomach growled at the odor of the stew Grandmother was dishing up for her. The decision was hers. "Yes," she replied. "I am Gray Dove." But she frowned, trying to recall the eyes of the dream dove, somehow familiar and yet so strange.

"Monique's brother's daughters have all gone to school at the Convent of St. Ann in St. Louis," Charles said. "All six of them." Leaning back in his chair, he sipped the glass of iced lemonade. Beyond the windows of the sitting room, Forester Creek Road lay dusty and empty in the August heat. Even the leaves of the cottonwood trees lining the road looked limp and wilted.

Watching Star open the window wider to capture any possible breeze, he continued, "The nuns who teach there are gentlewomen, and kindly. Julie wouldn't be scarred by the ugliness of old scandals that aren't her fault."

Star hesitated, looking out the window into the heat haze blurring the distance. Charles was never one to avoid a decision that must be made, even though the very thought of this one made her heart ache.

She crossed the room to look down into her old friend's face. It struck her suddenly how he had aged in the past year. His aristocratic face was thin and gray. Nowadays, he leaned heavily on the cane he had once swung jauntily. A sense of coming sorrow seeped through her like old pain.

He had been speaking of Julie, she reminded herself, and answered slowly. "I can't bear to be separated from her, Charles. She's only seven. I might lose her."

"I think not," he returned with some asperity. "Julie's an

unusual child . . . and she'll always be your child, Star." He drew in a long breath, seeming to struggle with an inner pain. "Life is a long series of losses, isn't it, my dear?"

Their eyes met, and the depth of sadness in his gave another meaning to the words. Gently, she laid her hand on his shoulder. "You've never lost me, Charles."

A long sigh escaped him, his weary gray eyes still holding hers. "No," he murmured. "But each time we had to part I felt lost. If only . . ." His voice trailed away.

"What's between us could never be lost, my dear," she said, and bent to press her cheek against his hair.

Charles raised his hand to gently smooth her head. "Never," he answered softly.

To Julie, the train seemed to hurtle from daylight into night as it rushed eastward across the endless prairies, its light slipping through the darkness. Two elderly ladies in the seat nearby had smiled at her and asked where she was going. The young woman with them had glanced flirtatiously at Will, several times. Two cowboys played cards in one of the seats, and a drummer snored with his head against his cases.

"Are you hungry?" Will asked, dragging the hamper Lydie had packed from beneath the seat.

"Not very," she said, admiring his lean smiling face, and casting a jealous glare at the young lady who was still watching him. When the train stopped at the big station in Cheyenne, Will had shown her where the ladies' room was so she could wash her face and relieve herself. Then he had bought her a soda water from a vendor.

Now he handed her one of Lydie's chicken sandwiches and she ate it with no further protest. When he leaned back, propping his feet on the seat opposite, enjoying his sandwich, Julie watched him with fond eyes.

How terrible it would have been to go on this long journey without Will. Even though she guessed that Grandmother was reluctant to have her go away to school in St. Louis, Charles had insisted. Will was leaving for Harvard, and he could see Julie safely ensconced at St. Ann's. Because she equated Charles, so tall and stately and white-haired, with the God Lydie talked about, Julie knew it was right to go if he said so. The best part of all would be the days traveling alone with Will. He was her hero, worshiped with blind adoration that only occasionally embarrassed him.

"Remember . . . when you are at St. Ann's," he interrupted her thoughts, "remember what I told you to say. Alex Cameron is your father and he is a very rich man. Your mother is dead and you live with your grandmother. That is all you need to tell, and you must forget everything that was said to you last year in school."

"I want to forget it, Will," she answered in a sad small voice.

"You look tired," he said, patting her head. "Here . . ." And he unfolded a blanket, spreading it on the seat beside him. "Put your head on my knee and go to sleep, little one."

With a yawn, Julie obeyed. "What will you do?" she asked, looking up from where her head was pillowed on his knee.

Smiling, Will tucked the blanket around her. "Read my book until the conductor puts out the lights."

Sighing with fatigue, she snuggled against him and closed her eyes.

The long, mournful wail of the train whistle filled the darkness. Julie turned on the hard seat, drifting between sleeping and waking. Will slept with his head thrown back against the seat, a ray of light from the lamp at the end of the car across his face. As she moved, he awakened and his gray eyes looked down into hers.

Julie's heart leaped and pounded in her chest. She remembered the dream creature of her vision who had gathered her up into itself and protected her from the night cold. The gray dove, with warm protecting wings and soft, loving eyes . . . the gray eyes of Will Forester.

Chapter 33

1882

The cold wind seemed to come straight off the snows of the high Wind Rivers. Alex hunched his shoulders against it as he walked toward the house from the stables. Patchy snow still lingered on the north side of the buildings and beneath the trees.

In the early dusk, light from the kitchen fell across the back porch, and through the window he could see Mrs. Schrader at her work. This was home . . . and he was surprised that the word had entered his mind. For a long time now, he had ceased to feel about anything, especially about home. When he knew that Katrin would never set him free, he had accommodated himself to that, living in the same house, speaking only when necessary. With Caroline gone, it didn't matter.

"'Evening, Mr. Cameron," the housekeeper greeted him in her usual restrained manner. "You want supper?"

It had been a long, cold ride in from the ranch, and whatever was cooking in the oven set his mouth to watering. "Soon as I change," he replied, and started for the door.

"Mrs. Cameron's in bed with a sick headache," the woman offered.

When Alex gave her a questioning look, her eyes slid away. Sometimes he thought she'd developed a sneaking sympathy for him beneath her unswerving loyalty to Katrin.

"You'd best look in on her," she added, and turned back to stir something cooking on the stove.

Pausing beside his wife's bedroom door, Alex drew a deep breath. When he left, she had been excitedly planning her trip with Bertha to Philadelphia for Maria's graduation from Miss Potter's finishing school. There had even been talk that the three of them might go on to tour Europe if arrangements could be made. Katrin had long ago made it abundantly clear that Alex would not be welcome to go with her to Maria's school. He'd let that go, as he'd let go any thought of affection from Maria herself.

From long experience, he knew Katrin used her sick headaches as a refuge from reality. It was only with an effort that he could force himself to open the door and enter her room.

Clad in a frilly lavender silk and lace robe, Katrin lay on her pink satin chaise. Seeing Alex, she shoved away the maid who had been applying cold compresses to her forehead. The woman scurried from the room.

"*Your* daughter!" Katrin cried out. "Your daughter!"

For one wild moment, Alex wondered whether something had happened to Julie. Then Katrin threw a letter toward him.

"It's from the headmistress. Read it and see what kind of daughter you've raised in Maria."

Bending to retrieve the paper, Alex's mouth twisted at the irony of it. In one of her ugly scenes, long ago, Katrin had told him Maria was not his daughter. It had stunned him at first, but he'd had Caroline then, and after that her daughter, Julie . . . a child he was afraid to love. Katrin had never been above lying to achieve her ends or to hurt him. Jed was dead, and Alex could not believe his brother would have betrayed him in that way.

He'd always regretted that his relationship with Maria was so distant, but he'd stopped trying to buy her love now that she was grown. Maria was Katrin's daughter . . . as though she'd managed to conceive the child by herself.

In stiffly formal prose, the headmistress of Miss Potter's school stated that Hannah Maria Cameron was no longer a student there. "Her rebellious behavior has long been a trial to us," the letter said, "but we had hoped to make a lady of her for her parents' sake. However, the incident with the riding master was beyond the realm of decency. He has been dismissed. We will arrange for Maria's return to Wyoming as soon as possible."

"What riding master?" Alex demanded.

Katrin covered her face and moaned aloud. "I only pray they'll keep it quiet. That Bertha won't have to know."

"To hell with Bertha!" Alex growled. "What about the riding master?"

"Can't you guess?" Katrin's voice rose, and cracked with emotion. "Can't you read between the lines? You . . . of all people." She shot him a baleful look, then turned her face into her pillow and sobbed. "She's your daughter after all."

"Papa!" Maria called as she descended from the train, clutching her modish feathered hat to her head, the skirts of her dark green traveling gown blowing in the stiff March wind.

My God, Alex thought, she's a beauty . . . and I never noticed until now. The contrast of her mother's bright golden hair with her father's dark eyes was stunning, as was her voluptuous figure in the well-fitted gown.

"Papa!" she cried again, and flung her arms about him.

She was his daughter, Alex told himself, hugging her close. Damn Katrin, this girl was his daughter too. She'd gotten herself into some silly kind of trouble, but it was worth it if she turned to him at last.

"Where's Mama?" Maria asked, looking around as Alex released her. The other passengers were hurrying into the ugly yellow depot building, the men holding their hats against the wind, the women clinging to their shawls under the gray, blustery sky.

In a conspiratorial whisper, she asked, "Is she terribly angry?"

"She's in bed with a sick headache," Alex replied wryly, knowing Maria would understand the significance of that information.

Unpinning her hat, Maria tossed her head. "Mama can just forget it," she told him, dark eyes flashing. A tendril of bright hair, loosened by the wind, blew enchantingly across her smooth cheek. "It was all a terrible lie. The headmistress hated me and wanted to get even." She gave him a beguiling smile. "Oh, Papa . . . it's so wonderful to be home again."

Something had happened that Alex could not quite fathom, but when Maria gave him another impulsive hug, he felt a part of his dead heart begin to come alive again.

Alex was excluded from the loud and furious confrontation between mother and daughter that took place behind the closed door of Katrin's bedroom. For himself, he thought it foolish of Katrin to make so much of Maria's being kissed by a lecherous riding master, just as foolish as that haughty headmistress. But perhaps part of Katrin's anger was centered in disappointment that she would not be traveling to Philadelphia to mingle with the other wealthy parents at Miss Potter's graduation ceremonies.

As though to punish her mother, Maria became attentive to Alex in a way she had never been before. In the evening, she brought him coffee where he sat reading beside the fire, lighting his cigar with a coquettish gesture he found immensely appealing.

"I'm bored out of my mind, Papa," she confided one night only two weeks later. The two of them sat alone beside the sitting-room fire, for Katrin had flounced off to her bedroom after yet another tedious and silly disagreement with Maria.

Giving him a tremulous smile, Maria continued, "Mama and I quarrel all the time . . . about nothing, as though she can't stop punishing me."

Alex reached over to pat her hand affectionately. He knew something about Katrin's never-ending punishment, and his heart went out to his daughter.

"I know you're going to the ranch for spring roundup. Could I go with you and stay for a while?" Maria burst out, her dark eyes sparkling at the idea. "Would you like that, Papa?"

"Things aren't very exciting at the ranch," he protested,

amused by her enthusiasm, but pleased that she had asked. Katrin wouldn't like it, he thought. She never visited the ranch now. His foreman, Buck Webster, had married and lived with his wife in the old ranch house.

"You could ride with me and show me the place. It's been so long I've almost forgotten what it looks like." Impulsively, she dropped down beside his chair, folding her arms on his knee and giving him a pleading look he found totally irresistible.

Maria took over the bedroom the Websters did not use and proceeded to annoy a very pregnant Mrs. Webster by leaving clothes strewn about and never offering to help with the cooking or the dishes. Sleeping in the bunkhouse, Alex chose to ignore Mrs. Webster. Indulgently, he catered to Maria's every whim, pleased that at long last his daughter had turned to him for company and affection.

Spring came in a rush that year. April brought warm and pleasant weather, the catkins on the willows bursting out all at once. The cottonwoods leafed, and everywhere there were birds coming home from the southland. New calves had to be gathered and branded.

As the ranch work increased, Alex had less time to devote to Maria, but she was sweetly understanding. "Let one of the cow hands ride with me, Papa," she told him. "I know how busy you are."

He chuckled, knowing how she loved to show off in one of the many fancy riding habits she'd brought along. Kissing her cheek, he went to ask Terry Burnside to look after his daughter, choosing him because he seemed to be more refined than most of the Texas cowboys who made up the crew now.

It had been a long hard day gathering cattle from the rocky benches to the east of the ranch, beginning before dawn and ending now with the last rays of sun fading in the west. Alex looked forward to Mary Webster's good supper and an evening of Maria's company. He was teaching her to play poker, proud of how quickly she grasped the intricacies of the game. Unsaddling his horse, he turned it into the corral and tossed his saddle into the tack shed. From the lighted cookhouse, he could hear the sounds of the ranch hands at their supper. Then another sound, low and strange, caught his attention.

Puzzled, he crossed to the stable, flinging open the door on the dusky interior. Beside the manger, Maria stood in Terry Burnside's fierce embrace, her mouth locked with his, Terry's hands clasping her buttocks as he pressed her against him.

At the sound of the stable door banging behind Alex, they broke apart guiltily. At once, Maria began smoothing her hair, trying to conceal the fact that her shirtwaist was unbuttoned. She attempted to smile at Alex, while Terry simply hung his head in embarrassed silence.

"Get your gear and make tracks." Alex spat the words out, trying to keep his voice low so that no one else would hear.

"Tonight?" Terry looked up, his young face shocked.

"If you're not out of here before dark, I'll beat the shit out of you." Alex couldn't look at Maria, only at the guilt-stricken cowboy. Finally, Terry shrugged and pushed past Alex to leave the stable without a word.

Giving him an imploring look, Maria laid her hand on Alex's arm. "Terry just didn't understand, Papa. I was only thanking him for riding with me, and he . . . he just took advantage." She began to cry.

"I know, sweetheart." Alex encircled her shoulders with his arm and hugged her close. "Those damn Texans got no upbringing. Maybe you ought to go back to town."

"Oh no!" Maria cried, wiping away her tears. A strange, hot light burned in the depths of her dark eyes as she pleaded, "I want to stay here . . . with you, Papa."

For the next few days, Maria seemed subdued. She cleaned up her bedroom and even offered to help Mary with the dishes. Then one morning after Alex and the crew had left to work the continuing calf roundup, she dressed in her best riding habit and commanded the stableman to saddle a horse for her.

"I figgered it's my duty to tell you," Mary Webster

confronted Alex. "She rides off every day by herself. It ain't safe fer a young gal."

"Thanks, Mary," Alex said, suddenly weary of the responsibility of his willful daughter. "I'll talk to her."

"I won't do it again, Papa," Maria promised with a lighthearted kiss. "It's just that I was bored."

Even though he accepted her promise, Alex felt uneasy. Something was not quite right, not quite straightforward. The next day when one of the men returned from his circle gathering cattle to complain that Hal Johnston had disappeared just when he needed his help, Alex's unease burgeoned into panic. He left Buck in charge and rode straight to the ranch house.

"She went out again," a tight-lipped Mary Webster told him.

Alex mounted his horse, determined to find Maria and send her back to Cameron City first thing tomorrow. A horse whinnied. Drawing rein, Alex turned and saw tethered behind the stables the horse Hal had been riding this morning.

"Bastard!" Alex muttered between his teeth. Tying his own mount to a corral pole, he looked around. The stables were empty except for old Bill who was shoveling manure. Cursing softly, Alex walked to the deserted bunkhouse.

They were on the cot, Hal's bare buttocks heaving as he thrust against the woman lying beneath him. Maria's head was thrown back, her eyes closed tightly, her wet red mouth open and moaning softly. Her hands clutched at Hal's back as her pale nude body answered his thrusts with wild abandon.

Sickness poured through Alex, blurring his vision. He stumbled from the room, his insides heaving. Dropping down on the bench beside the bunkhouse door, he sat with his face in his hands for a long time, certain that the heart he had thought Maria could heal had been ripped open again.

"She was screwing every cow hand on the place," Alex rasped. "Everybody knew it but me."

"For God's sake, Alex," Katrin cried, casting a glance at

the tightly closed bedroom door, then at her daughter who sat, stony-faced, staring at nothing. Her baleful eyes returned to Alex. "You don't have to talk like one of your whores."

Ignoring her, he crossed to the bedroom window, looking down on the willow-lined banks of Forester Creek. Spring runoff still filled the creek from bank to bank. Through the open window, he could faintly hear the roar of water as it poured over the falls far up the creek. It was the last time, he told himself, drawing cigarette makings from the pocket of his cotton shirt. It was the very last time he would let anyone get near him.

Katrin whirled on her daughter. "I hope to God you're not pregnant by one of those Texas tramps."

"I'm not." Maria gave her mother a cool glance. "I got my period this morning."

Throwing up her hands in despair, Katrin paced the room distractedly, stopping finally in front of Alex. "We have to get her married, that's all there is to it. If there'd been anyone suitable here, I'd have arranged it before she ever went east. I just hoped she could do better there."

"Lots of them were suitable, Mama." Maria broke in with a vindictive smile. "None were good enough in bed."

Katrin gasped and the color drained from her face. It was a moment before she regained her composure.

Alex groaned inwardly. Carefully making a cigarette, he avoided Katrin's questioning stare. Turning as he lit his cigarette, he saw her eyes narrow in thought, and a slow mean smile grow on her mouth.

Giving Alex a triumphant look, she drew her silk robe tight about her and crossed the room to confront Maria. "We're invited to Will Forester's welcome-home party tomorrow night. If you're so good at attracting men, I suggest you practice your wiles on Will. Catch him, and you'll have something worthwhile."

"Katrin . . ." Alex's protest trailed into silence at the fierce look she gave him. "Christ," he muttered, stalking from the room.

Why should he be surprised again at Katrin's lack of

scruples, that she would be willing to drop the problem of her out-of-control daughter into the arms of Will Forester? During his summers in Cameron City, Will worked with Charles and Alex in their multiple business interests. The young man was Charles's son in every way ... the same kindness, integrity, and intelligence. That he had always longed for such a son drew Alex to him. Even when Charles was gone, Alex knew the two of them would be good friends. Certainly, Will had better sense than to lose his heart to a girl like Maria. Alex intended to do all in his power to prevent such a thing from happening.

Moonlight silvered the trees and the sagebrush hills in the distance. Before them, the pale line of the dusty road faded into shimmering distance. The last lights went out in the schoolhouse, and the voices of the weary dancers going home drifted into silence.

The light seemed to catch in Maria's pale gold hair, as though it were spun of moonlight. Will's heart thumped, roaring in his ears, as the scent of her perfume drifted on the warm spring air. Unobtrusively, he slowed the horse to walk so that the buggy ride home from the schoolhouse dance would last longer.

She leaned over to touch her cheek to his shoulder, then moved away, murmuring, "I'm sorry. You must think I'm forward, but it's meant so much to me to have your company these past weeks." With a long sigh, she laid her cheek against his shoulder again. "I'd have simply died in Cameron City if it hadn't been for you."

Swallowing hard, Will leaned toward her, hoping she wouldn't move away this time. He felt an irrational urge to free her golden hair from its elaborate chignon and run his fingers through its spun silk softness.

The lovely, earnest face was turned to his, and her dark eyes gleamed in the moonlight. "You're so beautiful," he said, and she smiled.

"It's strange, isn't it?" he said, the pressure of her cheek against his shoulder like a firebrand. "You can know some-one all your life, then suddenly, one day you see them in a different way. Like the night of my welcome-home party . . . I couldn't believe I'd never noticed before how wonderful you are." It had caught him by surprise . . . her sultry beauty, her admiring glances. Even his mother had remarked on Maria's finishing school polish. But Will knew that wasn't what drew him to call on her every day since then; it was something deep and urgent binding him inexorably to Maria.

"I've grown up, Will," she murmured, sliding her hand along his arm. "I guess I had to grow up to appreciate what a wonderful, handsome man you are."

Without thinking, he took the reins in one hand, his other arm stealing about her yielding shoulders.

"It's such a beautiful night, Will," she said, snuggling closer on the buggy seat. "Do we have to go straight home?"

Will felt the fire ignite in his loins, and he struggled to subdue it. In all his twenty-two years he had never felt like this. But this was not one of the girls he and his Harvard friends visited to satisfy their youthful urges. Maria was a proper girl . . . a Cameron, educated and well brought up. But he blindly turned the horse up the Falls road leading to the rocky glen where Forester Creek roared down from the hills.

Through the material of his jacket, Will could feel her full soft breast pressing against his side. One of her hands took his at her shoulder, stroking his fingers, the other lay softly, innocently on his knee. All the breath went out of him, and he could not speak.

"The falls are beautiful in the moonlight," Maria murmured as he drew the horse to a halt beneath the cottonwoods where the rocky bank overlooked the roaring creek. Shadows of the trees moved over the adoring face lifted to his, and Will's arm tightened about her shoulders. In the distance, a whippoorwill called, sweet and sad, in the warm moonlight.

Maria's hand moved across his chest, leaving a trail of fire, resting softly on his shoulder. "I could stay here forever with you," she whispered, and pressed her soft mouth against his chin.

The touch of her lips was like a torch, igniting his whole body. Will felt himself harden with desire, and a moan escaped him. Maria was in his arms, her mouth hot and sweet beneath his, her arms tight about his neck, her breasts like burning brands against his chest.

"Will," she gasped as their mouths parted. "Oh, darling Will. I love you . . . I love you."

"Sweet . . . sweet Maria . . ." His lips devoured hers, his tongue probing in urgent need. She opened to him without hesitation, filling his mouth with her sweetness. Desire surged through him.

Somehow, the buttons on her blouse were open and his blindly searching hand held her soft breasts as his mouth sucked hungrily at them. Her hands seemed to be touching him everywhere, sending molten shafts of passion through his body. The roar of the water falling in the creek echoed the roar of need that pulsed through him.

"Maria . . . Maria . . ." he gasped urgently as she let him press her down on the seat of the buggy, his hand searching in desperate haste beneath her skirt. The few underclothes she wore were gone in one swift movement, his trousers opened, and their bodies joined in a need that could not be denied.

The buggy swayed and rocked with their frenzied movements. Tossing its head, the horse moved restlessly. The moonlight, the falling water, Maria's soft moans lifted Will into a world of rapture beyond reality. With an exultant cry, he thrust deep into her hot yielding body and emptied himself of passion.

"There's a letter from your grandmother," Priscilla said, giving Julie one of her admiring buck-toothed smiles. Flopping down on her bed in the austere little room she had shared with Julie for two years, she propped pillows behind her skinny shoulders and tore open her own mail. "How come your father never writes?" she asked for the hundredth time.

"He doesn't have time," Julie answered, aware of the sympathy in her friend's eyes, feeling the old familiar twinge of rejection. But it was spring now and Grandmother was waiting for her to come home. Surely Will Cameron would be home from Harvard too. Last summer they'd gone riding together several times and he'd treated her like a grown-up lady. Maybe this summer there'd be more time with the gentle, laughing young man who was her idol. Eagerly, she turned to her letter.

All the blood seemed to drain out of her as she read her grandmother's spiky handwriting. A terrible pain started somewhere deep inside, growing and growing until she wanted to scream out the hurt of it. As if from a distance, she heard Priscilla saying, "My mother says she loved meeting you when she was in St. Louis. You're such a sweet girl, she'd love to have you visit us at my grandparents' cottage in Cape May this summer."

Staring blindly at the letter, Julie fought back the tears burning behind her eyes. He was married . . . her own dear hero . . . her Will. Married to the beautiful, dreadful Maria who was her half-sister, according to Grandmother, but who never spoke to her.

Somehow, she'd thought Will would always be there for her with the same warm smile, the same gentle hands. She'd even shared the dream with her beloved friend Priscilla when they lay in bed after lights-out, talking dreamily about growing up and getting married.

How could she ever bear to go back to Cameron City, to see him married to Maria?

"Do you want to go to Cape May with my family this summer?" Priscilla asked again, a bit impatiently this time.

"Yes," Julie answered, making her voice steady with an effort, blinking back the threatened tears. She hugged her friend then, certain that Priscilla had offered her escape from the unhappy realities awaiting her back in Wyoming.

Chapter 34

Marriage was not at all what he'd expected, Will thought as he mounted the stairs to his father's office above the Cameron City Bank. He was late again, and his face warmed as he wondered if his father guessed the reason. How could he resist Maria's soft-eyed pleading to "come back to bed, Will, and love me just a little before you leave." A little always turned out to be a lot. When she lay in sated slumber, he would dress and go to work, still amazed at her endless desire for him. His married friends had told him they had to beg their wives for less than Maria insisted upon. On their honeymoon in San Francisco, they'd scarcely seen the city, indulging themselves instead in days and nights of passionate enjoyment of each other.

"Good morning, Papa," he said, entering the spacious office overlooking Cameron City's busy main street and the railroad yards beyond, where the August sun glared mercilessly.

Charles looked up from the papers spread on his wide mahogany desk, and smiled. "Good morning, Will. And how is Maria this morning?"

Will felt himself flush. "Fine," he replied, turning to hang his coat on the standing rack beside the door.

"Your mother says she's never seen anyone who seems to thrive on pregnancy the way Maria does."

It was simply a pleasant, fatherly observation and Will felt annoyed with himself for letting his relationship with Maria color every moment of his life.

"By the way," Charles continued as Will sat down at his own rolltop desk placed against the far wall. "Your shingle came on the morning train. There . . . by your desk. I'll have someone hang it this afternoon."

Will pulled the wooden sign out from the wall, feeling a thrill of pride at the elaborate gold letters on shiny wood: WILLIAM C. FORESTER, ATTORNEY-AT-LAW. He'd passed the bar examination easily. Maria had teased him to go back east to live, thinking that Boston would be one long series of parties and dressing up. But he was a married man now, with responsibilities, not only to his wife, but to his father.

"Looks good, huh?" Will asked, turning the sign to show Charles. Their eyes met and Will felt his own sting with emotion at the pride in his father's face.

Even more than his marriage, it was that face that had made his decision not to take the offer from a prestigious Boston law firm. Charles had failed in the past year. His white hair was thinner, his face drawn and gray. When he walked, he seemed to be struggling to conceal his pain, and he was always short of breath.

There had been so many years when Will was growing up, so many years when he'd needed his frequently absent father. Just since his mother agreed to move to Cameron City had they come to really know each other. Despite the protests of his mother and his wife, he'd decided to stay, hang out his shingle in Cameron City, and help ease the burdens of business he knew his father carried.

"Go over these mortgages with me?" Charles asked, and Will drew up a chair near his father's desk just as a soft knock sounded at the door.

When Star Cameron came into the room, Will was struck again by her unconscious elegance. She wore a doeskin riding skirt with a wine-colored silk shirtwaist, her figure as straight and slim as a girl's. He caught the look of affectionate understanding that passed between Star and his father. A sudden pang of envy went through him as he wondered whether his relationship with Maria would be as deep and abiding. He didn't really want a marriage like his parents', who were kind to each other without ever really communicating. Sometimes he wondered how they had ever had enough passion between them to conceive him.

Turning to him with a smile, Star asked, "How is Maria? Alex told me she's expecting."

Will nodded, looking pleased and proud. "She's doing fine." Maria did not visit her grandmother, she'd made that clear to him. He had seen Star at the wedding, unobtrusive in a dark silk gown, and absent from the reception at Forester House.

"She's thriving," Charles broke in. "I think she enjoys living in the Forester mansion on top of the hill above everyone in Cameron City." There was a faintly sardonic note to his voice.

Star studied him gravely. Will flushed, aware that Maria's demands on the servants had already caused his mother problems.

"I'm buying the Dunlap place," Star said, abruptly changing the subject. "Will you handle the paperwork and put it in Julie's name?"

"They couldn't make a crop, huh?" Charles observed.

"People who should know, say this isn't farming country." Star shrugged. "I'll pay them enough to get back east and start over."

"Alex will be glad to have them stop eating his cows," Charles said with ironic amusement.

"He doesn't know about this," Star replied. "Dunlap came to see me after Alex left on the cattle train last week. Anyway, it's my business."

"Is Alex going to St. Louis?" Charles's voice was low, and his gray eyes studied her face sympathetically.

"I asked him to." Her lips tightened and she looked down at the hands clasped in her lap.

Charles sighed. "I know you've missed our little Julie, Star, but a summer with a family like the Stanburys must have done a lot for her. They're solid people. I checked them out."

Star's head was bowed and she did not look up. Will thought she was struggling to hold back tears and he longed to touch her shoulder in comfort. The dancing eyes of the little girl he'd taken to St. Louis came into his mind. It seemed she had found friends there, but he hoped with all his heart that did not mean Star would lose her.

Julie was aware of her friends peering over the stairwell into the reception hall. Even though she was trembling, she kept her head high and a smile on her face as she descended the stairs.

"Your father is here," Sister Antonia had said. Stunned, Julie could only stare in silence while Sister fussed with her hair and her uniform, anxious that she appear presentable.

Now all the girls had crowded in the upper hall, elbowing each other in their eagerness to catch a glimpse of this fabled man from Wyoming who never wrote to his daughter.

In the shadowed hall, Alex stood uneasily before the great oaken doors of St. Ann's. Watching his daughter descend the long stairway, he felt his heart contract painfully. She'd grown tall, all arms and legs, but the plain gray uniform was somehow becoming to her dark hair and eyes and her olive skin.

"Here she is, Mr. Cameron," the black-clad nun said, smiling. "We're very proud of Julie. She's one of our best students."

Alex gave her a curt nod. "I'm glad to hear it," he said, unsmiling. With a puzzled glance, the nun led them into the visitors' sitting room.

They stood before the tall windows overlooking the rolling grassy hill sweeping down to the tree-shrouded chapel. The Mississippi River gleamed faintly in the distance. Surely anyone would be proud to have this handsome man for a father, Julie thought, studying him. He wore a well-tailored black suit with frock coat, highly polished high-heeled boots, and a gray broad-brimmed felt hat that was the badge of a cattleman. His rugged face was deeply tanned, and when he removed his hat, she saw the gray intermingled in his sandy hair.

The uneasy silence stretched between them. At last, Julie held her hand out tentatively. "I'm glad to see you, Alex."

A wry smile twisted his mouth as he took her hand. "It might be more appropriate if you called me Father while we're here."

"Very well," Julie agreed, regarding him gravely.

Again, Alex felt his heart twist. There was something in the contours of her childish face that brought memories of Caroline rushing over him in a painful flood. Abruptly, he turned to look out the windows. Drawing a cigar from his pocket, he made a ritual of lighting it, allowing himself time to regain his composure.

"How is Grandmother?" The words came in a rush as she suddenly realized the possible portent of his unexpected visit.

Seeing her distress, Alex patted her shoulder reassuringly. "She's just fine, Julie. But she misses you and she was concerned about you since you've been away so long. That's why she insisted I come here to see you . . . to make sure you're well and happy."

"I miss her too." Julie's eyes suddenly filled with homesick tears. "And Lydie?"

"She sends her love." He puffed on his cigar, watching her with carefully shuttered eyes.

It was so painfully hard to find anything to say to this man. "I wish Grandmother had come," Julie burst out, then drew in her breath, afraid she had offended him.

He looked down at his cigar. "It's a hard trip, as you know, and your grandmother isn't young." Smiling politely at her, he added, "She's anxious for you to come home when school ends next spring." Drawing a long breath, he added, "It's lonely for her without you."

"I know." Julie could not meet his eyes. She'd missed Grandmother too, and Lydie . . . but the whole town was occupied with Will and Maria's wedding. The copies of the *Cameron City Clarion* that Grandmother sent were filled with ecstatic descriptions of it. Without thinking, the words came out. "I guess you were all busy with the wedding this summer."

"Yes." The word was flat and final. Puzzled, Julie studied his suddenly cold face. For reasons she could not fathom, Alex was not happy about Maria's marriage to Will.

Because she still could not bear to think about it, she began to tell him about her summer at the New Jersey shore, about the elaborate "cottage" Priscilla's grandparents maintained at Cape May, and about her visit to Stanbury Oaks, the plantation on the river near Cape Girardeau, where Priscilla had grown up.

Alex listened attentively, smoking his cigar until she wound down with nothing more to tell.

Giving her a penetrating look, he turned away abruptly, crushing out his cigar in an ashtray. "You're learning how people of wealth and breeding live, Julie. I'm sure that's worthwhile."

Not quite understanding, Julie nodded in agreement anyway, then confided, "Grandmother has made the arrangements. I'm to start taking piano lessons this fall."

A choked sound came from him. Whirling away from her, he walked to the far end of the room and stood there for a long time staring blindly out the tall windows.

Watching him, Julie felt an ache spread inside her chest. Grandmother had told her on the day of her vision that she had the gift, not only to know the future, but to see inside another's heart. Tears filled her eyes now as she felt the pain and emptiness emanating from the tall, lonely man who was her father. She longed to go to him and comfort him, but something held her back, the same wall that had always separated them.

"Good-bye, Father." She faltered over the unfamiliar title, and was pleased when he smiled. They stood before the tall front door, Sister Antonia waiting beside the stairs.

His smile faded and he looked uncomfortable, as though unsure what to do next. "Good-bye, Julie," he said.

Glancing over her shoulder at Sister Antonia, and at Priscilla who was still hanging over the upstairs banister, she whispered to Alex. "All the fathers hug their girls when they say good-bye." It wasn't entirely true, although the ebullient Mr. Stanbury had even hugged Julie.

With a chagrined expression, Alex bent and gathered her into his arms. He was very stiff, the fabric of his coat rough beneath her hands, but she hugged him anyway and planted a quick kiss on his cheek.

"Good-bye, Father," she said again as he set her on her feet.

"Good-bye." Alex's voice was low and strangled and he did not look at her. Without another word or gesture, he opened the oak doors. They fell shut behind him with a sharp final click.

"I have never been welcome in this house, Alex," Star said just as the black maid opened the leaded-glass doors of the Forester mansion. Last night's snowstorm had blown away, leaving Cameron City sparkling under a pristine blanket of white. In spite of the brilliance of the sunlight, the February air was icy and Star shivered beneath her beaver fur cape.

With a carefully bland face, the maid told them the family was upstairs in the nursery. The house was overheated, and the dry hot air seemed smothering. Star gladly surrendered her fur into the maid's outstretched hands. As the woman disappeared down the hallway, Star flashed a sidelong look at Alex's frowning face. "You know it's true," she said in a low voice. "Monique will be furious that you've brought me here."

Alex's mouth tightened. "This is your first great-grandson, Ma. Even Monique won't object to your seeing Maria's baby." He studied her for a moment, then gave her a teasing wink. "Don't tell me you aren't dying to see him."

Slipping her arm through his as they climbed the stairs, Star steeled herself. Even though it was a freezing February day, the kind of day when people in Wyoming kept inside, Alex had brought her in his carriage to see his new grandson, born just yesterday. In his jubilant state, she could not refuse him.

Bursting with pride, she thought, giving him an amused glance now.

"Did I tell you they've named him Cameron?" he asked

for the tenth time. "Cameron Forester," he went on, bemused, not waiting for an answer.

The beautiful curving staircase seemed long to her, making her aware of the years. Only half listening to Alex telling of plans for his grandson's future, Star was suddenly struck by how incongruously far her life had come from her beginnings. From the primitive skin lodge to a mansion as grand as this one, she thought, and it was the lodge she dreamed of when in need of comfort.

A door stood open on a lavishly decorated nursery which was empty. "They must be in Maria's room," Alex said, holding her hand in the crook of his arm and leading her on.

A low gasp greeted their entrance. Alex's mouth tightened, but he did not hesitate, leading Star across the vast bedroom filled with ornately carved mahogany furniture, blue damask draperies, and thick carpets.

Maria lay ensconced in a huge bed. Star's eyes took in the quilted blue satin coverlet, the luxurious lace-trimmed pillows, the frothy blue robe Maria wore. The skin lodge was another lifetime.

Monique stood on the opposite side of the bed, staring stonily at them, not speaking. Will hurried toward Star, hands outstretched. "Come look at your great-grandson," he said proudly. "He's perfect . . . big and strong and beautiful."

Maria managed a cool, polite smile as she drew back the blanket from the baby lying in her arms. Star's heart contracted as she looked at the tiny face. Eyes screwed shut, small fists waving, the baby blew little bubbles from his pink mouth.

Tentatively, Star reached a hand toward him. One of the warm little fists closed about her finger. Such a pain went through her, she almost gasped aloud. Her gift was seldom one of joy, and in this moment, she recalled unhappily the first premonition she had felt on seeing Katrin. It was true, Katrin had brought unhappiness . . . and this child would bring heartaches.

"Quite a boy, isn't he?" Will's proud voice asked.

Star could only nod in reply, longing to warn him and knowing she could do nothing to change what must be.

"Cameron Forester," Alex boomed. "I can't wait to teach him to ride a horse."

"At last, Alex . . ." It was Katrin's voice and Star looked at her in surprise, for she hadn't noticed her in the room. "At last you have the son you've wanted all your life." Her lips were smiling as she said the words, but her eyes were hard.

Charles's face was gray and gleaming with clammy sweat. His breath came in short, panting gasps. Taking the wet cloth from an anxious-faced Lydie, Star carefully wiped his forehead. Charles let out a long breath, leaning back in the big leather chair before Star's fireplace.

"You shouldn't have walked from the office, Charles," she chided gently. "That's why you have a driver and buggy."

With a wan smile, he protested. "It's spring, Star. The first really good day of spring. I wanted to smell the lilacs and watch the birds."

Carefully, she smoothed back his thin white hair with the cool cloth. Charles drew a ragged breath. "My pills are in my coat pocket . . . there in the foyer."

At Star's glance, Lydie hurried to the foyer. When he had gulped down the pill, Charles smiled up at the two concerned women. "I'll be all right now. Just let me rest a minute."

Watching her friend's struggle, Star closed her eyes for a moment against the gift. The shadow she saw lying over Charles seemed to have physical substance. All the strength went out of her knees and she sat down abruptly on the chair beside him.

His breathing had eased and he waved the hovering Lydie away. "I'm fine now . . . honest, Lydie."

Lydie cast a questioning glance at Star, who nodded, then said in her deep voice, "I'll fix you a little bite of somethin', Mr. Charles."

Star followed her to the kitchen door, whispering, "Send Clint to bring Mr. Will."

Charles leaned back in the chair, closing his eyes. The sense of loss grew in Star as she watched his weary face. Gently, she took his hand in hers. The gray eyes opened, looking at her with tender warmth.

"Your girl will soon be home, won't she?"

How like Charles to, even now, be thinking of others. "Yes," she answered softly. "The first of June."

"Good." He closed his eyes again as though speaking had wearied him, leaning his head against the back of the chair.

Through the open windows, Star could hear the bees working in the lilacs, the cry of birds nesting in the newly leafed cottonwoods. A new cycle of life beginning. Charles's hand tightened on hers, and she thought of all the years that would have been empty without him.

Leaning toward him, she murmured, "I love you, Charles."

Without opening his eyes, he smiled sadly. "That's the first time you've said those words to me, Star."

"There are many kinds of love, dear friend." Star's eyes stung with tears of regret as she wondered why she had never before told him how deeply she cared for him.

Still holding her hand, Charles reached over to cup her cheek in his other palm. The gray eyes darkened with love. "It just may be, Star my love, that the kind we've had is the best of all."

Their eyes held in the long silence of farewell. Hearing voices in the kitchen, Star bent and gently kissed his mouth. Charles sighed, his grip on her hand tightened, and they were still holding hands when Lydie ushered a worried-looking Will into the room.

Wind in the trees awakened Star in the night. The sense of loss she had borne all day, ever since Will had taken his father home in the buggy, overwhelmed her now. She felt bereft . . . alone in the dark world of wind-tossed trees.

Old ways, she thought, only the old ways could comfort. Rising, she donned her doeskin gown and went down to the skin lodge to sing for the loss of her dearest friend.

Chapter 35

1883

Midday August sun beat down on the dusty main street of Cameron City. Restless, Will rose from his desk and walked to the window to look out on his father's town, wondering whether he would ever be through missing him. The railroad station was deserted now, the morning eastbound gone and the westbound not due until evening. Sagebrush-gray hills rolled away beyond the tracks, shimmering in the heat. At the hitching rack on the street below, the horses stood, hip-sprung, heads drooping.

Idly, he speculated on where the train would be now . . . pulling out of Laramie, or nearly into Cheyenne. Ever since he'd gone to the station with Star to see Julie and Lydie off for Cape May, he'd felt restless and out of sorts.

Alex should have been there, damn his self-centered heart. A man should be proud to acknowledge a daughter like Julie instead of ignoring her. Alex seemed to be forever running from reality . . . busy at his ranch, gone to Texas to buy more cattle, busy everywhere except Cameron City. When he was in town, he spent most of his time in the nursery worshiping his grandson.

Remembering the girl he had taken to St. Louis only three years ago, Will sighed. She'd changed. Girls do grow up, he reminded himself wryly, and this one was suddenly all arms and legs and huge dark eyes. But the change was more than physical. Once he'd delighted in the friendship they shared. Now she seemed unwilling to meet his eyes, and spoke to him only in inarticulate monosyllables. With a shrug, he turned from the window. Maybe she'd become aware of the difference between men and women. The thought saddened him, that he should thereby lose her innocent regard.

Just as he seated himself once more at the huge desk that had been his father's, the door flew open and Maria swept into the room.

"You didn't come home for dinner," she accused, her dark eyes flashing.

Leaning back in his chair, Will studied his wife. Childbirth had given a fullness to her exquisite figure, and in her white tucked lawn gown, trimmed with lace and ruffles, she looked every inch the fine lady. Fearing she might lose her figure, she'd hired a wet nurse for the baby, and prevailed upon Monique to send to St. Louis for a proper English nanny for the child.

She had no right to be so beautiful, and so selfish, Will thought, knowing how seldom Maria ever visited their child.

"Cameron City is boring me into my grave," she went on, pacing the warm room. "The least you could do is give me your company for dinner."

"I'm sorry, Maria," he said, seeing that she was working up to a tantrum. "Star asked me to take Julie and Lydie to the train this morning. Julie's going to visit the Stanburys at Cape May, and Lydie's going on to Atlanta." Discreetly, he did not add that Gussie had written asking Lydie to come because she was lonely and ill.

Maria paused in front of his desk, eyes flashing. "And that's more important than your wife?"

"I thought today was the Ladies Literary luncheon," he protested, knowing that the tangled relations of the Cameron family were always a volatile subject. Maria would never acknowledge her half-sister, whose birth, she claimed, had disgraced the family and her mother.

Sweeping off her wide-brimmed white leghorn hat, Maria groaned dramatically. "Spare me, please. I know the literary club is your mother's pride and joy, but I can't bear those twittering women."

Nor could she bear any other part of the town social life that his mother had tried to draw her into, Will thought sadly. Monique had endowed the building of a new Catholic church in memory of her husband. She'd established the Ladies Altar Society, and plainly hoped that her newly converted daughter-in-law would join in supporting church activities. Beyond her resigned attendance at Mass, Maria managed to evade all responsibility.

Producing a white lace fan, Maria began to fan herself furiously. Even the beads of sweat on her upper lip were becoming. "All you do since your father died is work, work, work." Her voice fell to a self-pitying whine. "And all I do is wait, wait, wait, for you to come home from this damned office."

To entertain you, play cards with you, take you to bed, he thought, struggling to quell the resentment rising in his heart. "My father tried to teach me his business in the last few months of his life," Will explained patiently as he had so many times before. "But I had no idea how far-reaching his investments were. It'll take me a while to learn it all and get things under control."

"What are all those clerks and bookkeepers for?" She glared at him, her voice sharp.

"You don't understand business, Maria—" Will began, aware that he was fighting his way through a conversation they had had many times before.

"I understand," she interrupted, rising to her feet. "You're too busy to take me on a holiday." She began to pace once more, fanning herself furiously. "The Billings are in Colorado Springs, you know," she added with an accusing glance.

"Maybe next month," he began, and she whirled on him, leaning across the desk to stare into his face.

"Always next month, Will . . . or next week or next year." Her lovely mouth twisted in an ugly sneer. "It's even wait until tonight . . . or tomorrow . . . when I want to make love."

"Maria," he protested, standing and reaching out for her.

Evading his grasp, she picked up her hat. With a stubborn lift of her chin, she stared at him. "I'm going to take a holiday, Will. I have to get out of this awful heat." In a dramatic gesture, she laid her hand against her forehead and sighed. "Papa's ranch is so much cooler. I've decided to go up and stay with the Websters for a week or so."

Frowning, Will studied her. "Do you think that will be good for the baby?" he asked.

Maria tossed her head, giving him a pitying smile. "I won't take him with me. He's better off here with Nanny."

Her face hardened then, and Will felt a stab in his heart as he recognized a look he'd seen on Katrin's face when she spoke to Alex.

"Sometimes I wonder what kind of man you are, Will." Her voice was low and cold as ice. "Maybe you're like your father, who married Monique for the Chartrand fortune. You find my father's money more interesting than me."

Aghast at such an insane accusation, Will stared at her.

Giving him a pitying smile, Maria tossed her head as she opened the door. "I'll be leaving in the morning."

Will stood staring at the door, a sense of defeat settling over him. Trapped . . . the word sprang into his mind. Trapped. When he thought of their courtship, he could recall only a wild whirl of rising passion. His own youthful sexuality had trapped him in a marriage with a vain and shallow woman he scarcely knew.

Alex swung down from the train in the gathering dusk of a chill September day. He would stop at his mother's before he went straight to the Forester mansion to see his grandson. If he was lucky, Lydie was back from her visit with Gussie in Atlanta, with supper ready. The long trip from Texas had involved many changes of transportation—railroads, stagecoach, horseback—and he was tired. He'd contracted for a good herd of cattle to be driven north to Wyoming in the spring. The cattle business was booming and he intended to make himself another fortune. Tomorrow he'd see Will at the office to discuss business and sign any papers necessary.

Buck would be starting roundup at the ranch and he wanted to be there.

"Oh, Mr. Alex!" Lydie exclaimed when she opened the front door. "Thank God, you're back."

A chill of apprehension swept over him. "Where's Ma?"

"Here, Alex." Star was in the doorway between the foyer and the sitting room, holding her hands out to him. It struck him suddenly that she had aged . . . and he had always thought her ageless. Impulsively, he bent to kiss her cheek.

"Bring some coffee, Lydie," she said, and led him into the sitting room. "You look so tired," she said when they were seated by the bay window opened to catch the cool night breeze. "I wish I didn't have to trouble you."

"Let's hear it," he said, grimly steeling himself, nodding his thanks at Lydie, who poured his coffee.

"You knew Monique intended to move back to St. Louis before fall?" Star began, setting her coffee on the marble-topped table between them. A faint breeze stirred the dried seed pods on the lilac bushes beside the window.

Alex nodded. "I know. And when Monique does something, she does it in her own time."

Star's eyes shifted from his as she turned to gaze out into the dark street. "Last week she had everything packed and shipped, then she insisted Will make the trip to St. Louis with her. Will made Maria come back from the ranch to stay with Cameron—"

"What!" Alex exploded, straightening so abruptly he spilled hot coffee on his hand. "Damn her! What was she doing at the ranch?"

"She told Will she needed a change, needed to get out of the valley heat."

"Bullshit!" Alex growled, mopping up the coffee with his pocket handkerchief. "She should have been here with her baby, the selfish little bitch."

"Alex, please listen." Star laid a placating hand over his. "Will brought her home before he left, but he hadn't been gone two days when she asked Katrin to stay with the baby and Nanny. She went back to the ranch."

Despair settled over Alex as the ugly scene between Maria

and Hal in the bunkhouse replayed in his mind. Katrin had been wrong, and he'd been wrong . . . marriage hadn't changed Maria. He tried to block out the ugly words that came to him: slut, whore. They weren't words to use about one's own daughter.

"You want supper, Mr. Alex?" Lydie interjected. As though trying to cheer him, she added, "Miz Beaufort sends her regards."

Alex shook his head. He'd better get home and make sure Cameron was all right. Given half a chance Katrin would ruin him just as she had ruined Maria. His heart felt like a lead weight inside his chest. Looking at his mother, he said heavily, "I'll go to the ranch first thing in the morning and find out what's going on."

"She's gone," Mary Webster snapped, her mouth a tight slash across her plain face. Wrapping her hands in her faded calico apron, she drew a deep breath as though gathering courage. "Even if it means Buck's job, Mr. Cameron, I won't have it. We got little kids and I won't have them see such goin's-on."

Alex looked across the sunlit ranch yard where two towheaded children were at play in the swing Buck had hung from the limb of a cottonwood tree. Once he had played here with his brother . . . once life had been simple. But the world had turned over since then, and the past had a way of coloring the future.

Painfully, he remembered Katrin screaming at him that Maria was Jed's child, remembered how Katrin had clung to the girl, protected and spoiled her, how he had tried, over and over, to buy the child's love with presents. But now there was Cameron Forester, he told himself . . . the future, and he wasn't going to make the same mistakes or let Maria ruin his grandson's life.

"You know where she went?" he asked Mary, keeping a calm demeanor as he rolled a cigarette.

"Took your best saddles and horses and left with that Tex Dunnahy." Mary's resentment colored her voice.

"God damn Texas cowboys!" Alex muttered. He didn't

want a cigarette after all, and he flipped it across the dusty ranch yard.

Mary gave him a pitying look. "He didn't force her, Mr. Cameron. She was happy as a lark when they rode outta here. Said they was goin' to Cheyenne and have themselves a time."

Tex groaned, thrusting violently against her as he exploded inside her. Maria laughed aloud. She'd already come again and again, but she grasped his buttocks and held him fiercely close.

"My iron man," she teased, laughing as she kissed his handsome face.

Panting and sweaty, Tex grinned as he rolled off her. "Jesus, Maria . . . don't you ever get enough?"

"You just might be the one to do it," she answered with an arch look. "Nobody else ever has."

"I'm ready, willin', and more'n able." He reached across her to take the package of prerolled cigarettes from the bedside table.

Watching him, Maria admired the lean masculine lines of his body, the tanned, rough-hewn face. He was good in bed. Better than any man she'd ever been with, doing things to her that Will would never have thought of, things that sent her wild with ecstasy. It didn't matter that she had bought the cigarettes from the lobby vendor, or that the hotel room was charged to her father's account. Tex satisfied her completely, and she meant to stay with him.

But as she lay back on the pillow, puffing cautiously on the cigarette Tex handed her, a faint sadness came over her. It was always this way after lovemaking, she told herself, this reluctant return to reality. But she wouldn't think about reality now, or about what lay back in Cameron City. Will had his son and heir and that's all he'd really wanted from her. She had Tex. With a seductive smile, she snuggled against him, running her hand down his body, wondering if he could be aroused again so soon.

A knock sounded on the door, and Tex cursed. "Who the hell is that?"

"Probably the maid." Maria rose and pulled on her robe. "I'll get rid of her." She cracked open the door and looked into her father's hard and angry face.

Walking from the train station to the Plains Hotel, Alex saw Cheyenne's boom on every side. New buildings were going up everywhere, with the sound of saw and hammer loud in the clear air. The streets were crowded with vehicles, the hitching rails lined with horses. From the saloons came the tinny sound of pianos and the low mutter of gamblers.

He could have stayed at the new Cheyenne Club. John Coble had proposed him as a member in that exclusive company of rich Englishmen and easterners who'd come west to make a fortune in cattle. But he'd stayed at the Plains ever since it was built, the staff knew him, and he felt comfortable there. When he was settled, he'd start looking for Maria, even though he was at a loss to know where to start.

"Mr. Cameron," the desk clerk stuttered when Alex had signed the hotel register. He was a callow youth, new to Alex. "There must be some mistake. You're already registered."

At once, Alex understood. With a grim smile, he stared the youth down. "Then I guess you better tell me my room number."

When Maria peered at him through the barely open door, rage boiled in Alex. In one violent movement, he shoved the door open and stepped into the room. Maria stumbled, flung backward by his entrance, clutching the thin silk robe about her nude body.

Sickness poured through him as he slammed the door and surveyed the room. The remains of a meal stood on a table in the corner, food congealing on the dirty plates, coffee spilled on the tray. A half-empty bottle of whiskey stood on the dresser with two glasses.

In the rumpled bed, a disconcerted Tex pulled the sheet up over his bare chest. Alex glared at him, thinking the man had a sly face, weak and handsome . . . the kind a silly woman like Maria would fall for.

Turning on her, he ordered, "Get your things. You're going home with me."

The silk robe clutched about her, Maria glared at him defiantly. "Like hell I will!"

Alex fought against the pain clogging his throat. Trying to keep his voice calm and even, he said, "For God's sake, Maria, you have a baby at home . . . and you have a good husband. Don't throw all that away for this. . . ." He gestured inarticulately at Tex, searching for a word bad enough. "For some slimy drifter willing to live off your father's money."

"I'm a grown woman," Maria answered in icy tones, her face hard. "I'll do as I please. And you have more money than you'll ever need."

Weak with defeat, Alex stared at his daughter, this stranger whose values were so far removed from his own. Anger bubbled to the surface again, anger for all this foolish creature was destroying in her selfishness. But she'd always had everything she desired, hadn't she, all the presents she'd asked for? Maybe Tex was just another present she wanted.

"But it's *not* your money," he said coldly. "It's mine, and it won't be spent on whores . . . male or female."

Hatred twisted the beautiful face and gleamed from the dark eyes. "We'll see about that," she retorted with a toss of her bright head. "Get it through your head, old man. I'm not going with you."

Shattering pain broke inside him, with the knowledge that she'd never loved him, never truly loved Will . . . or even her child. Maybe she was incapable of loving, even more than Katrin.

Alex tightened his hands into fists. He wanted to smash that lovely face, to destroy the man in the bed watching him warily. Sick rage boiled in him. He couldn't change something that had begun long before Maria was born. He slammed the door hard behind him.

Chapter 36

1886

Julie leaned on the windowsill where the shutters had been thrown open to catch the breeze, for it was warm already in May. Below, where dusk settled over the vast lawns of Stanbury Oaks, the servants were still cleaning up from the afternoon's barbecue. Faint sounds of musicians tuning their instruments drifted up from the lighted ballroom. Torches gleamed along the oak-lined drive, half illuminating the blaze of azaleas blooming beneath the trees.

How different it was from Wyoming, from Red Hill Ranch and even Cameron City. Everything here grew with lush abandon, and every tree, every bush filled the air with perfume. Briefly, she wondered whether Grandmother would like it, and was instantly certain she would not. In Wyoming you could see forever, and the wind blew for a hundred miles with nothing to stop it. A sense of nostalgia stole over her, at once dispersed by the sight of another fine carriage coming up the long graveled drive.

All day carriages had been arriving at the great white plantation house overlooking the Mississippi above Cape Girardeau. It was Priscilla Stanbury's fifteenth birthday, and her parents had invited the neighboring gentry to help celebrate for their only child.

"Julie, does my hair look all right?" Priscilla's question had a mournful note to it and Julie turned at once to comfort her always insecure friend.

Priscilla's loving nature and generous heart could not disguise the fact that she was plain. Her teeth were too

335

prominent, her nose too thin, and her hair a plain light brown, all of which she daily bemoaned before her mirror. At fourteen she was still half child, while Julie, a year younger, was already blossoming into womanhood.

"You look beautiful," Priscilla added, giving Julie an admiring look.

Smoothing the silken folds of her pale blue silk gown, Julie smiled at her friend. "So do you."

The maid who was still fussing with Priscilla's elaborate coiffure gave Julie a sharp glance and quickly looked away. Priscilla's bedroom was a bower of white lace curtains, thin silk draperies surrounding the carved wood tester bed, soft pastel-colored rugs on the shining floor.

"That's really your color," Julie added, rearranging heavy rose-colored lace at the shoulders of her friend's silk-satin rose gown. She meant it truly, for the glowing silk lent a becoming flush to Priscilla's pale complexion.

Priscilla sighed and squeezed Julie's hand. "I'll always wish I looked like you."

Her friend's ardent admiration embarrassed Julie, and she was thankful for the abrupt interruption of Mrs. Stanbury.

"It's time to go down now, darling," the plump, pale-faced woman said, smiling, touching Priscilla's hair lovingly. Her eyes fell on Julie, and her smile faded. "I thought you'd already joined the guests, Julie dear."

Certain that Mrs. Stanbury had not meant to be hurtful, Julie answered, "I'm not quite ready. I'll be along later." Glancing at the reflections in the pier glass, Julie knew that Priscilla's loving mother did not want her daughter's friend to outshine her at her own birthday party. Priscilla and her mother had given her so much, she could give them the gift of her absence at this important moment.

Mr. Stanbury stood at the head of the stairs, sweating in his black formal clothes, his round face beaming with affection as he offered his arm to his daughter.

From the hallway, Julie watched as the family descended the stairs together. The orchestra struck up the strains of "Happy Birthday," the guests' voices rose in the words.

Happiness emanated from Priscilla, transforming her plain face.

Julie sighed and went back into the bedroom, pretending to rearrange her hair. In the years she'd been at St. Ann's she'd become almost a member of the Stanbury family. Two months in Wyoming every summer, living a life that seemed more and more alien to her, then she'd go east to Cape May, New Jersey, and the elegant seaside cottage of Priscilla's grandparents. Christmases were spent here at Stanbury Oaks, with elaborate celebrations, dinners, balls, and gifts.

Lawrence Stanbury had done well to marry a rich Yankee's daughter, but he'd invested wisely and prospered on the wreckage of the Civil War. Both he and his wife doted on their only child. They'd accepted Julie into their lives completely because Priscilla loved her.

They'd taught her so much, she thought as she settled down in the green-velvet-upholstered window seat to gaze out at the festive torches lighting the dark grounds of the plantation. Just as her father had said, long ago, "You're learning how to live the right kind of life, Julie."

A pang went through her at the thought of her father. Since that first time, he'd come to visit her at St. Ann's every year on his annual trek to Chicago for the cattle sale. Each visit was as brief and uncomfortable as the first. But now there was another reason for his visits to St. Louis. Cameron was there, Cameron . . . whom her father loved with a fierce possessive love.

After Charles's death, Monique had moved back to St. Louis. Then, when all the terrible scandal happened—when Maria ran away with another man, leaving her husband and child—Monique had insisted on taking Cameron to live with her. After every visit, Alex complained that she was making a spoiled sissy of the boy.

How could Will have let his son be taken so far from him? Julie wondered. Had he been terribly hurt by his wife's defection, and the way Maria had cleaned out his bank accounts before she disappeared? Grandmother said he did nothing but work, keeping up a law practice in addition to running the bank. He'd sold Charles's ranch to Alex, taking stock in Cameron Valley Cattle Company in exchange. Julie seldom saw him when she was in Wyoming. He was distant and polite when they did meet, on the street or at her grandmother's on business. It seemed to her that he was frozen in pain, filling his empty life with work.

The sound of women's voices in the hallway startled Julie back into the present. Music and laughter drifted up the stairs. The party was under way. She could go down now.

A cut-glass chandelier at the bottom of the long sweeping stairway cast a brilliant light over the company gathered in the great hall, laughing and talking. Men in dark formal wear, and women in a rainbow of bright wide-skirted gowns, eddied about. Everywhere, candles glowed, flowers filled huge china vases. The whole room gleamed with a kind of incandescent light.

Julie threaded her way to the ballroom, searching for a glimpse of her friend. Radiant-faced Priscilla was dancing with a slender young man, smiling into his handsome face. He seemed vaguely familiar to Julie and she thought perhaps he had been at some Christmas celebration. The dark mustache he was cultivating was unfamiliar, but the curly brown hair and laughing blue eyes struck a chord in her memory.

"I want you to meet my dearest friend, Julie Cameron," Priscilla said gaily, leading the young man over to Julie's side. "This is Richard Ledoux, Julie. He's been away at school in Virginia." She gave him a languishing glance. "I'm so glad he came home in time for my birthday."

Richard bowed slightly and kissed Julie's hand. His eyes were so intent on her face, the look made her quiver deep inside.

The music struck up again, calling the dancers. Impulsive Priscilla seized Julie's hand and placed it in Richard's. "Dance with my friend, Richard," she commanded with a laugh.

"You were here at Christmas," he said as they took their places in the set.

"Yes." She looked at him in surprise. "How did you remember?"

"No one could forget that beautiful face," he replied, with a slight bow of his handsome head, his eyes burning into hers.

Startled by the extravagant compliment, she could think of no reply before they were whirled away in the movements of the quadrille.

"It's dreadfully hot in here," he whispered in her ear when the music ended. "Let's get some air."

Ignoring the stares of the chaperones, he led her out the open french doors, onto the wide pillared veranda. In the distance, the Mississippi River gleamed through the trees. Somewhere a mockingbird sang, and the air was heavy with the scent of jasmine.

Richard kept her hand in his as they strolled the length of the dimly lit veranda. Breathless, Julie was aware of a strange, sweet flow of sensation from his touch. When they paused beside one of the tall brick pillars, shaded from the moonlight, Richard lifted her hand to his lips. Julie sighed and closed her eyes.

Unexpectedly, Richard turned her hand over and kissed the palm. His mustache was soft, his lips hot against the sensitive skin. A new and compelling emotion swept through her, and she drew in her breath sharply.

"You're so lovely," he murmured, bending his head toward her, his eyes gleaming in the half-light.

Julie waited, certain he intended to kiss her, wanting it. Back at school they'd talked about kissing, after lights-out, wondering about men and women. Some of the girls claimed to have tried it, assuming an air of superiority because of their experience.

At the swish of skirts coming along the porch, Richard drew back quickly.

"There you are, Richard." Mrs. Stanbury's voice had a faint edge to it. "Your mother is quite upset with you for neglecting your sisters. Come along, now."

In a moment they were back in the ebb and flow of the party, amid chattering guests, music, the smell of perfume and punch. Priscilla, surrounded by friends, waved at Julie.

With a covert glance at Richard, dancing with one of his

three sisters, Julie joined Priscilla. She felt out of sorts with Mrs. Stanbury for interrupting Richard's kiss because she'd wanted it with all the beating urgency his touch aroused in her young body. All these years her romantic dreams had been filled with Will Forester. Now he seemed an old man. Richard was here, young and handsome and admiring, his mouth hot and seductive on her hand.

"Mother's planning a marvelous party for next week," Richard said in his soft, lazy voice. "I hope you'll come."

He had been at Stanbury Oaks almost every day since Priscilla's birthday . . . riding with the two girls, playing croquet on the wide lawns, or simply lounging on the veranda drinking juleps as he was just now. The southern spring air was heavy and still, filled with the rich perfume of magnolias.

"We wouldn't miss one of your mother's parties," Mrs. Stanbury said, smiling at him. With a sigh, she fanned herself against the heat, signaling the little black maid to refill her lemonade glass.

While their chaperone was occupied, Richard slid Julie a look of such blazing intensity that all the breath went out of her. They hadn't been alone for a moment since the party, but his glances told her more than words. When he touched her, to help her dismount from her horse, or kissed her hand in greeting and farewell, she feared her body would burst into flame.

A constraint had settled between herself and Priscilla, simply because she could not share this new and wonderful feeling. "I'm in love," she said to herself in the dark bedroom, experimenting with the idea, wondering if love was what made her whole body throb wildly in Richard's presence.

"Julie's leaving for Wyoming in two weeks," Mrs. Stanbury broke in abruptly. "It will be nice for her to see River House."

"Richard's family's plantation adjoins ours," Priscilla explained, her eyes on Richard in unabashed admiration.

"Yes," Richard said; his eyes met Julie's and her throat clogged with longing. "I'm anxious for you to see it."

River House was as beautiful as promised. It was situated on a grassy knoll at a bend of the Mississippi, and its driveway was lined with huge azaleas blazing with exotic color. Tall oaks dripped filmy veils of Spanish moss. The house had an elegance Stanbury Oaks did not have, with exquisite carved doors and leaded-glass windows. The huge pillars at the front rose a full two stories, gleaming white against the lush greenery.

The elegant supper was over and the dancing had begun. Richard danced with Priscilla first, then with his three sisters. All the time, Julie waited, almost unaware of the nameless, faceless young men who were her partners, her eyes following Richard.

At last, he danced with her. It was a minuet, so that only their hands touched, only their eyes asking and answering, the fire in his leaping each time they came together.

"I need some air," he said as the music died. His hand was hot on her waist, his voice ragged. As though dazed, Julie allowed him to lead her out through the wide-flung french doors. His hand tight and hot on hers, they went down the brick paths, beneath the scented magnolia trees, to the gazebo overlooking the river.

Urgently, he pulled her into the shadows of the gazebo. "Oh, God," he groaned, and took her in his arms, holding her so close she could scarcely breathe.

His mouth covered hers, hot and seeking, his mustache soft against her face. A great surge of response poured through Julie. Her lips yielded to his, eager, wanting his kiss, wanting his arms holding her so close her breasts crushed against his hard chest.

"Julie . . . beautiful Julie," he murmured, his lips caressing her throat. "I've wanted to do that since the first time I saw you."

"Oh, Richard," she gasped, scarcely able to breathe. "I love you."

"You're wild and exotic . . . like no other girl in the world." His lips traced the line of her shoulder, down the low-cut neckline of her white lawn ballgown to the cleft between her breasts.

She should stop him, she knew, but she didn't want to stop. The breathless sensations pulsating through her body were more wonderful than anything she'd ever dreamed. "I love you," she said again, lifting her hand from his shoulders to run her fingers through his soft wavy hair.

Richard's hand stole inside her bodice, freeing her breast to the hot moist seeking of his mouth. She gasped at the exquisite sensation pouring through her. He groaned aloud. Once more his mouth took hers, fiercely demanding. His hands slid down her back, cupping her hips to press her against the strange hardness of him.

"I want you, Julie." His voice came in bursts, his breath hot and panting. "I've got to have you."

Nothing in the world seemed to have meaning at this moment but the sensation of his body pressing against hers, his mouth like fire against her skin, his voice pleading. She loved him . . . she wanted him to love her. . . .

"Richard, dear!" It was Mrs. Ledoux's voice calling across the lawns, softly, barely audible above their harsh breathing.

Dropping his arms, Richard stepped quickly away from Julie, breathing heavily. "Christ!" he swore softly.

Desperately rearranging her bodice, Julie felt a painful ache settle between her thighs. She could not look at Richard.

"Just showing Julie the view from the gazebo, Mother," he called, his voice barely under control.

"I'm sure too much night air isn't good for her," Mrs. Ledoux said coolly, standing at the foot of the steps leading up to the gazebo, her face barely visible in the darkness.

"We'll be right in, Mother," Richard said. Clearing his throat, he took Julie by the elbow.

It was only back in the brilliantly lighted ballroom, dancing with Mr. Stanbury, that Julie realized it was she who had cried out "I love you," and Richard had not replied.

A mockingbird's song awakened Julie to a faint sense of unease. The Stanburys had been strangely silent on the drive home from River House last night, except for Priscilla, who had chattered about the party until she fell asleep with her head on Julie's shoulder.

Julie scarcely slept all night, remembering Richard's urgent whisper, "Meet me. I'll send a note." The strange, wild feelings he'd aroused in her were irresistible. She couldn't wait to kiss him again, to feel his mouth against her breast, his arms holding her against his strong young body. Maybe today, she thought, and sat up quickly, calling to the young Negro maid who slept in the dressing room between Priscilla's room and her own.

"Miz Pris still sleepin'," the maid informed Julie as she helped her dress. "But breakfast already served to the folks."

She would have breakfast quickly, Julie told herself, then wait for one of the grooms from River House to arrive with a note from Richard. This time, she was certain, he would say he loved her.

"Good morning, Julie," Mrs. Stanbury said as she joined her in the shaded breakfast room overlooking the garden.

The faint nagging unease burgeoned into the front of Julie's mind at the cool tones of her hostess's greeting. Elizabeth Stanbury had been almost like a mother to her, making her a part of their family all these past summers. Never had she spoken to Julie in such icy tones, or looked at her with such hard eyes.

Painfully, Julie wondered if Mrs. Stanbury guessed what had happened in the gazebo last night. Should she confess and ask forgiveness? But then she'd be sent home and she couldn't bear not to have Richard hold her again. Surely he'd ask her to marry him as soon as she was old enough. Then she could live in that lovely house and never go back to Wyoming.

"Ask Mr. Stanbury to join us," Mrs. Stanbury said to the maid. Sipping her coffee, she gazed out the tall windows across the brilliant azalea gardens to where the great river gleamed in the sunlight.

The Stanburys exchanged significant glances as he sat down at the table, dismissing the maid.

There was a long and aching silence. Julie's apprehension grew. The ticking of the tall grandfather clock in the hallway seemed to be the sound of approaching doom.

Clearing his throat loudly, Mr. Stanbury began, "You've been like one of our own family, Julie . . . a companion for Priscilla, and a joy to us."

"You've been wonderful to me," Julie replied in a low tentative voice, her heart thudding against her ribs. "I'm very grateful."

"Priscilla looks on you as her dearest friend." Mrs. Stanbury's voice broke on the words. Julie stared at her in pained surprise.

"But she's my dearest friend too," she protested softly.

"I think she just doesn't understand, dear," Mr. Stanbury said to his wife, who was dabbing at her eyes with a lace handkerchief.

Clearing his throat once more, he toyed self-consciously with the silver at his plate. "Perhaps it's different in Wyoming," he began at last. "Here in the south, family is of the utmost importance—bloodlines and all that."

His face grew flushed and he wiped a hand nervously across his balding head. "We are fond of you, Julie, but you must understand about the Ledouxs and ourselves . . . old families, neighboring plantations, shared interests. It's been arranged for years."

Puzzled, Julie stared at his unhappy face. Mrs. Stanbury stifled a sob.

"Richard and Priscilla," Mr. Stanbury said, meeting Julie's eyes straight on. "They're to be married."

Julie's heart seemed to burst with pain. How could Richard try to seduce her, make her fall in love with him, when he was promised to Priscilla? How could he? She wanted to cry out the words.

"I didn't know," she managed to say, looking down at her plate, determined she wouldn't weep. "Pris didn't tell me."

In all their exchanges of confidence, Priscilla had never mentioned it. Her crush on the gardener's son, and on the handsome brother of a classmate, had all been discussed at length. Julie was certain Pris hadn't thought of Richard in that way yet. Vaguely, she recalled Pris mentioning him in a proud and sisterly tone.

With a distressed glance at his sobbing wife, Mr. Stanbury nodded. "She was only partly aware of the arrangement, I guess. I'm sure she never thought about it as an actuality."

Mrs. Stanbury dried her eyes. "I'd hoped to have the wedding here . . . on her seventeenth birthday."

All the delightful seaside vacations at Cape May, all the wonderful holidays in this great house were ended now, Julie knew. A part of her life was ended because a selfish young man had wanted her kisses, and she had behaved like a wanton.

Had it been like this with her mother? she wondered, thinking that perhaps she'd inherited some kind of curse. Then her heart twisted in anguished knowledge that she could not begin to understand the love between her parents. Caroline had loved only one man: Alex Cameron. She had died bearing his child. Grandmother spoke of her with sad affection as a mother to take pride in . . . a fine lady. Trying desperately to hide her pain, Julie knew in the depths of her being that what she had felt with Richard had no relation to what her mother had felt when she sacrificed everything for love of Alex Cameron.

Suddenly, she wanted her grandmother . . .

. . . wanted to be held in those loving arms amid the scents of sage and herbs and soft doeskin. All these years, she had been living a dream that could never come true, denying her true heritage and trying to assume Priscilla's.

"I'd never hurt Priscilla," she managed to say, fighting back the sobs. "I love her." Tears spilled down her face and she cried out the aching words, "I want to go home . . . to Wyoming."

Chapter 37

A meadowlark's musical warble awakened Julie. Turning on her back, she stared up at the weathered pine ceiling of the ranch house bedroom, trying to fit the bird's notes into words.

"Money next week . . . dat's what he say," Lydie always insisted, and Julie smiled to herself in remembrance. Because she was in the midst of spring housecleaning, Lydie hadn't come to the ranch with them. Julie stretched and sighed. She could hear her grandmother in the kitchen making breakfast. The enticing scent of freshly ground coffee drifted through the half-open door.

Determined to not allow herself time to think, she slipped on her robe and went into the kitchen. Ever since she'd come home, she'd wanted to share the hurt with her grandmother, but shame held her back. How could she have thought herself in love with one burning look from a young man's eyes, and one kiss from a man who must have kissed a hundred girls as naive as she? Didn't he care that she would feel soiled and ugly afterward? And for her to betray such a friend as Priscilla, even unknowingly . . .

Priscilla had been dismayed by her sudden departure for Wyoming. Mrs. Stanbury covered it by saying Julie's grandmother wasn't well. When Priscilla tried to make plans for Julie's visit to Cape May later in the summer, her parents were silent. Julie quickly made the lame excuse, "I'll have to wait and see my grandmother."

Dismissing the unhappy memories, Julie forced just the right amount of cheer into her voice. "Good morning, Grandmother."

Turning from the stove, Star held out a steaming mug of coffee. Just as she had that first moment they met again at the station, Julie drew in a painful breath. Somehow it had always seemed to her that Grandmother would live forever. But she had aged in the past year . . . her black hair heavily streaked with gray, the lines around her eyes and mouth deepened, and her straight figure was beginning to stoop just a little.

It struck her suddenly that it was part of growing up to realize that nothing was going to stay the same, however much one might desire it. Things had already changed unbelievably, with Charles dead, Monique moved away, Maria deserting Will and her baby. But not Grandmother, she thought fiercely . . . not her.

Already dressed for the day in a dark blue riding skirt and chambray shirt, Star began laying slices of bacon in the iron skillet. Impulsively, Julie crossed the room to give her a hug.

Star smiled and leaned over to kiss her cheek. "Sit down, love. Breakfast will be ready in a minute." Her eyes followed Julie affectionately. "Does the ranch look good to you?"

The silence grew long. Julie sat at the table, toying with her coffee mug. Morning sun slanted across the smooth white pine floors. Through the open door, she could see Little Knife and a ranch hand saddling their horses for the day's work.

Unable to contain her unhappiness any longer, Julie drew a long breath and began, "Do you remember the summer before I went away, Grandmother? When I was so unhappy at school?"

Setting the plate of bacon and biscuits on the table, Star took the chair opposite Julie. "Yes," she replied quietly, her eyes warm and understanding. She waited.

"You said I had the gift of sight, inherited from you . . .

that I must cherish my heritage. Then I went to the top of the red hill and stayed alone until my vision came to me."

"The gray dove . . . I could never forget that, dear one." Star reached across the table to touch Julie's hand.

Covering her face with her hands, Julie struggled to hold back the tears. But all her misery burst out in agonized sobbing. At once, Star was beside her, holding her tear-stained face against her breast, stroking her hair.

In halting painful words, Julie poured out the whole story of her first intense infatuation, her first kiss, her betrayal of a dear friend. The last words fell off into broken sobbing.

"Dear love," Star murmured, bending to kiss the dark head pressed against her, longing to take away this youthful sorrow. "You didn't truly hurt anyone except yourself. Priscilla will marry Richard, and perhaps come to regret it. And you've come home to find your true self . . . as it was meant to be."

"Grandmother." Julie raised her head, the dark moist eyes staring up at Star. "I've lost the gift; I know it. Is it gone for always?"

"Like any gift, it must be used," Star said gently, smiling at the intent young face.

"Would it be right if I go on my vision quest again, Grandmother?" Julie asked hesitantly.

"It would be very right," Star answered, and smiled in relief. "Is it tonight you would go?"

Julie had hoped for the same strong vision of the protecting gray dove, but the first night she slept the dreamless sleep of deep fatigue. All through the next day, she lay on the hilltop, aware of the thunderheads drifting across the summer sky, the wind sighing in the pines, the far distance of Cameron Valley swimming in a heat haze.

Late in the afternoon, she dozed, awakening suddenly to the call of the meadowlark. "Julie must wait." She was certain of the words in its song. Dizzy with hunger, she wondered if it were an omen, if the meadowlark should be her *wyakin,* or if it only told her to wait for the true vision.

Again she slept, and awakened to the pale light of predawn, shivering in the cool air. A mourning dove called softly from the chokecherry thicket. Its mate answered: *ooah, cooo, cooo, coo.*

As though from a cloud's distance, Julie seemed to see Cameron Valley spread before her: the red hill, the water-laced meadows, the gray carpet of sage covering hills and plains . . . even past the turn of the mountain to the Old Ranch, where it all began. Like the gray dove's wings wrapped warmly about her, the land seemed to hold her to its breast. A profound sense of peace fell over Julie.

Aikits palojami . . . fair land. The Nez Percé words Grandmother used came to her. This was home. Her destiny lay here. She would never go away from it again.

It was the driest summer in Wyoming history, Alex told them. All the cattlemen were worried. He had come to supper at Star's house because he knew Will would be there with Cameron and he never missed a chance to be with his grandson. As always, Katrin refused to join them. Cameron would be here all summer and she would have her chance to entertain and spoil him.

Only half listening to the business talk between her father and grandmother and Will, Julie looked down the table at the small boy sitting stiffly in his chair. Dressed in a dark blue suit with a high-collared white shirt and string tie, Cameron looked desperately hot and uncomfortable.

When Monique consented to bring Cameron to his father for the summer, there had been a flurry of activity at the half-closed Forester mansion. Living alone there, Will kept a minimum of rooms open and a minimum of staff consisting of his housekeeper and cook, the stableman and his wife, who did the cleaning.

Monique arrived with her own retinue of servants, but she had done little socializing. When Julie saw her riding by in her fine carriage, it seemed to her Monique was ill. She had gained weight, but the excess flesh was pale, soft, and unhealthy looking.

Now Cameron shot a shy glance at Julie and she smiled encouragingly. He had wonderful manners, she thought, even though he had drawn in a sharp breath of surprise when Lydie joined them at the table. Understanding, Julie thought wryly that she'd spent enough time in Missouri to know that Lydie's position in this household was unique. She might be Grandmother's cook and housekeeper, but she was also Grandmother's friend. At least Lydie had quit dying her hair that hideous red. It was gray now, cut short above her plump, pleasant face.

"The range is overcrowded," Alex was saying, his face glum. "When the government put the cattlemen off the Cheyenne Reservation, they all moved west."

"Not to mention all the herds still pouring in from Texas," Will added.

"No more Texas cows for me," Alex stated with finality. "Damn skinny critters . . . all hide and hair. My cattle bring premium price because of my Oregon bulls. Next year I figure on putting Herefords in with my cows."

"Even your range is overcrowded," Will told him in a mildly ironic tone. "What about—"

"I'm selling the herd down this fall," Alex interrupted. "Won't be enough winter feed anyway with the buffalo grass drying up already . . . even before it ripens." He glanced out the open window into the hot still afternoon. "Damn, I wish it would rain."

Looking at her father's worried face, Julie wished for some way to help him. But when his fond and doting glance turned to Cameron, a twinge of jealousy squeezed her heart. Lydie brought the homemade ice cream for dessert and Cameron's gray eyes widened with delight. He grinned at Julie.

How could she be jealous of this charming little boy? she asked herself. Everyone was drawn to him. Grandmother even insisted he looked like Charles. What kind of madness had possessed his mother to run away and leave him? Maria had left Will too, which was even more unfathomable to Julie. She wondered how Will really felt about the wife who had treated him so badly. No one in the family ever spoke of Maria now.

Monique and Will simply told Cameron his mother had gone away and refused to elaborate. Alex would not discuss his daughter, even with Katrin. Distraught at first over Maria's behavior, Katrin kept her silence with so little objection Julie wondered if she secretly kept in touch with Maria.

Sorry for this lonely little boy isolated in a world of adults, Julie winked at him. "After supper I'll show you our Indian lodge, if you'd like."

Again the gray eyes widened, glowing with anticipation before he caught himself and answered politely, "I'd like that very much."

Debilitated by her illness, Monique Forester scarcely left the cool confines of her great house that summer. Cameron was left to the care of servants and his busy father. His doting grandfather soon replaced the stiff suit and collar with jeans and boots and gingham shirt from the general store. Katrin joined the throng of admirers and there was always cake and cookies in her kitchen for a hungry boy.

Alex took him to the ranch and stayed so long Monique grew concerned and demanded that Will insist he return to town. The weeks of indulgence and freedom with his grandfather had set Cameron out of control. For the first time, he found the company of other boys in the town and he ran wild with them.

July had melted into August with still no rain in Wyoming. Clouds piled up in the southwest and drifted across the sky, cotton clouds that bore no moisture.

On an errand to the store for her grandmother, Julie walked slowly through the stifling heat carrying the parasol Lydie had thrust at her as she left. The dusty main street was empty of traffic in midday. At the hitching racks a few horses stood with drooping heads.

The hot summer silence was suddenly broken by a crowd of little boys running past her, pushing her aside so that she stumbled against the water trough in front of the livery stable. Brushing off her skirt, she turned to call after them.

They had formed into a circle, shouting encouragement to two of their number who had fallen into the dust, punching and struggling.

"He's jest a dumb city dude whose ma run off from him," one of them shouted. "You kin beat him, Jess," another one urged.

At once Julie knew the identity of the fighter, and apprehension poured through her. She'd tried to lure Cameron to ride with her, tried to make a friend of the lonely boy, and he'd chosen to run with these town toughs, all of them older than he. Secrets were impossible to keep in a place like Cameron City. Even these boys had heard the scandalous stories about Maria, and now they were flinging her shameful behavior at Cameron.

Setting her mouth in a grim line, she stalked into the midst of the shouting boys. Cameron was down, the other boy astride him, punching his face. Blood spurted from his nose.

"Fight back, Cam!" she heard herself yell, and caught his startled eyes. Fear washed from his face, he grinned, heaved himself up, catching his opponent by the shoulders and bearing him backward to the ground.

"Hit him!" Julie shouted. A sudden silence fell over the spectators as they looked at her in amazement. Her face burned with the realization of her behavior. "Get out of here!" she told the boys. To her surprise, they obeyed, disappearing behind the livery stable, leaving Cameron sitting alone in the dust.

Wiping his dirty face, Cameron's opponent paused to shout, "Yer ma's a stinkin' whore!" Anger and shame flooded Cameron's face and he swallowed a sob. Julie was certain that, at four, he didn't know the meaning of the word, but he understood its ugliness.

Reaching out a hand, Julie pulled him to his feet. "We're going to your father's office and you can explain your behavior to him," she said in as stern a voice as she could muster. She wanted to weep with him, but she could think of nothing to say to erase the hideous knowledge the boys had flung at him. Ignoring the silent tears streaking his dusty face, she tried to stanch his bloody nose with her handkerchief. His shirt was torn, his face bruised, his clothes filthy from the livery stable dust.

"He was fighting," Julie said simply when they stepped into Will's office above the bank. Somehow she could not bring herself to tell him any more.

"Why?" Will asked, standing up and looking down in amazement at his disheveled son.

Taking his father's proffered handkerchief, Cameron held it to his still-bleeding nose. "They said I was a chicken city dude," he managed to mumble, avoiding his father's eyes.

Struggling to suppress his grin, Will picked the boy up and held him on his lap. "Lean your head back like this," he said. "That'll stop the nosebleed."

Cameron obeyed, lying limp across his father's lap, his head resting on the arm of Will's swivel chair. Julie let out a long breath. Surely Cameron and Will would talk this over between themselves when Cam could tell his father the truth. It wasn't her place to explain Maria to her son.

"Thanks, Julie." Will's warm gray eyes met hers and all the years ran backward. Once more she was a panicked, miserable child, rescued . . . lifted up in Will's strong arms and carried home to safety.

Her heart leaped inside her chest like a wild bird. "I think I owed you one," she said softly.

He grinned and she saw that he remembered too. "Yes." He glanced down at the boy he held, gently wiping Cameron's nose. "I guess we're even now."

No answer came to Julie's throat, clogged with emotion now, her whole being suffused by a wondrous joy. She knew, as she had known that long ago day on the train when it came to her that it was his eyes in her vision. The incident with Richard had been merely a rite of passage into womanhood. Will Forester was her destiny, as he had always been.

"It will be an early winter," Star told them.

They sat on the front steps of the ranch house in the falling dusk—Star and Julie and Will. A small fire burned just below them, covered by green weeds to make smoke in a vain attempt to drive away the mosquitoes. Julie slapped one of the pests on her arm. She was unwilling to forgo the pleasure of sitting out in the cool twilight just to avoid mosquitoes. They never seemed to bother her grandmother.

Cameron had gone to the stables with sugar lumps for his horse, an Appaloosa given him by his great-grandmother and named, with singular lack of imagination, Spot.

"Alex agrees with you," Will said, contemplating his cigar. "That's why he's started roundup early." He grinned at them. "Cameron wanted to work roundup, imagine that?"

Star chuckled softly. "Someday he will . . . someday."

Silent, Julie watched Will's face, knowing that in the fading light he could not see her eyes on him. After she'd told Star about Cameron's fight, Star had prevailed on Will to let Cameron come to Red Hill Ranch for a visit. The boy was silent and sullen at first. It was obvious to Julie he'd never told his father the true reasons for his fighting. Troubled, Julie asked her grandmother if they should discuss his mother with Cameron.

"*Sepekuse,*" Star replied sadly. "Let be, Julie. He's too young to understand."

Today Will had been to the Old Ranch to see Alex. En route back to town he'd stopped here to check on Cameron. Julie hoped he'd stay.

Concentrating on the way his dark hair curled around his ears, the long, strong fingers holding his cigar, Julie thought she couldn't bear to be thirteen another moment. Will treated her as though she were Cameron's age . . . a child. She wasn't a child. Richard had kissed her and touched her breast, arousing her to the certainty of her own womanhood. Clasping her arms about her knees tightly, she thought she heard a meadowlark call. "Julie must wait."

Will was silent for a long time, puffing at the cigar. "Mother's health is failing," he said at last, his face grave. "One day I'll have to bring Cameron to live with me."

"You should marry again, Will," Star said in a low voice.

"I'm married now!" The words had a bitter edge to them.

In careful tones, Star replied, "Maria's been gone long enough. You could get a divorce on grounds of desertion."

Drawing his breath in harshly, Will answered in a voice flat and devoid of emotion. "I was born, bred, raised a Catholic, Star. Divorce is unthinkable—even from Maria."

"Foolish . . . foolish . . ." Star breathed the words as though she could not hold them back.

Julie's fingers ached with longing to touch Will's unhappy face, to hold him close and comfort him. She was certain Maria had never loved him the way she loved him. Someday, she told herself, someday I'll be grown up and Will will love me in return.

"Katrin sends her money," Will broke out bitterly. "I've seen the bank drafts."

"Then you know where she is?" Star asked.

Will gave her a sharp glance. "No, not really. Apparently, she moves around a lot."

Now, Julie thought . . . now I should tell him what's happening to Cameron because of Maria. But the words did not come.

The cigar had gone out and Will scratched a sulfur match on the stone steps, carefully relighting it. "Mother and Cameron will be leaving for St. Louis next week," he said as though determined to change the subject. Turning to Julie, he smiled at her through the dusk. Julie's heart turned over. "Maybe you could travel with them on your way back to school."

A sense of time suspended caught at Julie. She glanced up at the eaves of the cabin where the medicinal herbs she'd helped Star gather were hung to dry. Beside her, she felt Star tense, waiting. Sliding her arm about Star's shoulders, Julie returned Will's smile. "I'm not going back to school. This is where I belong, and where I'm going to stay now."

Through the twilight, Star's dark eyes met Julie's, filled with infinite love and understanding, binding them together for all time.

Chapter 38

1887

Disaster lay over Wyoming like a cold winter fog when spring finally came in 1887. The first snow had fallen in November, as heavy as though it were midwinter. After Christmas a warm chinook wind blew up from the south. Old-timers welcomed it, declaring that the worst was over. But in the last week of January the blizzards came . . . wind and snow and cold without end, paralyzing the whole territory. Nothing moved in that vast expanse of white and howling arctic cold.

When spring came at last, it was not a fog that lay over the Wyoming cattle country, but the stink of dead cattle bloating in the sun. Buzzards filled the skies.

"Fifty to sixty percent," Alex told Star disconsolately. "I figure we lost that many." He looked tired and suddenly older, Julie thought, watching him pace her grandmother's sitting room. A fire burned in the fireplace against the cold of the spring day. The silver tray with coffee Lydie had brought in sat on the marble-top table, untouched.

Alex paused to light a cigarette. Blowing the smoke out explosively, he continued, "Heard it's more like ninety percent east of Laramie. The cattle business is dead . . . and I'm dead busted."

Giving him a piercing look, Star leaned over from her chair beside the fire, lifting the silver coffeepot to fill the cups. "It's not dead," she said briskly. "Just because you lost that fancy Hereford bull." With a sharp glance at Julie, she added, "When you pay that much for an animal, you ought to keep him in the barn and take care of him."

"I'm busted, Ma." Alex glared at her. "Aren't you listening? I sold the herd down short last fall and now I've lost a good sixty percent. I ain't even got breeding stock left."

Julie thought he seemed on the edge of panic. If only she could help him in some way, at least comfort him . . . but there was a line that neither of them ever crossed. She saw that her grandmother was studying him, her old eyes calm, her face serene.

"Perhaps you should stop and remember where you started from, Alex," Star said quietly.

Startled, he stared at her for a moment, then shrugged and began to pace the room distractedly, puffing on his cigarette. "I'm going to mortgage the lumber company to buy cattle and restock," he said, almost to himself.

"That will have to wait until Will comes back from St. Louis," Star replied. "If he can't borrow enough money to keep the bank afloat, you'll have to find another way."

"He'll get the money," Alex replied shortly. "The Chartrand resources are endless, if Monique will let go of some of it."

Star watched him in silence. Did she know what lay ahead? Julie wondered. She had tried to call on her own gift and found only a blank wall. They had been rich and lived well for as long as she could remember, but she knew that there had been bad times once.

Suddenly Alex paused in his pacing, turning to face his mother. "Will's bringing Cameron back with him for the summer." His eyes lit up. "Monique isn't well enough to make the trip, so Katrin's hoping he'll let Cam stay with us."

Remembering Will's bitter voice last fall speaking of the money Katrin sent to Maria, Julie was certain her father was doomed to disappointment. Despite his friendship with Alex, she doubted Will would trust his son to Katrin.

"I haven't told Katrin how bad things are," Alex added, almost defensively.

When he left, Star stood long at the window, watching him ride away, head down, shoulders hunched inside his heavy wool jacket against the cold wind. An aura of sadness surrounded the straight elegant figure, and Julie felt pierced to the heart by it. Crossing the room, she put her arm about Star's shoulders. Thanks to her grandmother, she had lived a coddled and protected life for fourteen years. Now it was time to pay back a part of a debt that could never truly be paid.

"It'll be all right, Grandmother," she said, pressing her cheek against Star's. "We'll make it. I'll help you."

With a soft laugh, Star turned and hugged her close. Looking into her face, she said, "I have to tell you the truth, dear Julie. Charles was never one to put all his eggs in one basket. The investments he made for me are as sound as those he made for Monique and not all in Wyoming. You needn't fear we'll ever be broke."

With an arm about Julie's shoulders, she turned to stroll back across the room. "If Monique refuses Will's need for a loan, I've enough to see him through. And I'll take the mortgage on Alex's lumber company myself."

Opening the door to her study, she gestured inside. Julie saw that her desk was piled with ledgers and files, as though Star had been poring over them.

"It's time now, Gray Dove," Star said quietly, and Julie felt a thrill of pride at her use of the name. "It's time for you to begin to learn to manage your inheritance . . . and your heritage."

Not until the end of summer did the stench of rotting carcasses cease to pervade the air. Star's horses had wintered far better than her neighbor's cattle, although every loss had been a sorrow to her. By August the meadow grass grew up to the horses' bellies as she and Julie rode the ranch with Little Knife. The diminished size of the herd saddened her, for every one of her horses was a friend.

"Indeed," she said to Little Knife in her native tongue, the language he had learned from Old Magpie. "The *hattia tinukin,* death wind blew over the land. *Sepekuse,* so be it.

Perhaps now the white man will see that you cannot take more from the earth than you return to it."

Little Knife had grown stout in his comfortable life as Star's foreman. He was known as John Littleknife now, and had married a half-breed girl. Their two sons went to school in Cameron City during the winter. With the aid of an old Texas cowboy named Percy McGrath, and various itinerant cow hands, he ran the ranch exactly as Star wished. Now, he shrugged and gave her a skeptical look. *"Tamtaiza uatiskipg,"* he replied. "Tomorrow will tell."

"Yahooo!" It was Cameron riding wildly toward them, scattering the quietly grazing horses across the meadow.

Star and Julie exchanged amused glances. As Cameron reined in the horse beside them, Star thought of Monique, knowing how appalled she would be to see her properly brought up grandson attired in soiled cowboy clothes and riding so recklessly.

"I thought we were going back to town tonight, Julie," he said, leaning to pat his winded horse.

"You'll have to change horses," Julie chided, frowning at him. "It looks to me like Spot's done in."

"That's all right," he said giving Star a bright, assured look. "Gran has plenty of them."

From the trees along Forester Creek, Will could hear the plaintive coo of mourning doves. The low, sad sound was like a knife piercing his heart. Shoving the papers on his desk aside, he stood up as though to shove emotion aside too. Even when he was alone, he kept a shield around his feelings, even when he lay with a whore he was simply satisfying a need, not giving of himself. When he thought about it, Will wasn't even sure how it had all happened. On a moonlit night, a beautiful young girl had whispered "I love you" and he had taken her in youthful passion, thereby changing both their lives forever.

Impatiently trying to shake the mood, he strode to the window and looked down the street, empty in the growing darkness. Lights gleamed from the houses in the distance, warm yellow lights where families were gathering home for the night. His life was satisfactory enough, he told himself. He had his work. He had a friend in Alex, and in Hans Becker, the young bachelor doctor who had just moved to Cameron City and who delighted in irritating Will with his radical ideas about free silver. And he had his son to raise. . . .

With a wry smile, he took a cigar from the humidor on his desk. Actually, he'd seen little of Cameron this summer. The boy had either been with Alex at the Old Ranch, or at Red Hill with Julie and Star. In town, he found time to charm Katrin, who doted on him, or run with the town boys when their chores were done.

Julie had promised she'd bring Cameron home today, and Will allowed himself a twinge of annoyance that she hadn't kept the promise. Because she seemed mature and responsible far beyond her age, he'd depended on her. He'd been shocked, but he'd listened when she told him Cameron had learned all about his mother . . . learned it in the coarse, ugly language of small boys. When he'd found the courage to talk to Cameron about it, the boy spat out the bitter words, "I don't have a mother," and ran away.

The summer was running out. A feeling that at five years old Cameron was already out of control lay uneasily in the back of Will's mind. Somehow, he had to find more time to spend with his son before the visit ended. He had to break out of this shrunken life of his, where the days were filled with nothing but work, only the puzzles of law and finance to occupy his interest.

Walking into the kitchen, he opened the ice box where the housekeeper had left the remains of Sunday's roast beef for his supper. It looked dry and unappetizing. He reflected on how smoothly things ran when his mother was in residence . . . the good hot meals ready on time, the clean clothes, and the shining house.

The front door slammed and he shoved the roast back into the ice box. With a sigh of relief, he thought that it must be Julie bringing Cameron home.

"Good Lord! What happened?" Will demanded as he met them in the spacious foyer. Cameron's jeans were torn, his face was pale, bruised, and scratched, and his arm was in a plaster cast held in a sling.

Julie glanced at the boy, then gave Will a wry smile. "He was showing off again—this time on a strange horse."

"Dr. Becker says it's part of growing up," Cameron added, with an air of bravado.

"Why didn't you have him on a gentle horse?" Will gave Julie a steely glare.

"Aw, it wasn't her fault, Pa," Cameron interrupted. Relieved that the boy's injuries seemed minor, Will nearly laughed. What would his mother think to hear her well-trained grandson address his father in that manner.

"Cam does tend to be a little reckless," Julie replied, with an affectionate pat on Cameron's head. With an air of competent authority, she added, "The doctor gave him some pills for pain. We'd better get him to bed right away."

When Cameron fell into a drugged sleep, Will and Julie left him, walking slowly down the wide staircase together. She'd seldom been in this house, but Julie thought it was beautiful, even with half the rooms closed up, the furniture draped in sheets.

Light from the gas lamp in the foyer gleamed on the crystal chandelier hanging there, candleless now. For a painful instant, Julie was back at Cape Girardeau, beneath the glittering lights on a hot spring night.

"Have you had supper?"

Will's voice jolted her back to the present. She met his gray eyes, warm and concerned . . . not the eyes of a lover. Julie let her breath out in a long sigh. "No."

Picking up the lamp from the foyer table, Will led the way to the kitchen. "Mrs. Parker left some cold roast if you'd care to join me." He turned, smiling, and her heart leaped painfully.

"It looks pretty awful," Julie said when he set it on the table. "Lydie's been teaching me to cook," she added proudly. "If you have some eggs, I'll make an omelet."

Will poured himself a whiskey and lit the cigar he'd left when the front door slammed. Seated at the kitchen table, he watched Julie move efficiently about the kitchen, whipping the eggs, slicing bread to toast in the oven, as she told him about Cameron's accident.

In a moment of astonishment, Will realized this was no longer the child he'd taken to St. Louis so many years ago. She was a young woman. The dark blue divided riding skirt fit neatly over rounded hips, and her young breasts thrust against the pink striped shirtwaist. There were bloodstains on the blouse, undoubtedly where she had held Cameron, and Will's heart began to pound in a way that astounded him.

"Cam loves it here, Will," Julie said when she had served the omelet and they were sitting opposite each other. She had managed to keep her feelings under control, she thought, and well hidden. She'd made him laugh, telling about Cam's escapades, and that had touched her even more deeply than the sadness that always seemed to dwell behind his gray eyes.

"I know," Will replied. Tasting the omelet, he smiled. "I'd hate to tell Lydie, but I think you've outdone her."

Laughing, she met his eyes, then quickly looked away. "Why couldn't Cam stay here and go to school?" This was a safe subject, she told herself . . . nothing personal, no need to meet his unsettling eyes. "Katrin and Alex would love to keep him," she began.

Will interrupted in a harsh voice, frowning at her. "Katrin! Between her and Alex they'd spoil him rotten." He took a sip of the coffee she poured for him. In a low bitter voice, almost to himself, he said, "Katrin's got the Pinkertons looking for Maria."

Julie stared at him. "I thought she was sending money, keeping in touch and hoping you wouldn't know."

Will's face hardened. "About a year ago, they lost touch. Katrin's been searching for her ever since." With an eloquent shrug, he dismissed the subject. Standing up, he grinned down at her. "Let's do the dishes."

The soft curve of her cheek as she bent over the dishpan, the gleam of lamplight on her dark hair tied back neatly with a wide pink ribbon, filled him with a yearning he'd thought he'd put away forever. All the hungry loneliness suddenly seemed to be centered in this smiling girl. Not her . . . not here . . . not now, he told himself and said briskly, "Well, the loan from Chartrand Brothers will save Cameron City Bank—and a lot of Cameron City ranchers."

"There'll still be a lot of foreclosures, won't there?" Julie asked, glad that her father had been saved, although she was certain Star would end up owning the lumber business.

"Oh, yes," Will conceded. "But where the loans are secured by land, we'll make out all right. There are an awful lot of people in the east wanting to buy land and start farming in the west."

Julie turned to face him, frowning. "But this isn't farm country, Will; it's cattle country."

"It's fertile land," he told her decisively, "and everyone has a right to it . . . not just cattle ranchers."

Surprised at his statement, Julie carefully wiped the dishpan and hung it up. Will's philosophy about the land was at odds with all she'd learned from Star and from Alex. Pained that there should be any area of disagreement between them, she quickly changed the subject.

"Are you going to take Cameron back to St. Louis?"

"No." Hanging up the dishtowel, Will looked at her. "I don't dare be away from the bank that long. Alex is going east to buy cattle. He'll take Cameron down to St. Louis."

Transported once more into the past, Julie mused, "Alex used to come to see me when I was at school in St. Louis and he came east with the cattle." Her mouth tightened and her chin went up. "But only because Star sent him."

The sadness in her soft young face made Will ache for her. Gently, he touched her shoulder. "Alex loves you, Julie. He just can't get past his own walls."

"No," she said, shaking her head, denying his words. At this moment it didn't matter whether her father loved her, or anyone else. The only love she needed was Will Forester's, now and forever.

His gray eyes darkened as she lifted her head and looked full into them. Desire pulsed through her veins. "Oh . . . Will," she murmured, and moved toward him.

The arms that closed about her were as familiar as though they'd held her many times before. All her dreams paled beside the touch of his mouth against hers, strong and warm, possessing all her senses. Every nerve seemed to leap into exquisite sensitivity so that she was aware of each muscle of his tall body pressed against hers. His hands were warm on her back, holding her so close that her breasts crushed against his chest. Will kissed her as though he could not stop and Julie surrendered all her throbbing being into his arms.

"Oh, God!" Will broke their embrace so abruptly, Julie staggered. Turning away from her, he wiped a hand over his agonized face. "I'm sorry, Julie . . . sorry. I guess I'm a little crazy tonight."

Laying her hand gently on his arm, Julie looked into his eyes. "I love you, Will."

Guilt washed over his twisted features, and he groaned softly. "I shouldn't have kissed you, Julie," he said in a ragged voice. "God!" He turned his back. "I'm old enough to be your father."

Her dream come true, Julie was caught up in a glowing fog of happiness. Sliding her arms about his waist, she pressed her cheek against his stiff shoulder. In a low, teasing voice, she said, "Not unless you became a father at Cameron's age."

Will stood rigid, resisting her embrace. Suddenly afraid, Julie dropped her arms. Her heart sank as he turned to face her, his eyes shuttered, his mouth tight.

"I'm a married man," he said harshly.

Tearing his eyes from her pleading face, Will strode to the back of the kitchen, took a lantern from the wall, and lighted it. "C'mon," he commanded, not looking at her. "I'll take you home."

Chapter 39

1888

"You gotta come, Mr. Forester." Mrs. Schrader's pale jowly face trembled, her eyes pleading. "I been keepin' house fer the Camerons all these years and I ain't never seen the missus like this."

Irritably, Will shoved aside the papers on his desk. With the opening of Oklahoma territory to settlement this summer, the influx of settlers to Wyoming had slowed down. But he still had more work than he could keep up with. The last thing on earth he needed was to deal with Katrin in the throes of what Mrs. Schrader had described as a nervous breakdown.

"Where the hell is Alex?" he snapped.

"He went to Cheyenne. The stockmen's association's having a meeting on what to do about the rustlers." The woman's voice shook with emotion. "I'd send him a telegram, but she won't let me." She peered fearfully at Will across the hot, close room. "Jest keeps yellin' that it ain't his business."

With a resigned shrug, Will picked up his hat. "All right," he said. "Let's go."

Katrin was in bed, groggy from what Mrs. Schrader called a "sleeping draft" administered by Dr. Hamlin. Soon after Will married Maria, he realized her mother was an intractable shrew, and he'd purposely seen as little of her as

365

possible. A sense of shock went through him at the changes in her. She'd always been a pretty woman, and dressed well. Now her flesh hung in pale unhealthy folds, the once-bright hair mussed and dulled by threads of gray. Her eyes were red from weeping.

Swallowing the pity and distaste that rose in his throat, Will sat down in the chair Mrs. Schrader hurriedly placed beside the bed. "Katrin," he said softly.

Glazed blue eyes met his, widening as she recognized him. Grabbing his hand, she implored wildly, "Go after her, Will. Bring her home. She's your wife. You can't let this happen to her." Suddenly she fell back against the pillows, covering her face with her arms. "Oh God! I can't bear it!" she screamed.

"See what I told you," Mrs. Schrader said righteously. "Poor dear . . ." She began to chafe Katrin's wrists, in an effort to quiet her.

Jerking away from her, Katrin thrashed about in the bed, moaning piteously, "I can't bear it . . . I can't bear it."

"For God's sake, Katrin," Will demanded, trying to break through her hysteria. "Tell me what's happened."

"I can't . . . I can't . . ." She tossed her head from side to side wildly. Mrs. Schrader managed to lay a damp cloth across her forehead and Katrin quieted for a moment.

"The detective . . ." Katrin whispered, staring at Will. "His name's Nichols and he's staying at the hotel. Go see him. He'll tell you everything."

Something cold as ice grew inside his chest, and Will thought his heart had turned to stone. Maria . . . the detective Katrin had hired must have found Maria.

Standing, he reached for his hat. His own mother, always the lady, and imperturbable as stone, would never have behaved like this; nor would the self-possessed Star Cameron. "If you can't get her quieted, Mrs. Schrader," he said, "you'd better send for the doctor again."

Mr. Nichols was in the saloon next door, the hotel clerk told Will. The bartender pointed him out; a cadaverous-looking man in a derby hat, he might have been an undertaker or a drummer rather than a Pinkerton man.

"I'm Will Forester." He held out his hand across the scarred wooden table where the man sat nursing a drink. The saloon was nearly deserted this early in the day.

"Figured you'd be along," Nichols said, returning his handshake. "The old lady plumb went to pieces when I told her."

"Then I guess you'd better tell me," Will said, steeling himself. Sitting down, he signaled the bartender for two whiskeys.

"Yes, sir." Nichols raised his glass to Will and drank his whiskey in one gulp. Leaning across the table, he confided in a low voice. "I found yer wife."

Looking at him with a stony face, Will asked simply, "Where?"

Nichols would not meet his eyes. "In a whorehouse in Denver. She works there."

Deliberately smothering the waves of impotent rage that rocketed through him, Will drew out his checkbook.

"The missus paid me," Nichols told him self-righteously. "But I'd take kindly to another whiskey."

Will signaled the bartender once more. "Give me the address in Denver," he said coolly, and wrote it down. Then he wrote a check to Nichols and handed it to him.

"Now, Mr. Forester," the man protested, downing the whiskey the bartender set before him. "I don't want you to think I was askin' fer more money. No, sir."

"That's all right, Nichols," Will said, standing up and looking down at the man with deliberately icy calm. "That check is yours for taking the next train out of town . . . in either direction."

The lilacs beside Star's kitchen door were in full bloom. In the warm afternoon, the scent of them was heavy and sweet. Will was swept by the poignant memory of the day he had first brought Julie home to Star, carrying the weeping child in his arms. Longing, fiercer than any he had ever known, swept through him. Last fall, for one brief moment, he'd held her yielding body in his arms, kissed her tender mouth. She was a girl, he told himself . . . only fifteen this year, and he was a man with a lifetime of pain behind him. But in that moment before he knocked on the door, he wanted her more than he had ever wanted anything in his life.

"Why, Mr. Will . . . what's the matter?" Lydie's black face was concerned as she peered at him through the open door.

"Is Julie here?" he said without thinking.

"Why no," Lydie looked surprised. "She's at the ranch. Star was feelin' a bit poorly, so Julie went alone. It's hayin' time and somebody needed to be there."

Dear God, he thought, it wasn't Julie he'd meant to ask for at all. He'd come to see Star, but it was Julie he wanted with all his heart. It was hard to remember her true age when she seemed so mature. Even now, she was a girl gone to do a man's job. After the hard winter, Star had sent east for a mowing machine and a hayrake. Now the wild hay in the meadows would be harvested and stored to feed animals in the winter. And Julie had gone to oversee it all.

"That's just your foolishness, Lydie." Star's voice broke in as she came into the kitchen, smiling at Will and holding out both hands. "I'm really just a little tired."

"I've got to talk to you," he said, forcing composure upon himself, walking past her into the sitting room.

"So . . . I suppose I have to go to Denver and get her," Will said as he finished telling Star the story. Puffing on his cigar, he paced the room, pausing to look out the front windows. There was the Falls road he'd traveled one moon-lit night with a young man's hot unreasoning blood pulsing through him. And that night had brought him to this moment.

"You should have divorced her long ago." Star's voice had a bitter edge.

"We've argued that before," Will told her with an ironic twist to his mouth.

"And I'm still right," Star snapped. With a decisive gesture, she stood up.

A sense of her strength penetrated through Will's anger. He looked at her straight slender figure, marveling that she must be nearly seventy years old. The black eyes were sharp as ever, the black hair only slightly streaked with gray, her skin still firm except for the wrinkles about her eyes and mouth. Immortal, he found himself thinking, surely Falling Star is immortal.

"Lydie," she called in a firm voice. When Lydie's questioning face appeared in the doorway, she ordered, "Come help me pack. I'm going to Denver with Will."

The house was in a run-down section of south Denver, a world away from the Brown Palace Hotel where Will and Star were staying. They sat in the carriage for a moment in silence, staring at its forlorn, peeling facade.

"You think I don't know about whorehouses," she had told him with some asperity when he protested her accompanying him. "Don't you know Gussie Beaufort was my best friend?"

Will had struggled to hide his grin. "I heard that, but I didn't believe it."

"Believe it," she said, and stalked out of the spacious, marble-floored lobby ahead of him, telling the doorman to call a carriage.

"Oh, fer God's sake!" said the sleepy-looking woman who opened the door of the shabby house to their knock. She slammed the door in their face. From inside, they could hear her screeching, "Kate, Kate; it's some of them damn do-gooders."

"Now jest what the hell do you want?" The frowsy bleached-blond madam in her well-worn pink satin wrapper skewered them with pale gimlet eyes.

"I was told I could find Maria Forester here," Will said, icily polite.

"Not here." The woman started to close the door and Will put his shoulder against it.

"The Pinkertons say she is," he told her in ominous tones.

"Goddamn Pinkertons," the woman growled. "Why don't they stick to train robbers and leave my business alone?"

"Do you have anyone here named Maria?" Star broke in.

The woman stared at her. "Yer an Injun, ain't ya?" she asked.

"Jesus!" Glaring at the woman, Will reached for his wallet. "We'd like to see her . . . whatever it costs."

"No accountin' fer tastes." Kate gave them a lascivious grin and opened the door, pocketing the twenty-dollar gold piece Will handed her. "Follow me," she called over her shoulder, leading them up a dark, narrow stairway. "Beats me why you'd want her. She ain't been worth a damn fer months now. Only thing she's good for is them queers who like dead bodies, if you ask me."

"Nobody asked," Will snapped, holding himself rigidly in control. He was sick with the need to have finished with this.

"Maria, honey," the woman called, opening a door in the long dim hallway. "You got visitors . . . twenty dollars' worth."

"What's the matter with her?" Star demanded, looking down at the inert figure on the rumpled soiled bed.

"Damn her," Kate's voice rose. "Wake up, you bitch." She leaned over and shook Maria roughly. "It's all that damn medicine she takes all the time. Nothin' but dope. She'd do anything for it. Even smoked it with some Chink miners come here once." Shaking her again without result, she muttered, "Worthless bitch. I'll kick her out fer this."

Peering at Will in the dim light, she whined, "You want yer money back?"

"Just get out!" Will shoved her and slammed the door behind her.

Watching as Will tried to rouse Maria, Star clung weakly to the bedpost. She had thought she was strong enough for this, that she could help Will through the horror she was certain he would find. But it was more than even she could bear, seeing that once-beautiful girl in the wasted, bloated piece of human wreckage lying there. It would kill Alex and Katrin to see her like this.

"Ask that . . . Kate, for some coffee, will you, Star?" Will broke into her painful thoughts. "I'll see if I can bring her around."

Will was very like Charles, Star thought in the hours she helped him work with Maria, trying to bring her to full consciousness. He had all Charles's goodness and compassion, but not Charles's sense of the reality of things, or he'd have rid himself of Maria long ago. This woman had deserted him and their son, betrayed him, shamed him, left him nothing but loneliness, and now when she was as low as a human being could sink, he had the compassion to hold out a helping hand.

Tears stung her eyes as she helped him with cold compresses and hot coffee. Somehow, time had tricked them all. Will Forester had married the wrong granddaughter.

"The other girls call her Crazy Mary," Kate offered, leaning in the doorway, smoking a cigarette. "She ain't never really clear in the head."

Nor would she ever be again, Star thought, as Will struggled to talk sense to the now-conscious Maria.

"She's a dopehead," the woman went on without emotion.

Exhausted, Will leaned back in the chair and turned cold eyes on her. Maria tossed restlessly on the pillow, mumbling to herself.

"If yer relatives," Kate continued dispassionately, "I'd be obliged if you'd git her outta here. Otherwise, I'll jest have to kick her out. Dopeheads ain't any more good in my business than they are anywhere else."

In the end, Kate relented enough to help them dress Maria and get her to the carriage, giving them the address of the nearest hospital.

Will's money provided immediate entry, a hospital bed, nurses and doctors. Too worn out to speak, Will and Star took a carriage back to the hotel.

Next day, a pompous bearded doctor delivered the verdict, shaking his head sadly. "I'm afraid she's beyond help, Mr. Forester. Even if we can wean her from the drugs, her mind is gone."

Will made a strange strangled sound in his throat. Star watched him, afraid, for he had gone through all this horror without the slightest hint of emotion, as though he were made of steel.

"There is a fine sanitarium near here that I can recommend," the doctor continued. Pausing, he added in careful tones, "It's rather expensive."

"That doesn't matter," Will said tonelessly. He looked cold and empty to Star, beyond comfort.

"It's a nice place, used to be a hunting lodge, built by some eastern millionaire," the doctor went on, confident now. "They'll take fine care of her there. And that will leave her family free to live their own lives."

Will's mouth twisted bitterly at the words.

"You don't divorce a wife who's insane," Will told her impatiently.

Star looked at his hard, bitter face, then glanced out at the sagebrush plains rushing past the homeward-bound train. Sighing, she forced herself to broach the subject again. She was exhausted, not just from the long train trip, but an emotional exhaustion that could not be relieved by rest. It was sweltering in the car. Someone opened a window, and cinder-laden hot air blew in with a rush.

"You have a right to a life of your own, Will," she said softly, fanning herself. "Don't wait until it's too late." For you and for Julie, she thought.

Will's face tightened. He stared straight ahead into the empty miles of sagebrush plain. "It was too late the day I married Maria," he said with finality, as though closing all the doors that led to life.

Chapter 40

1895

For the past six years the streets of Cameron City always seemed to be lined with settlers' wagons. Julie moved past the crowd of wan-faced, shabby women chattering in front of the general store beneath the dull gray sky of a threatening summer storm. Their numerous children, dressed in a patchwork of castoffs, played in the dusty street, laughing and shouting. Most of the men, those who weren't in the saloon, gathered in front of the land office, chewing tobacco and talking in laconic tones.

She saw them eye her curiously, enviously, and was all too aware of her fine clothes and the knowledge that they regarded her as the enemy. Cattlemen and all their ilk were enemies to these ragtag seekers of free government land.

It wasn't just the way they'd flooded into Wyoming after the hard winter had cleared the land of cattle, she told herself with a resentful glance at a seedy, hard-bitten man who quickly moved out of her path. It wasn't even that they plowed up the good buffalo grass and strung barbed-wire fences around the water holes. They lived off Aycee beef, the herd her father had struggled to bring back after the hard winter had nearly destroyed him. Nesters and rustling seemed to go together in Wyoming. Statehood was supposed to bring law and order, but things got worse every year.

It had all boiled over up in Johnson County where the

rustling was worst. The Wyoming Stockmen's Association had hired a gang of Texas hard-cases to clean out the rustlers. But when they'd surrounded a nester's cabin and shot him in cold blood, public outrage turned against the stockmen. A lot of prominent men in Wyoming were still busy trying to cover up their involvement.

Just as she turned into the sheriff's office, several horsemen dashed wildly down the dusty street, shooting pistols in the air, scattering the nester kids like a flock of scared chickens. The women cringed back against the storefront and the men stared as the riders galloped on, whooping and yelling.

The anger already simmering inside Julie boiled over when she saw Cameron was with them. She glared at his departing figure seated on a fancy silver-trimmed saddle, clad in a bright checked shirt and fringed leather vest with a wide-brimmed hat on his head. He seemed to think himself a desperado at twelve, and she'd heard he was running with the roughest element in town. If Will weren't so busy helping these miserable nesters settle on homesteads, he might take time to control his son. Alex was worried sick over Cam's behavior. Katrin had even come to the house to talk to Grandmother about it, hoping she could influence Cam to settle down.

Will should have made him stay in school in St. Louis after Monique died. She didn't want to think about Will, she told herself, trying to ignore the old yearning that would not die. They met at family gatherings or on business, always carefully polite with each other. Most of the time he avoided seeing her, and that was all for the best, she knew, since there seemed no possibility he would ever unchain himself from Maria.

She thought sadly of how Monique had tried to keep the secret of Maria from Cameron. Now she was gone. Surely it was Katrin's fault that Maria's situation was common knowledge in the town. Katrin had insisted Alex go with her to Denver to see Maria. It had been a shattering experience for both of them, as Alex told Grandmother. After a period of grieving, locked in her room, Katrin told around town that her daughter had died. But she'd told her dear friend Bertha the truth. From there it spread as gossip always does.

Cameron no longer pretended to anyone that he didn't know about his mother. His attitude toward Will bordered on defiance. Julie thought sadly that Cameron was too young to understand that Will was not at fault. But when the town toughs made sly jokes about his whore of a mother, locked up now in a nut house, Cameron had to be angry at someone.

"Howdy, Miss Cameron." Sheriff Jim Wilson took his long legs off his desk and stood up, grinning self-consciously.

His eyes went over her in frank appreciation and Julie felt herself flush. Jim Wilson wasn't the only man who looked at her in that way, who might have come calling on her with the slightest bit of encouragement. She easily kept them all at arm's length, intimidated as they were by her grandmother and her father, as well as by the fact that she was becoming a rancher in her own right.

Maybe her independent accomplishments made up for what she was missing, the things that were a normal part of other young women's lives. Even though she hadn't attended the wedding, Priscilla still wrote to her, still considered them best friends. Her letters extolled her husband and her two beautiful children. Refusing to admit to envy, Julie told herself that was Priscilla's life, not hers.

"Good morning, Jim," she replied, taking the chair he held for her and smoothing her gray merino skirt about her knees. The admiration in his sharp blue eyes pleased her. At least he didn't look past her the way Will Forester always did.

"It is now," he agreed with a wide grin. "What kin I do fer you?"

"Evict the squatters who moved onto my place on Bitter Creek," she said without preamble. "I've got over a hundred head of good Herefords on that property. If I'm going to build up the herd, I need all the water and grass for them." Anger at the threadbare family who had chosen a prime spot on the creek and begun building a cabin clogged her throat. When she'd ridden out there with Percy McGrath, one of

Grandmother's old ranch hands who was running the Herefords for her, they'd refused to budge. Waving their homestead papers in her face, they insisted they'd filed on this property legally.

"Grandmother bought that place from the original settlers, the Dunlaps, years ago. She gave it to me and I own all that land in fee simple. It isn't open to homesteaders."

"I'll get right out there, Miss Julie," he assured her, patting her hand. Realizing what he was doing, Jim blushed furiously and jerked his hand away as though he'd touched a hot stove.

Leaning both elbows on the kitchen table, Jim Wilson blew on his coffee to cool it. He nodded his thanks to Lydie. Afternoon sunlight lay rectangular patterns across the table and glinted off the silver ring Jim wore.

"I been to Bitter Creek already this mornin'," he said, sipping the steaming coffee and avoiding Julie's eyes.

"You saw the squatters then?" Julie asked, frowning at him.

"Their name's Yancy and they're from off some worn-out farm in Arkansas," Jim began, concentrating on adding more sugar to his coffee.

Julie exchanged glances with her grandmother, already certain that Wilson had failed in his mission.

"Got five kids," Jim added irrelevantly.

"And they're still on my property," Julie snapped, anger rising inside her.

Jim shook his head. "Miss Julie, they got papers for that land . . . legal homestead papers, filled out and filed for 'em by Will Forester."

"Will Forester!" Julie half rose from her chair, glaring at Jim. His eyes slid away from her furious scrutiny. Scarcely aware of Star's placating hand on her arm, Julie pushed back her chair and began to pace the room. "Damn Will Forester," she said. "Who does he think he is . . . God? Giving my land away."

Ever since she'd made the decision to stay in Wyoming, she'd worked beside her grandmother, learning the horse-breeding business. Star's special magic in gentling horses had become Julie's too. But it wasn't enough to quell her growing restlessness. She had to prove she could succeed on her own.

Until two years ago, she'd rented the Bitter Creek pasture to her father. Determined to start her own spread, she'd borrowed the money from Star, bought a hundred head of good Hereford cows, and turned them out on the meadows along Bitter Creek. Although the emotional barriers between Alex and herself remained, he had been helpful in getting her spread started, offering suggestions, even sending some of his cow hands to help.

Shifting uneasily in his chair, Jim gulped his hot coffee. Julie cast another glare in his direction. Why had she thought he'd handle this business for her? He was too young to be a sheriff anyway, and he hadn't brought in any of the rustlers and horse thieves that had plagued the ranchers in the area for the past few years. Star hadn't been bothered. Her Appaloosas were too well marked, and too hard to hide.

Reaching for his hat, Jim rose hurriedly. He shifted from one foot to another, obviously unsure how to handle her outburst. "I reckon you better talk to Mr. Forester about it," he said.

"You're damn right I will," Julie burst out. Leaving them staring after her, she stalked out of the room, and out the front door.

Like a blight on the land, Julie fumed as she rushed down the board sidewalk. Main Street was muddy from yesterday's rain and still lined with rickety homesteader wagons drawn by hungry-looking horses. They were changing the face of the land she loved, but they weren't about to steal her own personal piece of it.

The anteroom of Will's office was crowded with them, waiting hopefully. Rushing past them, Julie flung open the door and faced Will across the wide mahogany desk.

Startled, he stood up, his hands still full of papers. The man and woman sitting beside the desk stared at her.

"Julie—" he began.

"I want to talk to you," she interrupted through clenched teeth. "Now!" With a glare, she dismissed the couple who moved nervously toward the door.

While Julie waited impatiently, Will ushered them out of the office, speaking in low reassuring tones. All the years of frustration, of loving him and wanting him, burgeoned into an anger that threatened to engulf her. She loved that place on Bitter Creek because she had nothing else to love . . . the little cabin under the cottonwoods where old Percy lived now . . . the streams and meadows. Will Forester had denied her his love and now he was trying to deprive her of everything else.

"You're a traitor," she said in a low hostile voice as Will faced her. "You betray the men who settled this country— my father, your father—giving it all away to a bunch of ragtag seekers of something for nothing."

Will stared at her in stunned surprise. "Julie," he protested, holding up a hand to still her outburst. "What's this all about?"

Trembling with anger, Julie tried to force her voice into calmness. But bitterness colored her words as she spoke in a hard tone. "You know damn well . . . Those Yancys you settled on my Bitter Creek place. They're stealing my land and you're helping them."

Will frowned down at her. "The land was free, Julie," he protested. "I wouldn't have helped them file on it if it hadn't been."

Riveting him with angry eyes, Julie asked bitterly, "Are you getting rich from this, Will—stealing land, ruining the ranches? I'd have thought you had enough money."

"Money has nothing to do with it." Will's mouth was tight, and a muscle worked in his jaw.

"I see," she said in a voice dripping with sarcasm. "Purely altruistic . . . looking out for your fellow man . . ."

"Julie . . ." he protested once more, reaching out to touch her arm.

She stepped away from him. "How about helping out the fellow man you've known all your life, Will? People like my father. Those high-minded settlers of yours aren't fussy about what they eat—a hundred-dollar Hereford or a ten-dollar longhorn, it's all the same to them."

Will opened his mouth to speak, but she rushed on. "Alex had a hell of a time making it back after the big die-up. In the old days, a rancher didn't miss the cows stolen out of a herd of twenty thousand, but when you have a hundred cows . . . even one is a big loss."

"I know the rustlers are bad." Will raised his voice in order to interrupt. "But it's not my people doing the stealing."

Falling silent for a moment, Julie gave him a look of contemptuous pity. "You live in a dream world, Will, just like these nesters who think they've found a dream home. Wait until they've gone through a Wyoming winter." Fixing him with a venomous stare, she went on, "Your life is a mess, Will, your son runs wild, you don't have the guts to get free of your crazy wife." Her voice dropped, and she was suddenly ashamed of her words and filled with pity for him. "Is this all you have, these poor grateful people fawning over you, praising you?"

Will's face darkened with anger. Abruptly turning from her, he walked back to his desk where he stood with clenched fists, staring down at the papers lying there.

For one irrational moment, she wanted to take him in her arms and comfort him. But it was too late for them; perhaps it had always been too late.

Summoning all her strength, Julie determined to finish what she had started. "Whatever means you used to settle those Yancys on Bitter Creek . . . I want them off—now."

Will lifted his head and looked straight at her. His gray eyes were dark and cool. His voice was calm. "You can't fight the future, Julie . . . and people like the Yancys are the future of Wyoming—small ranchers, farmers, and families."

Once more, anger poured through Julie, blurring her vision, making her tremble inwardly. Bitter Creek was like her child, she told herself, and she'd never let it go.

"I can fight, Will," she said, lifting her chin defiantly. "Just watch me."

"Good Lord, Julie." His voice rose, impatient and angry. "Didn't the cattlemen shed enough blood in the Johnson County War? All Wyoming should have learned a lesson from that. You don't win by killing innocent nesters."

"Not so innocent." Her voice was caustic. "I'll take the sheriff out there and check the brands on the hides they've got buried from the cattle they've butchered. If that doesn't work, I know the men to hire to put them off the place."

Will's face blanched, as though for the first time he understood the strength of her resolve. "You wouldn't do that, Julie . . . not you."

"Watch me!" she cried defiantly. "If you want to start a Cameron Valley War, Mr. Forester, I promise you: I'll finish it."

Chapter 41

Percy found the men for her, four of them, with faces of stone and empty eyes. They wore their gunbelts with familiar ease. Julie thought it best not to ask questions, and it didn't make any difference whether they came from the Hole-in-the-Wall gang, or the Brown's Hole Wild Bunch. They looked tough enough to put the Yancys on the road just by intimidation.

"No shooting," she cautioned them when they met at Percy's cabin on Bitter Creek. "I don't want anyone hurt." Seeing their doubtful expressions, she quickly added, "I'll pay a bonus if it's done peacefully."

"Don't worry, ma'am." Percy grinned at her through his bristly gray beard. He was a short man and wiry, his sun-darkened face as wrinkled as a dried apple beneath a battered Stetson. "I knowed these boys a long time. They'll do the job to suit you."

But when she insisted on riding to the Yancy homestead with them, their objections were so vociferous, she told them, "Quit if you don't like it. I'll get someone else to do the job."

Exchanging resigned looks, they mounted up. Julie, on Handyman, her gray Appaloosa with white hand-shaped markings on its hip, followed them.

The Yancy cabin, built beneath a stand of cottonwoods

beside Bitter Creek, was so poorly constructed, Julie thought a Wyoming blizzard could whip straight through all the cracks between the logs. It was late summer, and no sign of Yancy plowing or putting in a crop. The only animals in the makeshift corral were two plow horses and a milk cow. A shaggy yellow dog ran barking to meet the horsemen.

A rawboned man of indeterminate age lounged in the low doorway of the cabin as they reined up.

"I done told you to move on, Yancy," Percy began in stern tones. "This ain't your land. You're squattin' here on Miss Julie's hay meadows."

In reply, the laconic Yancy merely spit tobacco juice into the dusty dooryard. Behind him, peering fearfully from the cabin's gloom, was his thin, pale wife holding a toddler in her arms. Two wide-eyed small children clutched at her skirts.

"Since you didn't take the hint," Percy continued, frowning at the man, "I done brought some boys from Hole in the Wall to help you move."

The words "Hole in the Wall" caught Yancy's attention. The reputation of the rustlers and robbers who hid out in the wild and desolate Hole-in-the-Wall country was legendary. His sallow face blanched and fear shone from his pale eyes as he stared at the men facing him. Revolvers rode easy on their hips and the rifles were loose in their scabbards.

"You don't mean right now?" Yancy whined. "Today?"

"Today, Mr. Yancy." Julie's voice was harsh with long-simmering anger. An old saying came into her mind as her glance went over the men sitting easy in their saddles, hands resting on their gunbelts: "Set a thief to catch a thief."

"The boys will help you load your wagon," she went on coldly. "I want you off the place by sundown. Otherwise, I'll bring the sheriff out to check the brands on all those cowhides you've got buried around here."

"It ain't right . . ." Yancy started to protest, his wife clinging fearfully to the threadbare sleeve of his cotton shirt.

"I've checked my deeds, Mr. Yancy," Julie said. "This property wasn't open to homesteading. You've made a mistake and you'd better move on before winter sets in."

"Be damned!" Yancy blustered. "I'll see you in court, Miss High an' Mighty."

The woman burst into tears. "Mr. Forester said it was open land." She turned pleading eyes on Julie.

"Mr. Forester was wrong," Julie returned in icy tones. Seeing their mother in tears, the children set up a wailing. From inside the cabin a baby answered their cries.

Feeling a bit sick, Julie reined her horse around. "Take care of it, Percy," she said. "Help them get loaded and moving. Don't hurt them."

"Told you to let me handle it," Percy growled. "No job fer a woman. Now git on back to my cabin. Me and the boys'll meet you there."

As she rode away, Julie saw that two of Percy's toughs had dismounted and were hitching up the Yancys' ramshackle wagon. The voices of the weeping children and their mother seemed to echo in her ears all the way back to Percy's cabin.

"Now, Miss Julie, you mustn't worry about them folks," Percy told her when she had paid off the boys from Hole in the Wall and thanked them for handling the Yancys as she asked.

Julie watched from the doorway until the willows along the creek finally obscured the riders from view. Summer wind stirred the cottonwoods around the cabin, and a family of mountain bluebirds sang in the branches of the tree nearest the house.

When she turned to take the cup of coffee he offered, Percy went on, "Why, you shoulda seen that place. Like Tom said, they'd have starved out or froze out this winter." He patted her shoulder. "You know people gotta understand Wyoming if they're gonna live here. This ain't no Arkansas weather."

Julie gave him a wan smile, still haunted by the memory of the weeping disheartened woman and her children. The man was obviously shiftless and incompetent. Percy was right . . . they'd have starved out. She sat in the chair he offered, sipping the bitter coffee.

Sitting down in his other chair, Percy studied her across

the stained wooden table. "Don't go feelin' sorry now," he insisted. "Anyways, seems Yancy was a miner back east and he's headed fer Rock Springs now. Figgers on gettin' a job in the coal mines there."

"Maybe they'll be better off," Julie replied, trying to make herself believe it.

"Damn right they will!" Percy said emphatically. Standing, he grinned down at her. "You want me to ride back to Red Hill with you?"

"No," she said, with a wan smile. "I want you to look after my Herefords and get a haying crew on that meadow by next week."

She couldn't tell Percy where she was going, Julie thought, as she pressed the Appaloosa hard on the road south. He'd be outraged, thinking she'd backed down after all the trouble he'd gone to, hiring those men and putting Yancy out.

It was nearly dusk when she caught up with them. The Yancys had camped in the sagebrush beside the road. It was a dry camp with a hot wind blowing dust and Yancy watering the horses from a bucket. They had a small campfire next to the wagon, and Julie could smell salt pork frying.

The woman screeched and gathered the children close to her as Julie reined up beside their fire. The baby in its basket awakened and began to cry lustily.

"Ain't you done enuff?" Yancy asked in a flat, whiny voice, pausing beside the fire, the empty water bucket in his hand.

"I don't think much of you, Mr. Yancy," Julie replied crisply, looking down at him. "But I do feel for your wife and children. I hate to see them suffer because you're a shiftless fool."

"You got no call," the man began belligerently.

"Shut up!" Julie commanded. "I came here to see your wife."

Mrs. Yancy's pale weary eyes met Julie's, and her heart ached for all the troubles behind this woman and the troubles she was certain lay ahead.

"The land you homesteaded was already owned by me," she said, speaking directly to the woman. "Mr. Forester made a mistake, and I'm sorry you have to pay for it."

Tears flowed down Mrs. Yancy's wan face as she held her sobbing children close to her, watching Julie apprehensively.

"It's only fair that I pay you for the improvements you made on the property," she continued, repressing emotion. As soon as the haying crew came in, she'd have them tear down the shanty of a cabin. The corral would likely fall by itself. This seemed a way to help the woman and save her pride at the same time.

From her pocket, Julie took the bank draft she'd written out while waiting for Percy and his men to return. "It's in your name, Etta Yancy," Julie said, holding the paper out. "You use the money to keep your family going while your man finds a job."

Hope sprang to life in the woman's eyes. When Yancy reached for the draft, Julie deliberately moved her horse and cut him off. Staring in disbelief at the bank draft, Etta Yancy looked up at Julie with such gratitude, Julie felt a twinge of guilt.

"They'll cash it at the bank in Rock Springs," she told her.

"Praise God," the woman said softly, tucking the draft into her blouse. For the first time, she smiled at Julie. "You didn't have to do that, did you, miss?"

"I had to do it," Julie answered in a muffled voice. Abruptly she reined the horse around, whipping him into a gallop on the road north. I had to do it for me, Julie thought, in order to live with myself.

Cameron City was closer than the ranch and the road easier to follow in the darkness. Still, it was very late when Julie turned her horse into the corral and walked up to the house on Forester Creek Road. The day's events had left her emotionally exhausted. She felt tired enough to sleep forever.

The kitchen was clean and empty. Julie stared in surprise at the trunk and two carpetbags sitting in the foyer, then followed the sound of voices into the sitting room.

"Julie!" Star cried, leaping up from her chair with all the grace of a girl. Lydie rose slowly, grimacing, setting the glass of iced lemonade on the marble-topped table. Her curly hair was white as snow now, in startling contrast to her dusky face.

"We sent a message to the ranch, but the boy said you weren't there." Star's expression was concerned, her eyes questioning.

Julie looked away, unwilling to share an incident of which she was not entirely proud. "I went by Bitter Creek to check up on Percy," she said. "Then decided I'd come on in to town."

"Good thing you did," Lydie chided. "Me and your grandma are leavin' in the morning. Gonna be gone a month."

"Where to?" Julie asked in surprise, for Star seldom traveled anywhere except to the ranch. There'd been that awful trip to Denver with Will. Then Alex had insisted on taking her to Cheyenne. All the bustle of that brawling little city upset Star and she took the next train home.

"Steamboat Springs." Star smiled, giving Lydie a sidelong glance. "Lydie thinks the hot springs will help her rheumatiz, and I wouldn't mind a little trip before winter sets in."

Julie frowned, studying her grandmother, unsure whether she was being entirely truthful about her health. No one knew Star's true age, but her figure was still slender and wiry, only slightly stooped. Each year the gray grew thicker in her black hair, but the elegant face was scarcely lined and the dark eyes as sharp as ever.

"Fact is"—Lydie flashed her white grin—"I couldn't git in there by myself. If they think I'm Star's maid, it'll be all right."

"That's ridiculous," Julie protested.

Lydie shrugged philosophically. "Ain't as bad as Georgia, Miss Julie."

"We'll put one over on 'em," Star said in a soft, amused tone.

"I'll get you some lemonade, Miss Julie," Lydie said, "and some supper if you ain't et."

Julie sighed and nodded. "I guess I am hungry, Lydie." Percy had offered food, but she'd been too upset to eat then.

Star's wise old eyes studied Julie closely, but she spoke in an offhand manner. "Will's back. He came by wanting to see you about something."

She didn't want to see him, Julie told herself. Avoiding Star's penetrating gaze, she walked into the kitchen. Especially after today, she didn't want to see him. If she'd been in the right, why did she feel so miserable about taking back what was really hers?

She'd tried to call on the gift of foresight that had made her buy the right property, invest her money wisely, and avoid the catastrophes that befell so many other people in the cattle business. If she could guess the future, why could she not see any future for her and Will . . . ever?

"Julie." There was a knock at the open ranch house door.

Recognizing the voice, Julie spun around from the table where she was sorting breeding records. Her heart raced wildly. Damn, damn, damn, she thought, why was it always this way? Just the sound of Will's voice, a glimpse of him down the street, could set her whole body yearning like a lovesick adolescent.

"Hello, Will." She forced herself to sound cool and calm, in spite of her inner trembling. He wore jeans and boots, a wool plaid shirt beneath his denim jacket, and she thought he looked as elegant as he did in town in a black frock coat and white linen shirt.

"I'd have been out earlier," he said apologetically, holding his hat in his hands, "but I got busy and didn't get away."

What could she say? She'd seen Star and Lydie off on the train, then rode to the ranch purposely hoping to avoid meeting Will. The calm September day was cool, a portent of autumn. She'd worked all afternoon on the records, planning to go over them with Little Knife tomorrow.

An awkward silence grew between them until Will finally asked, "May I come in?"

"Sure." Embarrassed by her lack of courtesy, Julie stepped back. Glancing beyond him, through the open door, she saw that the shadows of the cottonwoods were long in the lowering sun.

"Would you like a drink?" she asked, struggling to keep her voice even, to subdue the ache that filled her heart in his presence.

"Yes, I would," he replied. With a self-conscious smile, he took off his jacket and hung it over a chair back.

Opening the cabinet, Julie took out the decanter and glasses Grandmother kept there to serve visiting horse buyers and stockmen.

Will stirred the low fire and added a log, then sat down in the big leather Morris chair beside the fireplace, his eyes following Julie's graceful movements. The gray merino riding skirt fit snugly over her rounded hips, and her breasts filled the pink calico shirt in a way that set fire to his loins. The cut crystal of the glass and decanter she placed on the low table before him gleamed in the firelight.

"My father gave this crystal to your grandmother," he said, accepting the drink and turning the glass to admire it. He took a deep breath, struggling to suppress the longing that seemed about to overwhelm him.

"I know," she replied quietly.

Startled by her tone, Will searched her face.

"I know all about them," she continued, moving about the room, not looking at him.

"Did Star tell you?" he asked in surprise.

"She didn't have to." Julie turned to look at him with a rueful smile. "I have the gift, you know."

"Yes, I know," he said. Her dark eyes gleamed at his quiet acceptance and her expression warmed.

Again the silence stretched between them. Will felt a hot ache begin in his chest, spreading along his limbs, eating at him. The past few years he'd avoided Julie, afraid of the feelings he struggled to suppress. Then they'd quarreled over the Bitter Creek property and she'd made it easier by avoiding him.

"I came back from Cheyenne yesterday," he began, sipping Star's good whiskey with appreciation. "I wanted to see you right away . . . to apologize."

Julie waited, standing beside the fireplace, her dark eyes intent on him. Will drew a deep painful breath. She didn't intend to help him with this.

"The survey I got from the land office was wrong, Julie. You do own the Bitter Creek property." His eyes probed her unfathomable ones. "I hope you believe it was an honest mistake."

"Do the Yancys believe that?" she asked, her voice low and bitter.

"I intend to make restitution to them, Julie—out of my own pocket," he protested.

"It's too late," she said, turning her back and staring into the fire. "I kicked them out yesterday."

"You had the right," he said carefully, sensing her unhappiness from the rigidity of her slender body.

Covering her face with her hands, Julie struggled to hold back the sob that broke from her aching throat. "It was awful, Will . . . the woman and kids crying . . ."

Setting down his glass, Will rose and took her slender shoulders in his hands. He turned her to face him. But she would not look at him, and when he gathered her close in his arms, she buried her face against his chest and gave way to weeping.

Gently smoothing her hair, Will tilted her chin to look down into her face. "It's all right, Julie. The whole mess is my fault. I'll see they're taken care of."

"I paid them for the cabin and corral," she said, looking up at him with swimming eyes.

He should have guessed, Will thought, wanting to kiss her tear-streaked unhappy face. In spite of himself, he chuckled. "How much?"

"Two hundred dollars." She managed to choke out the words.

"Lord, Julie." He tried not to laugh. "They've never been so rich . . . and probably never will be again."

"It was a bit high," she admitted, smiling now, dashing her tears away with one hand.

Even now she'd stopped crying, Will couldn't let go of her. The feel of her slender body so close to his made his heart swell with longing. Her soft full breasts seemed to burn through the layers of calico and wool, setting his body ablaze with need.

His arms tightened and he looked tenderly into her luminous eyes. "Why don't you stop trying to be a tough cattleman, Julie?"

"Because I have to be one," she said, her hands resting warm against his chest. "When Star dies I'll be all alone."

"You'll never be alone as long as I'm alive, Julie." The words came from the very depths of his love for her.

Closing her eyes, Julie swayed toward him. Will's mouth covered hers and all the empty years seemed to drain away.

In complete surrender, Julie returned his kiss, all the unfulfilled longing, all the dreams she'd denied for so long poured into that kiss. Her arms clung to him, her body pressed fiercely against his. A strange and wonderful fire ran through her.

"Darling Will," she gasped as their mouths parted and he bent his head to kiss the soft curve of her neck. "I love you so."

He couldn't stop kissing her, reveling in the sweetness of her skin, the tantalizing brush of her eyelashes against his mouth, the yielding heat of her soft body.

"Julie . . . sweet Julie," he muttered brokenly, his mouth seeking hers again in a devouring kiss.

"My little love," he murmured, looking into her face as they broke apart. His gray eyes were dark with passion. "My love, I've wanted you for so long."

Julie's heart soared at the words. Longing poured through her, so intense she would have given herself to him there on the hearth rug. "Love me, Will," she whispered, her mouth eagerly seeking his.

Will's warm tongue teased her lips open and all the breath

went out of her as his kiss seemed to touch the depths of her soul. Their bodies molded against each other as though they were one being and a fire leaped through Julie in response to the hardness of his desire for her.

"Love me now, darling," she said softly, looking into his eyes. "We've waited so long. . . ."

She saw his struggle to regain control as he buried his face against her hair and muttered brokenly, "My love, my love, it isn't right."

"It's the rightest thing we've ever done," she told him, smiling. Cupping his face in her two hands, she kissed him, a deep, heart-shattering kiss. She could almost feel him melt against her.

Holding his hand tightly, Julie bolted the front door and led her lover home into her heart at last.

Chapter 42

Cool and gray, first light filled the bedroom. Julie started awake at the unfamiliar presence in her bed. Memory flooded back. Smiling, she turned on her pillow, reveling in the delicious soreness of her body, feasting her eyes on Will's tanned face, relaxed and vulnerable in sleep.

For the first time she noticed the streaks of gray in his thick brown hair, the fine lines about his mouth and at the corners of his eyes. Will was thirty-five, she remembered, too young to be gray, too young to have so many years of loneliness behind him.

No more loneliness, darling, she thought, for either of us. Gently, she slid her hand across the dark mat of hair on his chest. Will stirred and sighed in his sleep.

In a moment, she would kiss him awake, stir him to passion, and they would make love as they had all night through. But just now she wanted to savor the moment that fulfilled all her dreams. Why had she ever doubted her vision of a lover's gray eyes? Surely it was out of fear and lack of faith. Now the doubts had vanished and it seemed this morning that they had been lovers forever.

"Darling," she whispered, kissing his ear. She lay across his chest so that she could feel the beating of his heart against her breast. Loving the feel of his hard-muscled body,

Julie slid her hands down his flat stomach and felt him begin to harden in response to her touch.

Suddenly she was seized in a fierce embrace and kissed until she was breathless. "My beautiful Julie," Will murmured. "My love." With gentle fingers, he brushed her loose black hair back from her face and began to kiss her softly . . . her eyes, her ears, the pulse at the base of her throat.

A sweet insistent throbbing pounded between her thighs, rising in intensity. "Darling," she whispered, holding him close, the touch of his strong male body inflaming her senses. "Darling Will . . . love me."

Propping himself on one elbow, he looked down at her with an expression of gentle concern. "Are you all right, love? I didn't want to hurt you last night."

Tenderly she ran a finger down his stubbly cheek. The gray eyes darkened, a flame of desire burning deep behind them. In spite of his gentleness, he had hurt her the first time, but she had forgotten the pain in the wild soaring rapture that followed. All through the night they'd slept, awakened, and turned to each other with urgent need, rising with cries of love to unexplored heights of ecstasy.

"We've waited so long for each other, Will." She sighed, drawing him down into her arms. "We have so much to catch up on."

Will's hot fervent mouth answered her devouring kiss. Her whole body ached for him, and when at last he covered her, she surrendered completely, moaning softly with pleasure. Once more, he led her along rapturous paths into an exquisite explosion of sensation. All the breath burst from her lungs in a wild cry of fulfillment.

"Julie . . . Julie . . . Julie . . ." He cried her name at the moment of climax, and whispered it again as they both drifted into sated sleep.

Pillowing her head on his broad shoulder, Julie murmured, "Darling Will, you make me so happy."

The sun was high when Julie awakened. Will was gone from the bed and the odor of coffee and frying bacon drifted in from the kitchen. She could hear him whistling, a low unmusical sound.

In the bathroom she found he'd made a fire in the small potbellied stove, so there was warm water for her bath. Hurrying to dress, she didn't know whether to sing or weep, she was so filled with happiness. Dressed in her gray skirt and a clean white shirtwaist, she quickly put up her hair. Looking into the mirror, she found it incredible that last night's magic hadn't wrought some outward change. It was still the same Julie looking back at her, but not the same . . . ever again.

"Good morning, cook," she called gaily.

Will's whistling ceased as he turned from the stove, grinning at her and holding out his arms. Deliberately, Julie prolonged their kiss, clinging to him, until they were both breathless.

"Will you stay today?" she asked, standing close, her arms about his neck.

He seemed to hesitate for a moment. Then his big hands slid down her back, cupping her hips and holding her against him. "Wild horses couldn't drag me away from you," he answered with a grin. His mouth sought hers, and Julie leaned eagerly into his embrace.

A knock at the door drove them apart.

"Oh, Lord," Will groaned. "I've made a scandal of you."

Julie laughed. "Little Knife doesn't gossip with the Ladies Literary Society."

But Little Knife looked a bit uneasy and Julie was certain he knew what had taken place last night. For one thing, he'd had to take care of Will's horse or the poor creature would have still been at the hitching rack.

"You want me to ride out with you to check the mares and foals today?" Little Knife asked.

"No," she answered in lilting tones, aware from the way the foreman was looking at her that she must be shining with happiness. "Mr. Forester's staying over and he'll go with me."

Little Knife's swarthy round face broke into a wide grin.

"Good," he said. "That's good." Turning jauntily away, he added over his shoulder, "Me and the boys need to check fences in the south pasture. Those damn homesteaders keep cuttin' the wire."

The sky was a clear and flawless blue. Only the chill in the slight breeze and the mountainsides blazing with golden aspens spoke of summer's end. With Will riding beside her, Julie thought the whole world seemed to glow with an enchanted light. Happiness suffused her with a depth of awareness she'd never felt before. The scent of the grass, the grace of the horses, the sweet tones of calling birds, all seemed blessed with joy.

This Will wasn't the stern businesslike lawyer, but more like the fun-loving young man who'd taken her to St. Louis long ago. He'd even teased her about riding sidesaddle today, and managed to kiss her a dozen times while they were saddling the horses. Catching his eye, she reached out across the space between their horses, and he took her hand. Even that brief touch sent excitement tingling along her nerves.

After their circuit of the pasture, Julie reined in her mount. Taking her tally book from her pocket, she wrote down the count she'd kept in her head as they rode among the mares and their cavorting foals.

Looking up, she met Will's admiring eyes. "How can you keep that count in your head?" he asked.

"Old-maid ranchers learn to do lots of things," she replied, smiling. Watching the easy movements of his tall, lean body as he swung down from his saddle and walked over to her, she felt a rush of heat pour through her.

"Old maid, my foot," he scoffed, laying his hand on her knee. "You could have your choice of any man in Wyoming."

Except you, she started to say, and was drenched in joy at the realization that was no longer true. Sliding down from the saddle into his waiting arms, Julie lost herself in his kiss, pressing hungrily against him.

Aware that he was fully aroused, she slanted a teasing look at him. "Have you ever made love in a meadow in the middle of the day?"

His face was tense with longing, but it broke into a grin at her words. "Your wish is my command, beautiful lady."

Quickly discarding their clothing, they tumbled, laughing, into each other's arms on the soft damp grass beneath the willows. The red-wing blackbirds flew up at their approach, then settled back to scold. The horses cropped grass quietly, and the creek moved along its grassy banks with a low sweet murmur.

"Do you know how long I've loved you, Will?" Julie asked pensively, her eyes on his adoring face. Her fingers traced a path along his shoulders as her body responded to his caressing hands. "Ever since the day you brought me home from the fight at school."

Will paused in his loving tour of her body, his gray eyes darkened in that way she had come to recognize, filled with deep emotion. "Darling girl," he said. "It seems I've wanted you so long, I can't remember when it began. Maybe the night in my kitchen when I kissed you."

"And told me you were old enough to be my father," she teased, breaking the intensity of the moment.

Smiling, Will touched his mouth to hers. "Old enough and fool enough to have wasted all these years," he murmured sadly.

"Don't waste any more," she whispered. Running her fingers through his thick hair, she opened her lips to him. Their mouths joined in a deep, devouring kiss.

Driving passion swept through Julie. Trembling with the intensity of her need, she lifted her hips to take him into the center of her being. A rising tide of rapture caught her, blind and deaf and lost to everything except the exquisite joy of loving. Then the sky itself seemed to explode in her eyes. She cried out as his seed burst inside her, then wept in the certain knowledge her gift brought . . . that their love had made a child.

Suspended in silence, they lay together, reluctant even

now to be parted. In the distance a meadowlark called. Julie turned her head on Will's shoulder and looked into his warm eyes. "Once upon a time I thought the meadowlark said, 'Julie must wait.'"

His eyes darkened and his arm tightened about her. "Now," she murmured half to herself, "now I think it says, 'Julie loves Will.'"

Will smiled at her fancy. Pressing his lips against her temple, he murmured, "Or 'Will loves Julie.'" His mouth found hers then in a kiss that was drained of passion and filled with love.

Pillowing her head on Will's shoulder, Julie looked pensively up through the overhanging willows into the infinite blue sky. In the gloom beneath the trees a spider's silver thread caught the sunlight. Only the soothing murmur of running water broke the silence.

After a moment, Julie began to talk. She told him what she had told only Grandmother, of the wondrous vision she had found in her quest on the hilltop years ago.

Will propped himself on one elbow, his eyes intent on her face as she spoke. "It was your eyes on the gray dove that warmed and protected me," she finished. "I recognized it that day on the train to St. Louis, and always I knew that someday, somehow, we'd be together."

Turning questioningly to him, Julie drew in her breath sharply, for his eyes were moist. Holding her close, Will laid his face against her bare shoulder. She felt the hot wetness of his tears, and her heart was filled with the perfect knowledge that he understood.

Julie dropped two beefsteaks into the hot iron skillet. At once they began to sizzle and smoke rose in a cloud above the kitchen stove.

"Lydie says cook 'em fast," she said, smiling at Will, who was watching her from his chair beside the kitchen table. Love for him filled her until she thought her heart would burst. Needing to touch him, she moved across the room to stand behind his chair, her hands on his shoulders. She bent to kiss his temple and press her cheek against his hair. Will turned his head and captured her mouth with his. They broke apart laughing for no reason except sheer happiness.

Leaning back in his chair, Will scratched a match to light his cigar.

Her arms about his neck, Julie kissed the top of his head. In a dreamy voice, she mused, "In spite of our fight over Bitter Creek, it's a lovely place. Maybe we should build our house there after we're married."

Will tensed beneath her touch. He held the lighted match so long it burned his fingers and he dropped it on the table with a sharp exclamation. Taking the cigar from his mouth, he turned to look at her with a stricken face.

"Oh God, Julie." His voice was harsh and strangled. "I thought you understood."

Her hands dropped to her sides as he stood up to face her. All the breath seemed to have gone out of her as she waited. "Understood what?" she managed to say, and she shivered as an inexplicable coldness fell over her.

"That I can't divorce Maria." He swallowed hard, as though his throat hurt before he continued. "She's in an asylum in Colorado. How could I desert her?"

"She deserted you," Julie retorted, her voice echoing the pain growing inside her.

Will looked away. "I can't do it," he said miserably. "The law says I can't." Reaching out, he took her by the shoulders and drew her toward him. "I'll give you anything on earth you want, dear heart . . . anything—"

"Anything but a wedding ring," she interrupted, her pain burgeoning into fury. "Because my mother was Alex Cameron's whore, did you think I would be your whore?"

"My God, Julie!" Will protested, staring at her in shock. "How can you use that word for your mother . . . for yourself?"

"You've always run from reality, haven't you?" Julie cried bitterly.

"I love you, Julie." His face was agonized, his eyes pleading. "These last years have been hell for me . . . seeing

398

you, wanting you, and knowing I have no right. . . ." His voice fell as he reached out to take her in his arms.

Deliberately, she moved away. Her chest hurt as though a knife had been shoved between her ribs. "I won't live my mother's life!" Her voice fell, all the hurts of her life in that one pained whisper. "You can't have me, Will, unless I can have your name."

"If I could, don't you think I would?" Will moved toward her again, holding out his arms.

Quickly, Julie put the table between them. If he touched her, she would give in because she wanted him so desperately. All the ugly taunts from her childhood seemed to be ricocheting about inside her head.

"Just go," she said, steeling herself against the misery in his eyes and the pain that threatened to overwhelm her. "Go right now . . . saddle up and get out of here, and please . . . please don't come back."

Will's hand touched her shoulder and she ran from her need for him, slamming the bedroom door behind her and bolting it. It seemed forever before she heard the sound of a horse being ridden away. Only then did Julie abandon herself to tears that seemed endless.

"I thought Julie would meet us," Star said as Alex gathered up the bags and trunks she and Lydie had brought from Steamboat Springs. She glanced over the crowd come to meet the evening train at Cameron City's little depot, almost willing Julie to be there. Beyond the faintly gleaming railroad tracks, the sky was an explosion of gray and pink and gold. The wind was filled with dry scents of autumn.

"She's still at the ranch," Alex said offhandedly.

The uneasiness she'd felt all day grew with the words. A sense of foreboding filled her so strongly that she would have gone at once to the ranch if she hadn't been so weary from the long train ride. Age was catching up with her, she thought grimly.

Alex took them home in his buggy, helping open the house that smelled closed and musty because Julie hadn't been in town to air it as she'd promised. When they'd finished, he sat down in the leather chair by the fireplace, watching as Lydie propped Star's feet on a footstool and settled a pillow at her back.

Lydie's black eyes snapped with humor as she told Alex, "Them fancy hot springs did wonders for my rheumatiz, but not so much for Star." She favored him with a toothy grin. "She kept tellin' the attendant she was so weak she had to go in the baths with her maid or they wouldn't have let me in. I think she started to believe it herself."

Star caught the concerned glance that passed between them. "Nonsense," she told Lydie tartly. "Now quit fussing. You're making me nervous."

"I'll put some coffee on," Lydie replied blithely, and disappeared into the kitchen.

"How are things?" Star asked Alex, aware that he wanted to talk.

"Damn nesters!" he burst out immediately. "They're stealin' me blind. Buck and me figure they got away with near a hundred head just while we were working roundup."

"Maybe it isn't just the nesters," Star replied mildly. "Ever since the hard winter, there've been a lot of old-time cowboys drifting around without a place to light. Some of them have ended up making a living rustling cattle."

"Hell!" Alex exploded. "The nesters even protect them . . . let them hide out on their homesteads. An honest cattleman hasn't got a chance," he finished gloomily.

Sighing, Star studied her son's worried face. Would he be like his father, she wondered sadly, unable to bend and accommodate the tides of change sweeping over the country? The days when the cattlemen owned the grass to the end of the horizon were gone. There would be small ranchers, farmers in the sheltered valleys . . . another new world in the many she had known.

"Come spring, if any of my cows are being sucked by a calf with some nester's brand, you can bet there'll be hell to pay." Alex glared at his cigar and fell silent.

"Have you seen Will?" Star asked, the sense of foreboding rising once more to the front of her mind.

"Oh yeah, I forgot to mention that," Alex replied. "His uncle in St. Louis died. He had to go back . . . something about the estate. I think he's the executor."

She watched as his face grew even more troubled until the reason burst out of him. "That damn Cameron . . . I don't know why Will lets him run wild that way. He won't listen to me, even now that he's stayin' with me and Katrin. Nothin' but a kid, and I had to bail him out of jail for helpin' bust up the Longhorn Saloon last week. And that no-good bunch of toughs he runs with . . ."

"I'm afraid Cameron has to learn everything the hard way, Alex," she said. "There's enough of his mother in him that he never listens to good advice." And that mother had brought him shame, Star thought. She sensed the rage behind his recklessness and his facade of charm.

Alex studied his cigar for a moment before he spoke in a tired voice. "Will's marriage to Maria was a disaster engineered by Katrin. Sometimes I think he blames Cameron for all that unhappiness."

"As you blame Julie for Caroline's death," Star said softly.

Alex's head shot up and he stared at her in disbelief. As she watched, something seemed to shatter inside him. Tears swam in his dark eyes. Star was silent, knowing she could offer no comfort.

"I gotta go, Ma," he said roughly, not looking at her. "I'll look in on you tomorrow."

The next day when Star arrived at Red Hill Ranch, Julie greeted her lovingly. But she seemed subdued, lost in thought even when listening to Star's amusing tales of the swells she and Lydie had encountered in Steamboat Springs. She offered no explanation for not looking after the house in town.

In the afternoon they rode together, checking on Star's beloved horses. Little Knife had killed a deer and Star prepared a feast of tenderloin and fried potatoes. Julie ate little, moving the food around on her plate as though it displeased her. All through the long evening, Star waited, certain the dam must break, that Julie had to let her unhappiness out eventually. She kissed Star good night and went to her room early, still completely self-contained.

When Star was putting morning coffee on to boil, she heard the sounds from Julie's bedroom and understood. Closing her eyes tightly, she wished for the magic to assume Julie's pain. Full circle, she thought sadly. The bright-haired woman she had dreaded on sight, and now her bright-haired daughter, had brought sorrow to the loved ones of Falling Star.

Opening the door, she went into the bedroom where Julie still hung over the chamber pot, retching. In the bathroom, Star wet a washcloth. Sitting beside Julie on the bed, she gently wiped the cold sweat from the girl's pale face and laid her back against the pillow.

Julie closed her eyes tight, her face working in a fierce effort to suppress emotion. When she could speak at last, her voice was a cry of pain. "I'm pregnant, Grandmother." Her mouth twisted bitterly. "Like mother, like daughter."

"Are you sure?" Star asked, already knowing the answer.

"I started with morning sickness the day after I missed my period," Julie replied, her voice trembling.

"Will?" Star knew the answer to that question too.

Julie nodded, tears welling in her eyes.

"You'd better let him know," Star said gently, taking Julie's clammy hand in her own.

"No!" Julie sat bolt upright, glaring at Star. "He won't marry me. He's got a wife, he says . . . that crazy slut who deserted him."

"Julie . . ." Star murmured, trying to draw the girl into her arms. But Julie resisted, stiff and angry.

"Some stupid sense of eternal responsibility . . ." Julie's voice trailed off into a sob. "Oh, Grandmother," she cried, and surrendered into Star's comforting embrace.

The paroxysm of weeping passed. Julie dried her eyes, but Star saw that the bitterness remained.

"I won't tell him, Grandmother," she said, her voice hard and certain. "And he'll never see his child if I can help it."

Chapter 43

1896

"Why won't she come to town?" Alex demanded. He paced the length of the sitting room, pausing to stare out the windows where the summer wind blew fading roses into a rain of bright petals. "I can understand why she wouldn't trust old Hamlin, but there's that young doctor Becker."

"You know why, Alex," Star replied patiently. She handed Lydie the sheets to be placed in the trunk they were packing to take to the ranch. "She hasn't been in town since last fall."

"Star and me can bring that baby as good as any doctor," Lydie broke in, slamming the trunk lid for emphasis.

Puffing on his cigar, Alex resumed his nervous pacing. "What the hell's the matter with Will? He should've done something, should have taken care of her."

Aware that the situation, almost a repeat of his own past, was deeply disturbing to Alex, Star watched his pacing with sympathy. Knowing he covered his worry with sharp words, she explained patiently, "Will did try, Alex. When he came back to get Cameron, after he knew he had to stay in St. Louis all winter. The story was around town already. . . ."

"Pregnancy's one thing you sure cain't hide," Lydie stated, glancing up from the diapers she was counting on the dining table before packing them.

"He went to the ranch," Star continued. Alex puffed

403

furiously at his cigar, listening. "Julie locked herself in and wouldn't see him . . . told Little Knife to send him away."

Alex let out a long ragged breath. "She ain't got the guts her mother had."

"Alex!" Star glared at him, outraged. "Caroline had you by her side every minute." The anger dissipated at once, for she saw fear in his eyes. His beloved Caroline had died bearing a child; now the same kind of travail lay ahead of Julie.

"She could have sent me away, Ma." There was a tremor in his voice. "I was married too . . . remember?"

Tears stung Star's eyes. Her hands trembled on the trunk lid as she followed his glance across the room to the piano, which stood on the far wall of the sitting room as it had for so many years.

His voice was low. "Cameron says Julie plays beautifully. Mozart, like Caroline used to play for me." Sensitive to the wounds she knew had never healed, Julie never played when Alex was in the house.

Watching his face twist in the agony of a grief that was over twenty years old, Star wondered if there would ever be peace for him anywhere. Once she had been sure of it, but the possibility seemed to recede with the years.

"Julie was a good companion for Cameron," she said, hoping to divert him from sad memories. "Then he thought he'd outgrown her and took up with the town ne'er-do-wells."

Alex carefully relighted his cigar, taking control of his emotions. "He's at it again," he said with a wry glance at Star. "Ever since he came back from St. Louis. Katrin was thrilled to have him stay with us, and so was I. She pets and spoils him and he doesn't appreciate it. Won't listen to a thing I say."

"Will can get him under control when he gets back," Star said doubtfully.

"Yeah, maybe." Alex puffed his cigar thoughtfully. "Too bad Will had to look after his uncle's estate. I guess it's complicated, with six daughters fighting over it, and the brother who lives in France."

He took a long drag on the cigar, then ground it out in the big ashtray Star kept for his use. "I'm taking Cameron with me to the ranch for calf branding if I can get him to leave off practicing steer wrestling for the Fourth of July rodeo. It's time he learned the cattle business anyway."

The worry lines in his tanned face deepened, and he seemed lost in thought. Star knew the past was a burden on his heart. He was troubled about Cameron and troubled about Julie. Slipping her arm through his, she walked through the kitchen with him, wishing for some comforting words she might say before they parted.

"I guess me and Katrin don't have much of a marriage," he burst out suddenly. "But we get along all right. She goes her way and I go mine. Will should have let us have Cameron after Monique died. At least he'd have had some kind of supervision."

Wishing she might have had him too, and passed on to him something of his Nez Percé heritage, Star sighed. "He's fourteen, Alex," she told him, sorry for the vision quest Cameron would never undertake. "One day he'll grow up, and you'll be proud he's your grandson."

Alex managed a grin at the consoling words, but his eyes were doubtful. "I'd thought to make a cattleman of him. He's too wild to ever be a lawyer like Will. But the way the country's changing . . . maybe that's wrong too."

"It's a good business," Star assured him. "Teach it to him if you can."

Alex shook his head doubtfully. His troubled eyes met hers. "I'm not a cattle king anymore, Ma. Just an ordinary rancher doing the best I can."

She smiled into his unhappy face. "That best looks very good to me, Alex."

His face softened and he reached out to hug her briefly. Star's heart ached when she saw how much her words of praise meant to him. Standing on tiptoe, she kissed his cheek.

"Taz alago, Lone Hawk," she said.

Alex's face broke into a grin. *"Taz alago, Nakaz,"* he said.

She could hear him whistling as he mounted his horse and rode away.

Lydie had changed the bed, and Little Knife's wife, Mindy, took the bloody sheets away to soak in the washtubs. Exhausted, Julie lay in a half doze, her face pale against the white pillow.

"I'm glad you didn't tell me how bad it would be," Julie murmured, opening her eyes as Star wiped her forehead with a damp cloth, smoothing back her dark sweat-drenched hair. The ranch house bedroom was already growing warm as the burning July sun blazed from the morning sky.

"It's over now," Star said, helping Julie slip the clean nightgown over her head.

"You'll fergit how much it hurt when you see this darlin'." Lydie laid the blanket-wrapped baby in Julie's arms. "Ain't she a honey?" she asked as Julie drew the blanket away from the round red face of her child.

"Like a newborn kitten." Julie laughed. "Ahhh . . ." She let out a long breath as the baby opened her eyes and stared up at her. Love poured through her and she kissed the tiny wrinkled face softly.

From beyond the window, a meadowlark's call echoed in the still-warm air. Tears stung her eyes with the memory of the golden autumn day this baby had been conceived. All through the long, lonely winter she'd taught herself never to think of Will. Star's books had kept her company, with occasional visits from Star and Lydie and Alex. She'd settled into a calm routine, shutting Will's memory from her mind. Now, for one flashing moment she longed to share with him her joy in this tiny being they'd created. Then the buried anger bubbled to the surface. He'd rejected her for some stupid sense of responsibility. Even Alex had done better by her than Will had done by his daughter.

"Her name is Caroline," Julie said, and pretended not to notice the look that passed between Star and Lydie.

"If she's half the lady her granny Caroline was," Lydie told her in a solemn voice, "she'll be jest fine. You need to rest now, Miss Julie," she added briskly, reaching down to lift the baby into her arms. "Me and Great-Granny will take care of this little love while you're sleepin'."

Star bent to kiss Julie's forehead, then tucked the sheet lovingly about her, watching as she drifted into sleep.

In the kitchen, Lydie had laid the baby in the cradle. She was crooning a soft lullaby as she moved about fixing the breakfast they'd missed because they were delivering a baby.

Amused at Lydie's possessiveness, Star stood in silence for a moment looking down into the child's face. Gently, she picked her up and held her against her breast. A deep sense of joy pervaded her whole being as the baby's heart thumped against her own. It was exactly as it had been the first time she held Julie in her arms . . . the same bonding, the same sense of kinship. This child was gifted. The circle was complete.

The weather stayed hot and dry with empty cotton clouds drifting across an intense blue sky. Life at Red Hill Ranch centered around Caroline as the three women took daily note of every change in her.

Julie refused to listen to any nonsense about staying in bed for a month. Within a week, she was up and helping care for the baby. Within two weeks, she was busy trying to convince the two older women that Caroline did not need to be held constantly.

"She sure is a good chile," Lydie said, watching fondly as Julie sat in the big Morris chair beside the fireplace, cuddling her sucking baby to her breast. Gently, Julie smoothed the thick black fuzz on top of the little head. The pumping of the tiny heart against her breast filled her with a new kind of joy each time she held the child. The baby's eyes opened, staring up at her. Something in that look was so like Will, Julie's heart wrenched with pain. Shutting her eyes against it, she tried to shut her mind too. But he was always there in her inner heart, no matter how she denied it. She'd returned his letters unopened, even those from faraway France, where he'd been obliged to go to settle his uncle's estate. In spite of her resolve, the ties between them remained, strengthened now by this small being they had created. And yet she swore she would not share their child with him.

"Why, it's Mr. Alex," Lydie said as a horse snorted and blew just outside the cabin.

The front door was open to catch the breeze, and Star quickly crossed the room to look out. Her heart seemed to fall inside her chest as she watched Alex walk up the steps, his face dark and frowning.

"Has Cameron been here?" he asked without preamble, standing in the doorway, squinting against the change of light.

"We haven't seen him," Star said, and apprehension filled her heart. After the rodeo, Cameron had gone to help Alex at the Old Ranch just as he'd promised. Knowing they were busy with calf branding, Star hadn't expected to hear from them until they were finished.

"Damn his hide," Alex growled, then broke off abruptly as his glance fell on Julie and the baby. "Well . . ." he managed to say, seeming totally at a loss. "I didn't know that—well, you should have sent word about the baby," he ended defensively.

"You wouldn't have been any help," Star told him with a smile. Her hands grew clammy as she watched his face, wondering if he guessed how important this meeting was to all of them.

Julie buttoned her blouse and wiped the baby's milky mouth. Almost defiantly, she looked up at Alex standing beside her chair, staring at the baby, his face working in an effort to control emotion. "This is your granddaughter, Alex. Her name is Caroline."

His rough-hewn face crumpled. Tears flooded his dark eyes. Alex turned quickly and walked out of the house.

"Go after him," Star commanded, taking the baby from Julie. "You mustn't let this pass."

Alex stood with his arms folded on the top pole of the corral, his head bent. With a stab of pain, Julie realized he was crying.

Her heart filled with sorrow for him, she put an arm about

his broad shoulders and said in a low tentative voice, "Father?"

His tanned rugged face was wet with tears as he turned to meet her questioning eyes. "I'm sorry, Julie," he said, and drew her into his arms.

In those words, Julie knew they had thrown away the regrets of the past like old discarded clothes. The grief Alex had clung to for so many years would be comforted. She would have the father she had longed for all her life.

Holding her away, Alex looked into her face, smoothing her cheek with gentle fingers. A tremulous smile softened his hard mouth. "My little girl," he said. With heart overflowing, Julie hugged him, pressing her face against his shoulder, where she let the tears come at last.

All these years he'd kept aloof from this girl, Alex thought sadly. He'd been so afraid to care for another person as he'd cared for Caroline. What a terrible waste . . . and Alex raised his eyes to the hills where a wind stirred the pine trees. Suddenly, as though bursting out of the drifting white clouds, two hawks skimmed across the treetops. His arms tightened about his weeping daughter, and he seemed to hear Caroline's beloved voice telling him she carried this child. The vision was true, he knew with a sudden sense of pervading joy. The daughter he held in his arms was the one fated to be Lone Hawk's companion.

Granddad said whiskey made a man crazy and he wouldn't allow it on his ranch. But Cameron found it made him feel strong and brave, grown up and ready to take on the world. It had made him mad as hell when the cow hands brought in those Aycee cows with the calves bearing old Jack Greenfield's brand. And it made him even angrier when Granddad ordered all the suspect cows and calves driven into a fenced pasture where the sheriff could inspect them later. If Granddad didn't have the guts to do anything about Greenfield's blatant rustling, he'd do it himself. Nobody got away with stealing from the Camerons.

Back in town it hadn't taken him long to round up his

friends. They were always ready for excitement. He bought whiskey for all of them and laid out his plan while they sat around a table at the back of Sam's Bar. They weren't welcome at the Longhorn anymore.

Greenfield's place adjoined Alex Cameron's Old Ranch on the east . . . handy for mavericking Aycee calves and rustling Aycee cattle. Hot excitement ran along Cameron's veins as he rode with five of his buddies, made brave by whiskey, across the sagebrush flats leading to the Greenfield homestead. Before them they pushed a herd of range cattle, most of them branded Aycee along with a few of Greenfield's own cows.

The drab ugly cabin looked deserted out there in the flats without a tree for miles. "Damn Ioway pilgrim," Cameron yelled at the others, reining up on the low hill overlooking the makeshift farm with its scraggly cornfield and chicken run.

Looking around at the young men surrounding him on their horses, Cameron grinned. There was Ray Jones, blank-eyed with liquor, and Carey Perkins, who tied his six-gun holster down like a real gunfighter. Restless and footloose, most of them were older than he. But he'd grown tall over the winter and his voice had changed. He even shaved once a week. Age had nothing to do with it, he thought arrogantly. He was the leader. Ever since the day when, sick with rage, he'd held his gun to Carey's throat, none of them mentioned his crazy whore of a mother.

"Hey, gang!" he called recklessly, finishing off the pint of whiskey and tossing the bottle into the sagebrush. His voice rose to a shout as he spurred his horse into a run. "Let's send the thievin' bastards back to Ioway!"

The cattle surged before them, gathering speed as the riders shouted and fired their guns into the air. A cloud of dust rose from the dry earth as the herd pounded down the hill toward the homestead. The cornfield fell before the onslaught of stampeding cattle. The fence of the chicken run was torn loose and squawking chickens died beneath thundering hooves. Suddenly, amid the shouting and the bawling of cattle, a rifle barked from the cabin.

Struck sober by the sound of a second shot, the wild-riding boys fell silent. One after another, they reined up their horses, looking around in bewildered uncertainty. They hadn't expected any resistance. Another rifle shot rang out and Cameron felt a sharp hot pain in his thigh.

"Jesus!" he cried, grabbing at his leg. Blood poured through his fingers. Jerking on the reins, he turned his horse to follow his friends, who were already fleeing in a cloud of dust. Something slammed into his shoulder and he was unseated, falling hard into the sagebrush.

Struggling to rise, he screamed at the fleeing horsemen, "Help me, you bastards. Help me!" They disappeared over a rise without looking back. Weakness poured through him and he slumped to earth. His blurring vision held only sky and sagebrush.

"It's that no-good kid of Will Forester's," Cameron heard a voice say, dim and far away. Through a haze of pain, he made out Jack Greenfield's ugly face.

Old man Greenfield leaned over his son's shoulder and cackled. "Damn poor shot, Jack. A little to the right and you'd'a made a steer outta him."

"Aw hell." Jack stood up. "I didn't mean to hurt the little bastard. I'll let his granddad know he's here."

Why had she always felt so responsible for Cameron? Julie asked herself, watching as the men loaded the boy into the wagon she and Star had driven from Red Hill Ranch. Was it because he'd been motherless too . . . or just because he belonged to Will? One of Jack Greenfield's young sons had brought the news. Star hadn't wanted her to come along, but she felt impelled to go. The baby would be safe with Lydie, and somehow she was certain Cameron needed her.

In the end, Little Knife drove the wagon over the rough road to the Greenfield place. The Greenfield boy had caught up with Alex halfway to town and he arrived before they did.

"Comfortable?" she asked now as Cameron's pale face

looked up at her from the feather bed where he lay in the wagon. Sweat poured from him in the hot afternoon sun. Julie was sorry for his pain, but she had to stifle the urge to shake some sense into him.

Shame washed over his features, and he looked away from her. "They just rode off and left me," he said in a low voice. "I might have been dead and they didn't care."

"If you were dead, you couldn't treat them to whiskey at the saloon every day," she said crisply. "That's the kind of friends you had, Cam."

"Do you hate me, Julie?" he asked, his gray eyes dark with shame.

"No, Cameron," she said, taking a pillow Star handed her and tucking it beneath his head. "I don't hate you, I love you. But it's time you grew up and I'm tired of waiting."

His attempt at a smile ended as a grimace of pain when Star tightened the bandage on his shoulder where the bullet had knocked him from the saddle.

"Not very smart, Cameron," Star said unsympathetically. "Getting yourself all shot up for behaving like a damn fool." She nodded toward where Alex and Greenfield were walking together around the homestead, assessing the damages. "Now your grandfather has to pay for all the mess you made."

A groan of more than pain escaped Cameron. "My father's supposed to be here this week." He turned his agonized face away from them. "He'll be furious with me. We already had a quarrel about my coming home before he got back from France."

Julie was silent, the mention of Will blotting out everything else for her. He would be coming home soon, and she hadn't thought out what she would do then. She didn't want to see him or share their child with him. He'd hurt her too much to ever forgive.

Trying to control the sudden onrush of emotion, Julie walked away from the wagon. Behind her she heard Star's severe voice. "Your father will be glad you're alive, Cameron. And like the rest of your family, he'll hope you've learned something from this."

Cameron closed his eyes and Star saw tears slip down the face that was still very young and vulnerable. Gently she smoothed back his damp curly hair and bent to kiss his forehead.

"We're going to take you home now," she whispered. "And this time, my son, you'll be really home."

Chapter 44

A pale silver twilight lay over Cameron Valley as the last streaks of gold faded in the western sky. Harnesses jingled and the horses blew from the fast pace Little Knife had kept. Sawing on the reins, he pulled the team to a halt in front of the house at Red Hill.

At once, Alex jumped down from the wagon seat and hurried toward the cookhouse where the ranch hands were eating supper. "Need some help here, boys," Julie heard him call.

Her breasts were swollen and aching. Milk had seeped from them, staining the front of her shirtwaist.

"I have to feed the baby," she told Star, who had sat in the wagon bed beside Cameron all the way back. Listening anxiously for the sound of the baby's hungry cries, Julie climbed down.

Star must have seen the anxiety in her face, for she smiled reassuringly. "Lydie would give her a sugar tit. She'll be fine." Cameron moaned softly, and she bent to speak to him in a soothing voice.

Evening wind rustled the cottonwood trees. The cooling air was pleasant against Julie's face after the hot, dusty ride from Greenfield's. It was a moment before her eyes adjusted to the change of light when she entered the cabin. She could hear the baby whimpering softly and at once began to unbutton her shirtwaist.

First, her searching glance fell on Lydie, seated in a straight chair near the fireplace. Her arms were empty and she barely glanced at Julie. Even though she was smiling, her black face glistened with tears.

Following Lydie's eyes, Julie drew in a long aching breath. Her heart seemed to lurch and fall inside her chest. Will Forester sat in the big Morris chair, holding Caroline in his arms and gazing adoringly into her face.

All her anger and resentment surfaced at once. Stifling the urge to tear the baby away from him, Julie demanded harshly, "What are you doing with her?"

Will's eyes met hers, darkening with longing in that way she had tried to forget. Julie's throat clogged with emotions she'd been certain she'd repressed for all time.

"She's mine too," Will said in a gentle voice.

All that might have been was there between them, the barrier of a wife who was no wife. She'd loved him so, and he'd failed her. With a painful twist of her heart, Julie knew she loved him still. Determined not to risk that hurt again, she composed her face into hard lines.

The baby's whimpers grew into full-blown wails. "She's hungry," Julie told him, reaching for the child.

Will stood, carefully surrendering the baby into Julie's arms. "She'll be as beautiful as you are," he said in a low voice. His eyes held hers, and she saw there the depth of his love and need for her, undiminished in the months apart.

Longing flashed through her. Julie turned abruptly away from his yearning gaze. She wanted his arms about her, his mouth on hers, wanted him as intensely as she had always wanted him. Nothing had changed, not even the painful knowledge that Will valued her less than his principles.

"Her name is Caroline Cameron," she told him. Guilt-stricken when she realized how spiteful the words sounded, Julie closed the bedroom door quickly behind her.

With the assistance of Little Knife and two ranch hands, Cameron was installed in Star's bed. His filthy clothes removed, he lay in groggy silence while Star bathed him and packed his wounds with herb poultices. Willow bark tea brought a grimace to his face, but he drank it dutifully. Exhausted and in pain, he lay back on the pillow, his young face flushed with guilt as he looked at his father standing at the foot of the bed.

"I guess Granddad told you what happened?" Cameron's voice was shaky.

Struggling with his own guilt over the son he had neglected for so many years, Will managed to keep his voice even. "You're lucky the bullets went clean through. You could have been killed. Greenfield's not a bad man. He was only protecting himself."

With one last burst of bravado, Cameron protested, "He was mavericking Granddad's calves."

"That was Alex's business, not yours," Will said reasonably. "He'd have handled the problem without any drunken Wild West antics." Shame-faced, Cameron did not reply.

Studying the vulnerable face of his son, Will was assailed by regret . . . for the marriage that never was a marriage, for the son he'd half blamed for that failure. His cousins in St. Louis, all the people of Cameron City, saw him as a success, but he had failed at the most important things. If only Julie would give him another chance, he thought, this time he'd do it right. The way she'd reacted to his presence tore his heart, even if he deserved it. And yet, he was certain he'd glimpsed in her eyes a yearning as deep as his own.

"Granddad wants me to live with him and Grandma," Cameron began tentatively. "He thinks I could learn the cattle business and take over his ranch someday."

"If it's all right with you, Will," Alex interjected. Carrying a cup of coffee, he walked into the bedroom and looked down at his grandson with a concerned face.

"Does Katrin . . . ?" Will asked, and Alex laughed.

"She dotes on the boy, Will. He's the center of her life when he's with us." Hastily, he added, "But I won't let her spoil him . . . I'll promise that."

Will nodded, saddened by the knowledge of how little

rapport he had with his son and certain life with his grandfather would be best for Cameron. Time enough when the boy recovered from his wounds to try to help him understand the past that had haunted him. And time then to tell him the final truth about his mother . . . after he'd told Alex and Alex had told Katrin.

Enticing odors of the stew Lydie was cooking for supper filled the cabin. The coal-oil lamps were lighted and Julie was busy setting the table. Star carefully left the bedroom door ajar so that she could hear Cameron if he stirred. She'd added a few drops of laudanum to his willow bark tea and he was sleeping heavily.

Going to the cupboard, she took down the cut-crystal glasses and poured two whiskeys for the men seated by the screened and empty fireplace. Alex looked worn out but contented, and he grinned at her as she handed him the glass. He would have his son, Star thought, knowing that the unhappiness Katrin had brought would be diluted now. They might have conflicts over the boy, but he would bring them comfort in their sundown years. And Julie would have her father at last, now that Alex had made peace with his long grief for Caroline. Beneath the fatigue, Star felt a sense of completion, a circle closing.

Will's troubled eyes met hers as she handed him his whiskey. She gave him an encouraging smile, saddened to see his glance go beyond her to Julie. The baby was fed and sleeping, but Julie stayed in the kitchen helping Lydie, purposefully ignoring Will's presence.

Sitting down on the leather sofa-bed, Star gratefully took the cup of coffee Lydie brought her. This day had wearied her more than she dared admit, and she fought down the sick weakness she often felt now when she was overtired. Silent, she watched Will studying his drink, waiting for him to speak, for she knew he brought another piece of the circle.

"On the way home from St. Louis," he said at last, "I went to Denver." His voice was so low, Alex frowned and leaned forward to catch the words. Julie and Lydie were suddenly still, turning to listen. The faint sad cooing of a mourning dove was borne on the wind. Then Little Knife called to the ranch hands, the sound muffled in the quiet dusk.

"I meant to see Maria." Will cleared his throat, tightened his lips, and continued in a dispassionate tone. "To see if there was any way I could get a divorce." He threw a pained glance at Julie, who stood immobile as a statue.

"When I got to the sanitarium, they told me she was dead." Covering his agonized face with one hand, he continued in a muffled voice. "She'd been dead for six months and they never notified me . . . just kept cashing my checks."

"God!" Alex sat stiffly, staring straight ahead as though looking back at all the pain Maria had caused. For him, she had died long ago in Cheyenne and his grieving was finished. It came to Star then the thing she must tell Cameron, that he must beware all his life of a bright-haired woman.

Will raised his head, his eyes seeking Julie. Her face was wet with tears, but she turned away and would not meet his pleading gaze. "Julie," he said, and all the years of longing were in that one word.

All through supper and cleaning up afterward, all through Alex's insistence on telling Will how he intended to divide his property between his grandson and his daughter, Julie had managed to avoid meeting Will's gaze. She could feel those penetrating gray eyes on her, unswerving as though he could not tear them away.

Maria was dead, the half-sister she'd scarcely known. That distant, sinister figure forever standing between herself and the man she loved was gone.

What did the future hold? she wondered later as she stepped from her bath and dried herself. To deny the gift is to lose it, Star had told her once, and Julie knew how vehemently she had denied it, fearful of the pain it brought. Now she could not guess what lay ahead. She only knew a rancor toward Will still simmered in her heart. All the long, lonely months, when their child grew inside her and he was far away, stood between them. Julie wondered if she were strong enough to forgive him.

In the bedroom, she could hear the baby fussing. Milk was seeping from her full, heavy breasts and Julie smiled to herself at the wonder of this intimate connection between mother and child. Slipping a white muslin nightgown over her head, she went in to feed her baby.

The door to the kitchen was closed, but she could hear Lydie singing to herself as she set biscuits to rise for breakfast. Julie stopped short, her heart pounding at the sight of Will Forester standing beside the cradle looking down at his daughter with an expression of wonder and awe. Heat surged through Julie's veins, her fingers ached to touch his face, and her mouth softened with longing for his kiss.

"She's beautiful," Will said. His face was grave as he turned to her. "Exactly like you, dear love."

Memories of hurt and pain dissipated like smoke in the summer sky. All that remained was the love they'd shared, a love that would never end. There was nothing now to keep them apart.

She went to him, yielding gladly to his fierce embrace, her mouth searching for his and claiming it with passionate abandon.

"Oh God, Julie," he murmured against her throat. "My love, my dear love . . . I've needed you so."

Unable to speak, she held on to him hungrily, lost in the dear familiarity of the tall lean body pressed against hers.

Holding her away, Will smoothed back her loose black hair, his gray eyes dark with love. "I brought something for you." Reaching into his pocket, he held out a gold band, a wedding ring set with tiny gold nuggets instead of stones.

"Tell me it isn't too late, Julie . . . that you forgive me."

A deep pervading joy grew inside her and she knew it had

returned. The gift was hers once more. Will Forester was a man of unswerving honor, a man for the lifetime they would have together.

"We've already forgiven each other, darling," she whispered, holding him close. Looking down at the fussing baby, she smiled. "There's our forgiveness, Will . . . and our future. It's just the beginning."

Hearing the baby's cries, Star opened the door into the bedroom, then closed it quietly. Julie lay propped against the pillows, the baby tugging at her breast, its cries soothed. On the edge of the bed, Will sat watching, his face incandescent with love. With a sigh, Star shut the door. The circle was closing.

Amid all the bustle of making ready to transport Cameron into town next morning, Julie was sharply aware of her grandmother's movements. Last night, she hadn't joined Julie in the bed they were to share while Lydie slept on the sofa-bed, and Alex and Will went to the bunkhouse. This morning she seemed to move as though carefully calculating the energy needed for each step she took.

It is time, something said inside Julie's head. Her heart twisted agonizingly, yet she knew its truth. Last night when she surrendered to Will's arms and made whispered plans with him, she had been aware of the return of her gift. It had brought happiness then. This morning it brought pain.

"Aren't you going to ride with me, Granny Star?" Cameron asked when they had finished the noon meal and loaded him into the wagon. They'd settled him so that shade from the wagon seat fell on his face, but a shaft of sunlight gleamed in his sandy-blond hair. Star's heart caught in sudden pain. For the first time she was aware of Cameron's startling resemblance to Hugh Cameron, the Shining Bear. There was the same curly dark gold hair; the cut of his features and the shape of his mouth were all Hugh's. Only the gray eyes came from Charles.

"Not this time, my son." Star reached across the wagon rack to smooth back his tumbled hair, knowing that he would soon sleep from the laudanum she had given him. *"Kuse timine,"* she murmured, bending to kiss his forehead.

Cameron stared at her. "What does that mean?"

"Go with good heart."

He smiled, already half drifting into sleep. *"Kuse timine,"* he repeated. *"Kuse timine,* Granny Star."

"And so I shall," she told him. Stepping back from the wagon, she signaled Alex, with Lydie sitting beside him on the seat, to drive away.

"We'd better get started if we want to get to town before dark," Will said, watching as the wagon moved into the heat haze lying over the sagebrush plain. Tired of waiting in harness, the horses hitched to the surrey stamped and blew nervously.

Looking steadily into Star's face, he told her, "As soon as we get to Cameron City, Julie and I will be married—at your house if that's all right. Then I'll have Dr. Becker make up Caroline's birth certificate. She'll be legitimate." He studied Star's face gravely. "That's important to Julie," he added.

"Yes," Star answered with an effort. Somehow she kept drifting away from the present, forgetting to listen to the voices speaking to her now. Smiling, she moved around the surrey and kissed Will's cheek. "It will set things right for Julie . . . and for you."

From the pocket of her skirt, she drew a small well-worn black velvet bag. Taking Will's hand, she laid it in his grasp.

"These were your grandmother's—the Forester pearls. Long ago, they were given me by your father. . . ." Her voice trailed off as a myriad of memories crowded her mind.

Will's eyes were moist. "He loved you very much," he said softly.

"Yes," she murmured, her voice strangely distant. Then she straightened and smiled at him. "As you love my Julie . . . for all your lives. Give these to her on your wedding day."

"Are we ready?" Julie's voice interrupted them. But Star's eyes still held Will in love and understanding. Reaching out, he touched her hand. She smiled, but now her concentration was centered on Julie.

Will turned to help Julie down the steps, smiling fondly at his sleeping baby.

As though drawn by Star's steady gaze, Julie walked directly to her and laid the child in her arms. Closing her eyes, Star gave herself over to communion with the small spirit she held against her breast. The baby sighed and moved in her sleep. Star kissed the soft, sweet-smelling cheek, willing a long and happy life for this Caroline.

"There is a thing to be done before you go," she said, turning to Will. "Keep your daughter and wait in the house until Julie comes back to you."

He cast a puzzled frown at Julie, who scarcely seemed to notice him, so intent was her concentration on Star.

"Please, Will," she said in a low voice. Their eyes met and he nodded, understanding now. Gathering the baby into his arms, he walked slowly back into the cabin.

"Come, Gray Dove," Star said, slipping her arm through Julie's. Seeing how the hand on her arm trembled, Julie clasped it with fierce protective love.

"We will go to the hilltop now," Star said in Nez Percé. "There the *hattia tinukin* blows for me."

"No, Grandmother," Julie protested, and fell silent at the distant visionary glow in Star's eyes.

It was like another time, in another life, Star thought, on the Night of the Falling Stars when she had helped Old Grandmother climb the hill. Life was a circle, never ending.

Star had to stop many times, gasping for breath, but at last they reached the crest of the hill. Star sat down on a flat rock, panting, and drew Julie down beside her. "Remember this place of your vision?" she asked.

Tears swam in Julie's dark eyes as she nodded. "I remember, Grandmother." Although she and her grandmother spoke the old language, Nez Percé, only occasionally, the words seemed to come easily to her now.

With trembling hands, Star unclasped the necklace from about her neck. "This was Old Grandmother's strongest medicine as it has been mine," she said, reaching to place the chain that held the ancient blue stone about Julie's neck. "Now it will be your *wyakin.*"

Through a mist of tears, Julie looked into Star's suddenly aged face, deeply aware of the import of this passing of power from one generation to the next. "So it will be with Caroline?" she asked, and Star nodded.

"You are the best of two cultures, Gray Dove," Star continued, willing her voice to remain strong and steady. "But you must always be mindful of your Indian heritage. Those who do not honor the past will find no honor themselves."

"Grandmother!" Julie cried in protest as full understanding of this moment dawned in her eyes. Quickly, she drew Star into a close embrace, as though to protect her.

"Go now," Star said, gently pushing the girl away. "Your life is there . . . just beginning." And she pointed to the ranch house where the surrey waited. Will had come from the house, walking back and forth in an effort to still the wailing of his daughter.

"Give me this time alone," Star whispered, wiping Julie's tears with gentle fingers. "I will come to you tomorrow."

"Little Knife will bring you to town?" Julie asked, afraid, still wanting to deny what the gift told her was reality.

"Go now, my daughter," Star said. "Your life is waiting."

Falling Star watched until the surrey had disappeared beyond the horizon, leaving only a dust cloud hanging in the warm blue air. She sat very still, feeling the blood pulse through her body, feeling the beat of her heart ease and slow.

Wind sighed in the pine trees . . . *hattia tinukin,* as she had told Julie . . . the wind of death. Sunset filled the sky with a blaze of color, crimson and gold fading into gray. The evening star hung huge and bright on the horizon as darkness crept across Cameron Valley.

Out of the pine trees moaning softly in the wind, a light appeared, moving toward her. When she could perceive its form, a soft cry burst from her lips.

It was a fine strong horse, and the bear who sat astride him was a great golden-colored creature with fur that curled down over his huge chest.

Falling Star rose and held her arms out to welcome Shining Bear.